SHIVA IN STEEL

Tor Books by Fred Saberhagen

THE BERSERKER SERIES

The Berserker Wars
Berserker Base (with Poul Anderson, Ed Bryant, Stephen Donaldson, Larry Niven, Connie Willis, and Roger Zelazny)
Berserker: Blue Death
The Berserker Throne
Berserker's Planet
Berserker Kill
Berserker Fury
Shiva in Steel

THE DRACULA SERIES

The Dracula Tapes
The Holmes-Dracula Files
An Old Friend of the Family
Thorn
Dominion
A Matter of Taste
A Question of Time
Séance for a Vampire
A Sharpness on the Neck

THE SWORDS SERIES

The First Book of Swords
The Second Book of Swords
The Third Book of Swords
The First Book of Lost Swords: Woundhealer's Story
The Second Book of Lost Swords: Sightblinder's Story
The Third Book of Lost Swords: Stonecutter's Story
The Fourth Book of Lost Swords: Farslayer's Story
The Fifth Book of Lost Swords: Coinspinner's Story
The Sixth Book of Lost Swords: Mindsword's Story
The Seventh Book of Lost Swords: Wayfinder's Story
The Last Book of Swords: Shieldbreaker's Story
An Armory of Swords (editor)

OTHER BOOKS

A Century of Progress
Coils (with Roger Zelazny)
Dancing Bears
Earth Descended
The Mask of the Sun
Merlin's Bones
The Veils of Azlaroc
The Water of Thought
The Face of Apollo

FRED SABERHAGEN

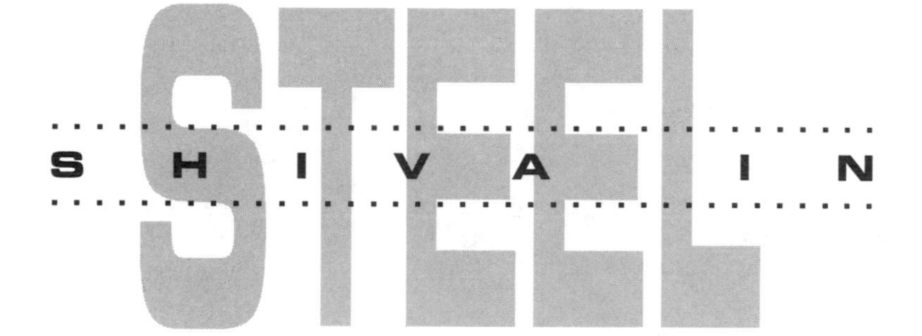

A TOM DOHERTY ASSOCIATES BOOK

NEW YORK

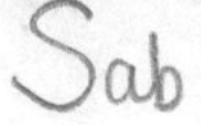

This is a work of fiction. All the characters and events portrayed in this novel are either fictitious or are used fictitiously.

SHIVA IN STEEL

This book is printed on acid-free paper.

A Tor Book
Published by Tom Doherty Associates, Inc.
175 Fifth Avenue
New York, NY 10010

Tor Books on the World Wide Web:
http://www.tor.com

Tor® is a registered trademark of Tom Doherty Associates, Inc.

Library of Congress Cataloging-in-Publication Data

Saberhagen, Fred.
Shiva in steel / Fred Saberhagen. — 1st ed.
p. cm. — (The Berserker series)
"A Tor book"—T.p. verso
ISBN 0-312-86326-8
I. Title. II. Series: Saberhagen, Fred, 1930– Berserker series.
PS3569.A215S48 1998
813'.54—dc21 98-21191
CIP

First Edition: September 1998

Printed in the United States of America

0 9 8 7 6 5 4 3 2

SHIVA IN STEEL

ONE

Five thousand light-years from old Earth, on an airless planetoid code-named Hyperborea, inside the small Space Force base that was really a sealed fortress, unexpected visitors were rare, and even more rarely were they welcome.

The lone ship now incoming had been a total surprise to everyone on the base when it was detected about an hour ago by the early warning net of robot pickets that englobed the entire Hyperborean system. Since that sighting, Claire Normandy had been fidgeting in her base-commander's office, distracted from her other duties by watching the interloper's progress on the larger of her two office holostages.

Normandy was neat and slender, with straight black hair and coffee-colored skin. Her usual voice and manner were quiet. In her job she assumed authority, rather than continually striving to demonstrate it. At first encounter, most people tended to think her dull and colorless. Less immediately apparent was another tendency, a love of gambling when the stakes grew very high.

The commander's uniform today, as on most days, was the workaday Space Force coverall, suitable for wear inside space armor, when the need for that arose. Her age was hard to estimate, as with most healthy adults; and within broad limits, chronological age was not a very meaningful measurement.

The unscheduled caller's reception at the base was not going to be particularly cordial. It had been tentatively identified as a privately owned spacecraft named *Witch of Endor,* engaged in mineral prospecting and a variety of other small-business ventures, owner and operator Harry Silver. Once, some fifteen years ago, Claire had had a brief encounter with a man of that name, and she had no reason to doubt that this was the same person.

Informed of the *Witch*'s approach by superluminal courier just minutes after the far-flung robotic eyes of base defense had detected it at a distance of around a billion kilometers, Commander Normandy had opened communications with the pilot as soon as the distance delay for radio communication fell under a minute. When the visitor, speaking calmly enough, had pleaded recent combat damage and a need for repairs, she had ordered his ship to stand by for inspection. In a matter of minutes, one of her patrol craft had matched velocities. Her people had gone aboard the *Witch* and one of her own pilots was now bringing the civilian craft in for a landing at the base.

Her alertness was heightened by a certain message that had come in by long-distance courier a few hours earlier and been promptly decoded. Claire was still carrying the hard copy of that message in her pocket. For a moment, she considered taking it out and looking at it again—but really there was no need.

It came from from sector headquarters on Port Diamond, and was signed by the chief of the Intelligence Service there. Below the usual jargon of routing and addressing, it read simply:

GOOD EVIDENCE KERMANDIE SECRET AGENT IDENTITY UNKNOWN HAS TARGETED YOUR BASE FOR PENETRATION. OBJECTIVE UNKNOWN. YOU ARE DIRECTED TO APPLY HEIGHTENED SECURITY MEASURES TO ANY RECENT OR NEW ARRIVALS, PARTICULARLY CIVILIANS.

When Claire had first laid eyes on the message, her immediate inner reaction had been: *What civilians?* There were seldom any here, and at the moment, not even one. And her second reaction, not long delayed: *What evidence?*

She supposed she would never be given an answer to the second question. As for the first, about civilians, now it seemed that she might soon be going to find out.

When she tired momentarily of focusing her attention on the intruder, she turned, gazing out through a clear window at a dark horizon, the jagged line of an airless and uneven surface only a fraction of a kilometer away, but five thousand light-years from the sun whose light had nourished the earliest years of her own life—as it had, long ago, those of the whole race of Earth-descended humans. The rotation of the planetoid beneath her feet was swift enough to set the stars and other celestial objects in visible motion, rising in an endless, stately progression from beyond that jagged line. Months ago, she'd learned that she need only stare for a little while at that perpetually sinking horizon to induce a feeling that the world was somehow giving way beneath her.

The whole cycle of rotation was several minutes long, and during various segments of that great circle, the light of distant galaxies predominated.

Looking out as it did over the landing field, the commander's office window offered a view of several robotic interstellar couriers, poised for quick launching. Each was sited in its own revetment, widely spaced along the near side of the artificially flattened surface that served the base as landing field. Half a kilometer away, on the far side of that field, set into a naturally vertical wall of rock, were the hangar doors through which arriving vessels were admitted to the interior docks and berths that had been carved out of the rock into several subterranean levels of hangar space.

The *Witch of Endor* was going to touch down a couple of hundred meters from those doors, the first unscheduled visitor to land on or even approach this planetoid in more than a year. The ship's sole occupant before the Space Force had come aboard, the man identifying himself as the ship's owner, Harry Silver, had made no objection to being boarded, but rather, had been relieved to hand over the controls.

Two days ago, or even yesterday, Commander Normandy would not have been made quite so edgy by an unforeseen arrival; but today she had been eagerly expecting quite a different set of visitors, vitally important ones, and they were already almost two hours overdue. Any suggestion that the day's schedule of events was going to be disrupted was most unwelcome.

In fact, she was anticipating at every moment another signal from the robot pickets of her early warning array, giving notice of the arrival, in-system, of a task force of attack ships. If everything was going according to schedule, those six Space Force vessels—three light cruisers and three destroyers—should have been dispatched two standard days ago from Port Diamond, a thousand light-years distant. It made no sense, of course, for her to be gazing with naked eyes toward the stars in that direction as if it might be possible to see the approach of the task force. But time and again, she caught herself doing just that.

Commander Normandy's second-in-command was a diligent lieutenant colonel named Khodark, but her adjutant was an optelectronic artifact, a computer program, sometimes classified as an expert system, known as Sadie. Sadie's usual holostage persona had a vague, but no more than vague, resemblance to the commander herself.

At the moment, Sadie's head was visible inside the larger office holostage, looking out with a certain expectancy on her pleasant virtual features, as if she could be curious as to why the Old Lady should be somewhat on edge today, and should stand gazing out the window at nothing much at all.

In fact, no one else on Hyperborea besides the base commander, not even virtual Sadie of unquestionable loyalty, knew that the task force was scheduled to arrive. Three light cruisers and three destroyers ought to create quite a stir among her people when they showed up. And that would be time enough for an announcement.

The transparency through which Commander Normandy stared at the universe was an extraordinary window, even for a port in space—it had been formed of statglass, ten centimeters thick with protective elaborations. And what it showed her was no ordinary view.

What she saw, in concrete, mundane terms, was the aboveground portion—which was less than half the whole—of a human outpost, set in rather spectacular surroundings on a minor planet in orbit around a brown dwarf, which in turn was only the junior member of a binary star. The dwarf, not quite big enough or hot enough to be a real sun, had in the commander's view the apparent size of Earth's moon as seen from the surface of the Cradle World. Its light, dull red, dim, and often depressing, came in some of the station windows—whenever, as now, anyone wanted to look at it. Generally, the majority of the four dozen or so people on-station preferred virtual scenery—green hills, tall trees, blue sky, and shining water, easily generated on screen and holostage—when they wanted any at all. For the past month, most of them had been too busy with their jobs to give much thought to the esthetics of their environment.

Few of the jobs on this base were routine, and all of them were demanding.

Even as she watched, she saw the flicker across a portion of the sky that meant another robot interstellar courier coming in. The traffic was so frequent that on an ordinary day, she would scarcely have given the sight a thought.

Complications, always complications.

On the large chronometer set into one wall of Commander Normandy's office, a certain unmarked deadline was drawing near—now no more than seven standard days away. If everything went according to plan, today's expected visitors, the six ships and crews of the task force, were going to be departing Hyperborea before that deadline. Then they would be lifting off on the last leg of the journey that would take them to their objective. The schedule did allow a little spare time for the unexpected things that always came up—but spare time was a precious commodity that should never be squandered pointlessly. Even two hours lost at the start was enough to create the beginning of concern.

Only this morning, the commander had issued an order canceling the passes of three people who had been scheduled for a weekend of such recreation as they might be able to find down on Good Intentions, so everyone on the base knew that something special was up, though not even Sadie knew what it was.

If all went well, and the crews of the task force completed their mission successfully, they were going to kill a thing that had never been alive. Their mission called for them to demolish a brutally efficient form of death, which was also a master of strategic thinking. A spiritless thing that nevertheless made deep plans, and moved and struck with the power of a force of nature. It was a terrible foe, the mortal enemy of everything that lived.

Humanity called it a berserker.

For centuries now, Galactic life had been engaged in a

great defensive war. The death-machines that Solarian humans called berserkers had been designed ages ago by a race now remembered only as the Builders, because so little else was known about them. Demonstrating great cleverness and the absolute reverse of wisdom, the Builders had gone all out to win an interstellar war by creating an ultimate weapon, meant to eliminate all life from the worlds held by their antagonists.

The ultimate weapon had done its job to perfection, but any rejoicing among the Builders must have been short-lived indeed. Berserkers had proven to be more easily launched than recalled. The race of their creators had been the next to disappear, processed efficiently into oblivion by the remorseless death-machines. Only very recently had stark evidence surfaced, strongly suggesting that at least a few members of the Builders' race were still alive—but only in the depths of the Mavronari Nebula, effectively out of touch with the rest of the Galaxy.

Now, hundreds of centuries later, the mechanical killers still fought on, endlessly replicating and redesigning themselves for greater efficiency, steadily improving their interstellar drives and weaponry. Even finding possibilities of improvement—as they saw it—in their own programming. Whatever the precise intent of their original designers, the berserkers' goal was now the abolition of all life throughout the Galaxy.

Humanity—organic intelligence, in all the biological modes and manifestations that phenomenon assumed on various worlds—was the form of life assigned the highest priority in the great plan of destruction because human life was the only kind capable of effective resistance. The only kind capable of fighting back with purpose and cunning and intelligence.

And of the several known varieties of Galactic humanity, only the Solarian, the Earth-descended, seemed capable of matching the berserkers' own implacable ferocity.

For ages, the conflict had dragged on, often flaring into all-out war. It pitted Galactic life—which in practice, meant Solarians, the sons and daughters of old Earth—against the machines that had been programmed ages ago to accomplish the extermination of that life. From time to time, the conflict died down in one sector, while both sides rebuilt their forces, only to burst out in another. If annihilation of the berserkers seemed an unattainable dream, at least there was every reason to hope that they might be prevented from achieving their programmed goal.

Two personal holograms, one mounted on Claire Normandy's desk, the other on her office wall, beside the big chronometer, showed a smiling man of an age as indeterminate as her own, in the company of one obviously young adult. The suggestion was that the commander was certainly old enough to have a grown child somewhere. And in fact, she did.

On the other side of the chronometer hung a silent holographic recording of a man—not the one who smiled in the other picture—giving a speech before an enthusiastic crowd, some of whose heads showed blurrily in the foreground. The speaker was dressed in a distinctive costume; a long shirt of fine material, secured with a leather belt over trousers of the same thin stuff. His name was Hai San, and everyone who knew anything about Kermandie, or about history in this sector, knew who he was. Hai San had been killed, martyred, by the Kermandie dictatorship six or seven years ago.

The junior officer she'd sent to pilot in the *Witch of Endor* was calling in now from aboard the approaching ship, a young man's head and shoulders showing in a solid-looking image on the small office holostage. He reported briskly that there were no problems and that landing was now only a couple of minutes away.

Tersely, Commander Normandy acknowledged the communication.

There was still no sign of the task force of ships she had been expecting. More to relieve her growing tension than for any other reason, she swung open a door and left her office, striding purposefully down the narrow, slightly curving corridor outside. Other uniformed figures passed her, walking normally. Inside the walls of the base, an artificial gravity was maintained at the usual standard, near Earth-surface normal.

Most of the station's interior was decorated in tasteful combinations of green and brown and blue, streaked and spotted at random with contrasting hues of brightness, imitating the colors of Earthly nature. Here and there, people could look out through statglass windows, which in time of trouble, could be easily melded into the walls. Corridors were seldom wider than was necessary for two people wearing space armor to pass, while living quarters tended to be relatively spacious. Given several cubic kilometers of rock to work with, and a generous budget, the diggers and shapers who built the base had not stinted on creating habitable space.

She filled her lungs appreciatively. Today's scent in the corridors, chosen by popular vote a few days in advance, was fresh pine.

As Claire Normandy walked, she cast a security-conscious eye about the interior of the station, trying to see whether there was anything in plain view, at this level, that a casual visitor should not be allowed to see. Nothing leaped out at her.

The commander used her wrist communicator to make a general announcement to everyone aboard the station. "Your attention, this is the commanding officer. We are going to have a civilian visitor coming aboard in a few minutes. We will not, repeat not, be giving the gentleman a tour of the base. But I don't know how long he may be with us, perhaps for several days. So I want you all now to take a look around your immediate environment, wherever you happen to be, with security in mind, and do whatever may be necessary to tighten things up."

The strongest source of natural illumination for several light-years in any direction was a small white sun, the dominant member of the binary star in terms of illumination as it was in terms of gravity. Now, as a consequence of Hyperborea's rotation, this real sun's harsh light, as it rose on the opposite side of the installation, carved out stark shadows on the planetoid's black rock.

All in all, this place seemed an inconspicuous corner of the Galaxy, so out of the way that the garrison could still nourish hopes that the berserkers hadn't spotted it in the two or three standard years since the base had been established.

Reentering her office, she looked again at the holocube on her desk, and the two recorded images within looked back at her.

Got our visitor on visual, Commander." That was from the officer who today happened to have the duty of handling traffic control on the small landing field. He sounded moderately excited, which was only natural. For several months now, the job had entailed nothing but the dispatch and recovery of robot couriers.

Normandy turned back to her holostage and made adjustments to get a closer look. Harry Silver's ship, *Witch of Endor,* was now close enough for the telescopes to show what looked like recent damage, at least superficial battle scars, marring the smooth shape, approximately that of a football, with ghostly silver. In another minute, it was settling gently toward a landing, outlined against angles of dark rock that had never known air or moisture. The patrol craft that had intercepted the visitor came into view a little behind it, following it down.

A panel at the bottom of the holostage was now displaying what modest amount of information the base's extensive data banks contained on the *Witch*'s owner of record. Usually the dossiers made available in this way were fairly accurate. This one was short and obviously incomplete, but perhaps it would be helpful. A quick look confirmed what she was able to remember about the man. Claire Normandy was not particularly perturbed by what the record told her—but neither was she greatly reassured.

She decided that she wanted to see Silver with a minimum of delay. She instructed her virtual adjutant Sadie to ask Mr. Silver to step into her office as soon as he came aboard.

"I know him," she then remarked aloud—more to herself than to anyone else, since only an artificial intelligence happened to be listening.

Though there were no actual criminal convictions listed in Silver's record, when read by an experienced eye seeking enlightenment between the lines, the document suggested that he had been involved in interplanetary smuggling in the past, in the nearby Kermandie system and elsewhere. The printout Commander Normandy now held had nothing to say regarding exactly what the man was supposed to have smuggled, but she thought there could hardly be much doubt on that point—illicit drugs were the usual contraband.

The presence of any civilian on base just now was somewhat upsetting—and yet, there was something attractive in the prospect of simply talking for a while to someone from the outside. Like the people under her command, the commander might have chosen to spend an occasional day or two on the system's other world, Good Intentions—but she had chosen not to do that.

Of course, the demands of security came first. How convenient it would be to simply order Silver to remain aboard his ship for the next few hours, keeping him out of the way—but such a course would certainly alert anyone to the fact that something out of the ordinary was taking place on the Hyperborean base. Besides, from his ship, he'd certainly be able to get a good look at her expected visitors when they came in—as surely they must within the next hour or so.

Claire Normandy was trying to recall the details of her only previous meeting with Harry Silver. At that time, fifteen years ago, she had been newly married and fresh out of the Academy. There was no doubt it was the same man, though changed from how she remembered him. Today, when he finally walked into her office, his dark eyes did not seem to have much life left in thcm.

Silver was a man of average height and wiry build; what she could see of his hands and hairy forearms, below the rolled-up sleeves of a standard ship's crew coverall, suggested superior physical strength. Looking around the carefully designed room, he ran a hand through moderately short and darkish hair. He was not Claire's idea of a handsome man, partly because of a nose that had at some time been pushed slightly sideways. "Maybe my nose has changed since last we met. Could have it fixed, but it's probably going to get hit again. This way, it doesn't stick out so far."

Silver's story, as he had already told it to to the crew of the patrol craft, made him, like several thousand other people, a refugee from the adjoining Omicron Sector. The gist of what Silver had to say came in the form of an urgent warning: Not only had the berserkers over in Omicron defeated humanity there, but they had been ahead of us in tactics, in overall planning, at every turn.

Claire got the definite impression that this man had forgotten their previous meeting more thoroughly than she had. At first glance, she found in his appearance and manner none of the uneasiness or furtiveness that in her mind would have suggested the criminal—not that she had wide experience in making such determinations. She decided not to mention their earlier encounter.

Invited to sit down, Silver did so, and with the movement of a tired man, put his booted feet up on an adjoining, unoccupied chair. Then he said: "Thought I better put in at the handiest system and try to find out what's going on—and also get my ship checked out. That last blast might have strained the hull more than's good for it. Things were knocked loose. I lost a chunk of fairing when your pilot put the brakes on here for landing—not that I'm blaming him."

"We'll do what we can for your ship. First, Mr. Silver, if you don't mind, I'd like to hear more of what's been happening in Omicron Sector. Not only to you, but events in general."

"Sure. Our side's been getting its rear end kicked during the last three, four standard months."

"Have you any theories about why?"

"Probably none worth debating. In hardware, it's about even, as usual, between us and the damned things. And I don't think our fleet commanders were idiots . . . though they were made to look that way a couple of times."

"How about your own personal experience?" She could have asked him coolly, *How are things on Kermandie, Mr. Silver?* just to see what kind of a response she got. She had no real experience in such matters, but it seemed to her that surely no true secret agent would be so easily caught. And above all, she had enough to do already, more than enough, without trying to conduct any kind of investigation.

Silver, though not openly reluctant to talk about his recent adventures, was vague about the details of the skirmish that had come so close to demolishing his ship with him inside it; nor had he much to say about how he had managed to get himself and his small ship out of the doomed Omicron Sector. Normandy had already had a report from her techs saying that the *Witch's* weapon systems and shields had badly needed repowering when it landed at Hyperborea.

"The work on your ship will have to wait a little while, I'm afraid."

"Oh? Why's that? Your docks didn't look busy."

"We have certain maneuvers scheduled." At the moment,

all base docking and repair facilities were being held on standby, ready to minister at once to the slightest need of any of the ships of the incoming task force.

Again, Harry Silver declined to talk much about the details of his escape. "You can check out my black boxes about that," he'd said, meaning certain recorders on his ship—and the technicians of course had been doing do. In general, their findings confirmed his story.

There were other matters that Silver was much more willing to discuss, especially the terrifying effectiveness of the berserker tactics he'd just experienced.

Let's get back to the big picture." Adjusting the controls of the large holostage that dominated one side of her office, the same instrument wherein Sadie most often appeared and on which she'd marked the approach of Harry's ship, Commander Normandy now called up a solid-looking schematic, representing about a third of the territory that had been explored with reasonable thoroughness by Earth-descended humans and in which Solarian settlements had been established. One third of Solarian territory equaled no more than two percent of the Galaxy's mind-boggling bulk. A mere two percent of the Galaxy still comprised billions of cubic light-years, and the display showed only a representative few hundred suns, an infinitesimal fraction of the billion stars within that selected volume.

The territory made visible was arbitrarily divided into sectors, according to the system devised by strategists at Solarian headquarters. Near the center of the display was the sector in which Hyperborea was located. One of the adjoining sectors was code-named Omicron.

Commander Normandy moved a finger, causing the location of the Hyperborean system to light up in the form of a tiny green dot. "How did you happen to bring your ship here, Mr. Silver? I mean, given that you were fleeing Omicron Sector, why choose to come out in this particular direction?" Now the wedge-shaped space designated as Omicron glowed transparent green. Given Silver's stated position within that wedge at the start of his escape, it might have been more logical for him to head in another direction.

Silver claimed that he'd latched onto and followed the tenuous old trail left in flightspace by some now-unidentifiable Solarian scoutship. According to this explanation, it was sheer chance as much as anything else that had brought him to Hyperborea. "I remembered about the settlement in this system, and I expected that my ship was going to need some dock time."

Adjutant Sadie had been listening in, and now a graphic version of her head, reduced in size, appeared to assure the commander that if Harry Silver had indeed been using the standard charts and autopilot programs, it was quite likely they would have brought him to the Hyperborean system.

As far as the standard charts were concerned, which almost never showed military installations of any kind, the system contained only the old civilian colony.

Silver said he'd preferred not to check in at the Kermandie system if he could avoid it. "Those people can be hard to get along with sometimes."

Claire Normandy nodded in agreement. It was a sentiment shared by the great majority of people. "You didn't stop there at all, then?"

"No." He looked at her blankly for a moment, then went on. "I remembered the coordinates of your system here, and the civilian colony on the other planet—of course, this base wasn't here last time I passed through." He gazed around him at the solid new walls. "That must have been five standard years ago—no, a little more than that."

"No, we weren't here then."

When he'd emerged into normal space, Harry told her,

out on this system's fringe, he had been surprised to dctcct not only the expected evidence of life and commerce on the small world of Good Intentions, nearer the brown dwarf sun, but also signs of active Solarian presence on Hyperborea. Naturally, he'd signaled, and soon discovered that he'd already been spotted and that a patrol craft was coming to check him out.

Silver's dossier showed that he was, or had been, a berserker fighter of considerable skill and experience. The record was sketchy, and even left room for speculation as to whether he might once have been a Templar.

Claire shot one more glance at his dossier, visible only on her side of the holostage, where virtual Sadie was holding it in readiness for her. There was nothing at all, other than a definite tendency to rootlessness, to suggest that the man before her might now be employed by the Kermandie dictatorship.

"Given your military record, Mr. Silver, we are taking your information very seriously. Thank you."

Her mind would not, could not, let go of the possibility that his apparently fortuitous arrival had some connection with the great secret project under way—she had to make it a conscious decision that she could safely dismiss that possibility.

When the talk lagged for a moment, Silver had a question of his own. "So, you're running a weather station here, hey?"

"Yes." The commander didn't elaborate. The official purpose of the base on Hyperborea was to keep track of Galactic "weather," a matter of some importance to military and civilian spacefarers alike. It was a valid function, and some such work was accomplished, but the real effort here went into the refitting and support of certain recon craft—most especially for the super-secret ships and machines of the mysterious branch of military intelligence known as Hypo, or its twin, the Earth-based group code-named Negat.

"Wouldn't have thought that a weather station here would be of a whole lot of value. Not that much traffic."

"There's enough work to keep us busy."

Commander Normandy couldn't decide at first whether it would be a good idea or not to raise with her visitor any questions on the shadier portions of his record, as it lay before her.

Eventually she decided not to do so. The man was, after all, just passing through.

For a moment, she allowed herself to dream that it might be possible to order him locked up for the next few hours—maybe on some pretext involving quarantine? But no, she really had no justification for any such drastic course of action. Neither could she very well try to persuade him to leave within the hour, not with his ship damaged as it was.

Obviously, Silver's dossier was incomplete, recording only fragments of his past. And there was no reason to suppose that it was up to date—her data banks held those of perhaps a billion other Solarian humans, chosen for a variety of reasons, and many of the records of course were old, and some of them doubtless inaccurate. Keeping up those kinds of records was not a high priority here.

Meanwhile, the commander had delegated to her inhuman adjutant, Sadie, the task of assigning Mr. Silver temporary quarters. Ordinarily, finding space would be no problem, for the facility had been built with the possibility of rapid expansion of its staff in mind, and there were numerous spare rooms. Today, however, the crews of six ships were coming, and it would be convenient for at least some of them to bunk aboard the base, brief though their stay would be.

When she returned from her short reverie, her visitor was sitting with his eyes closed, and she wondered if he could be actually asleep. In a few moments, she was convinced: Silver had apparently dozed off in his chair, facing the window and its jagged horizon of black rocks, stabbed at by sharp, steadily shifting light. The interior illumination of the office was soft just here. Well, that would be convenient, if he would go to his room and just sack out for the next eight to ten hours. After a brisk skirmish and a long flight, he might be ready to do exactly that.

She kept trying to remember what she might have learned about him at the time of their meeting fifteen years ago, what estimate she had formed then. So far, she wasn't having much success.

The next thought that crossed Commander Normandy's mind as she stood looking at her visitor was: *This man's life has not been dull, whatever else one might be able to say about him.* For a moment, she knew a kind of pointless envy. By any ordinary standard, the word could hardly be applied to her life either.

Was Harry Silver a spy, or was he not? She couldn't really believe it. Not for Kermandie. And spies, she supposed, didn't fall asleep on the job—not in a room where there might be useful information to be gathered. But whether she was right or wrong about the man in front of her, what would any Kermandie agent be after here?

Whatever he's been up to, he must be very tired, she thought, and somehow the fact of his obvious weariness tended to allay the vague doubts she had been feeling about him.

In slumber, her visitor's face was almost unlined, looking more youthful than before; but there was something in the way the vintage light of the remote galaxies fell upon his countenance that suggested he was very old.

After she had watched him for a while, a strange idea drifted up to the forefront of her consciousness: A large component of that light had been on its way here, to this precise time and place, heading unerringly for her window and Harry Silver's face, for something like two billion years.

TWO

Harry Silver, feeling as uncomfortable as he usually did when he had to put on his armored suit, could hear his own hard boots crunching lightly on black rock as soon as he stepped out of the airlock. It was a capacious double door that pierced the base's thick and sturdy wall at ground level. At the instant Harry stepped through the outer door, the station's artificial gravity released his body, turning him over to the minimal natural attraction of the planetoid, costing him almost all his weight.

For the time being, his suit radio was silent, for which Silver was grateful; the amount of talking he'd been required to do in the past couple of hours was unusual for him. Before climbing back into his armor and exiting the airlock, he had informed his somewhat reluctant hosts that he was going back to his ship to have a look at her—he'd been prevented from assessing the damage earlier by Commander Normandy's urgent request to see him as soon as possible. Now he intended to get one good look at his ship as she sat grounded, set his mind at rest to some degree, and then he was going to sit down for a while. Luckily, he'd been able to put the ship on autopilot and get some sleep while approaching Hyperborea, but he could feel the effect of days of strain. Some coffee would be good.

The patrol craft had touched down only briefly and was already back in space, presumably carrying out some kind of mission. The *Witch* of course was still sitting just where the Space Force pilot had set her down, only about two hundred meters from the airlock in the wall of the base from which Silver had just emerged, and a somewhat lesser distance from the much bigger doors that gave access to the underground hangar decks. Now Silver was bouncing along toward his craft, his body almost drifting in the weak natural gravity, his boot-crunches coming at irregular, long intervals. The gravity would have been even lower here, practically nonexistent, except for certain oddities of exotic matter at the planetoid's core.

As Harry went bouncing forward at a steady pace, he looked around him. His story of fleeing Omicron Sector to escape the berserkers was true enough—but it wasn't chance that had brought him to this planetoid. There was a certain object that he wanted very much to find—and it seemed entirely possible that this was where she'd left it.

Damn Becky, anyway! Harry hadn't seen her for seven years, but still she bothered him, popping up in his thoughts more than any other woman he'd ever known. About a month ago, before the situation in Omicron had finally become impossible, he had started dreaming about her again. In his dreams, she was in some kind of trouble; he couldn't determine what, but she was calling on him, expecting him to get her out of it. Fat chance. In real life, Becky Sharp had understood very well that he wasn't the kind of man people called on when their lives started to go wrong.

The horrors and destruction visited by berserkers on Omicron Sector, the wiped-out fleets and ruined planets, the menace that had forced thousands of relatively fortunate survivors to flee for their lives, had provided him with an excellent excuse for his visit to this rock—he wondered if the commander had suspected the truth, that he wasn't an entirely random refugee.

The truth was that he'd come here to Claire Normandy's world with the hope of locating something Becky must have had in her possession—but he thought it extremely unlikely that Commander Normandy knew anything about that.

One thing he'd never dreamed of discovering when he'd planned a visit to this system was a great, bloody, thriving Space Force installation. Quite likely the presence of the base, with its automated defenses and its dozens of curious, suspicious human witnesses, meant that he wouldn't be able to conduct the search he'd come here hoping to carry out.

Looking round him again, taking in the view of nebulas and star-clouds as his almost weightless saltation carried him toward his ship, Harry had to admit to himself that Hyperborea might be, after all, a reasonable place to establish a weather station. Could it be that was really all that the commander was up to, she and the four or five dozen people she seemed to have under her command? The Galactic wind, that wraith of particles and forces drifting among the stars, through the near vacuum of normal space, was intense in the vicinity of Hyperborea. As might be expected, the subspace currents, the flows of virtual particles and virtual forces, in the adjoining regions of reality were also particularly fierce.

Not that any of this was directly apparent to a suited human moving almost weightlessly over the planetoid's airless surface, or looking at the celestial sights. Hyperborea offered some spectacular views of sky in basic black, adorned by several globular star clusters and an assortment of glowing nebulas relatively near at hand. Less prominent, but more impressive if you thought about it, was an impressive backdrop of distant galaxies.

The strongest source of natural illumination within four or five light-years was the Hyperborean primary, a small, white sun. The primary of the Kermandie system, a somewhat bigger star than this one but almost four light-years distant, made one piercing, blue-white needle point, below the horizon at the moment.

At the time of Harry's last visit to these parts, about seven standard years ago, the only human settlement in the Hyperborean system had been a civilian community already in place for centuries on Good Intentions. That planet was much larger than Hyperborea, a good distance sunward, only a few million klicks from the brown dwarf, almost near enough to receive from it some decent warmth. Good Intentions and Hyperborea both went around the dwarf and so were never more than a couple of hundred million kilometers apart. That was only a few hours by ordinary spaceship travel, which was almost always subluminal this deep in a solar system's gravitational well. The brown dwarf, in turn, carried its modest family of planets with it in its own orbit round the system's massive white primary star.

A long way out, antisunward from where the brown dwarf revolved with its brood, several nameless—as far as Harry knew—Jovian-type gas giants showed as tiny disks against the Galactic background; those huge planets were engaged in an unhurried orbital dance whose full turns were measured in Earthly centuries.

Good Intentions, the almost Earth-sized rock that had long supported the tiny civilian settlement of the same name, came the closest of all these bodies to being hospitable to life. It bore a certain natural resemblance to the Cradle World of Solarian humanity; but unfortunately, the similarity was not really close enough to allow people to live outdoors on Good Intentions without protective suits or respirators—at least not for longer than a couple of days. Good Intentions, most commonly called Gee Eye, was just so tantalizingly, perilously, close to being naturally habitable that members of one cult after another, down through the centuries, had persisted in making the experiment. Some of the less stubbornly committed had lived to tell about it. Terraforming Gee Eye into a friendlier place was considered impractical for a number of reasons, most of them economic.

Commander Normandy and the few of her people that Harry had directly encountered so far seemed vaguely suspicious of him—he could feel this attitude toward the visiting stranger, but he couldn't tell where it came from. He supposed that whatever version of his record had shown up on their database must look fairly shabby. Probably it cataloged all, or most, of the brushes he'd had with the local laws of several worlds. And there was always the possibility that some error had got in, making matters look even worse than they really were—that had happened to him more than once. But he had to admit that even the absolute truth about his past might not appear worthy of commendation, especially if regarded from a conservative viewpoint.

At the moment, the *Witch of Endor* was sitting unattended, all hatches closed and locked. Harry's little ship was in the shape of a somewhat elongated football, about eight meters where her beam was widest, giving a cross section somewhat too great to allow it to pass through the hangar doors used by the couriers and various small vessels that made up the military station's regular traffic. Such Space Force craft tended to be long and narrow, though some of them were more massive than the *Witch*.

Harry was just about to lay a gauntleted hand on his ship's lightly wounded side, where a spent fragment from some berserker missile had gouged a path, when there suddenly erupted a cheerful hailing on his suit radio, shattering the past minute or so of blessed silence. Even before looking around, he muttered oaths, too subvocally deep for his microphone to pick up. He would have much preferred to be left alone while he was outside, but evidently that was not to be.

The source of the hailing, now identifying itself by a waving arm, was an approaching figure whose space suit was marked with a tech's insignia and fitted on the outside with extra receptacles for tools. A couple of maintenance robots, metal things shaped like neither beast nor human, one hobbling and one flowing along on silvery rollers, came with the human tech. There didn't seem to be any neat way for Silver to decline the other's company. The fewer things he did to work on the suspicions of his uneasy hosts, the better.

"Hello, Mr. Silver, is it? I am Sergeant Gauhati here." Judging from the tool in the sergeant's armored hands, a thing like a complicated golf club, Harry thought he was probably engaged in testing the force-field generators that must lie buried below the surface of the landing field.

Harry grumbled something inhospitable.

Already he felt practically certain that the sergeant's maintenance task was only an excuse. The base commander had sent someone out to keep an eye on him. All right, so he and his dented ship had dropped in on her unexpectedly. So what? What the hell was Normandy worried about, anyway? He was no bloody goodlife spy—there could hardly be anything in his record to suggest *that.* And everything was peaceful in the vicinity of Hyperborea as far as he could make out. But he could not dispute the judgment of his instincts in the matter; for the Force to plant a base in an out-of-the-way spot like this, *something* had to be going on here besides an earnest, ongoing contemplation of the interstellar weather.

Harry's new companion had now caught up with him. Waving his deformed golf club about, the sergeant began to babble about how beautiful this section of the Galaxy looked from this particular vantage point. To Harry, he sounded like a would-be poet who had been too long pent indoors with people who refused to listen to him. Harry soon decided that those people had good judgment.

Another sight that made a big impression on the sergeant, to hear him tell it, was the striking effect produced by the clouds of distant external galaxies that were visible in the clear spaces between the vastly nearer and smaller clouds of the Galaxy's own stars and nebulas.

The other's voice came chirping at him: "Is it not impressive, Mr. Silver? Is it not beautiful?"

"Yep. Sure enough." The babbler's suit, like most Space Force models, bore a nameplate stretching across the chest: Sergeant Gauhati, sure enough. Harry made a mental note to try to avoid the sergeant during the remainder of his visit.

Ah, the romance and the joy of it! "Think of all the people in human history who've wanted to see something like this. And how terribly few have ever had the chance."

Harry would have preferred to let all those yearning trillions deal with their own problems, choose their own ways to go to hell. He silently congratulated himself on not trying to punch the other out. Privately he felt that he deserved a prize for such forbearance, but he knew he wasn't going to get one. And something more than mere tolerance was advisable if he wanted to allay everyone's suspicions of the mysterious civilian visitor. He said: "Well, it's a living. Or almost."

His heroic effort at making chitchat was not much appreciated; the sergeant didn't seem to be paying attention. "I love space," the man proclaimed, raising one arm in a grand gesture and sounding perfectly sincere.

"Yeah?" Harry didn't love space in spite of, or maybe because of, the fact that he had spent so much of his life immersed in it, far outside of any friendly planetary atmosphere. "I don't."

Astonishment, expressed by gesture. Obviously, the sergeant's attitude was something that everyone should share. "You don't? Why?"

Harry thought about it for a minute. Then he made an

abrupt wave at their surroundings. "Because there's nothing there."

"Nothing?" Only the whole universe, the outraged tone implied.

"I mean nothing—apart from a few soft, wet spots on a couple of rocks—that's friendly to a human being."

He might have added that he, personally, found space a fundamentally uncomfortable place to be. But he kept quiet about the annoyances, the itches and chafings and constrictions, that his suit was inflicting on him, because there was nothing wrong with the suit. It was his own, and as near his exact proper size as made no difference. The fact was that he always felt uncomfortable in space armor, no matter how well it fit, and despite his long experience in wearing it.

Stoically, Silver now resumed his effort to inspect his ship.

Some of the crew of the patrol craft had already gone over the *Witch* once, beginning as soon as they'd boarded it, in search of any dirty tricks that berserkers might have tagged it with during his reported skirmish with them over in Omicron. This was a routine procedure after any combat—but they'd taken a good look at the inside of the ship as well as the outside, so it would seem they thought they had some reason to be cautious about Harry himself.

Other than his ship, Harry Silver owned very little in the way of material goods. But, as always, he had hopes. This time he thought he might have real prospects—if only these people would let him alone for a little while.

Now Harry wanted to make sure the local techs hadn't overlooked any serious problems, and also to get a rough estimate of how difficult it might be to get the minor damage repaired; and he hoped he could figure out some way to get someone else to pay for the repairs—but above all, he wondered whether he could depend on the *Witch* to be spaceworthy in an emergency. Could the repair job, or part of it, be put off until later?

Lately, emergencies of one kind and another had been coming at him thick and fast, and he had the feeling that the next one lay at no enormous distance in space or time.

Of course, five years ago when Becky had sent him a message from Good Intentions, when she had possibly deposited here on Hyperborea the thing he'd now come hoping to find, she would have been working alone and in secret haste. And that, as Harry knew only too well, was when the odds went way up on getting yourself killed in some kind of accident.

For several years, he'd managed to convince himself that it didn't matter whether his one-time partner had robbed him or not; no, Harry Silver wasn't the kind of man who'd spend the valuable days of his life in pursuit of anyone, especially a woman, for no reason other than to take revenge for a financial swindle. But he couldn't escape the fact that the loss of that amount of wealth did matter. It had kept on looming larger and larger, until now he could no longer convince himself that he could be indifferent.

Again and again he replayed in his mind that last talk he'd had with Becky six, no, seven years ago. The last time he'd actually seen her—on Kermandie, that had been—and how they had made love.

And then, just about five years ago, that final letter. It had reached him on a world far distant from this one, coming across the void through regular civilian interstellar mail, with the mark of origin certifying that it had been dispatched from Good Intentions. The message had been short, and at first glance, had seemed simple and clear enough—and yet, because of certain things it left unsaid, the more he thought about the text, the more he wondered.

For one thing, she hadn't told him what she'd done with

the stuff. Of course that really wasn't the kind of information that was wise to put down in writing.

Whether or not he could now manage to get his hands on the box of contraband Becky *might* have left here on Hyperborea—and whether the stuff inside the box would still be in marketable condition—was going to make a very large difference in Harry Silver's future. He had spent most of his life as a poor man—or at least had spent most of it thinking of himself as poor—and he had hopes of being able to get through the remainder in a state approaching wealth.

Meanwhile, Sergeant Gauhati had resumed poking around with his deformed golf club. Anything but easily discouraged, he kept on venting bursts of babble, generally leaving between them intervals of silence big enough for his captive audience of one to have interjected a comment if he should happen to feel like it. Now and then Harry did manage to come up with something, just to maintain appearances. In between, he still had plenty of time to think.

Hell yes, Harry told himself now. I might as well take a chance and send out the Sniffer right away to look for it. If I'm cagey about it, I can do it right under the nose of Sergeant Watchdog here. What's the worst that could happen? But framing the question that way was a mistake, and Silver quickly decided he didn't really want to think about the worst that could happen, which might lead to an arrest for smuggling.

Meanwhile, what he had now been able to see of his ship was reassuring. The hull wasn't torn open, or even badly dented—it was more a case of the outer finish being marred. Yes, it would be nice if he could recover the piece of fairing that had come loose on its final approach, but the difference in performance would be only marginal at worst. He could drive his ship and survive without it.

And meanwhile, the sergeant kept on cheerfully rhapsodizing about the glories of the universe. Now he'd spotted something in the sky that reminded him of a string of jewels his mother used to wear. Next time, thought Harry, he'd ask the commander to assign some spy who couldn't talk the job of following him around.

What the sergeant had spotted was the flicker of another robot courier on its approach. For a weather station, the traffic was indeed pretty heavy, Harry thought.

Having seen all he really needed to see of his ship's outer surface, Silver opened the main airlock and went in, not taking off his armor or even his helmet when he got into the cabin, because he expected his stay would be quite brief. He didn't even bother to turn the gravity up to standard level. What he did do right away was to get the Sniffer out of its locker.

Sniffer was of course a robot, designed chiefly to be useful in prospecting for minerals. Standing on its four legs, the robot looked vaguely like a knee-high metal dog, being roughly the size and shape of an average organic canine. It took Harry only a few moments to set in a few commands, telling Sniffer what to search for, and to program the beast with a rough map of the planetoid's surface the way it had looked nearly seven years ago—that was the most recent map he had. Then he was almost ready to turn the machine loose.

But before doing that, Harry decided, it would be not only polite but conducive to Sniffer's survival to somehow immunize the robot against the local defense system. Weather station or not, this place was on edge and, Harry would bet, well armed. He'd already discovered that the defenses were alert. If local fire control, whether human or automated, spotted some unknown machine crawling around the rocks, it was likely to shoot first and then later try to help Harry figure out what had happened to his robot.

Opening communications with the world outside his ship, he called: "Yo, Sergeant?"

"Mr. Silver?"

Gauhati sounded surprised to be invited into the ship. Harry didn't expect to enjoy the presence of his visitor, but he hoped the invitation would serve as convincing evidence that Harry Silver had nothing to hide.

He wasn't really worried about the sergeant stealing anything, but you could rarely be absolutely sure.

Having cycled through the airlock in what seemed a puppy-like eagerness to be sociable, Sarge took off his helmet, revealing pale curly hair and a young face glassy-eyed with the joy of life. He stood in the middle of the cabin, scratching his head as everyone tended to do on taking a helmet off. Harry got the impression that his visitor was making a distinct effort not to appear to notice anything.

"How about some coffee, Sergeant? Or tea if you like. I'd offer you something stronger, but that would hardly do while you're on duty."

At first, as if in obedience to some reflex, the sergeant declined. But as soon as he was pressed, he changed his mind and accepted.

Pouring himself a dose of coffee from the same fount, Harry chatted about the Galactic weather. He refrained from trying to pump the sergeant about his duties, or about the business of the base in general.

Having made what for him was a considerable effort to gain the goodwill of his shadow, Harry began with his story of wanting to send the robot out to look for his piece of fairing. "But I don't want my robot blasted. Think it'd be safe?"

Gauhati clearly didn't know offhand. To get an answer, he had to confer on radio with someone inside the base, but the business was handled in a routine manner and didn't take long.

A quarter of an hour later, Harry and the sergeant were both buttoned into their suits and back outside, Gauhati in the middle distance puttering about with his tools again, doing whatever it was he was nominally supposed to be doing. Sniffer had been certified friendly and dispatched upon its mission, bounding away almost weightlessly over the rocks, wearing like a dog license a small black box that would serve as an IFF transponder and hopefully keep the robot from being slagged or blown to atoms as a suspected berserker scout. With the black box bouncing a little around its neck, the autodog got its bearings and then headed out at a good speed. There was a lot of territory to search, but Sniffer had its methods, and some neat tools to use.

Having seen his robot on its way, Harry went on with as complete a walk-around inspection of the inside of his ship's hull as he could manage—his unwelcome escort also keeping busy, at some unconvincing make-work job, not too far away, while still babbling, from time to time, his appreciation of the way the universe was organized and displayed. He gave Harry the impression that he thought it had been done just to keep him amused.

Harry hadn't more than halfway finished checking out the interior of his ship before inexplicable things started happening in nearby space. He had all his screens turned on, and they gave him a better view than he would have had if standing outside.

This was something quite different than the arrival of one more robot courier, or even a succession of them. He had a confused impression that other ships, and what seemed to be parts of ships, had suddenly begun settling on the rocks around him, drifting down from the sky like leaves in the puny natural gravity, and obviously trying to get as close as they could to the base installation. Harry tensed, for a moment on the brink of starting to power up. But a moment later, he relaxed again. This obviously was no berserker attack. It wasn't an incursion of the bad machines, because there was no sign of the weather station's defenses waking up around him. Somehow, Harry would have been surprised if this particular weather station were not very toughly defended indeed.

Now there came down a small rain of minor debris, the

chunks ranging in amplitude up to the size of a barn door. This was material that had evidently been sucked along through flightspace with the arriving ships, and only fell clear of them on their arrival. The deck of his ship trembled under his boots as a piece the size of a kitchen refrigerator came down at a good velocity, only a couple of hops away. Someone, hell, it could be a whole squadron, had recently been shot all to pieces—and here he'd been complaining about losing a little fairing.

The imitation meteor shower turned out to be a very brief one. Meanwhile, Harry counted no more than two actual ship landings—one of them was pretty hard, almost a crash.

The new arrivals were of moderate size. The one Harry got a good look at he estimated as two or three times the size of the *Witch.* It looked to him like a Space Force craft, though there was no way he could immediately be certain. He saw a streak, a puff of dust on the horizon that dispersed in vacuum, vanishing against the star-clouds almost as soon as it appeared, and once a perceptible tremor of impact came racing through dark rock to touch his booted feet.

Whatever was going on, it was no planned exercise, and it was certain to mean turmoil, people and machines going on full alert, rushing around every which way. Well, that pretty well sank his hope of getting a report back from Sniffer any time soon; private business of any kind would have to be put off until later. One thing you did learn in getting older was how to have a little patience.

Not having received any urgent warnings or orders to the contrary on his suit radio, Harry went through one more quick walk-around inspection. Then, feeling partially reassured about his ship's condition—*Witch* could lift off in a matter of seconds, if necessary, though weapons and shields were still depleted—he went into the cabin again, just long enough to throw together a bag of personal belongings. Then, closing up the airlock behind him, he went skipping lightly back toward the station, curious about what was going on. Sergeant Gauhati, for once keeping his mouth shut, had already headed back in through the airlock—or rather had started to do so, but then stalled, obviously under orders not to allow the suspicious civilian any time to himself outside his own ship.

Glancing back over his shoulder, Harry thought: *Go to it, Sniffer. Bring me back a fortune.*

And then his thoughts were wrenched back to his immediate situation as the base defense system finally, belatedly, chose that moment to go into what could be nothing less than a state of full alert. His helmet howled with a signal impossible to ignore, then began a general call to battle stations. Not having any such place to go to, he managed to ignore that.

What had looked like raw projections of natural rock altered their shapes, turning into efficient-looking projector turrets. The entire sky abruptly hazed over with a dull red, all but the brightest celestial objects disappearing as force-field defenses deployed against incoming missiles or landers. The whole foundation of the base, just as he was about to reenter the huge structure, went quivering, as if with some impending transformation.

Just as Silver, his duffel bag slung over his shoulder, was about to step into the base airlock adjoining the landing field, he turned on an impulse and glanced back—in time to behold half a dozen machines, the size and shape of groundcars, emerge from some unknown nest, moving fast, darting and rushing to the newly landed ships. Ambulances, Harry quickly realized.

He stood there watching for a few moments longer, and then he had to jump out of the way as the same machines, coming back to the base by a different route, began rushing past him. Through glassy covers on the boxes, Silver could catch glimpses of wounded men and women. Fresh casualties, a good many of them, were obviously being extracted from the just-landed ships.

He gave the machines that were bearing the wounded priority of entry at the airlock, then followed them inside.

THREE

That the alert was not called until long seconds after the ships' arrival indicated to Harry that it had not been triggered by the mere fact of the Hyperborean sky being suddenly full of spacecraft and debris—instead, the immediate cause of alarm was most likely some item of news brought by the people whose ships were piling in on the field in such disorder. And their bad news was probably the story of how they'd managed to get themselves so horribly shot up.

What Silver could see of the base defenses, now that they'd come alive—a thin haze in the airless sky, a couple of turrets now protruding above rocks in the distance—suggested that they were every bit as formidable as he'd come to expect they'd be.

When he got back inside the base, he took care to leave his armor on; everyone else in sight was wearing theirs, or getting into it, some with an awkwardness that showed this wasn't a drill they practiced every day. Finding a spot at the intersection of two broad corridors, with the door to the base commander's office in sight, Harry propped himself against a wall and waited, holding his helmet under one arm and carrying his duffel bag of personal gear hooked onto his suit like a backpack. He'd tried to choose a spot where he could keep out of the way of hurrying folk who looked like they might have some real business in hand. He noticed that the artificial gravity had been adjusted to a little lower than normal, and he assumed he wouldn't have to wait long before someone told him what to do next.

He was in a good position to see Commander Normandy come out of her office, from which she emerged just long enough to take a look at some of the wounded as they were being brought along the corridor, evidently on their way to the small base hospital. Harry thought that he could see her dark face turning a shade lighter. She was going to be sick. No, she ordered herself sternly—he could see the effort in her face—she was not.

Looking up, the commander caught sight of Harry Silver and beckoned to him. Again he thought that he could practically read Claire Normandy's thoughts: Here was one situation she could deal with immediately, one essential thing that could be done, instead of staring at horrors over which she had no control.

Stepping into the commander's office for the second time since his arrival, Harry noticed immediately that the huge window that had earlier caught his attention was no longer a real window. Doubtless, a panel of something even tougher than statglass had slid up over the portal on the outside, and it had turned into a situation screen—and even the screen had now thoughtfully been covered with white noise, so Harry wasn't going to be allowed to see whatever gems of information it might hold.

He thought he had a pretty good idea of what Claire Normandy wanted to tell him, but there was no chance of their getting down to business right away. Almost immediately Harry's armored body was bumped from behind by someone without armor who came elbowing his way in through the doorway, moving with an urgency not to be denied. This was a man Harry had never seen before. A shaken man, a wounded man, wearing no space suit because he had a bloody bandage and a sling on one arm, showing he'd just come from the medics. He was wearing a Space Force dress uniform with a captain's insignia on the collar.

Commander Normandy recognized the captain at once, though her manner suggested they were acquaintances rather than friends or long-time comrades. When she offered the captain the chair that Harry had earlier occupied, he more or less collapsed into it and then stayed seated, the fingers of his good hand clutching one comfortably curved arm as if he feared the solid floor beneath his feet might give a sudden heave and pitch him somewhere that he didn't want to go.

"We were ambushed," the captain got out in a high voice somewhat the worse for wear. He seemed to have a dozen other things he urgently wanted to say, but at the moment, none of them were ready to come out.

Taking advantage of the pause, projecting calm authority—she did it well—the commander introduced him to Harry as Captain Marut. The captain's face was a lot paler than the commander's. His dress uniform looked somewhat tattered, as if he'd been through a couple of nuclear explosions while wearing it and hadn't yet had the time or opportunity to change. One of the sleeves of his tunic had been ripped completely off, so the bandages could be properly applied to his arm.

The captain was not a big man, or husky; in fact, he was almost frail, if you stopped to consider his actual dimensions. But with lots of energy, all of it mobilized right now. Large nose, curly hair, intense eyes, at the moment bloodshot with stress and fatigue.

While Marut was resting momentarily, gulping water from a cup someone had handed him, trying to organize his thoughts, Commander Normandy turned back to Harry, but just as she opened her mouth to speak, the adjutant interrupted her with a string of jargon meaningless to the outsider. Another urgent problem that it seemed only the commanding officer was competent to solve. Harry moved aside a couple of steps and took up an attitude of patient waiting, setting down his helmet and duffel bag on the floor where no one would trip on them and he could grab them in a hurry.

When Harry, his presence more or less forgotten, had spent a couple of minutes in the company of the wounded officer, he began to understand that it wasn't fear or shock that made the captain shake, that knotted the grip of his fingers on his chair arms, so much as it was anger.

The story came out somewhat incoherently, but basically it was simple enough. The commander of the task force must have been killed when his ship was hit—the evidence said that that vessel had blown up with all hands lost. They'd tried to get off a courier to Port Diamond, telling headquarters there about the disaster, but there was no way of knowing if that robot messenger had vanished safely into flightspace before the enemy could swat it. Other ships in the task force had been boarded—

"Boarded?" Normandy interrupted. "Are you sure of that?"

"They told us so," Marut assured her. "Before they went silent. But check the boxes."

"We're doing that."

Harry was thinking that given a successful boarding of one or two task-force ships, it was more than likely that the berserker boarding machines had managed to extract valuable information from those vessels and their crews before destroying them.

Maybe they'd even managed to discover the task force's intended mission.

The commander's thoughts were evidently running in a similar track. "Who was on those ships, Captain? That is, who might have been taken prisoner? Only the regular crews, or—"

Marut was solemnly shaking his head. With an air of reluctance, he informed his questioner that one or two of the people on those ships had been Intelligence officers.

Marut himself, of course, had no idea what secrets those officers could have been carrying in their brains, or if the enemy had killed them quickly, or if perhaps they had managed to kill themselves. But obviously the matter worried him. Much could depend on the identity of those people taken prisoner, if indeed anyone had been captured. And on whether those unfortunate ones had managed to silence themselves, activate their deathdreams, before serious interrogation could begin.

I seem to be . . . I seem to be the ranking officer among the . . . among the survivors." Marut looked around him, as if the fact were only now sinking in. "It's going to be up to me to send Port Diamond a detailed report before we go on . . . but that can wait."

Then, it seemed, there would be nothing to do but wait for further orders from headquarters—of course, by the time those orders arrived, the deadline for carrying out the assigned mission would have passed.

From what the captain was saying now, it sounded like the task-force commander and his staff had been opening sealed orders when the enemy struck. But Marut couldn't be sure about that.

Commander Normandy was looking at the speaker strangely. "Captain, did you say 'before we go on'? You're not thinking of proceeding with the mission, are you?"

His eyes turned on her blankly. "I intend to carry out my orders." *How could there be any question about that?* "Only two ships left out of the original six—both are damaged, and I don't know if we'll ever get one of them off the ground again. I'll have to recruit more forces somehow. What do you have available, Commander?"

Still, no one had mentioned in Harry's hearing the exact nature of the mission that had been so violently interrupted. Whatever it was, it was going to have to be scrubbed—the shot-up task force was no longer adequate to the task—to any task. This was obvious to everyone—even to Harry. Obvious to everyone, it seemed, except to Captain Marut. It was still impossible for that officer to realize that he didn't have enough hardware left, or enough people either, to attack anything.

"—let alone the kind of escort Shiva must be traveling with," said one of Marut's officers, who had come in, helmet under his armored arm, to join the talk.

Shiva. Obviously a code name, one that evoked strong and unpleasant emotions in the people who were using it. Like several other items in the conversation, the name landed in Harry Silver's consciousness and lay there, an unidentified object on his mental workbench, waiting until it could be connected with something that would make it meaningful. Meanwhile, he kept on patiently standing by and listening, aware that in the turmoil, he was hearing things that would not ordinarily have been allowed to reach his ears.

And sooner or later, someone would take note of the fact that he had been allowed to hear it.

Now and then one of the people who were continually coming and going in the office glanced over at Harry; he stood there in his civilian armor with his helmet off, looking bored, like some kind of salesman who had dropped in to sell the base exotic foodstuffs or entertainment modules, and was waiting to be told what to do now. He gave no sign that he was taking any interest in anything that the military were talking about.

At last, Commander Normandy turned to him again. This time, circumstances allowed her to get a little farther: "Mr. Silver, I brought you in here to explain to you—" But once more, as if it had been planned, there came the inevitable interruption.

The way Normandy and Marut kept shooting glances at the big chronometer built into the office wall, together with certain phrases in their conversation, strongly suggested that the deadline they were worried about was a matter of real urgency. And it wasn't just minutes away, thought Harry, watching them, but a matter of hours, or maybe even of standard days. There was a different kind of tone to the urgency. Was Marut totally crazy for wanting to go on with the mission, whatever it was? That was an interesting question.

For the second or third time now, being persistent though reluctant, the commander was telling Captain Marut: "Then I'll get off a courier to Port Diamond right away, tell them we're forced to cancel the mission."

"No! Wait!" For the second or third time, she met with an urgent objection. The captain, it seemed, would rather die than submit to having his mission officially canceled. But so far, he hadn't come up with any reasonable alternative.

And still more people kept popping into the office, one or two at a time, some of them on holostage and others in person, all clamoring for the commander to make decisions: There were more wounded crew, a handful of still-breathing remnants of people, survivors of the combat crews of the merely damaged ships, who were still being taken out of the remnants of their ships in medirobots—it seemed that some were having to be pried out of the wreckage, with great difficulty—and hurried aboard the station.

With all this activity going on, the door leading into the commander's office from the corridor was open most of the time, and still the medirobots were rolling past, one or two at a time at irregular intervals. Silver hadn't been counting, but it seemed to him that he'd now seen at least twenty smashed-up people being brought out of those smashed-up ships, and he wondered how many more there were going to be. He wondered also how the medical facilities of this small base were coping with what must be a nasty overload—but maybe they, like the defenses, were more formidable than he would ever have guessed just by looking at the outward appearance of the place.

Over the next half hour, an additional three or four ships' medirobots, each containing a shattered but still-living human body, were brought aboard the station, and the same number of units—he couldn't tell if they were the same ones—went back out, empty, yet again. They must be laboriously prying people from the wreckage out there, peeling away damaged armor somehow, bringing them still alive out of a ruined hull invaded by vacuum. Silver inadvertently got a close look at the contents of one incoming unit and turned away, not blaming Commander Normandy for feeling ill.

By now, Silver had heard repeated confirmation of the basic numbers involved—in Marut's squadron there had originally been six tough ships, three cruisers and three destroyers. And now there were only two destroyers left, and both of them were damaged, and both their crews badly shot up.

Another of the things that Harry Silver began to wonder while he stood waiting, adding up scraps of information, was why a fighting squadron, especially a shot-up one, would put in at a weather station, even in an emergency. One good reason would be if the surviving ships were just too badly damaged to reach any other friendly port—but that did not seem to be the case here, according to the information he could overhear coming from damage control.

You wouldn't choose a place like Hyperborea just to obtain the services of medirobots—had the squadron commander's overriding concern been the condition of his wounded, he'd certainly have found a greater number of human doctors, and probably an even better supply of helpful hardware, less than an hour's travel sunward, on Good Intentions. By now,

Harry had also learned that among the perhaps sixty or eighty people who crewed the small base on Hyperborea, there were just two qualified physicians, who were now overwhelmed with more work than they could handle.

The facts strongly suggested that Marut and his squadron had been intending to put in at Hyperborea all along.

Confirmation of this idea lay in the fact that Commander Normandy hadn't been surprised to see Marut when he arrived, only horrified at the condition of his squadron. Everyone else on the base now gave the impression that they'd been taken by surprise to see warships dropping out of the black sky in such a headlong rush to get here that they cut it very close with their reemergence into normal space. That meant that Claire Normandy, and she alone, had been expecting the fighting squadron's arrival. Which in turn indicated to Harry that its mission was some kind of a deep secret.

By now, some ten minutes had gone by since the commander had brought Harry Silver into her office, meaning to tell the civilian that she was commandeering his prospecting vessel, which, though showing signs of damage, was certainly in better shape than any of Marut's craft. But her attempts to do so kept being forestalled by interruptions, by the necessary demands of people concerned with matters even more urgent. This happened half a dozen times before she could hit Harry with the announcement she'd been trying to make.

When at last the woman in charge was able to deliver her message to him, Harry only nodded, slowly and thoughtfully, and did not put up the argument that the officers had evidently been more or less expecting.

Getting his ship wasn't all she had in mind. "Mr. Silver, let me ask you something plainly."

"Shoot."

"Do you represent, in any way, any agency of the Kermandie government?" The look on his face was evidently answer enough. "I didn't really think you did," Claire Normandy concluded, a trace of humor showing through her stress. "But if you had, I might have given you a message to pass along to them . . . never mind, forget I brought up the subject."

And even before the commander had finished speaking, there it was again—Harry could hear, for the second time since his arrival, someone in the background talking in tones of fear about someone or something called Shiva. Silver was able to identify the name as that of one of the gods of old Earth, but ancient mythology seemed an unlikely subject for an urgent conversation at this time and place.

Instead of arguing about having his ship taken from him, he said: "Commander, obviously you've got some kind of major dispute with berserkers coming up. I don't like 'em any better than you do, and I'm eager to be helpful. But just so I can be a little intelligent with my helpfulness, maybe you can answer a question for me: Just what in hell is this Shiva that we're all so worried about?"

The commander seemed to consider several responses before she finally settled on: "A berserker."

"Special one, evidently. Is it just so damned big, or what? New weapons, maybe?"

Suddenly her features reminded him of delicate ice crystals. "I don't have time to discuss the subject today, Mr. Silver."

"All right. Let it pass for now."

The Space Force regulations regarding security were more numerous, and more rigidly enforced, here on the frontier. Claire Normandy almost invariably followed regulations, though she had no reason to suspect the presence of any goodlife agent, or Kermandie agent for that matter, in her crew.

Goodlife—a name coined long ago by the berserkers themselves—were humans who sided with the cause of death.

Rare, warped minds who favored dead and murderous machinery over live humanity—such were uncommon anywhere, and almost nonexistent in the Force. There was no doubt, however, that they did exist. "Almost" was very far from good enough.

There were several reasons why an unfriendly agent might want to get close enough to her crew to be able to observe them at their work—but it was hard to imagine just how the hypothetical spy hoped to accomplish that.

For the moment, Commander Normandy looked a little more worried than before, as if she might be trying to remember just how much in the way of military secrets Silver could have overheard while standing in her office. Any breach of security was her own fault, of course, for bringing him in—but there was no use fretting over that now. When true disaster struck, when fate stopped merely taking potshots and pulled the trigger on a machine gun, no one could dodge every bullet.

She assured Silver that the Space Force would see that he was compensated—according to the standard scale—for the use of his ship, or for its loss if things happened to fall out that way.

Again, he didn't try to argue the point.

Not that she was really offering him any opportunity to do so. "And now you must excuse me, as we are very busy."

In return, he gave the commander a nod, and a parody of a salute that she never saw, having already turned her back to plunge into yet another urgent discussion. Silver scooped up his helmet and his bag of personal gear and lugged them out of the office, methodically tramping away through corridors, locating without much trouble the small room he'd earlier been assigned as quarters. And in the back of his mind as he tramped, he was thinking: *Kermandie government?* Me? *What in all the hells was* that *all about?*

He supposed he'd be able to find out sooner or later. Once

in his room with the door closed, accepting the assurance of his instincts that the enemy was not actually at the gates, he got out of his space armor, scratching his head and sighing with relief.

And there in the snugly comfortable little room he waited, sitting in the one chair, for a couple of minutes actually twiddling his thumbs. The possibilities of amusement in that activity being soon exhausted, he began working simultaneously on a short drink—he'd thoughtfully brought a bottle of Scotch whiskey in from his ship—and a chess problem, which his room's holostage set up for him. The device was quite accommodating, allowing him to choose from a wide variety of styles in the appearance of the virtual board and pieces. Harry selected characters from *Alice in Wonderland.*

No use trying to get any rest now, he wasn't going to have time. Ah, peace was wonderful. But Silver didn't expect that he'd be granted much time to enjoy it.

FOUR

After a while, Harry used the room's communicator to call his ship. When the housekeeping system aboard the *Witch* answered, he checked to see whether any messages had yet come in from Sniffer. Nothing yet.

He'd been in his room for almost an hour, quite a bit longer than he had expected, and was considering trying to catch a nap after all, but then the holostage chimed an incoming call, and the head and shoulders of Commander Normandy appeared, disrupting a rather interesting end game, the original chess problem having long since been solved. Speaking without preamble and in a forceful voice, the commander requested the codes required to make his ship's drive work. Evidently the Space Force techs she'd sent out to the *Witch* had been stubborn enough to keep trying for many minutes to crack the programming locks, but eventually they'd given up.

"Codes?" Silver squinted, one eye going almost shut, at the little stage on which the commander's shapely head, asserting her official priority, had obliterated most of his imaged chessboard. "I can't seem to remember any."

Commander Normandy was being the maiden of ice again. "All right, Mr. Silver. I am impressed by your downlocks, and I want them removed, right now."

He held the glass in his hand up a little higher so she'd be sure to see it. "A downlock code, hey? Did you try looking that up in the ship's manual?"

Captain Marut's head now appeared on-stage, looking over the woman's shoulder. He actually seemed to have calmed down a little. "Silver, I'm not sure that the type of code you're using on your ship is entirely legal—in fact, if we look into it, I bet we find it isn't. I wonder who put it in?"

"Can't seem to remember that, either."

It was Commander Normandy who proved equal to the situation. Sweet moderation was back, at least for the time being. "The point is, Mr. Silver, we need your ship, or we may need it, and the military necessity is too urgent for us to play around. You told me earlier that you were eager to be helpful. What is it you want? Something more than standard compensation, I assume?"

"Nothing so unreasonable as that, Commander." Harry leaned back, rocking gently on his chair's springs. "My problem is, I've stumbled into a situation where I don't know what's going on. I can lose a ship if there's no way to avoid it—wouldn't be the first time. But I do want to know why. Surely you can tell me more than you have so far—which is just about nothing."

Captain Marut started to interrupt with renewed mutterings about legality, but the commander gave him a look that quieted him. In this, she was going to remain in charge. "All right, I'll explain. I'm taking a chance on you, Mr. Silver, because of the positive things in your record, and because of the fact that in our situation, your willing cooperation may be even more important than your ship."

"Oh?"

"The point is, we are in grave danger of missing what may be our only opportunity to neutralize the berserker advantage that devastated the Omicron Sector. Shiva happens to be our code name for that advantage."

"Ah." Earlier, she had said it was a particular machine. "And what would this advantage look like if I ran into it?"

"Have you ever seen a berserker's optelectronic brain, Mr. Silver?"

He stared at her for a long moment before replying. "Yeah. Matter of fact, I have. Why?"

It wasn't the answer she had been expecting. "Well . . . actually I suppose it doesn't matter whether you have or not. They come in a variety of shapes and sizes and materials." Normandy was visibly weighing a number of factors, most of them things Harry could only guess at, and confirming for herself her idea that what she wanted from him could best be obtained by this kind of an appeal. Cards on the table.

She went on: "Shiva is the code name that headquarters has assigned to a certain piece of berserker hardware. More precisely, to the pattern, or to the pattern of patterns, of information that that piece contains. One particular berserker brain that has somehow grown to be tremendously capable, monstrously good at making strategic and tactical decisions."

He nodded slowly; the information fit with everything he knew from other sources. And it was bad news indeed—if true. What he couldn't understand was how the commander could be so certain about it; probably she just wanted to sound absolutely firm and convincing.

"All right," Harry said. "We've got a name for what just devastated Omicron. So now—?"

"If the berserkers took prisoners from the ambushed task force, and we must assume they did, chances are good they already know what I'm about to tell you. So I think the security risk in my doing so is minimal. The mission of that task force was to intercept Shiva and knock it out."

"That still *is* our mission," the captain put in firmly. "We are going to carry it out."

Claire Normandy paused long enough to turn her head, favoring her aggressive colleague with an unreadable look. Then she confronted Harry again. "However that may be, this base may be in grave danger of attack. Any way you look at it, we face a desperate local shortage of fighting ships and crew, particularly pilots."

As long as the information was flowing, Silver was eager to squeeze out all he could. "Wait a minute. You say you're going ahead with some kind of interception. How do you, or headquarters, or anybody, have any idea where this Shiva is?"

Marut's expression, his slight head shake, seemed to say that such a question was irrelevant. Worrying about it was someone else's job.

Harry tried again. "Was your task force expecting to pick up reinforcements here on Hyperborea?" No verbal answer for that either, but he thought the glum look in the two officers' faces signaled a negative. Silver kept pushing: "All right, say you have somehow managed to locate this super berserker. You even know just when it's going to be at some precise place. Headquarters assigned you six good ships to hunt it down—but now you want to tackle the job with one or two beat-up wrecks, plus maybe a couple of borrowed patrol boats?

"And if we throw in the *Witch,* which isn't even a fighter, you still won't be more than half your original strength. Imagine what kind of escort must be defending this Shiva if it's so damned important. Unless you've got some resources I haven't yet heard about, your plan doesn't make any sense."

The two officers were both glaring at him, but for the moment, they had nothing to say.

Harry kept at it. "And I still haven't heard an answer to the key question: What makes you think you know where Shiva is?"

Marut was ready to clap him in irons. "When we want your strategic assessment, Silver, we'll ask for it."

"You probably think you'll commandeer it."

But Normandy was determined to remain in control. "We do have the required information, Mr. Silver, about where and when to intercept the target. And we're even pretty sure about the strength of its escort. You can take my word for that."

"Maybe I can, but I don't. Sorry, Commander. I've taken people's words on things—well-meaning people—and lived to regret it. I've heard a lot about vital plans and inside tips and absolute essentials—heard about 'em, hell, I've tried to sell them—and some really are, and some aren't. Now, a minute ago you told me that my willing help might be more important than my ship."

"That is correct."

"Well, if you want my help, you'll have to explain that much to me at least."

Her cool gaze weighed him for a moment. "Stay where you are, Mr. Silver. I'll call back in about one minute."

The two human heads disappeared simultaneously, and briefly his latest end game was back. Silver sat staring unseeingly at the inhuman faces of the Red King and White Queen, and the little pawn between them. If they thought . . .

Meanwhile, in the base commander's office, Claire Normandy ordered Sadie to screen out all distractions for a couple of minutes. Facing Marut across her desk, she said: "We're going to have to decide this locally. There's no time to consult with headquarters."

"I agree, Commander."

"I'll give you the best advice I can regarding Mr. Silver, Captain. Looking at his record, it's absurd to suspect him of being goodlife. I'm now convinced that he is no one's secret agent—his abrasive manners alone seem to me proof of that—and if you're determined to push on with the attack, you're going to need every bit of help you can get."

That last point scored with the captain. But he was still reluctant. He had eased his wounded arm out of its sling and was tentatively trying its movement. "I have my doubts about his dependability. I wouldn't take a man's defiant attitude as proof that he's reliable."

"Again, I suggest that you look at his record."

"I have, ma'am. It's pretty spotty."

"Yes, I admit that. But I think the parts that most concern us are reassuring."

"With all respect, Commander, you say you haven't seen him for fifteen years, and knew him only slightly then. People change."

"I don't see any real alternative to using him. Captain, if you are as determined as you say to improvise some kind of fighting force to go ahead and tackle Shiva—"

"Commander, that is the job that I and the people under my command *are* going to do. We have our orders from CINCSEC, and I hope you're not considering trying to countermand them?"

Claire Normandy's attitude seemed to say that she had already given that idea serious thought. "No, I'm not," she said at last, "given the importance of your objective. It's only by a lucky chance that we know where and when to try for Shiva, and if you and the survivors on your crew are willing—"

"We are."

"But coming back to Harry Silver. Whatever your impression of the man may be, he's one of the best combat pilots you'll find anywhere."

The captain remained dubious.

"Not only that, Captain, but he's familiar with the Summerland system."

"Ah."

Only a couple of minutes had gone by when Commander Normandy's head once more erupted in the middle of Silver's chessboard and she began an explanation—at least a partial one—of what she wanted from him and why:

"It is more than likely that we are going to want to commission you as a pilot. Put you back in uniform."

"Oh?" At this point, the news didn't exactly strike Harry as a big surprise. And he understood that he had no legal grounds for argument. The Space Force had the right not only to commandeer his ship in an emergency involving berserkers, but it could also draft anyone it wanted to for the duration. But he had to say something. "Piloting what? Someone just took my ship away."

The commander sighed. "I want more than your unwilling body, Mr. Silver. So before I start telling you what to do, I'm going to give you some explanations."

Harry agreed mildly. "That would be nice."

"I'd like you to come to my office. Talking face-to-face is almost always better."

More often than not, capable and well-trained human brains, working in tandem with the best military hardware, including state-of-the-art optelectronic computers, could at least hold their own against whatever hardware and software berserkers could put up. But when the humans were pitted against Shiva, this was turning out not to be the case.

"As far as we know," the commander said, looking at Harry across her desk, "no one has yet laid eyes on Shiva—I mean, of course, whatever fighting machine that brain happens to be housed in—and survived. But we have learned something about it. What we are talking about here is not new physical weaponry, but a new level of command computing. The pattern is of a single, guiding machine intelligence, making both strategic and tactical decisions for the enemy in Omicron Sector."

Harry nodded. Captain Marut was sitting silent in a corner of the room, evidently thinking his own thoughts.

Commander Normandy resumed. "The origins of Shiva are obscure. It first appears on the scene in a certain skirmish won by the berserkers about two standard years ago. A few months later, there was another, larger battle in which the enemy enjoyed uncommonly fine leadership—and shortly after that, another. By the increasing scale of our defeats, the size of the units and the fleets involved, it is possible to chart the monster's rise through the layers of berserker command. Just *how* this one machine has learned or otherwise acquired such fiendish capability is a question that demands an answer—but no one has come up with anything like a certain explanation.

"Our best hope is that the existence of this monster can be attributed to some chance or random factor—an accident, a contamination, an improvised repair. It's even a theoretical possibility that Shiva is simply the beneficiary of a lucky string of random events, taking place outside the computer but deciding battles in its favor. That possibility of course is very remote, more mathematical than real.

"We can only pray that no blueprint exists, that there are not a hundred or a thousand similar units already under construction."

"Logically, wouldn't that be the first thing they'd do once they realized that they'd somehow come up with a winner?"

"Of course—but no device as complicated as an optelectronic brain can be duplicated as simply as a radio or calculator. Sometimes it's not even possible to examine the most intricate parts, where quantum effects dominate, without destroying whatever unique value those parts may have."

Another possible explanation for Shiva's string of conquests was that the berserkers had achieved a breakthrough in computer science and/or technology. One particularly frightening suggestion was that they had found a way to get around at least some of the quantum difficulties that plagued all such devices on the smallest level.

"Therefore, there is a very good chance that Shiva is truly one of a kind," the commander went on. "Trying to examine it closely enough to duplicate it might destroy whatever makes it unique. This gives us, as human beings, reason to hope that if we demolish it, there will never be another."

Yet another idea put forward was that the device might have managed to successfully incorporate some living, if no longer sentient, components—for example, a culture of human neurons, scavenged from prisoners. It had long been realized that live brains could do certain things better than even the most advanced computers. Yet this was open to the fundamental objection that no berserker had ever been known to incorporate live components within itself—and there was a general agreement among experts that none ever would.

"They've been known to hold prisoners," Harry observed.

"Oh, absolutely—as hostages, or sources of information, or as the subjects of experiments. But never as functional components of their own system."

However Shiva might have come by its special powers, humanity's survival was going to depend on finding some means to nullify them. If the master killer should be promoted to some larger command—or if the enemy high command should manage to duplicate Shiva's capabilities in other machines—the results would be disastrous for all Galactic life.

"Theorists have also debated the possibility that Shiva's success depended on the help of some renegade human, a goodlife military genius, whether Solarian or otherwise. But there is not a shred of hard evidence to support such a conjecture.

"In the known history of the Galaxy, few forms of humanity other than our own have ever demonstrated any military competence at all. And there is no reason to suspect that any exceptions are involved in the present situation. And no Solarian human with any outstanding competence in military tactics or strategy has been reported missing, as far as I am aware."

"Would headquarters pass on that information to you if they had it?" Harry wanted to know. "To the commander of a weather station?"

"This base is rather more than that, Mr. Silver, as I'm sure you have deduced by now."

Harry was nodding slowly. "And you, as its commanding officer, have more responsibility than shows on the surface. Probably more rank, too."

"Be that as it may," the commander said. And Marut, sitting in his corner, raised his head in mute surprise to look at her, as if he had just sighted some new obstacle in his path.

"All right," said Harry Silver, and looked at them both. His voice took on a stubborn tone. "Which brings me around again to my original question, which I asked about half an hour ago. You've been explaining all around the edges, but we haven't got to it yet—how do we expect to find this super-smart piece of hardware just waiting for us somewhere? Don't tell me we've got a spy at enemy headquarters."

The commander sighed. "Has your brain been fitted with a deathdream, Mr. Silver?"

"Hell, no."

"Therefore it would be a bad idea for you to carry the answer to that question—even assuming that I could give it to you. People who know certain things should not go into combat, into situations where there is a real risk of being captured. Even if you did have a means of instant suicide available, it's far from certain that you could activate it before interrogation began. The berserkers have known all about our deathdreams for some time."

"Ah," said Harry after a moment.

"That is why we are particularly worried," she added, "about the prisoners who were apparently taken from several task-force ships. Some of the people aboard those ships evidently had information that should not have been carried into combat."

"Those particular people," said the captain, "were to have disembarked here, stayed on Hyperborea."

"But they didn't," Harry observed. "Well, Captain? What do you think about it? Wouldn't you like to know how headquarters thinks it knows where Shiva can be found?"

"No." Marut was shaking his head calmly. "I have my orders." After a moment, he added: "When it comes to classified information, none of us should know anything beyond what we absolutely need to do our jobs."

"Really?"

"Really."

Commander Normandy went on with her briefing. If the unknown sources on which Solarian intelligence depended were correct, Shiva was scheduled to arrive, eight days from now, at the berserker base—once a Solarian colony—whose code name was Summerland, and which lay at no great distance, as interstellar space was measured, from Hyperborea. Only about eight hours of superluminal flight. No doubt the code name, Summerland, had become wildly inappropriate since the berserkers moved in, but that had been the name of the human colony and everyone stubbornly refused to change it. Since it had been overrun, it was a good bet that nothing of even the inanimate works of humanity survived there.

"Summerland," said Harry Silver in a muted voice, and for the moment, he had no more to say.

"I understand you know the place quite well?" the commander asked.

"Yeah. Lived there for a while."

"You were aware that several years ago, it became a berserker base?"

"I have heard that, yes."

"Well, that's our interception point. Where Shiva's going to be."

"If you really know that much, where is it at this moment? Somewhere in this sector?"

"Mr. Silver, you will get no answer from me to any further questions on the subject."

When the conference in the commander's office broke up, Harry went to get something to eat. The mess hall was small but reasonably cheerful, and there were promising aromas in the air.

There was Sergeant Gauhati. Harry determined to avoid eye contact and to sit down somewhere else. The room looked like it could seat around forty or fifty people with plenty of elbow space. Officers tended to congregate on one side, enlisted spacers on the other, but all ranks evidently shared the same mess here. And unless there was another food-service facility, one the visitor hadn't seen as yet, the total number of people on this base must be rather small.

He carried his tray to a small table, where he sat down alone, not looking for companionship. He had plenty to think over. By now, Harry was firmly convinced that he himself was the only civilian on the planetoid. None of the casual talk he overheard even came close to bringing up anything that sounded like a military secret. He was wishing now that he'd kept his mouth shut and hadn't asked to hear any.

He couldn't quite identify the entree on the day's special, and hadn't bothered reading the posted menu, but the stuff passed the taste test. It gave a convincing imitation, at least, of lean animal protein and a promise of satisfying the appetite, instead of simply killing it.

Someone was standing in front of Harry, and he looked

up, startled. Marut, holding a tray a little awkwardly in his one good hand, asked: "Mind if I join you?"

"Help yourself."

The captain sat down. "Just had word from the officer in charge of docks and repairs here. I am definitely down to one destroyer, the other isn't salvageable."

"Does this change your plans?"

"Not at all. I propose to go on, with whatever force I can muster, and achieve the interception at the scheduled time and place."

Harry leaned forward across the little table. "Look—let me say it one more time. Assume for the moment that you do know where and when to catch up with Shiva. When they planned your mission on Port Diamond, they assigned half a dozen tough ships to do the job. Seems to me that to try it with half your original strength, or less, will simply be throwing human lives away."

Marut's voice stayed quiet, but tension was building in it. "*You* look, Silver—we have no other option. And if your achievements as a combat pilot are really as good as the record indicates, I can't imagine why you don't see that. I assume that in spite of your griping, you're coming with us? Or would you choose to sit here in safety?"

"Safety, huh?" Harry pulled thoughtfully at the lobe of his left ear. "I expect the commander will get around to making the big choice for me if she doesn't like the way I decide things on my own. Tell me, Captain, just out of curiosity, exactly what tactics did your original plan call for?"

"That's classified information, and furthermore, I see no point in going into it now."

"You're probably right. Might be dangerous to tell me anything classified. Anyway, I suppose you'll have to work out a new plan now?"

"No doubt I will. We will. But it hasn't been done yet."

The rest of the meal passed mainly in silence.

. . .

On leaving the mess hall, Harry went to his cabin to get some sleep. As he kicked off his boots and shed his coverall, the narrow bed looked very good.

Cursed with a fine imagination, Harry, as he stretched out and called for darkness in his room, could readily picture what Summerland must look like now. The clouds of dust and vapor, raised by the berserkers' cleansing process, must have thinned enough to let a little sunlight into the lifeless lower atmosphere.

So it was no surprise to Harry that when sleep came, Summerland whirled through space before him in a system where a greenish sun cast a green light on everything.

Dreaming, he drifted closer, and for a time, everything on the world before him was, impossibly, just as he remembered it. And although his waking vision had never beheld Becky Sharp anywhere near that system, he knew in his dream that she was somewhere there, just out of sight . . .

FIVE

Early on his second day aboard the base, Harry renewed his assurances to the commander that she could have his ship, at the standard rate of compensation, the money to be put into his hands within thirty standard days. How far beyond this donation his willing cooperation was going to extend, he wasn't sure just yet. He'd tell them all he could remember about Summerland, even though that wasn't a subject he wanted to think about just now. As to whether he'd volunteer to drive some kind of ship in Marut's planned action—he didn't absolutely refuse. But right now, Harry's inclination was not to go along. As part of the deal, however, he would get his suit on right away, head back out to his ship and reconfigure the downlock codes, any way she wanted them.

Legally, the commander's emergency powers allowed her to draft him, or just about anyone else, into the Space Force for the duration of an emergency as nasty as the evidence suggested this one was shaping up to be—but as a practical matter, Harry wasn't worried about having his arm twisted. Not yet. Marut would probably prefer to get his revenge on Shiva without the help of any damned reluctant civilians—even if he did have to take their ships.

On the evidence Harry'd heard so far, even when admitting the importance of the objective, the mission Marut was proposing sounded like a sure bet for compounding the disaster of the ambush. Harry still couldn't understand what made them think they knew where Shiva was going to be. Well, lucky for them if they were wrong about it.

The commander didn't push him when he showed reluctance. Instead—and this made him wary—she sweetly expressed her appreciation of Silver's newly patriotic and cooperative attitude, at least with regard to his ship.

Then she suggested—firmly, in the way of commanding officers everywhere—that since their deadline for launching toward Summerland was still six days away, it would be a good idea to fit the *Witch* with some new hardware. For example, a c-plus cannon. She just happened to have a spare one—the new, compact, relatively low-mass model—sitting in the arsenal. A likely piece of spare equipment for your typical weather station. Sure. The *Witch* was not really built to be a fighting ship, but she was versatile, and if her armaments could be beefed up according to Commander Normandy's specifications, and with a pilot like Harry in the left seat, she might be almost a match for a regular destroyer.

Harry wasn't familiar with that particular model of weapon, and thought that tacking one on his small ship sounded a little ambitious, but he made no protest. He'd already, in his own mind, said good-bye to the *Witch*. She was a good vessel, but there were a lot of other good ones around. He'd stand by to cooperate with the techs.

And now there was time for a little personal discussion.

After briefly harking back to their meeting of fifteen years ago, Harry asked: "How long've you been here, Claire?"

Claire Normandy, not reacting one way or another to the familiarity, said she had now been on station here for a little more than two standard years—minus a couple of months of leave.

Harry came back to business. "The captain seems hell-bent on going on with this mission, whether I sign up to go with him or not."

"Yes, he is."

"Not my business, really—or it wouldn't be if he wasn't taking my ship—but do you think that's a good idea? My ship and your two little patrol boats aren't going to work as replacement for three battle cruisers and one destroyer."

"It may not be a good idea, Mr. Silver. But so far, it's the best we have."

From time to time, Marut grabbed a little sleep, ate something, had his wound looked at by a medic—it wouldn't do, Harry supposed, not to be in top shape when Shiva blasted him into atoms—and soon plunged back into the effort of improvising his new command.

The majority of survivors naturally seemed somewhat discouraged. Tirelessly, the captain kept exhorting: "We're not beaten yet, people."

In his spare moments, Captain Marut tried to keep up the morale of his surviving troops. Once or twice he visited the critically wounded, silently regarding their mangled and often unconscious forms as they lay in the two rows of medirobots that were jammed next to one other in the small, overloaded base hospital.

One or two of these people caught some of Marut's fervor and assured the captain that they were ready to press on with the mission—or they would be when the deadline for liftoff arrived. Harry, listening to a secondhand version of what was said, couldn't tell if the crew were really that gung ho or if they were simply humoring their commanding officer in hopes he'd soon return to his senses.

Among the task-force crews, casualties to qualified pilots had unfortunately been even heavier than to the other specialists.

Gradually, Marut revealed the tactics that he meant to use. He wanted to arrive at the Summerland system with his makeshift force no more than a couple of hours ahead of Shiva and its escort, and *take over* the berserker station there.

When another officer pointed out that any berserker base was bound to have powerful defensive weapons, the captain said he hoped to seize control of that armament and use it to blast the machines carrying and escorting Shiva as they approached.

The officer protested: "Nothing of that kind has ever—"

"Been attempted. I quite realize that. So the enemy will have no reason to expect it now. We'll have an advantage of surprise."

One way to look at it, thought Harry, was that the captain's chief purpose in life had now become revenge on an enemy that had slaughtered his comrades.

Some of the other ways of looking at it were no better. Harry wondered if maybe it griped the captain even worse that a disaster like this could abort his career.

What a plum the Shiva assassination mission must have seemed when they were talking it over back on Port Diamond. How the officers would have jockeyed and politicked, when possible, for such an assignment. But now what had been a chance for glorious achievement, leading to promotion, widespread publicity, perhaps even political grandeur, was turning into a fiasco. Now, to Marut, any risk must seem worthwhile in the effort to retrieve his fortunes.

. . .

The base on Hyperborea had never possessed any offensive capability—that had never been its purpose. It was not home to any substantial number of fighting ships, and lacked the facilities to support them. Commander Normandy also had at her disposal a few armed launches, narrow little craft, used as shuttles around the planetoid and on errands to and from other ships hanging in low orbit. These launches had room in them for little more than their two crew members, but Marut's reconstituted task force could have them too, if he could figure out some way to use them. And that was the extent of the direct help Commander Normandy could provide.

Hyperborea did also house and deploy a good flotilla of the most advanced superluminal couriers, the majority of them at any given moment berthed deep within the rock.

Those couriers had been coming and going at a high rate over the last standard month, and in fact, the landing field was empty of them now, though a supply ready for launching as required was ready underground. Information kept on coming in, a bit here and a bit there from the data-snatching buoys and probes, regarding the monster berserker commander codenamed Shiva by its victims.

There was only one other inhabited solar system physically close enough to make it possible that help might be obtained from it before the deadline. As a matter of form, an appeal for help was sent by fast courier to the authorities—there was really only one authority—on the planet Kermandie, four light-years distant. The expected rejection arrived by return courier in less than twenty-four hours—as everyone who knew anything about that paranoid dictatorship had assumed it would. But now the fact that the appeal had been made was on the record. It would be there the next time the question of interstellar sanctions against Kermandie came up in council.

. . .

True to his word, Harry had gone back to his ship and turned over the codes to the human techs, still glum with failure, who met him there. When a test had satisfied the technicians that they could now move the ship and use it, they left it to go on about more immediately urgent business—right now, work on Marut's one salvageable vessel had priority. Once more, Silver found himself alone.

Again he checked for messages, and this time, to his silent elation, found that a coded transmission had come in from Sniffer. The search robot, while remaining somewhere out in the field, had transmitted several pictures, which the man now decoded and examined in the privacy of his ship's cabin—under the present conditions, there seemed no chance of his getting away from the base to see the site for himself. The defenses were ignoring the robot dog, which had already become familiar to them, but both humans and machines would be sure to take note of a man in civilian armor, especially if there was anything out of the ordinary in his behavior.

Sniffer's pictures came up, one at a time, in three-dimensional form on the smaller of the control cabin's two holostages. The total absence of any sunlight in the images reinforced an impression that they had been made somewhere underground. The robot's lights illuminated a cramped, irregular space among big black rocks, and they showed two objects of great interest to Harry. One of these he thought he could recognize as the very thing he'd come here on the chance of finding: a small box made of some hard, durable substance, of rectangular shape, neutral gray in coloring, and presumably of sturdy construction. It was just about big enough to contain an average-sized loaf of bread.

But it was the sight of the second object that brought on sudden sickness in the pit of Harry's stomach. Wedged tightly between rocks, only a couple of meters from the small box, was an inert suit of space armor, custom-made and individualized, bearing painted and engraved markings that allowed Silver to recognize it at once as Becky Sharp's. The suit was jammed in a position that looked extremely uncomfortable, the head slightly downward between two huge slabs of stone.

Inside the armor there would presumably be a human body, frozen flesh and bone now every bit as inert as the useless protection in which they were encased. No doubt both the suit and its wearer had been exactly where they were for a long time; taking into consideration everything he knew about what Becky had been doing and what she might have done, Harry Silver decided that five years would be just about right. The statglass faceplate of the helmet was turned away from Sniffer's probing cameras, so there was no chance of his getting a look inside the helmet—not that after five years, he would have wanted to see in.

Looking at the images, Silver went through a bad few minutes. In fact, they were much worse than he would have expected had he tried to imagine something like this happening to Becky. He shifted the recorded images to the bigger of his cabin's two holostages, but that didn't help at all. During this time, he remained dimly aware of the noises being made by the crew of Space Force techs and their machines, clumping around outside the hull, getting ready to perform modifications on the *Witch.* But fortunately, the people outside couldn't see him or hear him.

He was still sitting there, staring at the stage, when Commander Normandy called and asked him to come in for another face-to-face meeting.

"Be right there."

But then, for a little while, he didn't move a muscle. He just went on sitting.

Fortunately, he'd had several minutes quite alone before her call came in.

By the time Harry was once more sitting down in a room with the commander and the captain, he had himself more or less in hand. It was probably a conference room near her office, with a dozen chairs, only five of them occupied when Harry sat down around a businesslike table.

The main reason the commander wanted to talk to Harry Silver at this time was his supposed expertise on the world called Summerland, where now a berserker base existed and there was reason to expect that a mechanical monster code-named Shiva was going to show up at some precise time in only a few days.

Marut had brought one of his aides with him. Together, they had a dozen questions for Harry, all of them about Summerland and the other bodies that shared its solar system. The standard astrogational charts and models gave the basic facts, of course, but left out a lot of details that the planners wanted to fill in. Some of their questions he could answer, and some not; he promised to try the database on his ship, though he doubted it held much more than the basics. Summerland had not been a major concern of his for some time.

In Harry's present mental state, it took a while before Marut's basic idea really sank in: The captain, using whatever makeshift squadron he was able to assemble, was actually planning a landing, some kind of a commando assault, on the distant planetoid that had become a berserker base.

The captain's physical wounds were obviously bothering him yet, but Harry was beginning to wonder whether the psychic damage might not have been worse. Marut still had his arm sling draped around his neck, and used it about half the time, but he kept picking at the bandages as if he were ready to tear them off, working on some subconscious theory that the injury would go with them.

When Harry tuned in again on the conversation going on around him, he heard the commander asking Marut: "Do you suppose the machines that jumped you knew where you were going? What your mission was?"

"I don't see how they could have known that, ma'am. Unless there's been some goodlife spy at work." Then he turned deliberately to Harry. "What do you think of that idea, Mr. Silver?"

"How the hell should I know?"—and he found himself coming halfway up out of his chair. Deliberately, he made himself settle back. "Sorry, Commander. Are you suggesting goodlife spies at CINCSEC? It seems unlikely." They were all looking at him, wondering what had suddenly set him off. Well, they'd just have to wonder.

But if Marut jabbed at him verbally just once more, any time during the next few minutes, he was going to get up and smash the little bastard's face in, never mind if the man had only one good arm to defend himself with. But happily, the captain seemed ready to move on to other matters.

The damage done in the ambush to the people and machines of the original task force, the enormity of the setback, was looming larger and larger. No more than a couple dozen of its people, out of an original complement of hundreds, had survived that berserker attack—and twelve of the survivors were still occupying an equal number of the station's medirobots, down in the crowded little hospital.

Where else could the captain turn to get some help?

The commander herself warned Marut not to expect much in the way of assistance from Gee Eye: "That's not a major spaceport down there, nor is it a favorite retirement destination. I think you'll be lucky if you can find a dozen people qualified out of their ten thousand. And how many of the dozen are going to volunteer . . . ?"

"And how many of those who volunteer will we be willing to accept after we get a look at 'em? But we have to try."

Claire Normandy agreed that it would be better if someone other than herself did the talking. Captain Marut volunteered to make the appeal—but then bowed aside in favor of one of his junior officers, who was admitted to have a more diplomatic manner.

The commander gave him some advice. "Tell them only that you need a few people—a very few—for a special mission. That some kind of space combat experience is required. And we might as well tell them at the start that it's dangerous—that'll be obvious anyway, and maybe we'll get a little credit for honesty."

The only real neighbors of the handful of people on the military station were the ten thousand or so living on Good Intentions. As Captain Marut was given the story by Lieutenant Colonel Khodark, the commander's second-in-command, "neighbors" was too strong a word. The Gee Eyes were the only other population within reasonable radio communication range, and that was all. Theirs was an old, old colony. According to the official histories, it had been founded for scientific purposes, even before Earth-descended humanity had been caught up in the berserker war.

There was of course also an unofficial history, in the form of legend or folktale, stating that the colony had begun life as a smugglers' base. Folktales were silent on the subject of how the place had got its name.

Over the last century or two, the people of Gee Eye had never been close to the mainstream—if indeed such a thing existed—of Galactic Solarian society. Traffic in and out of their modest spaceport was always low. The history of the place testified that it had an attraction for cranks and visionaries.

"What keeps it going?" Captain Marut asked.

"Not tourism, though our people go there sometimes just for a change, to get off the base for a little while. The population is largely folk from other worlds who want to get away from it all, I suppose. There are a couple of small Galactic Council facilities," Khodark replied.

"Do they all live in one town down there, or what?" The captain looked as if he felt vaguely uneasy, trying to imagine a mere ten thousand people spread out over the whole land surface of a planet almost the size of Earth.

"My understanding is that there are now three towns," Khodark explained. "Near enough to each other to be served by one spaceport. Plus a few outlying habitations, none of them at any great distance from the port."

Silver had actually visited Good Intentions at one point in his career, which was more than Commander Normandy had done—he had been in a surprising number of places. He could remember only one town there, but no doubt things changed over the years, even on Good Intentions.

Naturally, Marut wanted every fighting ship that he could get, and now he had his heart set on the few making up the small, separate defensive fleet of the planet Good Intentions, what the people on Gee Eye called their Home Guard.

Not that there was any prospect of his actually getting those. Harry Silver could have told the captain, and the commander did tell him, that the leaders of Good Intentions were not about to send their small flotilla off on a dangerous gamble in some remote and unknown place. And there seemed to be no way they could be compelled to change their minds.

"Trouble is, we'd have to fight a battle with them to get any of their ships away from them."

No one on the base was sure of how many private ships might ordinarily be based on Good Intentions, what type they were, or indeed, whether such craft existed. Records kept by the early warning array, which tracked all traffic in and out of the system, indicated that there could not be very many and that none had any fighting ability worth mentioning. But whatever the number, all of them seemed to have been driven elsewhere by their owners as soon they got wind that some kind of berserker emergency was shaping up. Certainly no parked hulls were visible in the latest long-range scans of that planet's lone spaceport, where normally two or three showed up.

Staring out through the broad statglass window of the commander's office, Harry thought about how soon he might be able to get down there to Gee Eye. More and more, he was nagged by the urge to see if he could learn anything about Becky's last days. If he actually took part in this upcoming battle, or wild-goose chase, or whatever it turned out to be, and lived through it, and if he still had a ship to use when it was over, he'd give it a try.

Once or twice, as this latest planning session continued, Silver had to be called back from some apparent daydream—the people and things in front of him tended from time to time to disappear, and there were moments when all he could see was a painfully positioned suit of armor, caught between masses of rock that Zeus himself couldn't have pried apart. And the only words he was able to hear clearly at this moment were purely in his mind, spoken in a voice that had never uttered a single word inside this room, and never would.

"Are we boring you, Mr. Silver?"

Harry looked at the man who'd said that, one of Marut's junior officers, who in response, blinked, sat up straighter in his seat, and closed his mouth. Commander Normandy said something calm and neutral, bringing the discussion back to business. Over the last day, she'd been getting in a lot of practice at doing that.

Now several of the Space Force people were looking at Harry in a different way, not challengingly, but oddly. Probably, he thought, they were beginning to wonder if he was on some kind of drug.

Let them wonder.

What did the station's database have to say about the facilities and assets available on Gee Eye? Nothing that suggested a lot of help was likely to be forthcoming from there. According to the database, there were a few schools, a monastery, founded and then deserted by some now-vanished cult. A hospital or two, one of them some kind of facility run by the Council government.

Meeting over, Harry went his own way again. Once he got back out to the *Witch,* he needed only to transmit a few simple orders to get his prospecting robot back onboard and tucked away into its locker. He supposed he could unlimber the Sniffer again, any time he wanted to, and send it back to that same hole in the rocks to pick up the little box, the special contraband that Becky had . . . well, that she must have had in her possession when she sent Harry that last message. That letter had been mailed on Good Intentions, and he had assumed it was about the last thing Becky did before boarding some kind of ship, likely her own, and heading out for parts unknown—intending one quick stop on Hyperborea before she left the system.

But somehow he could no longer get excited about the contraband, which only yesterday had played such a big part in his future—what had looked like his future yesterday, today had only a tenuous existence. Right now he could no longer get very excited or worried about anything that might be going to happen to him tomorrow or the next day. There seemed to be only one thought that could still stir his interest: the idea of hitting someone, or something, very hard.

Damn her! Damn her anyway, for getting herself killed like that!

. . .

And there was one other vaguely interesting thing: Certain indirect clues, mostly having to do with the numbers and types of people he encountered in the mess hall and the corridors, were causing Harry to suspect the presence on-base of some big, powerful, highly secret computers. No one ever talked in his presence about any such installation, but the people he saw, or many of them, had something of the look of computer operators.

When he had mentioned his thoughts on the subject to the captain, Marut had dismissed them with the short comment that it was none of their business. They had no need to know.

"Maybe you don't, Captain. I wonder if I do."

SIX

A few hours later, Harry was sitting in the cabin of the ship that he still thought of as his own, pondering imponderables and reading a list that the cabin's smaller holostage held up for him. The list bore a high security classification, but the commander had given it to him anyway. Compiled by Captain Marut, it gave the order of battle for the revised mission plan. Shorn of official form and jargon, the gist of it was something like this:

• Item: One destroyer, whose only official name seemed to be a string of esoteric symbols—her crew had given their ship a kind of nickname that they used when they talked shop among themselves, but Harry wasn't sure he could pronounce the word, and he wasn't going to try. "The destroyer" would do. Marut's one surviving ship still showed extensive scars from the berserker ambush, but her captain was firm in claiming that she had been restored to full mechanical effectiveness. Six out of the original crew were in the base hospital. Nine spacers, a full third of her current shorthanded crew, were replacements, some of them survivors from the crew of the scrapped destroyer. There were still several positions open, and they were going to have to be filled somehow before going into combat.

• Item: Two patrol craft, known prosaically as Number One and Number Two, borrowed from the base. These were smaller than destroyers, and less heavily armed and shielded. But they at least had the advantage of being operated by their regular crews, some of Commander Normandy's people. Adequately trained, though some of them had never been tested in a real fight.

• Item: One civilian ship, the *Witch of Endor,* in the process of being refitted for a fight. Some heavy offensive arms could be installed, but when the job was done, her shielding would still inescapably be weak by military standards.

• Item: Four armed launches, down another notch in size from the patrol craft, and incapable of independent superluminal flight—they would have to be towed to the near vicinity of Summerland, another detail of the plan with plenty of room for things to go wrong. As part of a force setting out to attack a berserker base, they seemed to Harry good material for comic opera.

• Item: Three, or four, or maybe even a dozen—it was still uncertain how many could be cobbled together before the deadline—space-going pods or machines, even smaller than the launches. Marut's tentative new plan called for using these as imitation berserkers, convincing enough to fool the defenses of a berserker base for some substantial fraction of a minute. The miniature fakes, like the armed launches, would have to be towed to the scene of action.

Before Harry had been forced to spend much time in contemplation of the utter inadequacy of this array, an alarm interrupted his unhappy musings. Lights flashed on the stage in front of him, and a discordant ringing sounded in his ears.

Something, somewhere in the Hyperborean solar system, had automatically triggered a base alert.

The first indication that an intruder had entered the system came from the base's automated early warning array, a deployment of robotic sentinels throughout a vast volume of space and adjoining flightspace surrounding the Hyperborean sun. Tens of thousands of units, each self-sustaining and comparatively simple, spaced millions of kilometers apart, were arranged in vast, concentric spheres, the outermost of which lay at a distance of several astronomical units antisunward from Hyperborea.

The signal was physically carried to the base by a courier moving at superluminal velocity, a risky procedure this deep in a system's gravitational well, but absolutely necessary if the warning was to stay at least slightly ahead of the object whose presence it was intended to announce. The courier arrived at the base only a few minutes after it was dispatched, and an orange alert was at once imposed.

Had Harry's ship been even marginally spaceworthy, he would have scrambled at the alarm's first tingle, without waiting for orders. But the techs had had to drop their tools in the middle of the job, leaving the *Witch* in a shape impossible to get off the ground, let alone enter combat. Harry could do nothing but grind his teeth in frustration as he ran a quick survey of the landing field on his ship's screens and stages. He observed that the destroyer was still sitting where it had been, but none of the human techs were anywhere in sight at the moment. Presumably, they'd all responded like good spacers to the alert, and were already inside the comparative safety of the fortress's protective walls, crewing some kind of defensive positions. Probably they would be wearing gunners' soup-bowl helmets, in effect wiring their brains into almost direct control of the base's heavy, ground-to-space defensive weapons.

Sitting ships were sitting targets, not the place to be when things got rough. Harry got himself out of the *Witch* and in a few moments, he was out under the stars and galaxies, loping unhurriedly toward the base, looking around as he progressed. This time, at least, there were no wrecked ships falling from the sky. Rather, the reverse, in fact.

As Silver loped along, headed for the base's nearest entry port, he could watch Marut's crew running, or riding some transport, toward their waiting destroyer, and then, only moments after the last armored figure had been swallowed by the ship's airlock, the destroyer lurching up from the ground, a full-power liftoff without sound or flare, and rapidly vanishing into the decorated blackness of the sky.

As one of her duties upon declaring a full alert, Commander Normandy had promptly relocated from her workaday office to her battle station. This meant going much deeper underground, and she did not go willingly, for she yearned to be out in a fighting ship with Captain Marut, or with her own people who were crewing the small patrol craft. But those were only momentary yearnings, as she went where the duties of the base commander required her to be.

Two of the armed launches, as many of them as were currently considered combat-ready, also got up into low orbit, though they weren't as quick about it as Captain Marut had been.

Once back inside the base, Silver made his way through deserted corridors to his room, the better to keep out of the way of people who had useful things to do. This, of course, was not the time to pay a visit to the bar, which he assumed would be closed down anyway. Once in his little cabin, he sat around in his armor, sweating, swearing to himself at the irritation of being afraid to take it off. After giving the matter some consideration, he did go as far as removing his helmet, trusting that here inside the walls, he'd be given warning enough to put it on.

Every now and then, he tried to think about chess.

Only a little later, when the second and third and fourth reports on the intruder had come in, suggesting that the situation was more or less under control, that the war god wasn't swinging his full-sized hammer at the base, not at this minute anyway—only then did Harry clamp on his helmet and move restlessly back out to his ship. He'd thought of something useful that he could be doing.

The next stage of the alarm, long minutes after the first, arrived by c-plus courier in the form of an urgent message from Good Intentions, saying that their independent defense array had picked up, entering the solar system, a mysterious presence that fit all too well the profile of a berserker scout machine. When could they count on help, and how much help, if it became necessary?

The folk down on Gee Eye had to wait an ominously long time for their answer. By the time their query arrived at the base, everybody on Hyperborea had their hands full, and few were paying any attention to their civilian cousins living sunward.

The second report from the early warning array came in about twenty minutes after the first, and was somewhat more circumstantial. The presence of a berserker intruder was confirmed. Only a single enemy unit had actually been detected, and the main object of the berserker's interest appeared to be Good Intentions rather than Hyperborea.

Working on the theory that the information she had been given so far was accurate, the commander dispatched a courier to Port Diamond with a coded message describing this latest development for the people at headquarters.

Ordinarily, the two patrol craft attached to the base, and their well-trained crews, would have been dispatched without assistance to investigate the intrusion—but Captain Marut was straining at the leash, and the commander judged it a good idea to let him assume command of the Space Force, including most of the ships with which he was planning to tackle Shiva.

She also realized that it would have been something of a gamble to commit all of her mobile forces to the defense of the civilian colony of Gee Eye against what seemed only a probe, or a light attack. But in fact, she was not gambling much—when someone asked her about this, she replied that if a heavy attack was about to land on her own planetoid, the few ships she had sent away weren't going to be of much help anyway. The base on Hyperborea relied for protection mostly on its fixed defenses.

Less than two hours after the sounding of the base alarm, the hastily assembled posse of three ships—one destroyer, two patrol craft, and two armed launches—with Captain Marut in command, having driven out to hunt down the intruder, sighted the enemy.

The enemy replied to a volley of Solarian missiles with a couple of volleys of its own, at a range of several tens of millions of klicks, a large fraction of an astronomical unit. On the present occasion, this was little more than ritual sparring, for the missiles at subluminal speeds took the best part of an hour to reach the point at which they had been aimed; and only then could they seriously begin to hunt, questing for a target that might well be long gone by the time they got near its original position. The type of missiles launched by Solarians in this sort of combat had to do a lot of independent computing, a lot of nice discrimination between enemy and friendly hardware. They were about the closest things to actual berserkers that Earth-descended humans ever allowed themselves to build, close enough to make many people feel uneasy; but for effective combat at these immediate ranges, there was not a whole lot of choice.

Another effective mid-range weapon was of course the c-plus cannon. It could project slugs a few score million kilometers—up to half an A.U. No doubt Marut would have liked to mount such a weapon on his destroyer, but there were several technical reasons why such an installation was not feasible. Nor were any of the Solarian ships now available in-system armed that way. The patrol craft were too light; Harry Silver's *Witch* was just barely massive enough to carry the lightest model of the weapon.

To his surprise, this time Harry actually felt a twinge of disappointment at not being able to get into the action. Almost anything would be better than this sitting around and waiting.

At least one argument had been avoided by the forced grounding of his ship. Marut's position in the matter was that even when the *Witch* was ready, someone else ought to be placed at the controls, while the civilian stayed on the ground and out of the way—he warned Commander Normandy: Give Harry Silver back his own ship and the man would be long gone.

Shortly after the first message from the inner planet reached the base on Hyperborea, an almost continuous string of radio messages from Good Intentions started to flow in. Some were clear, uncoded transmissions, the people down on the sunward world evidently thinking security be damned, this is an emergency. This time, it looks like bad things could be happening to us.

Gee Eye's own homemade warning system, not nearly as extensive as the Space Force net enclosing the whole solar family, had somewhat belatedly picked up the intruder, and ever since that moment, the leaders of the sunward planet had been clamoring for the enemy to be beaten off.

The townspeople cried piteously for Space Force help. Haven't they all been paying taxes to the Sector Authority? Actually, that was a doubtful proposition, but it seemed unlikely that anyone was going to check up on it.

For all anyone on the base knew, the intruder could well

be a scout from the same berserker force that had earlier ambushed Marut's task force.

Naturally, the Gee Eye people knew nothing about that. They were scrambling their own modest fleet, really only a small squadron of home-defense ships, and activating what ground defenses they possessed—if Claire Normandy's database told the truth about the latter, they were certainly not enough to seriously slow down any serious berserker attack.

So far, Gee Eye's Home Guard fleet seemed to be taking an inordinate amount of time to get into position.

Claire Normandy detailed one of her subordinates to reply minimally, and in the proper code, assuring the Gee Eyes that the danger was recognized and steps were being taken. The subordinate was to promise nothing specific in the way of help, but instead, to prepare the neighbors for a detailed appeal for volunteers.

Even assuming that Harry Silver could be induced to volunteer, more skilled people were desperately needed—all the details of the revised plan of attack on Shiva had not yet been worked out, but whatever they turned out to be, the experienced spacers required to make the plan work would be in short supply.

Before the alert was sounded, the commander had ordered a computer search for people with the special skills and experience the task force needed. The only database in which it made any sense to look was a fairly recent, fairly decent, representation of the population of Good Intentions. Under Sadie's direction, her little office unit needed less than a minute to do the job, winnowing the list for anyone who fit the profile.

"You mean anyone at all, Commander?" Sadie asked.

"Anyone." Then Claire rubbed her forehead with irritation. "No, scratch that, put in one exclusion. Leave out anyone who's ever been indicted for goodlife activity."

In all, the base data bank contained, among much other

information, details on about a billion individual human lives. Included in that number were the great majority of the ten thousand people now living on Good Intentions. Unsurprisingly, it turned out that not a single person of that approximate ten thousand had ever been accused of being goodlife. Even so, the harvest of people experienced in combat was about as slim as the commander had earlier predicted it would be.

"What will happen if we simply try to draft these people?" Sadie asked.

"I don't know, but I want to avoid that road if I possibly can. Put out the call for volunteers."

With everyone on the base but Harry Silver either spaceborne in a fighting ship or at an assigned battle station on the ground, Harry suddenly found Hyperborea a lonely place. All the good flight-crew people available except himself—and the base commander; he'd heard she fit that category—were already millions of kilometers away and fast receding. Whether they were putting their modest force up against a mosquito or an armada, it was still impossible to say.

For the moment, he was separated from all human society, and as far as he could tell, unobserved. Harry decided he might as well use the time to advance his private goals. It seemed unlikely that he'd have as good a chance again in the foreseeable future. It was the work of only a moment to once more unlimber the Sniffer from its locker. Quickly, he gave the robot orders, sending it back underground with instructions to pick up the box of contraband and bring it to the *Witch*.

Damn, but it made Harry's joints ache to think of Becky lying there for sixty standard months or so in her wedged-in space suit. The hellish cold of deep space would have seeped into her dead joints years ago. What was left of her now would be as hard as the surrounding rock. He wanted to do something about that, perform some kind of ritual at least, but he couldn't come up with anything. He didn't believe the woman he remembered would have cared about having a fancy funeral, or any particular religious observance, and she had no close relatives alive that Harry knew about. But when he thought the situation over, he decided that he might as well pick up the contraband. In fact, Becky would probably have wanted him to have the stuff, though she must have been angry at him when she set out to hide it here—if hiding it had been her purpose.

He couldn't think of any other object that she might have had in mind.

Nagged by a craving to know more of the circumstances of her death, Harry considered trying to follow the Sniffer to the spot and examining the ground in person—but in the end, he decided against that course. For one thing, he doubted he'd be able to force his own suited body very close to Becky's inert form, wedged in a narrow crevice as it was. Even Sniffer had had trouble getting in there. The holostage images sent back by the robot could be made to display the exact dimensions of all the objects in them, and he could see that trying to get himself between the rocks would certainly be a tight fit. It was quite possible that over the past five years, the crevice had grown narrower as the rocks shifted. Harry supposed that the major excavations carried out by the Space Force, in the course of digging hangars for the base, might have had something to do with that. Even if Becky's suit had so far resisted being absolutely crushed, it looked like it was now wedged in so tightly that getting it out would be a major operation. The rock masses were so huge that sheer inertia dominated, never mind the feeble gravity.

While waiting for Sniffer to fetch his treasure, Harry once more scanned the holographic images that the robot had sent back during its earlier jaunt. Then, deciding there was nothing useful to be learned, he destroyed them in the cabin disposal.

After that, he sat in his captain's chair in the *Witch*'s control cabin, flanked by two other seats that were seldom occupied, and brooded: What would be the point, anyway, in trying to dig her out? For one thing, he'd have to explain how he'd happened to locate her body. And then the business about the contraband would be likely to come out. And it was hard to see how the lady herself would be any better off.

Now it was finally, truly, sinking in on him that she was dead.

Trying to give himself something more positive to think about, Silver fired up his ship's communication gear and tried to pick up more stray transmissions from Space Force ships, anything that would give him some indication of how the ongoing search operation, or skirmish, was progressing.

Less than half an hour had passed in this fashion, and Silver was still sitting isolated in his ship's cabin when the Sniffer came bounding and sliding back over the rocks, past the robots that were now standing idle around Harry's ship, waiting for the technicians to return and resume work.

The maintenance robots haughtily paid Sniffer no attention, and in a few moments, the autodog was back in the cabin, standing in front of Harry. Inside its chest, where an animal's heart and lungs would be, was a small cargo compartment, and at a code word from Harry, the door of this came open. Reaching in an armored hand, he brought out the little box, which felt as if it were of sturdy construction, no bigger than an ordinary loaf of bread and not a whole lot heavier. Immediately the moisture in his cabin's air began to freeze on the surface of the container, filming it in a layer of ice.

The box of contraband appeared to be only latched shut, not locked. Harry got a tool out of a locker and applied some heat. After the box had warmed up to the point where it was merely frozen, Harry opened the lid, observed that the contents were pretty much what he had expected, then closed the container again and tossed it as if carelessly into the bottom of a locker. The commander's people had already gone over the interior of his ship, and it didn't seem likely that anyone would have a reason to search it carefully again.

Meanwhile, Sniffer stood by, some accident of its programming causing it to give a fair imitation of a faithful dog, alert and ready to do its master's bidding. Harry squinted at the robot, but had nothing to say to it—that'd be the day, when he started socializing with machines—beyond erasing from its memory the records of its work since arriving on Hyperborea; and in another minute, the Sniffer was back in its usual place of storage.

There was no reason at all to suppose that berserkers had had anything to do with killing Becky—they liked to fry their victims thoroughly, whether in armored suits or out, rip them to shreds, sterilize them, vaporize them, make sure that not even bacteria or viruses could remain alive. But Harry, now that numbness and grief had had their first innings with him, was still aware of a powerful urge to hit out, to strike back at something or someone. The damned machines would make a more satisfactory target than people, the people around him now, who'd had no more to do with killing her than the berserkers had. So if the Space Force wanted him to sign up for Marut's crazy mission, he was ready. As soon as he saw the commander again, he was going to tell her so. If they were taking his ship, they might as well have him, too.

Listening to such scattered bits of enigmatic radio traffic as came drifting back from the berserker-hunters in their current scrap, Harry kept gritting his teeth, and knew that he was ready.

Meanwhile, his ship's communication system kept on picking up odds and ends of human signals, drifting in from a few light-minutes away. These were messages exchanged among the ships that had gone out hunting berserkers, and between those ships and their base. Most of the traffic, of course, was in code that Harry's communicator couldn't read. But the relatively low number of messages, and a certain tone that he thought he could read between the lines of the few words that did come in the clear, suggested that some enemy had indeed been sighted, but things were going reasonably well.

Harry found himself, in his imagination, taking the point of view of Captain Marut—there was no chance that anyone else would be in command out there. Now the skirmish, which had died down temporarily with the enemy in hiding, suddenly flared up again. Sitting with his eyes closed, he had the imagination and experience to make it quite convincing.

Scraps of radio information suggested that the crew of one of the armed launches was attempting to position its craft in just the spot where the enemy, if startled into sudden withdrawal, would be likely to plunge into flightspace.

Other devices were being tried. Marut was deploying the space equivalent of a barrage balloon—a kind of spreading-out device that extended mechanical or force-field tentacles for kilometers in many directions, presenting a deadly barrier against any ship or machine attempting to drop into flightspace. Just as deadly, in its own way, as a c-plus cannon. Even if it did not score a direct hit, it could fill a region, cubic kilometers, of space and/or of flightspace with a murderous barrier, shredding and pulverizing any ship or machine that tried to make a transition locally.

Harry, listening in, could easily fill in the gaps from experience and imagination.

Naturally, the berserker, outgunned as it was, wasn't being idle all this time. Now one of the Solarian patrol craft had been hit, Harry couldn't tell how badly, while making an all-out effort to stop the enemy. There were going to be more human casualties today, but Harry now got the impression that the berserker scout had definitely been stopped.

"We think we killed it before it could get off a courier," said one clear voice. "But we can't be absolutely sure."

After waiting for a few more minutes to make sure—with berserkers it was always necessary to make sure—Silver suddenly picked up a comparatively long exchange in clear text, strongly suggesting that the shooting was over; some kind of minor victory was implied. At the very least, no fresh disaster had befallen. All consistent with what Commander Normandy had told him when he called her in her office.

What communications Harry could pick up from Marut suggested that the captain was actually a little disappointed that there was no other target around for his crew to shoot at. A listener got the impression that the little man would have liked to keep his little fleet in space for some gunnery practice, but knew he couldn't spare either the time or the resources for that.

Marut was giving his ships, reluctantly it seemed, the order to return to base.

Warily welcoming this kind of news, and having done all he could, for the time being, to advance the readiness of his own ship—not to mention his own personal fortunes—Harry shut things down, clamped on his helmet, and went out through the airlock. In a moment, he was bouncing, in a motion that must have made him look lighthearted, back to the base again.

Then it occurred to him to wonder what he was waiting for; now that he'd decided, why put off action until he saw Claire Normandy again? The peak of combat urgency was well past, and she could afford to turn her attention elsewhere. Harry decided to call her right away and tell her he'd made up his mind.

Hello, Commander." He paused, then took a shot. "Would you be in the computer room, by any chance?"

Her expression altered subtly. "What do you mean? Has someone been talking to you about a computer room?"

"Not at all—just putting two and two together. Anyway, I just called to offer congratulations. Looks like you can put today's action in the win column."

"Thank you, Mr. Silver." Pause. "I suppose you've also arranged some way to listen in on our radio traffic?"

"Just a little, here and there. Look, Commander, next time you people head out after the bad machines, I mean this Shiva, I'll come along."

"I'm not personally heading out, Mr. Silver. As I suppose you realize, my job is here. Captain Marut will be in command of the revised task force, and I'm sure he'll welcome your participation." She paused momentarily. "May I ask what brought about this decision?"

He shrugged. "I just wouldn't want to miss the chance. Especially now that my ship will have such a great new toy to shoot with. Where do I sign?"

The commander's image looked at him curiously, but then accepted his change of mind unquestioningly. "I'll have a form for you to sign. See me anytime, Mr. Silver, and I'll take care of it."

Trying to remember what model of holostage the commander had in her office, Harry supposed that probably a connection could be established that would allow him to sign up while remaining aboard his own ship. Transmit a binding signature. He was on the verge of suggesting that they complete the formalities that way—but then something, he wasn't sure what, held him back.

SEVEN

As soon as the technicians were relieved of their duties as gunners on base defense, they got back to work on what had been Harry's ship. They unlimbered all their exotic gear from a heavy hauler, and, yes, it looked like they were actually installing a c-plus cannon. Harry thought he could successfully resist the temptation to oversee their efforts, especially as he didn't understand half of what they were doing, and they tended to ignore his questions. And anyway, his assigned room aboard the base would be quieter.

Yawning, he added up the number of hours that had passed since his arrival on Hyperborea. He'd slept only once in that interval and was overdue for some sack time. He returned to his quarters.

Odd dreams were commonplace with Harry Silver, and now, as he drifted in the shadowy borderland of sleep, he had one involving Becky. He found himself standing, having no trouble staying alive without helmet or armor, amid the airless black rocks at the very place where Sniffer had found her body. But Becky and her suit were no longer there; there were only the massive rocks, and his robot dog, not really much like a dog, that came to stand beside him. Even as Harry understood that he was dreaming, he knew also that something important was waiting to be discovered. But he was afraid to find out what it might be.

Harry had seen no reason to set a wake-up call, and he got in a good sleep of more than six hours. When he woke up, he lay for a few minutes reflecting on the fact that the deadline for intercepting Shiva was that much closer. A new standard day had started, local time.

As he showered and dressed, shaved, and ordered a minor hair trim from a machine in his private bath, the vague fear engendered by his dream hung with him, like the aftertaste of some unpleasant food. He got a change of clothing from his duffel bag and checked out what his room could offer in the way of laundry service.

He continued to think things over while going to the mess hall for some breakfast, the one meal of his personal day he really hated skimping. Having been informed on awakening that a yellow alert was still in effect, he went in armor, carrying his helmet under his arm. Today he seemed to be in luck: real melons, which, he was told, were grown in a greenhouse established behind the kitchen; fishcakes so realistically constituted and gently seasoned that they might actually have come from the fresh-caught bodies of his favorite fish; hot tea, and bread still warm from the oven.

A dozen other people were in the mess hall—to judge by their manner, a crew of some kind just coming off a shift of work. Not a flight crew, though. Again, Harry thought to himself that most of them looked like computer people, though he would have been hard put to describe the details that gave him that impression. Maybe it was a vague air of being nonmilitary, though in uniform. Their official insignia was unfamiliar and told him nothing helpful. He nodded a good morning, but stayed at his own table.

One of the people paused at his table, long enough to exchange a few words. "Looks like there could be some more action soon."

"Don't tell me any military secrets. I don't know if I'm cleared yet for classified information."

Conversation over, Harry returned to his private thoughts.

So. Five years ago, Becky had sent him a message. Hard copy, printed on real paper, exemplifying the kind of care that many people took with messages they thought of true importance. Of course the letter, dispatched by regular mail from the little settlement down on Good Intentions, had contained nothing that might incriminate either sender or receiver—except maybe by Kermandie rules. It had taken about a month to catch up with Harry on a distant world. Not a lengthy communication, but a reasonably upbeat one, full of vague talk about starting a new life, a feat he assumed Becky had intended to accomplish in some solar system other than this one. She hadn't specified where in the Galaxy she was going, no doubt because she didn't want an angry or a contrite Harry coming after her.

Obviously, Becky hadn't disposed of her ship right there on Gee Eye, because she'd needed it for at least one more trip. She'd been heading out of this system, bound for her new world—wherever she thought that would be—when she stopped here on Hyperborea for the last time. Carrying the box of stuff and evidently intending to hide it in a secure place—maybe she was planning to write Harry another letter, later, telling him where it could be found.

Coming to Hyperborea, she'd landed on what had then been an utterly barren rock, innocent of human habitation. Never dreaming that in a couple of years a swarm of engineers and a small army of their machines would be here, digging in to construct a Space Force base.

Harry sighed. Maybe that was an accurate reconstruction of events—but not necessarily so. He could think of at least one alternate version, in which Becky had hidden the contraband in that deep crevice during some earlier visit to Hyperborea. And when she stopped here for the last time and was trapped, she'd been on her way out of the system, intending first to retrieve the box, to take it with her . . .

But hell, he supposed the details didn't matter now. However she got to Hyperborea on her last visit, whatever her reason for crawling around among these godforsaken rocks with the box in her hand, the massive walls had shifted on her and she'd been caught. Pure accident.

All right. Accidents happened. Even smart people screwed up sometimes, or were overtaken by sheer bad luck. But whatever the actual details of the tragedy, what had become of Becky's ship? Now it was nowhere to be seen. And with all the Space Force activity here over the last few years, no object as large as a spaceship could possibly have escaped notice on a planetoid this small.

Try once more. Suppose that shortly after her death, someone else had come along, happened upon an abandoned ship conveniently available, and had simply made off with it. That was a possibility. Otherwise, the Space Force base-builders would certainly have found it when they arrived to start construction.

Maybe the Space Force *had* found it—and in that case, Becky's ship, which Harry remembered as being very similar to his own, was almost certainly still here on Hyperborea. It wasn't sitting out on the field, but it could be stored in one of the deep hangars—assuming it could have been brought in through the hangar doors, which were too tight for the *Witch.* But no, Harry realized abruptly, her ship couldn't be here, anywhere, or the commander would be trying to mobilize it, along with the *Witch,* for this upcoming maximum effort.

Something in the back of his mind didn't want to leave the problem alone. Humoring the impulse, he tried once more. Suppose Becky hadn't been alone when she made her last stop on this rock. She'd had an unknown companion, or companions, who'd treacherously murdered her and then stolen her ship . . . but had left the valuable contraband behind. No. Damned unlikely.

Every scenario Harry could think of was unconvincing, crippled by serious difficulties. At last he gave up—for the time being. Maybe his trouble was that he kept expecting everything to make sense, and the thing about real life was that it often didn't.

After shoving his breakfast tray into the disposal slot and nodding a good day to his new acquaintances, Harry walked out of the mess hall wondering what to do with himself. But he wasn't the kind to wonder about such a thing for very long.

There was a lounge, the kind of place that he preferred to think of as a tavern—the sign on the wall outside named it a Social Room—just down the corridor from the mess hall. The social room had the look of a place in which it would be possible, at most times, to buy drinks, with some emphasis on the kind that contained alcohol or other substances in common recreational use on one or more Solarian planets. Right now the facility was closed, no doubt because the yellow alert was still in effect. But that meant little to a man who knew how to persuade the standard-model robot bartenders to open up. In Harry's opinion, these robots were among the noblest servants of humanity, in spite of—or maybe because of—the fact that they were also fairly simple machinery. Harry had met their kind often enough before, in a great many similar facilities on a great many other planets.

The service staff in this so-called social room, like most such machines, moved about on rollers, and none of them were any more anthropomorphic than they absolutely had to be to deal properly with such things as glasses, bottles, and various forms of payment. Berserkers sometimes tried, so far without success, to build imitations of the Solarian-human model, and so for centuries, humans had very rarely made any of their own machines resemble people.

It wasn't hard for a man of Harry's experience to persuade the inanimate system manager that the last remnants of the alert had just been canceled. The door promptly opened and the lights came on and he walked in, seeing a wide choice of tables. Soon a statglass window, much like the one in the commander's office, cleared itself, offering a fine view of the landing field—not much out there at the moment to intrigue the tourist, owing to the paucity of ships. A waiter approached, moving on rollers in the form of a narrow pyramid of adult human height, gently swinging inhuman arms.

Helmet detached and resting within easy reach on the table in front of him, Harry treated himself to one drink, and then another, thinking it would probably be a wise strategic move to conserve the bottle in his room as a reserve. He ordered up a bowl of pretzels to go along.

Whoever had designed the room, if it could be called that, had tried, with some success, to imitate an Earthly garden. Stuff that looked like moss and short grass was growing over much of the floor. Out of the virtual scenery disguising one wall emerged a real, live babbling brook, only about a meter wide and no more than ankle-deep. The little stream curved and gently splashed its way over and around some stones amid a profusion of real ferns and moss, along with a few un-Earthly plants, before vanishing into the base of another wall, with muted sound and a little drift of mist suggesting a waterfall just beyond.

Looking into a nearby mirrored wall and crunching on a

real pretzel, Harry asked himself aloud: "I wonder what the road to Good Intentions is paved with?"

No one was around to hear the question except the robot bartender, and the machine, as its kind were wont to do, did its limited best to come up with a profound reply.

"They say that of the road to hell." Its voice was clear enough, carrying to Harry's table from its source in another pyramid behind the bar, but no more human than its shape.

Harry turned his head. "No, they don't," he corrected it sharply. "What they used to say was—oh hell, never mind." But then, even after saying that, he paused for a reply, and getting none, was irritated into trying once more. "You're not making much sense, barkeep. I was asking a question, and you took what I said to mean . . . never mind."

There followed a silence, in which Harry felt like a fool, trying to start an argument with a thing. The robot had accepted his rebuke meekly—well actually, of course, it was only looking for clues in human behavior and responding to them as programmed. It would just as blandly have recited the multiplication table, or rolled over to his table and tried to tickle him, if someone had programmed it to do either of those things.

Of course what it had actually been programmed to do, in its character of servant, was to remain silent when challenged verbally. It was supposed to maintain only a shadowy presence, projecting an air of quietly purposeful activity behind the bar, where its rounded, inhuman head slid back and forth as it went about its work. Well, that was how a good Solarian machine was expected to behave, anyway.

After officially downgrading the original red alert through orange and all the way to yellow, in steps half an hour apart, Commander Normandy had turned over the watch to her adjutant and got in a much-needed six hours or so of slumber. After waking up and dealing with the routine chores she found awaiting her, she went looking for Harry.

When both Harry's assigned room and his ship denied his presence, she was struck by another idea. She reached for a communicator, then changed her mind—she hadn't taken her daily walk as yet.

Only gradually had the commander, once established at her battle-station console in the computer room, overcome her suspicions that the enemy's move in the direction of the civilian colony was simply a diversion, while the real blow would be aimed at Hyperborea.

She had ordered a slight shifting in the deployment of the robotic pickets of the early warning array, so that the emphasis was more on defending the planetoid and its base.

From the beginning to the end of the action, the Space Force people noted that the Home Guard ships of Good Intentions were dithering about ineffectually, neither attacking the enemy nor staying out of the enemy's sight. If the intruder was simply a berserker scout, as seemed to be the case, the defenders were behaving in the worst possible way—the enemy could tally up their numbers in perfect safety. Normandy changed her mind about making an all-out effort to mobilize the Home Guard as part of the new, improvised attack force.

Commander Normandy hadn't had as much sleep as Harry following the skirmish, but she'd had a few hours. As a rule, that was about all she needed.

She'd been vaguely hoping that today's scent in the corridors would be fresh pine again, but instead, the program had come up with oceanside salt air. One of these days, they were probably going to get a murmur of surf as background music.

Somehow, she wasn't surprised, on reaching the lounge, to find the door already open and the music already playing. There was only one customer on hand at the moment. Guess who. The commander wondered whether to make an issue of his unauthorized tampering, then decided to let it pass. She probably ought to have canceled the alert entirely an hour ago. Raising her wrist communicator, she ordered Sadie to do so now.

Standing erect beside his table, she announced: "I thought I might find you in here, Mr. Silver."

"Call me Harry." He raised a half-empty glass in a deft salute. "Join me in a drink?"

"Don't mind if I do." Claire turned to the waiter. "A nip of that pear brandy, if it's still available." As the machine glided away, she sat down opposite the civilian visitor. A quick look reassured her that he displayed no obvious signs of intoxication. No, she didn't think it was substance abuse that people had to worry about with Harry Silver. "Glad to have you aboard. I was hoping you'd volunteer. Drop in my office, and I'll have the paperwork ready to make it official."

"Seemed like the thing to do. I suppose we have to fill out the paperwork?"

"I'm afraid the Space Force insists."

"No way I could possibly remain a civilian and still drive a ship for you?"

The commander thought it over for ten seconds while turning around in her hand the small glass of pear brandy, clear as water, that had just arrived. "You'll be driving some kind of ship for Captain Marut, as part of his reconstituted task force. But I'll see what I can do, if you'll be happier that way. This qualifies as an emergency situation, and that gives me considerable latitude in how I do things. In your case, I think we can stretch a point. Captain Marut will have to have some input."

"Thanks. You could make me a captain too, just to keep him out of my hair. Better yet, make me a commodore." Harry's face lit up suddenly, and he raised a finger for emphasis. "Best of all, bust him down to spacer third class!"

"You're right, Mr. Silver, I could make you a captain. But I won't."

"Oh well, it was worth a try. How is the conquering hero this morning?" Harry could see the destroyer out on the field, with a couple of maintenance robots fussing around it. "Is he happy with his victory?"

"Certainly. Is there some reason why he shouldn't be?"

"Not at all. A win is a win. I was just hoping it might make him feel a little less . . . suicidal in planning his next project."

"You keep using that word, Mr. Silver, and I don't like it."

"I don't either. In fact, it's one of my least-favorite words."

In the aftermath of the skirmish, Normandy and Marut were both more firmly convinced than ever that a few key people were desperately needed to give their revised plan of ambushing Shiva any chance of success. In the time available, the only possible place to obtain such help was Good Intentions. Faced with this fact, Commander Normandy was having a difficult time deciding exactly what tone to take, what attitude, conciliatory or threatening, when next she appealed to the authorities and the people on that other world.

She would have much preferred to manage with the people in her own command, or to get assistance from someplace other than Gee Eye. But neither of those choices was available.

Harry, deadpan, said he didn't think he could be of much use to her in deciding matters of diplomacy, which had never been his strong point.

Claire Normandy assured him that he didn't have to worry about being asked for his advice. She also took the opportunity to bring him up to date on the details of the successful extermination of a berserker scout.

They were still in the middle of their discussion in the social room when Virtual Sadie's head popped up on a nearby stage, bringing Commander Normandy word that the mayor of Good Intentions, named Rosenkrantz—at least it sounded like that to Harry—was calling up to announce that he and his chief of public safety would shortly be arriving in low orbit around Hyperborea.

"Sorry, Commander. But the mayor's very insistent this time. He says to tell you that he and Guildenstern are on their way for a short-range conference."

The commander sighed. "What's he want, Sadie?"

"He's bringing the volunteers who responded to your appeal. Says there are only six of them."

"That's half a dozen more than I was afraid we'd get. Rosenkrantz is bringing them personally? Then he must want something else."

"He's complaining again, ma'am."

"Ye gods, what's he got to gripe about now? Pieces of berserker falling on his head?"

"Did you say 'Rosenkrantz and Guildenstern'?" Harry interrupted, squinting.

The commander shook her head at him, conveying the idea that he ought to keep his mouth shut for a minute. "Tell them to go away, Sadie . . . oh, hell, no, never mind. I'll take the call when they're ready." She shut Sadie off.

Short-range conference'?" Harry asked. "With Rosenkrantz and Guildenstern? Did I hear right?"

"You did. Their initials really are 'R' and 'G,' respectively. Their real names are almost unpronounceable for people of the most common linguistic backgrounds, and they realize this, and don't seem to care much what we call them. Up to a point, that is."

"Do I take it that you don't get on with them all that well?"

"If you take it that way, you won't be far wrong . . . as for the conference, we've done it a couple of times before. They park their ship in a low orbit, and we can chat without a time delay. But I don't have to accord them landing privileges, which would mean inspections and red tape. And as for getting along, R and G don't seem to get along with each other very well. In fact, I suspect the reason they're both here is because neither would trust the other to come alone."

Soon an announcement came that the visitors were now in low orbit and had requested landing privileges. Commander Normandy coolly refused. "Unless you've come to volunteer. If you insist on landing, I'll assume you're here for that purpose and place you under military discipline."

"You wouldn't dare!" The head of Mayor Rosenkrantz was bald on top, but sported a long, fierce black mustache.

"In a limited sense, that's true, gentlemen. It wouldn't require any daring on my part at all."

That gave them pause. "Your candor is refreshing," said Chief Guildenstern at last. His broad face on holostage was choleric, almost matching the red shade of his close-cropped hair.

"I'm glad you find it so. Now, what can I do for you?"

When their dialogue with the commander got under way in earnest, it was soon obvious that the mayor and the chief of public safety of Gee Eye were united in demanding protection for their world against berserker attack. Both men held unshakably to the idea that the fundamental purpose of any Space Force installation must be to protect Galactic citizens in its immediate vicinity. Doubtless the pair had their political differences at home, but on this subject they sounded like identical twins.

"We're not going home until we get some kind of guarantee of protection." That was the mayor speaking.

"Then you'll be hanging in orbit for a long time. All I can guarantee is that I'll be doing my duty, and so will the people under my command."

Now it was the chief's turn. "Well, what else could your duty be? I mean, no one here believes that story that you're just a weather station. Some of us think you've taken leave of your senses."

"I don't see how that follows, Chief. We do have other assigned missions that we must accomplish."

"And what are they?"

"I can't discuss that now. In any case, the military situation is very complicated. Can we agree that I know that situation much better than you do? Can you agree to trust me?"

"In what way?"

"Let me borrow some of the ships of your Home Guard force."

Both of Commander Normandy's interlocutors were already shaking their heads. On this point the pair needed no time at all to reach a consensus. The mayor said: "Sorry, Commander. All our ships are needed for home defense, and we can't see our way clear to sending any of them away. I don't think you would either, in our place."

"And many of our crews would be reluctant to go."

"I'm not asking any of your citizens to risk their lives aboard." Having been granted an opportunity to see the Gee Eye Home Guard in action, or at least trying to get itself into action, Normandy and Marut had already decided they didn't want them—but some of their ships would have been very welcome.

Rosenkrantz could sound very statesmanlike. "The answer must be no. Our first priority is the defense of our own world. And for that, we need our own experienced people."

"That's a disappointing decision, Mr. Mayor, and not a very wise one. Right now the most effective means you have of defending your home world is to give me all the help you can."

"We're bringing you six volunteers, all of whom meet your stated qualifications." This was Guildenstern, with a faintly malicious smile. He put a little emphasis on the final words.

"That's excellent, and we thank you. I've dispatched a shuttle to bring them down. Now, to return to the subject of my borrowing a couple of ships from your Home Guard—"

"That's impossible!" Guildenstern had been getting redder and redder as the talk went on. But now he paused, and there were tones of mockery in his voicc as he said: "But I've been given to understand that a large number of volunteers are actually on their way to your assistance, Commander."

The commander was taken aback. "Really, Chief? From where?"

"Why, from Good Intentions. They're even bringing their own fleet. In fact, I understand they've already dispatched a courier to you."

That brought on a period of silence, during which Claire Normandy looked as puzzled as Harry, observing from slightly offstage, felt. Dispatched a courier? From a world distant by only an hour's travel in normal space? That conveyed a great sense of urgency, as it would mean saving only a very few minutes' time, at considerable expense. But no courier had yet arrived.

Normandy asked: "Could you amplify that a little, please? You've brought me six volunteers on your ship—"

"That's right."

"But who are these others you just mentioned? You said that a *fleet* was coming?"

"Well, that's what we hear. Probably their courier message will explain it all better than I possibly could."

Mayor Rosenkrantz hadn't yet given up on his own agenda. Now his image on Commander Normandy's holostage pointed a finger at her. "These other missions you say you have to carry out, but refuse to talk about, are doubtless all very worthwhile. But—"

"Yes, believe me, gentlemen, they are."

"I hope you're not going to listen to that madman who calls himself an emperor."

"Say again, please?" Claire seemed to have no idea what the man was talking about, though for Harry, a light had suddenly dawned.

Guildenstern pressed on. "Commander, will you answer me one question?"

"If I can."

"What is the fundamental purpose of the Space Force?" No need for Claire to come up with an answer, he had one ready. "To protect the Galactic citizens who support it with their taxes, right?"

"Mr. Mayor, we are an instrumentality of the Galactic Council. As such, I'm doing my best to protect all the settled worlds in—"

Guildenstern was growing hoarse with anger. "The people here don't understand this call for volunteers, Commander. *You* are supposed to be protecting us. It's not up to *us* to fight for you."

Normandy did her best to respond. Harry sat by, listening through all the futile arguments, sipping gently at his second drink, thinking that Claire doubtless needed it worse than he did. Of course, what the leaders from Gee Eye really wanted to hear from the Space Force was that they would be protected at all costs and had nothing at all to worry about, and no one with any concern for the truth could tell them that. Not even if Claire had had nothing else to do with all her people.

The visitors' tone varied between threatening and pleading—they demanded to be told what was really going on. Had the enemy really been driven off? Yes. Was a bigger attack to be expected? No one knew.

That Claire Normandy was simply telling them the truth did not seem to have occurred to them. That's right, she assured the Gee Eye leaders, this time it hadn't been a false alarm. If their own defense forces were trying to tell them that it was, it was time for them to have their military thoroughly overhauled. This intruder, or the force attacking Gee Eye, was assumed to have come from the berserker base at Summerland, for the simple reason that all other known enemy bases were much farther away.

Normandy said: "I assume you'd like some help from me if and when the enemy does return?"

There was a silence on the beam. Then the chief: "What are you saying, Commander? Are you saying that if we're attacked again, you'd withhold help?"

"I'm saying that unless *you* give *me* all the help you can right now, I might not be here next time. This base might not be here. Don't bother asking me to explain that, because I won't. Just take my word for it."

"I call that dirty blackmail!"

"Call it what you like. But there it is. We probably can't win the war by anything we do here or—or anywhere else—over the next couple of days. But we just might lose it if we fail."

"Are you expecting another attack?"

"I have just canceled our on-base alert. I have no specific information to suggest that a bigger attack is coming, and I can't guess any better than you can whether it really is."

Guildenstern, with anger quivering in his voice, told her he hoped that she and the emperor would get along.

"Can you explain that, please? I didn't understand. Who is this emperor you keep mentioning?"

She had the distinct impression that both men at the other end of the beam were surprised at her ignorance. "Others can explain that better than we," said Mayor Rosenkrantz.

As soon as the six volunteers had been transferred to a launch, the ship carrying Rosenkrantz and Guildenstern lifted out of orbit, their pilot announcing tersely that he was setting a course for home.

"Thank you for coming, gentlemen," offered Commander Normandy politely. "We'll be in touch."

"Good luck, Commander." Only the mayor voiced the wish; she got the impression that the chief of public safety was too angry at her to utter another word.

When the heads of the people from Gee Eye had vanished from the holostage, Commander Normandy told Harry Silver:

"It doesn't matter to them that we are not at all well equipped for planetary defense. Apart from our own little rock, that is."

"Want me to talk to 'em next time?"

"Thank you, no, Mr. Silver."

"Call me Harry. Until I get my uniform on, at least."

"We had better remain on business terms, Mr. Silver. Call me Commander Normandy. And speaking of your uniform, when are we going to take care of the paperwork?"

Harry drew a deep breath, but before he was forced to answer that one, Adjutant Sadie's virtual head popped into existence on the stage.

The words in which Sadie delivered her report were, as always, clear and concise, but this time they didn't seem to make much sense. A battered, obsolescent courier had just arrived within point-blank radio range of the base and had promptly transmitted a recorded clear-text message from an unknown man who said his name was Hector, claimed the rank of admiral, and declared himself to be speaking in the name of the emperor.

"I hate to bother you with this right now, Commander, but—"

"It's all right. Let me see the recording."

When it came on, the commander began to watch it, with an eagerness that rapidly faded into bewilderment.

The speaker on the recording appeared in a resplendent uniform and did indeed call himself Admiral Hector. The gist of what he had to say seemed to confirm what the leaders on Gee Eye had been saying, pledging what sounded like substantial support to the gallant people of the Space Force in their heroic mission.

Nothing in the message gave any explanation of why the sender had considered it necessary to use a courier for in-system communication.

A rumor sprang to life and spread through the base. Substantial help was soon going to arrive. Hope soared swiftly, at least among the more ingenuous. Ordinarily, the presence of an admiral could be taken as meaning that a real battle fleet was not far off.

Those among the Space Force people on Hyperborea who knew nothing of the emperor didn't even realize at first that the courier had come from Good Intentions—they assumed it had originated in some other solar system, perhaps at a considerable interstellar distance. Or from a ship en route, in flight-space.

But the early warning system had registered no such arrival.

Elation gave way to bewilderment. "Wait a minute. Is this stuff about admirals and emperors some kind of code?"

"It's not one that our cryptanalysts can recognize as such. No, I think it's meant to be taken at face value."

"He says his fleet is on its way here? How many ships?"

"That's how the message is worded. Just 'fleet.' It doesn't say how many."

"About time we had some good news. Watch for some kind of flight of ships approaching. Hold them in orbit above a thousand klicks."

But no fleet arrived. A swift computer search of the charts for the now-devastated Omicron Sector turned up no political unit claiming to be an empire, or ruled by any official with the supposed emperor's name.

Others on Hyperborea, who knew or could guess the basis for the rumor, were not led on to soaring hopes. Any joy that anyone could derive from the message was short-lived. The truth about the Emperor Julius was available from several sources. Even from Harry Silver, as soon as the commander had a chance to let him talk to her.

EIGHT

From what Harry had been able to see of Marut's crew since the skirmish, they were on something of a victory high. Battle damage this time had been minimal on the Solarian side. Only one of the patrol craft was back, but the other had suffered no damage, merely stayed behind to gather debris; it was Space Force policy to pick up berserker materials for study whenever it was practical to do so.

A couple of armed launches had lifted off to take part in the skirmish, and they had now returned to the base as well.

Commander Normandy was eager to meet the six volunteers brought up by Rosenkrantz and Guildenstern, and to welcome them aboard the base. She had them escorted to her office.

There were just five men and one woman in all, out of a population of something like ten thousand, who met the simple criteria she'd laid down for selection, and were willing to volunteer to serve in combat.

The short list read:

Frans Cordyne
Karl Enomoto
Christopher Havot
Honan-Fu
Cherry Raveneau
Sandor Tencin

Six capable and eager people could certainly make a difference in the efficiency of the new task force, and here were six volunteers who brought some useful skills, if their records could be believed. They were standing in an irregular line for the commander's inspection.

Each of the six, following instructions, had brought along a single bag or case of personal belongings, so an irregular row of baggage lay at their feet.

Three of the volunteers had reported for duty wearing what were evidently the uniforms in which they had once seen action, and those three saluted when she appeared. All were going to be issued new uniforms in any case—a robot came to take their measurements. Two were Space Force veterans, and one, Sandor Tencin, had served in the Galaxy-wide organization of dedicated berserker-fighters called Templars. Why he had abandoned that vocation was not immediately clear.

Stand at ease, people," the commander advised them.

The six were of varied ages, and in general, they gave an impression of solid capability.

Frans Cordyne was a retired spacer, an older man having little to say but projecting an air of competence, who had evidently opted to let his hair drift into a natural gray. A medium-sized mustache of the same shade had been engineered to grow in smooth curves.

Karl Enomoto was dark and round, with a serious manner that went well with his serious determination, as shown by his record, to achieve financial success. After surviving combat on several occasions, Enomoto had retired from an administrative Space Force job, evidently determined to spend the next epoch of his life in the pursuit of wealth. The dossier showed that he had been beginning to have some success.

Christopher Havot, one of the three not in uniform, looked the most enthused at her appearance. He was a well-built young man—perhaps, on a second look, not so very young—with an open, attractive face and an engaging smile.

The man called Honan-Fu—the people of his tribe, scattered on a multitude of planets, tended to single, though often compound, names—was the least warlike in appearance of the bunch, and generally gave the impression of being about to apologize for some intrusion. He spoke the common language with an unusual accent.

At a first look, Cherry Ravenau's enormous blue eyes gave her something of the appearance of a frightened child. This impression was soon dispelled by the attitude in which she stood, one fist on a hip, and by the muttered obscenity with which she greeted the arrival of authority. That seemed a mere ritual though, and she was willing enough to serve in this emergency—to protect her child. She didn't have much faith in the Gee Eye Home Guard; any serious protection would have to be provided by someone else.

"I want you to know I have a small child at home," she remarked when the commander stopped to shake her hand in welcome. Ms. Ravenau's enormous blue eyes made her face remarkable.

Then why are you here? was the commander's first, unspoken, reaction. But all she said was: "I appreciate your volunteering, Ms. Ravenau."

In general, the attitudes of the six on their arrival, as shown by the expressions on their faces, tended toward the stoic and fatalistic. Only Havot, the most outwardly enthusiastic, had never been enrolled in any military organization. However, his record as a fighter, using a shoulder weapon against berserker boarding machines, was very real. On the small form filled out by each volunteer, he'd listed his occupation as dealer in educational materials. His combat experience seemed to have come about accidentally a few years ago when, as a civilian, he'd been caught up in an armed clash. The available details were extremely sketchy, but they strongly suggested that he had shown a great natural aptitude.

Two or three of the six had known each other fairly well in the main settlement down on Gee Eye. It crossed Claire Normandy's mind that she might ask them what they knew about the Emperor Julius, Admiral Hector, and their fleet, but then she decided that this was not the time for that.

The amount of combat experience varied widely among the six. Enomoto's record showed the most in terms of sheer time and danger endured on active service, but he was credited with no exceptional achievements. The experience of one or two was only nominal.

There was also a wide disparity in the military ranks these veterans had held. Not all were pilots. One, Honan-Fu, he of the mournful and apologetic aspect, possessed documented skill as an exceptional gunner.

Now each of the six was assigned a room, given twenty minutes to settle into quarters, and told where and when to report at the end of that interval.

The welcoming speech that the six volunteers received from Captain Marut, some twenty minutes later, was a little more businesslike than Commander Normandy's. "We have only a few days in which to get ready, and for that reason, we are going to omit the usual drill of military courtesy." Looking at the lifelong civilian, Havot, he explained: "I mean such matters as whether your insignia is put on properly, and how and when you should salute. I probably don't need to remind you, but let me do so anyway, that military *discipline* remains very much in force."

On leaving the lounge, Harry told himself that he ought to go at once to the commander's office and complete the paperwork attendant on his commissioning, so he too could put on a uniform. But his feet were carrying him in the opposite direction. He didn't understand the reason for his reluctance, but so it was. Anyway, it was a good feeling to be able to walk around again without armor.

On his walk, Harry encountered Captain Marut, just come from giving the volunteers his version of an inspiring speech. The captain's bandages, if he was still wearing any on his arm wound, had diminished to the point where they could not be seen under his sleeve.

Marut was full of enthusiasm now, especially elated that his one functional destroyer had performed as well as it had, even in its battered condition, and with its crew operating short-handed.

He was even reasonably tolerant of Harry's presence. "I hear you've finally volunteered, Silver."

"We all have our crazy moments."

Harry considered that there were plenty of reasons to moderate the rejoicing. Using a ragtag collection of little ships to blast a single berserker scout was one thing, and hurling the same outfit against Shiva, and the kind of escort Shiva must be traveling with, was quite another.

"The commander tells me," Marut was saying to him, "that you have some familiarity with berserker hardware."

"I've seen a few pieces here and there. I wouldn't call myself an expert."

"But possibly you could be of some help. We have to learn how to make our fake berserkers as convincing as possible."

Silver nodded slowly. "Yeah, I would think that if you're

determined to use fake berserkers, that would be a good idea. This means you still intend to sneak up on a berserker base and infiltrate it somehow?"

"Can you think of a better way to accomplish our mission?"

Harry could only shake his head.

"Then I'd like you to come with me for a few minutes. If you can spare the time? I've got the commander's permission to root around a little in the Trophy Room."

Marut walked swiftly, and seemed to know just which way he was going. Down another side corridor, which terminated in a large room whose rock walls had a crudely unfinished look, was a small warehouse full of assorted berserker hardware.

The only way into the Trophy Room from the interior of the station was through an airlock, though just slightly less-than-normal atmospheric pressure was maintained inside. At the end of the long corridor that offered the only access, bold signs, permanently emblazoned on walls and door, warned that everyone who entered was required to wear full body armor. Personnel entering were to consider themselves in deep space confronting the enemy. Every item of the room's contents had already been gone over at least twicc for booby traps or other dangers, but still . . .

An armed human guard, as required by regulations, was standing by in the corridor—in case any signs of unwelcome activity should suddenly become apparent in the berserker material that was now being brought in.

The guard's weapon was a standard carbine, and no doubt it had been frequency-tuned for harmlessness against any friendly, familiar surface.

Basically, such weapons were energy projectors, whose beams cracked and shivered hard armor but could be safely turned against soft flesh. The beam induced intense vibrations in whatever it struck; in a substance as soft as flesh, the vibrations damped out quickly and harmlessly. Hard surfaces could be protected by a spray of the proper chemical composition. In combat, the formula was varied from one day, or one engagement, to the next, to prevent the enemy's being able to duplicate it. An auxiliary machine, the insignia on its flank identifying it as part of the defense system, was even now busy spraying the corridor, walls, floor, and overhead with a new tone of reflective paint.

A marksman could, if he wished, hold an energy rifle of this type in one hand, bracing its collapsible stock against his shoulder. The front end of the barrel was a blunt, solid-looking convexity. More usually, the weapon rode like a backpack on the outside of an armored suit, and was equipped with its own small hydrogen-fusion power lamp, providing kick enough to stop a runaway ground train—or, with a little luck, a berserker lander or boarding machine.

The most expert marksmen generally preferred the alpha-triggered system to the blinktriggered, as it was just a couple vital zillionths of a second faster. The former was also a shade more reliable, though it took a little longer to learn to use. It too was aimed visually, at the point the user's eyes were focused on, but was fired by a controllable alpha signal from the operator's organic brain.

Aiming and firing of the BT version was also controlled by the user's eyes. Sights tracked a reflection of the operator's pupils and aimed along the line of vision; the weapon was triggered by a hard blink. BT was more likely than AT to fire unintentionally; experienced users of either system tended to avoid looking straight at anyone or anything they wanted to protect.

Commander Normandy, having for the time being concluded her business with the volunteers, joined Marut and Silver almost as soon as they arrived at the Trophy Room.

That was the unofficial name of this smooth-walled cavern. There was an official designation as well, the Something or Other Storage Facility, which no one ever used in conversation because no one remembered what it was.

Harry looked around him thoughtfully. "Lots of junk," he remarked, "for a weather station to be storing."

"Most of this was brought here from Summerland," the commander told him, "when it became apparent that base would have to be evacuated."

"I see." Silver knew, from years of experience, what a Trophy Room was like. He'd seen bigger and better-stocked ones than this. They were common on bases in frontier sectors, though many contained not a single scrap of enemy hardware.

Silver had long assumed that somewhere, in one of the Trophy Rooms on one of the many bases in the Solarian-settled portion of the Galaxy, there had to be at least one premier facility where some of the cleverest human brains in the Galaxy engaged in an intense study of berserkers, trying to wring new drops of knowledge out of every bit of hardware, arranging and rearranging every fact that was known about them into new patterns, seeking insight and revelation.

Not being privy to the decisions of high Solarian strategists, Harry didn't know where the primary skunk works was. Forced to bet, he would have wagered that the most advanced such facility probably existed on Port Diamond—and very likely there was another one, almost its equal, on Earth or Luna, though certain tests deemed dangerous were more likely to be carried out at a considerable distance from Earth.

When Harry thought about it, he could remember specifically how the one on the base at Summerland had looked—he might have seen some of this same junk there. Maybe the berserkers who'd taken over there were now using the same space for the same purpose, that of studying the enemy's technology. And Harry's imagination, unbidden, showed him the kind of trophies that it might now contain: all kinds of Solarian hardware, from weapons to garden tools to toys.

Ships bringing material for deposit in the Hyperborean Trophy Room came right down to the surface of the planetoid; but rather than landing in the normal manner and unloading cargo to be hauled in through the corridors of the base, they docked directly with the room's special entrance and transferred material as if moving it from one ship to another in deep space. Regulations required such behavior, and Harry had never been able to make up his mind as to whether those regs really made sense or not—they had probably been written in the aftermath of some kind of a disaster, when metal objects thought to have been thoroughly pacified had turned out to be still infected with the programmed spirits of death.

The purpose of maintaining such a collection, of course, was that any especially interesting material discovered, or any information gleaned from its examination, would someday be shipped off to Earth, or to Port Diamond, the two sites in the known Galaxy where the most serious research on the nature of berserkers was conducted.

Today more miscellaneous berserker parts were being towed in to the Trophy Room on Hyperborea, to be added to the pile. Some of the remains resulting from the latest skirmish were no more than dust, conveyed in bags and bottles, sievings of space in the vicinity of the place where the trapped berserker scout had died.

Undoubtedly, more similar stuff was still drifting about in nearby space, ready to be harvested. This was only a sampling of what had appeared to the gatherers to be the most interesting material.

Silver found it interesting to note people's reactions when they got to see a place like this one. Some were utterly fascinated, while others were only made uncomfortable. He hadn't yet found any way to predict who was going to fall into which category. In his own mind, the two basic responses were entangled, mingled with other reactions more difficult to identify.

Within the Trophy Room, a special section had been set aside, a kind of vault, in which defeated berserker brains, if any could ever be taken reasonably intact, were held as unliving prisoners. So far, the special vault here on Hyperborea, like most of the others that Harry had seen, held only a few token bits of material, hardly more than chips. Not brains in any important sense. Maybe they had once been parts of berserker brains, but they weren't now. This was not the circuitry that identified life for destruction, and marked out thinking life for special attention.

Marut lifted a specimen in its small statglass case. "I'd say maybe this bit came out of something that was hit by a c-plus cannon slug."

Harry grunted. It was a strange-looking little chunk, blackened and twisted, but he'd seen stranger. If Marut was right, it wouldn't be much good for study. That kind of impact tended to knock out all programming information and to produce some really bizarre results—pieces of debris that changed shape while you looked at them, alternating at random times among two or three configurations. Harry had heard that some of them eventually disappeared altogether, dropping into nearby flightspace, or into their own private spacetimes, almost inaccessible from any domain of spacetime that humans had learned how to reach.

The impact of a slug compounded of various isotopes of lead, arriving at the target with parts of its interior moving faster than light could travel in the surrounding medium, tended to be decisive no matter how well the target machine or ship was shielded and armored.

· · ·

Marut had come here hoping he'd find something that would make his desperate plan a little more feasible. Come hell or high water, he was determined to strike at Shiva. Any small advantage he might gain could make a tremendous difference.

There was no doubt that Marut, in the reaction he showed to this berserker stuff, fell into the first of Silver's categories—fascination. He was evidently less familiar with this stuff than Harry was.

Harry supposed that the captain must have been considered at least tolerably knowledgeable about berserkers too, or he wouldn't have been among those chosen for the mission against Shiva.

Commander Normandy, on joining the men, offered her official congratulations on the destroyer's successful blasting of the enemy courier.

The man with the still-bandaged arm acknowledged the praise abstractedly.

Now she had to renew her efforts to calm the captain down. Being in this room seemed to excite him, and the small victory had made him keener than ever to press on with his new plans for attack.

Following the recent skirmish on the approaches to Good Intentions, a couple of metric tons of similar material, residue of the defunct berserker scout, was being brought home to the storage place on Hyperborea. It arrived, towed in a container behind a launch or lifeboat from a patrol craft, twelve standard hours, or a day, after the last blast of the skirmish had been fired. Chunks of jagged metal and miscellaneous materials, towed carefully. The container holding the stuff would be parked in an orbit around Hyperborea until specialists could go over it carefully, looking for booby traps of various kinds as well as for information.

· · ·

As Silver became more deeply involved with the commander's and the captain's plans for defense and attack, they picked his brains for all the information possible on Summerland.

Less than ten years ago, there had been a human base on Summerland, and in fact, several members of the Space Force crew on Hyperborea had spent time there, in varying amounts. A few people could remember one or more children having been born there. And visual records of the place were plentiful—it had once been beautiful.

Harry'd been explaining to the commander about the Sniffer robot he carried in his ship, how it could be set to look for things—or for people—and how it did a better job overall than any organic bloodhound.

Somewhere in the Trophy Room there was a berserker device—now no longer functional, of course—that did much the same thing. This led to comments on the many general similarities in design.

"After all," said the captain, "the war's been going on for a long time. Sometimes they copy us, sometimes we actually copy them."

And Commander Normandy, despite all the greater problems she had to contend with, remembered Harry's request to immunize the Sniffer. Actually, he'd needed her approval to tag his machine, before he turned it loose, with something that made it "smell" friendly, show the proper identification, to the defenses.

Pausing briefly in her inventorying of the Trophy Room, she inquired: "While we're on the subject of battle damage, did you ever locate your missing bit of ship, Mr. Silver?"

He'd had plenty of time to prepare an answer for that question. "I'm not sure. Sniffer brought me back a picture of something wedged in the rocks, but the fragment looked badly damaged, and it was a bit too large for my robot to haul. It could have come from one of the captain's ships. Anyway, that was just about the time other events began to demand everyone's full attention. I think my fairing can wait until we get some bigger problems settled; the *Witch* can be made fully operational without it." Harry delivered his reply with full confidence that the commander wasn't going to check up on it, given the other demands on her time.

Meanwhile, just being in the same room with all this berserker hardware could give a man a chill—especially those parts of it that looked like components Harry'd seen before, when they'd been in full working order and animated by their own internal, infernal, programming. Despite all the evidence that everything in the bins and on the shelves had been thoroughly neutralized, Silver kept half-expecting something in the room to stir, to put out a gun barrel or blade, or extend a crusher in the form of vise-grip jaws, and then, with a single precise movement too fast for any human eye to follow, annihilate the next live body that came within its reach.

Berserker hardware. No human mind had guided the mining and refining of this metal, the fabrication of these parts. There was quite a variety, of which one or two chunks were probably large enough to serve as the basis for a disguised attack force or raiding party.

Silver squatted beside one of them, and put out a bare hand—he'd taken off one of his gauntlets, against the rules—to touch the surface. The act brought back evil memories, and Claire Normandy saw him briefly close his eyes. She didn't harass him about this open flouting of the rules.

Some of the berserker wiring and software would be allowed to remain in place in the adapted units. If Marut's plan was to succeed, the thing would have to be accepted by real berserkers as a regular, working shuttle unit of their own breed.

. . .

Captain Marut paced through the cramped space restlessly, mumbling oaths, adding what were probably obscenities, in some language Harry couldn't even recognize. The captain didn't look as if he were the least inconvenienced by the requirement of wearing full armor. He probably preferred to live that way, Harry thought.

Of course Marut hadn't been able to find among the berserker trash the part he really wanted, something that might be adapted to get one of his ships going again, or augment one of the weapon systems on the destroyer that could still move under its own power. Harry thought that what the captain was really looking for, and wasn't going to find, was some magic way to restore the ships and people he had lost. But there were other things here, weapons, components of infernal machines, that humans could adapt, could use, if only they could get close enough to the enemy to come to grips.

The captain, thought Harry, was in danger of turning into a kind of berserker himself, the kind of leader who very often got a lot of his own people killed.

Not that Harry, at the moment, minded very much. In his present mood, a boss with that sort of attitude was looking better and better to him.

"You couldn't make a real space-going machine or ship out of this. But you might be able to disguise your war party."

"That's all we need." Marut seemed to be trying to convince himself that it was so.

All the poor slob really needed, Harry thought, was the four or five good ships and well-trained crews he'd lost. He wasn't going to find them here, but that fact hadn't quite sunk in as yet.

The Trophy Room had been considerably enlarged, more space dug out of rock, to hold the four little space shuttles, each of which could be stripped of certain auxiliary equipment, thereby expanding the small cargo bay. It occurred to someone that this space was sufficient to house, in concealment, one human wearing space armor.

Marut's eyes were suddenly glowing with a dangerous light. "Silver, are you thinking the same thing I am?"

"I doubt it."

"Do you know . . . suppose that one of these gadgets could be towed behind an armed launch, or a larger warship?"

"I could suppose that if I tried. What then?"

"Suppose we took out certain things—this, maybe this." The captain's armored fingers slapped, in rapid succession, two different slabs of metal. "A small amount of new hardware would have to be added—no more than we could manage."

"Then what?"

"Then we put a spacer in it."

"A human being inside?"

Marut was being unexpectedly inventive. "You got it. Hell, we couldn't trust any pure machine with that part of the job—with what comes after we land on Summerland."

"You're serious about this?"

"There'll be plenty of volunteers among my people." Then he turned to the commander. "Ma'am, can we get your workshop to make up some duplicates of these? In outward appearance, I mean."

So, on the commander's authority, the four little shuttles were brought out of the cavernous Trophy Room and taken to the base shipyard, or dock, under the landing field, where they were to be partially rebuilt and retrofitted.

A message was brought to Commander Normandy in the Trophy Room. After reading it in private, she announced that she had just received fresh confirmation of Shiva's plans.

"It's going to be at the base at Summerland?"

"That's right."

Harry squinted at her. "And just at the predicted time? I suppose it's useless to ask where this tip comes from?"

"Yes, Mr. Silver. Quite useless."

"How long's it going to stay there?"

"Just long enough for the usual maintenance, I assume." Berserkers, like Solarian ships, had to power up from time to time, in one way or another. This often involved bringing aboard tanks, or frozen blocks, of hydrogen to fuel the power lamps—of course no ship or machine could carry onboard sufficient energy to propel its mass across many light-years at transluminal velocities; riding the Galactic currents through subspace was the only way to accomplish that. But just tuning in to those currents tended to burn a lot of power.

Marut, growing more and more enthusiastic, was willing to open up a bit about the tactics that the task force had originally planned to use. "We were to pop into normal space, about a hundred thousand klicks from Summerland, within five seconds after Shiva showed up for its scheduled docking—you say you know the place, Silver? Somehow, we have no really decent hologram."

"I can sort of visualize it. And could you really have managed that? Timed your emergence that accurately?"

"We had a good task force put together. We had everything we needed. Of course we expected our plan to work. Otherwise, we would've come up with something different."

The three soon left the Trophy Room, adjourning their discussions to the commander's office. There she was able to call up the most recent recon holos of Summerland, which showed the recently established berserker base, resembling an evil castle in some fairy story, squatting in what had once been a verdant valley—where now a lifeless river ran, still steaming, between bare, rocky hillsides, down to a lifeless sea. Doubtless the enemy still had units perpetually prowling, sifting, straining, making sure that on Summerland not a single molecule remained to twitch with signs of life.

"We were lucky to get these. We haven't had a whole lot of success with robot recon craft, and until this Shiva thing came up, it was very doubtful that sending a live crew to do the job would be worth the risk. The defenses appear to be rather ferocious."

"And now—"

"We're not running any more recon missions. For one thing, I don't want to take the chance of alerting the target base that something is up; and for another, we simply don't have the time. We have to decide everything on what we know right now."

There was no telling what else the berserkers might have built since the last holos were taken. There was no reason to doubt that the ground defenses of the new enemy base would be powerful. And it had to be assumed that Shiva would be traveling with a formidable escort.

Harry said flatly: "I'd put our chance of success with such a stunt under ten percent."

"We'll have a much better grasp on that when we've run a formal computer simulation. Several of them."

"Sure," said Harry. But he was shaking his head. If you ran enough simulations, and kept tinkering with them, you were bound to be able to get one at last that showed you the result you wanted.

"You don't seem to understand, Mr. Silver."

"What is it I don't understand?"

"Even if, which I don't believe for a moment, a good, honest simulation were to grant us less than a ten-percent chance of bagging Shiva with the force we can now put up—we still can't let the opportunity pass without giving it a try. If we fail to kill this monster now, how in hell is humanity ever going to stop it?"

Harry had no answer for that one.

"You said you came here from Omicron Sector, Silver."

"That's what I did."

"And your own ship was damaged there. You must have had a fairly good look at what was happening."

"I saw some of it." Harry still didn't feel like talking about his skirmish in getting out of Omicron. "Though I don't know what that has to do with anything. I stick by what I said before, this scheme you're coming up with now, putting people in pieces of junk, having them pretend to be berserkers—it just isn't going to work. And you just don't have the horses to go in there fighting."

Marut drew breath as if for some forceful reply, then apparently decided to let it wait until some other moment.

Harry said: "I suppose they ran some simulations for your mission before you started out from Port Diamond."

"Of course we did. Exhaustively."

"Sure. And I suppose the chances then were estimated at better than ten percent. As the mission was originally planned, with six fighting ships in a task force—"

"Don't be idiotic, man!" Marut glowered at him. "Our estimation of success was much closer to ninety percent than ten."

"All right, even if it was ninety percent then, *now* it'd be like trying to stop a tank by throwing eggs at it."

It was clear at this point that the revised plan for an attack on Shiva had Commander Normandy's approval, or at least her acquiescence. Now people from the station crew and people from the task force were already hard at work, along with such appropriate robotic assistance as Claire could summon up. If Marut's wild scheme was going to have any chance of success, not a minute could be wasted. The usual cautions and procedures, required by strict regulations, for dealing with all captured berserker assets had gone by the board—the last trace of murderous programming poison had to be got out of this hardware so it could be used for something else.

Later in the day, Silver, along with several other pilots, got to take their new miniships for a test drive, not getting more than a few klicks from the base.

"Actually, we ought to spend a few days, at least, getting the feel of this. But there's no time," said one of the pilots.

"Days? I'd say a month was minimal," said another.

Clamped into the combat chair, helmet on his head, Silver put the armed launch—or maybe the unit newly disguised as a berserker shuttle—through its paces.

The other pilots' respect for Harry Silver went up substantially when they saw how well he performed with the helmet on his head and his hands grasping the slow controls—those in which delays on the order of a large fraction of a second were not critical.

If the mission was to have any chance of success, heavy improvisation was called for at every step.

"All right, we might have the hardware to make a stunt like that barely possible. But we still don't have the people," said the first pilot.

Most especially, they didn't have the pilots. Soon it was obvious that even with Silver counted in, there was going to be a critical shortage of the trained, experienced people needed to carry out the revised plan of attack. It was going to depend on a flock of half a dozen tiny single-crew ships, maneuvering skillfully in the near vicinity of the berserker base.

If they only had half a dozen more, as good as Silver was—but even he wasn't sure, considering the matter as objectively as possible, that there were that many in the Galaxy.

NINE

By now it was clear that Rosenkrantz and Guildenstern had been telling the truth about one thing: A new swarm of volunteers was indeed about to arrive. They were actually from Good Intentions; they were coming on the ship called *Galaxy,* and every one of them was a follower of the man who called himself the Emperor Julius.

Fortunately, a good many of Claire Normandy's Space Force colleagues were ready and able to enlighten her as to what it was all about. Harry, who'd spent some time on Gee Eye years ago, could help, too. But not Captain Marut, whose face was as blank as the commander's when the subject of the Emperor Julius and his fleet came up.

Harry said to her: "Are you serious? You've been here for two years and have never heard of him?"

"Perfectly serious. Who is he? I have some hazy recollection of what an emperor was supposed to be—bearer of some kind of ancient title."

"That's right. Well, Julius and his followers have been squatting on Good Intentions for upward of five years—"

"I've told you I pay no attention to affairs down there."

"—and he claims to be the ruler of the Galaxy."

"He claims *what*?"

Harry, and others among Commander Claire's associates, did their best to explain the emperor to her.

The captain was relieved that evidently none of the titles of rank in the cultists' military organization—if one could call it that—had to be taken seriously. There was to be no disruptive attempt by anyone to weaken his, the captain's, authority of command over the new task force.

Captain Marut immediately began to speculate as to whether it might be possible to use this cannon fodder to conduct a diversionary attack, under cover of which, the serious attackers, masquerading as berserkers, would be able to get close enough to the berserker station to launch a landing party. But it would be best to make as few changes as possible in the plan already taking shape.

What name the Emperor Julius had been born with, or where or when that event had taken place, perhaps no one on Hyperborea now knew—or much cared.

Normandy thought it all over. Then she asked: "How is one supposed to address an emperor?"

Captain Marut, who had spent most of his life in distant sectors, had never heard of the emperor either.

"You're accepting his claim?" The captain couldn't believe it.

Claire Normandy briskly shook her head. "I'm not placing myself under his command, or treating him as a genuine head of state. But he's volunteering, isn't he? He and some unknown number of followers, and their fleet, while thousands of others are sitting at home demanding to be saved. I can say an awful lot of nice things to people who are actually going to volunteer, and who bring their own ships."

Marut shook his head slowly. "All the evidence confirms that it's one ship, ma'am. And nothing but a crazy cult."

"The distinguishing characteristic of cult members is likely to be fanaticism. If Julius now commands a holy war against berserkers—well, we could use a little of that on our side."

The only contribution that the general historical database could make was to suggest "His Imperial Highness" as the proper form of address for an emperor. "Your Magnificence" was listed as an alternate.

It seemed noteworthy that the database had nothing at all to say about this particular emperor, or his supposed empire—it contained biographical information on only about a billion contemporary people, less than one out of a thousand of the Solarian citizens of the settled Galaxy.

Within an hour or so of the arrival of the battered courier, a lone vessel whose live pilot identified it as the flagship of the imperial navy was picked up by the local Hyperborean defenses and went through the usual routine of being intercepted by one of Commander Normandy's patrol craft and taking a Space Force pilot aboard. The stranger was not much bigger than a patrol craft itself, though measurements taken at a distance had indicated she was somewhat too stout to be able to slide herself in through the hangar doors.

The commander's eagerness to obtain help had not yet caused her to discard caution. Only when she was solemnly assured that everyone on board the *Galaxy* was a bona fide volunteer for military service did she grant the vessel permission to land. And then she insisted on putting her own pilot aboard to carry out the maneuver.

An hour or so after the battered robot courier had delivered its surprising message, the emperor's ship, the only unit of his supposed fleet that had so far appeared, and bearing the volunteers' imperial insignia, was on approach for a landing on Hyperborea.

Soon the people on the ground were able to get a good video image. The insignia on the emperor's ship was of a large and rather clumsy design, featuring curved lobes that might have been intended as the Galaxy's spiral arms. It looked like a collection of stock shapes, borrowed from whatever source happened to be handy and stuck together without much thought.

When Commander Normandy got her first good look, by holostage, at the mob of volunteers Julius had jammed aboard his ship, her first impulse was decisively confirmed—she would send all of them, or nearly all, right back to Good Intentions. Discipline, not to mention experience, seemed almost totally lacking.

When she had first heard this group was coming, her imagination had leaped ahead to picture a horde of rigid fanatics who, even if inexperienced, would be ready to charge forth and do battle in any direction that their emperor aimed them. She'd been envisioning Templars on steroids, with nuclear grenades clipped to their belts, howling for a chance to die in battle.

The reality was somcthing of a disappointment.

Instead of Templars, fate seemed to be landing on her little rock a collection of misfits, marginal incompetents, people who had probably joined the emperor because they were not particularly welcome anywhere else. As fighters, they could be assumed to be almost useless. The extra scores and dozens of unskilled hands and useless mouths, if allowed to remain, threatened at once to become a problem on the small station. At the very least, they would be getting in the way.

Once the *Galaxy* was down, a quick laser scan of her measurements confirmed that she was too big to fit in through the hangar doors. The imperial flagship would certainly have to remain parked out on the field.

The Emperor Julius didn't just walk through a door, he made an entrance. But one watcher at least, Harry Silver, who'd seen some other famous entrance-makers in his time, had the impression that this one was just going through the motions, that the man's heart wasn't in it any more.

"Have you more ships on the way?"

"I regret not." Julius remained serene in his regret, though it was undoubtedly sincere.

"I thought perhaps your followers in some other solar system . . ."

"I regret that there will be no additional ships."

Events confirmed the sad admission. Unfortunately, the two admirals—or admiral and commodore—had almost nothing to command. However large the emperor's fleet might once have been, it now consisted of the one ship only, under a flag that no one on the station could remember ever having seen before: the same design as on the hulls, of clumsy curves that might have been intended as the Galaxy's spiral arms. The crew was top-heavy with rank. Almost everyone seemed to be a commissioned officer.

Marut was at a loss. He had never encountered anything of the kind before. Berserkers hadn't stopped him, but human folly could.

Marut, or one of his people, asked one of the Julian officers: "How large is the emperor's domain?"

"His Imperial Highness reigns over the entire Galaxy." The claim was made straightfaced, with a calm demeanor—though the admiral would have to be crazy to expect anyone here to believe it.

"I see." *Then how is it some of us never heard of him until two days ago?* The question wasn't asked aloud. There didn't seem to be much to add in the way of comment. The commander had been nursing hopes that maybe there was a whole planet, somewhere . . . but even if there was, of course what counted were people and ships that she could put on the line before the inexorably approaching deadline.

"But most of the *people* in the Galaxy have never heard of him!"

There was no crack in the admiral's serene demeanor. "Now that he has assumed active leadership in the holy war, first billions, then hundreds of billions, will rally to his banner, and to his name."

"Sure they will—I hope they bring some ships and weapons with them."

Harry had formed no idea of what the emperor was going to look like, and was startled by what he saw. Julius, somewhat shorter than average, had some natural resemblance to Napoleon Bonaparte, one of the great conquerors of pre-space Solarian history, who had also made himself an emperor, placing the crown on his head with his own hands. The modern version was obviously aware of the likeness, and cultivated it at least to the extent of arranging his scanty, dark hair into a lock that fell over his massive forehead. Silver wasn't sure that many of his followers would have recognized that name.

It was probably all wasted effort, or it would have been if the object was to impress the folk on Hyperborea, but the man kept trying. Harry had to admire that, in a way. And he wondered if he, Harry Silver, was the only one on the base who got the point.

The emperor made his first appearance on the station wearing a rather special uniform, decorated with a sash and many medals. But the most eye-catching feature was the ceremonial sword at his belt—on a second look, it might have been a real sword. The long blade was hidden in its sheath, and some observers, who had never heard of swords before, weren't sure what the unfamiliar object was.

The latest rumor, as unconfirmed as rumors usually were,

said that Julius himself, and one or two of those with him, were the only members of his group who claimed to have bona fide combat experience—and there were some grounds for suspecting that the records indicating that experience had been falsified.

One of the first things Julius said on disembarking was that he wanted a meeting on strategy, face-to-face with Commander Normandy, as soon as possible. Sadie, the adjutant, put him off with diplomatic phrases; he was quietly angry at being forced to deal with a mere program.

Actually, the commander was somewhat relieved that this visitor's ship could not fit into the hangar, because she would not have allowed it entry anyway now that she'd had a look at Julius and his crew. But she had not yet despaired of finding among them some of the people that she needed.

The emperor, after debarking from his ship and leading a portion of his flock through the temporary tunnel to the hangar, unerringly picked out the person who was in charge, even though Commander Normandy was in her combat armor, which didn't ordinarily display much identification.

Julius, wearing what Harry could easily believe was an emperor's full-dress uniform, went straight to her, followed by several of his motley band of refugees, and bowed lightly.

"Commander Normandy, I place myself and my forces under your command."

Hearing the same little speech from almost anyone but the Emperor Julius, Harry Silver would have been disposed to laugh at it, and to favor the commander with a pitying look because she had to put up with such garbage. But when Julius spoke the words, no one seemed impelled to snicker.

Nor did Commander Normandy seem in need of pity. It was ridiculous, but something in his voice, his look, stirred even in her a surge of hope. Instinct said that this was someone who could be relied upon. "Thank you, er, uh, Emperor Julius." And she offered a handshake.

Julius accepted both hand and title with a gracious nod. The latter was, after all, no more than his due. And if there was just a hint of gracious condescension in the way he took her hand, well, it was not so marked that anyone could have objected to it.

And the first impromptu conference between the leaders necessarily took place in the hangar.

The commander said: "I had hoped to have a small welcoming ceremony—in the lounge. But . . . how many of your people have come with you?" The inside end of the rescue ramp was still disgorging cultists, unarmed people blinking at the scene around them and smiling nervously.

"Almost a hundred."

The base was simply not prepared to receive or house that many, eager volunteers or not.

My own people are almost going to be outnumbered, was Commander Normandy's immediate private thought. *But not for long*—because she had already decided that most of the emperor's folk were going home again, before they had time to unpack.

They would not even be leaving in the ship they came in. "That stays here. It looks like it might be very useful."

But some means of getting people off the ship had to be worked out when it developed that there were only two space suits—and very few of the hundred knew how to use a suit. An enclosed, pressurized tube-ramp used years ago in construction was dug out of a deep locker, and when extended, served to establish a connection between ship and hangar. The mass of cultist volunteers were brought in by that means to normal air and gravity.

Also, it appeared likely that only a few of them possessed the talent or training to do anything useful in a military way. These, the emperor insisted firmly, were going to serve as the *Galaxy*'s crew. With surprising willingness, he gave in on another point—the great majority of his hundred, however eager they might be to enter battle, were going to have to turn around and go right home.

To persuade his followers of the need for this withdrawal, Julius had to put in some minutes of serious effort, first cajoling and then ordering them to do so. Hundreds of other cult members had begged and pleaded with the emperor to bring them with him when he ascended into the heavens to do battle, but he had insisted that they stay behind. There appeared to have been a thorough kind of screwup at embarkation. Originally, only those who met the Space Force qualifications were to have been allowed aboard his ship—but somehow, a few exceptions had been made, and then a few more.

The lounge, or wardroom, was not, by a long way, the biggest interior space available on the base—but it was the only area of sufficient size, apart from the hangars, to which the commander was willing to admit a collection of eccentric strangers, particularly at this crucial time. She'd even been nervous about letting the cultists hang about in the hangars, virtually empty as they were, but there hadn't been any good way to avoid letting them pass through.

Anyway, the lounge offered a far more welcoming environment than those stark caverns. The high, arched ceiling, especially when augmented with a little virtual tinkering, suggested a noble grove of trees, a close approximation of Earth's native sunlight twinkling from above leafy branches, stirred now and then by a gentle breeze. Here the emperor and as many as a dozen of his entourage could be received, with equal numbers on the other side, to provide something like dignity and public ceremony; and Commander Normandy had asked that the emperor and no more than a dozen of his immediate party, or entourage, be brought there.

A small delegation of Commander Normandy's own officers appeared, some of them grumbling and yawning, still fastening their tunics. Dress uniforms at the ceremony instead of coveralls. People who were off duty at the moment, and who would otherwise have been asleep, had been drafted into a kind of welcoming committee.

Whether Julius and his entire following were all insane or not, they were at least sincere volunteers, and Claire Normandy remained determined to offer them a welcome and a heartfelt thanks—even if her next move was going to be to send most of their hopeful shipmates right back home.

Arrangements for the welcoming were hastily cobbled together: "Flags will be displayed, and something like a ceremony attempted—we're going to have to work with him, and with his people. At the very least, I'm going to have to take his ship."

Examination by the commander's techs had confirmed that the emperor's ship was really a pretty good one—at least it was undamaged, and it did carry some weaponry. It could make the difference in the planned assault on Summerland. But even had it been a clunker, she would have commandeered it.

"Get the people off her and figure out some other way to send them home."

"On what? We may have to house them for several days."

"I know. Put up cots in the hangar."

"We don't have that many cots."

"Then put sleeping bags on the deck, dammit. Improvise something. There's plenty of space in there. We must be polite, but they are not to be allowed to wander."

"Yes, ma'am."

When the emperor, and a small party he had personally selected from his associates, appeared in the doorway of the lounge, Harry Silver was already on hand, having taken his position at a table on the far side of the room, about fifteen meters from the door through which the latest visitors must enter. First he heard a door opening and closing in the distance, way down a corridor somewhere outside the imitation forest glade, and then a muted babble of voices, all bright with mutual politeness, gradually coming closer. He was trying to pick out the emperor's voice without ever having heard it before, and not having a whole lot of success.

Silver wasn't looking forward with enthusiasm to the announced ceremony, but he'd be damned if he was going to let a pack of cultists run him out of the only watering hole available. He took up an accustomed, and for him, easy position, standing on the fringe of events, left out of the ceremony altogether, with a drink in his hand and his gaze that of a detached observer, cynical and sour.

There was no doubt at all about which man was Julius, shorter than almost every other male in the room. His uniform was impressive; worn by a smaller personality, it would have looked gaudy and over-elaborate. "Jaunty" would not be quite the right word for the emperor's attitude—it was more serious than that. Certainly "ambitious." Maybe "grandiose." He was a man who radiated . . . something. Exactly what was hard to say, but definitely something. All eyes went to him as iron dust to a magnet.

Meanwhile, in front of Julius, beside him, after him, flowed the expected escort of aides and hangers-on, now reduced to a reasonable number, looking worried and trying to be haughty. All of the high-ranking officers in the cult's nonexistent navy wore odd uniforms and guarded expressions. The others, mostly in civilian clothes, were a handful of strangely assorted people, including—

Becky.

Harry Silver's drink fell from his grasp, and in the next instant, his hand, making a reflex grab for recovery, knocked the glass off the edge of the table, thudding and splashing to the floor—but not until later did he remember that he had dropped it.

Fierce demons of emotion—elation, anger, outrage—

flared up inside him like explosions, with the result that he nearly fainted when a second look and a third look assured him that yes, it was really she, the woman he had thought dead, who was standing there with the others, a beam of virtual sunlight lighting up her hair. Just a person, a living person, like everyone else. What really made her stand out from the rest of the emperor's entourage was that Becky was about the only one who had the class to look uncomfortable.

Two or three enlisted people from the station's crew—and one or two from Marut's—standing near Harry were looking at him and at the glass he'd dropped, shaking their heads slightly. No doubt they were positive that he was drunk. Whether or not Harry Silver had been on the verge of getting drunk a minute earlier, he sure as hell was sober now.

He moved a couple of steps to one side, to get a better look at Becky over someone's shoulder. The lounge was full of people now, and she hadn't seen him yet.

Her hair was done up in a different way than he remembered, and it seemed also to be a different color, though he couldn't really be sure—how many nonessentials he'd forgotten! He supposed she must be wearing different clothes than when he'd seen her last, though he was damned if his mind could show him a clear picture of any set of garments that she had ever worn. Otherwise, the years had hardly changed her at all from the picture presented by his memory.

He heard one of the other women who had entered the lounge with Becky call her "Josephine." In the next moment, it was the emperor himself who turned his head and spoke to her, saying something that Harry couldn't hear, in a casual and familiar way; and suddenly what she'd written in her last letter, about starting a new life, took on a whole new meaning.

Commander Normandy, entering the room from another direction, had now launched into her brief formal speech of welcome. Everyone in the room was standing, in the universal attitude of people prepared to endure speeches in respectful silence. In the background, soft but stirring music played; someone had thought to enliven matters that way.

Silver stood watching, unable to think, unable to move, until eventually her eyes came around to him.

TEN

Becky's eyes met his at last, and Harry saw her small start of recognition. But it was plain that the impact on her was nothing like the hammer blow he'd just experienced. Well, she'd had no reason to believe that he was dead.

Then who in hell is in that buried suit? It took Silver a moment, conducting a mental review of Sniffer's holographs, to realize that for all he knew, it could be empty. The armor was hard and solid enough to hold its designed shape independently of the presence of a wearer, dead or alive. The ghastly corpse, so vividly imagined, took on a kind of quantum quasi-existence. Why would anyone go to such lengths to hide an empty suit? With a little effort, Harry could think of several reasons, especially in the case of armor so easily identifiable. The ghastly corpse, whose existence he had never doubted until now, vanished like a ghost at sunrise.

Vaguely, Harry became aware of a couple of Space Force

bystanders staring at him; probably they were worried that the drunken civilian was about to create a scene. But their reactions, or anyone's, counted for nothing. She was alive. She was alive! A constricting shell of frozen grief, already congealed and hard as armor, had been shattered in a moment. It was like a tree on his homeworld shedding a whole winter's worth of ice at once.

He didn't know whether to openly recognize Becky or not, or what name to call her by if he did. Another woman had just called her Josephine. She'd been living a new life, a different life, for five years now, and Harry was afraid he might precipitate trouble. Fortunately, the base commander's ceremony was still in progress, with people droning little speeches at one other, postponing the need for him to do anything at all.

One of the enlisted men standing near Harry evidently thought it was the sight of the emperor that had upset him, and edged a little closer. "Don't care for the imperial aristocracy?" the spacer asked in a jesting whisper.

"Not much, no."

Silver couldn't just stand there any longer. Somehow or other, not trusting himself to take a last look back at Becky, he got himself away from the reception.

A couple of hours passed before Harry had any chance to talk with the woman he'd just seen resurrected. He would have preferred to have their first meeting in years someplace where they could hope no one was eavesdropping—maybe inside the *Witch.* But with all the techs clambering around, their chances of privacy there were pretty low.

He'd sat in his room for a little while, thinking that she'd come looking for him as soon as she had a chance. But maybe she wouldn't. And maybe something he didn't know about was preventing her from doing so.

Well, if she was trying to find him, and he wasn't in his room, she'd know where to look next. In fact, it was just as likely that she'd look first in the other place.

The lounge was fully open now, with the remnants of the welcoming ceremony still in evidence. Harry settled himself in a kind of booth at one side of the woodland glade, where he and whoever might join him would be able to look out directly, between virtual trunks and branches, at the all-but-empty landing field—they had before them the real thing, visible through statglass. The bar was fully open again and things in general had largely returned to normal. Whatever that might be. Windows were allowed to be windows once more.

The landing field consisted basically of five or six hectares of flattened, graded rock and gravel with, at the moment, just three lonely ships in sight: Marut's destroyer, still being checked out and tightened up after the successful skirmish; Harry's *Witch*; and now the emperor's *Galaxy*. Of the three, *Galaxy* was parked closest to the hangar doors, and still connected to one of those portals by the evacuation tube. The two patrol boats were presumably somewhere out on reconnaissance.

Blocking off one end of the vast unused hangar space underground, the maintenance people and their machines had created what was in effect a miniature shipyard. Up on the surface, Captain Marut's second destroyer was no longer recognizable as a ship, having been cannibalized and disassembled until only a few odd piles of parts remained visible.

Following the course that Harry had predicted for her, Becky soon came looking for him in the bar. The very place where the welcoming ceremony had been held. No one had yet bothered to take down the flags. Someone's idea of inspiring music was still working away at a muted volume, trying to decide whether it wanted to be a melody or not.

At the moment, the two of them had the place to themselves; everyone else seemed to be busy with various ideas of important business.

She'd already changed out of the clothing she'd been wearing as part of the emperor's retinue. She had on a Space Force coverall now. Somehow borrowed, probably; as yet, it bore no designation of unit or rank.

"This was about the first place I tried," she explained innocently. If she hadn't succeeded here, of course she would have found out where his room was and tried that. "If you weren't in here, I would've tried the library."

"Didn't know there was one. Real books?"

"So I've heard."

"I'll have to check it out. What'll you have?"

"Scotch on the rocks sounds nice." Becky swirled into a seat with a graceful movement that somehow made her look for a moment as if she were wearing an evening gown.

Summoning the robot waiter, Harry ordered the Scotch. When it had been set down on the black shiny surface of the table, he offered his companion a silent toast with his own raised glass.

She choked a little on the stuff.

Harry said: "I thought the emperor's people didn't believe in using alcohol."

"They didn't—don't. As of today, I'm officially not one of the emperor's people anymore."

"I see." She had never been much of a drinker, either, as Harry recalled; but tossing one down was evidently a good way to signal to the world that her allegiance to Julius was behind her.

"I just handed in my resignation," Becky offered.

"Uh-huh."

"They claim you can never do that, but I did it anyway. That was good," Becky concluded with a sigh, having on her second attempt disposed of half the glass. She tossed her head and ran her fingers through her hair, a gesture that he remembered.

Harry observed: "When we were all in here earlier, I heard one of the women call you Josephine."

"Oh, yeah. You have to take a new name when you join, and that's one of the names they like to give people. When I first joined up, there were four other Josephines—at least. Now I'm the . . . I *was* the last one."

"What happened to the others?"

"Bailed out before I did. Like a lot of other people."

"No more Josephines. I see. Were all of you his wives?"

"No. Not all of us. There were grades of wives and concubines. It's a long story."

"Then I guess it can wait till some other day."

Becky's hair was longer than Harry remembered it, and curly, as she now sat twisting it in one hand.

So far, Harry hadn't so much as touched her, not even her hand, and he kept wondering what was going to happen when he did. He'd always wondered how her body that looked so frail sometimes could be so tough.

"So," he said. "You want to talk about the Emperor Julius?"

"I don't care. I can take him or leave him alone, as they say." Her fingers went to twisting her hair again.

"You still have some good feelings about him?"

"Sure. He's really not so bad—if you have to have an emperor. I just got pretty sick of having one."

"Are they going to be mad at you for dropping out?"

"Lots of others have, dropped out I mean. Some more are going to. But what're you doing here, Harry? You could've knocked me over with a virtual photon when I saw you."

"I get around a lot."

"I know that. Are you still . . . ?" She let it die there, assuming he would pick up on the meaning.

He was about as sure as a man could be about anything that they weren't being overheard. Not right here and now. Commander Normandy didn't seem the one who would routinely spy on people. He said: "I found the stuff, Becky, right where you left it. My Sniffer came up with it yesterday." Then he thought, yesterday, can that be right? It seemed like a long and weary month ago.

All she said was: "Oh."

Harry relaxed a little; he'd been afraid she was going to pretend she didn't know what he was talking about. He added: "I also found your dead body."

That made Becky blink, but after blinking, she only stared at him blankly. He supposed he'd have to spell it out: "When I found the armored space suit you'd shoved down there"—now understanding flickered across her face, slowly followed by remorse—"I somehow got the idea that you were still inside it."

"Oh, Harry!"

"It looked to me like you'd got caught in some kind of a land shift while you were crawling around studying the minerals, or whatever you were doing, and there you'd been stuck for the past five years. Getting more and more impatient, waiting for me to come help you out." He paused. "There wasn't anybody in it, was there?"

"No. Oh, Harry, I'm sorry! I knew that damn fancy suit had been seen, and I didn't want them tying it to me. I just wanted to put it somewhere where *no one* was ever going to find it—let alone you. How'd you ever happen to be down *there?"*

The music kept on dribbling and babbling in the background. He felt like telling the barkeep to shut it up, but maybe silence in the background would be worse. The ceiling's visual attributes were being muted now, in some kind of random progression of effects, changes so gradual it might not be noticed that they were happening; the high arches looked more like the inside of a Gothic church than a grove of trees.

Meanwhile, out on the big blank space of the real landing field, visible in sunlight at the moment, one small maintenance robot was moving, making everything else look all the more intensely motionless, so that the scene looked like a painting. He shrugged. "The Sniffer told me there was something else down there, something I was looking for. So far, no one knows that I found anything."

Becky hesitated just long enough to be convincing. "Oh,

you mean the stuff in the box. I wanted to ditch that, too. That would have been easy, but . . . ever try to get rid of a suit of space armor, Harry?"

"Can't say I have."

"Just making a hole in it—just making a *dent,* for God's sake—would take a bigger weapon than I've ever carried. Cutting it up into little pieces would take a lifetime, and then you'd still have all the pieces to dispose of somehow."

"You could have just sent the armor drifting off into space."

"I thought of that. But they're pretty good now at looking for that kind of thing."

He sipped his drink. He wasn't going to ask who was pretty good, or who would be combing space in the vicinity for that particular suit, or why. He suspected it would most likely be some kind of Kermandie agents. Maybe later on they would discuss all that.

Becky was going on: "—so, I got myself a new suit on Gee Eye, and then I came back here and shoved everything I wanted to hide down into a cranny in the rock, where I thought no one was ever going to look. How was I to know that you'd come poking around?" Now she sounded almost offended.

"That's all right. I didn't know myself until a month or two ago that I was going to be here."

"Were you really sore about not getting the stuff, Harry? When I never arranged to hand it over?"

"I managed."

"I'm sorry. I suppose you missed out on a lot of money. At the time, I just felt scared, and lost, and I wanted to get away from all that. And I guess I thought I was doing you a favor, too, by getting rid of the stuff, because it's dangerous. But you've got it now, and you want it, so that's good. I'm glad. But maybe it won't even be worth anything, after all this time."

"I don't know if it will or not. I'll have to check it out when I get a chance. By the way, what happened to your ship?"

"That's another long story. I had to turn it over to the . . . to Julius and his group when I finally joined. Part of the setup is, you bring them all your property."

"I bet."

"So the ship was communal property for about a year, just sitting on what passes for a ramp, at what passes for the emperor's private spaceport. It was never used. Everyone was afraid to go near it without being told to do so—then someone ripped it off. Lifted off one day and was never seen again."

Harry nodded. Now finally the lounge music had shifted to something that he was able to put up with. Somewhere in the room, a limited robot intelligence had finally apprehended that the imperial welcoming ceremony was over.

Becky couldn't seem to stop apologizing. She slid a little closer on the padded bench. "When we were partners, it got to be like I just couldn't take it anymore, the way my life was going—not that it was your fault, Harry."

"I didn't suppose it was."

"I looked at the stuff, and I looked at everything I had been doing, and I thought I just couldn't live that way any longer. I wanted some peace. So I quit. I'm sorry."

"I wish you'd stop telling me how sorry you are. There must be something else we can talk about. How's your love life? Rotten, I hope."

"Sure, Harry."

"And so, after you ditched everything that tied you to your old life, in an effort to find some peace and quiet, you stayed on Good Intentions, gave away your spaceship, and became Josephine and took up with that lunatic."

Becky shrugged her narrow shoulders and looked sad. Ever since he'd seen her in the doorway, he'd been fighting down an urge to take her in his arms. Whatever her reaction to that might be, it would be sure to bring on complications neither of them needed at the moment.

Instead, Silver asked: "What're you going to do now? Assuming we can get all this other business settled." He gestured vaguely toward the ceiling, as if there just might happen to be some berserkers lurking in that direction. In answer to her questioning look, he added: "Impending big shoot-out with the bad machinery."

"It looks bad this time, doesn't it? Whenever they call for volunteers, watch out. That's what my daddy always used to warn me. I don't know anything about what's going on. Except that I couldn't stay on that damned planet any longer, even if I had to volunteer for a war to get away."

"You couldn't just walk out on Julius? They kept you confined with lock and key?"

"No. No, they didn't do that. I could've put my suit on and walked over to the other town. Either of the other towns, but they were both getting tired of taking care of more and more defectors, and I would've still been on Gee Eye. Gods and spirits, Harry, I had no idea you'd be here!"

"How could you have?" He started to take a drink, then set down the glass untasted. "It looks bad, all right. We're going to lift off in a couple of days and go out and fight a battle."

Something about his tone of voice made Becky fall silent for a while. Then finally she came up with: "Then maybe at least I won't have to worry about what to do next."

Now it was Harry who found he was unable to let the past alone. After a while, he said: "So you gave up on me, just to get tied up with this Napoleon? He's a loser, if I ever saw one."

She was puzzled. "Na-po-lee—who?"

"Never mind."

"That's not his name. His name's—"

"The Emperor Julius, yeah, I know. I also can tell that he's a loser, whatever name he uses."

Slowly, Becky nodded. "But he wasn't always. Five years ago, I didn't think he was a loser."

Maybe you thought I was. He didn't say that aloud. *Maybe you were right.*

After a while, Becky said: "Commander Normandy says she's sending most of the people who came on the emperor's ship right back to Gee Eye—they might already be on their way."

"They will be, as soon as she decides which kind of ship she can best spare to carry them. Probably a couple of launches. But not you, lady. If you don't volunteer to fight, she'll see to it you're drafted into this war and you won't be sent back anywhere. Your record as a damned good pilot is right there in the database for everyone to see, and at the moment, that's just about the only thing that the commander notices about anybody. That and combat experience, which you also have."

"Are you drafted too, Harry?"

"Sure. Just haven't got my uniform yet. They said they weren't sure they had a helmet big enough for my head."

Becky turned to look toward the landing field, which lay before them utterly lifeless and awesomely empty in the amber glow of the dwarf that wasn't quite massive enough to be a real sun. Not even the one little robot was moving now. "You said we're going out and fight a battle? When will our ships get here? I didn't see any in the hangars."

Harry took another drink.

ELEVEN

On returning to her office, the commander found waiting for her a small pile of communications that had arrived within the hour, carried to Hyperborea on a crewless interstellar courier that had been delayed many days in flight. There was nothing very odd in this, as such delays, caused by natural events, were fairly common. Most of the messages would not be decoded on base, but simply forwarded to their respective destinations.

One note, however, was addressed to her, and so had been duly decoded. It was a query from certain authorities in Omicron Sector, dispatched before the final evacuation and fall of all those worlds. What it amounted to was a terse query: Had anybody in the Hyperborean system seen the fugitive Harry Silver? He was wanted in Omicron Sector on several charges, one smuggling, others unspecified.

Note in hand, Claire sat thinking, fingers drumming on the edge of her holostage display. Almost a standard month had passed since this query was dispatched, and by now, the people who had wanted Harry Silver back in Omicron for legal reasons were very likely dead, or if very lucky, were refugees like Harry. Possibly they would eventually set up some kind of government in exile, or whatever the right term was, but right now, they had bigger things to worry about. She certainly did.

Commander Normandy put the decoded message away in her private drawer. She'd deal with it later, if she were forced to do so.

After thinking for a moment, she called up the adjutant. "Sadie, was it you who decoded the query regarding Lieutenant—I mean, Mr. Silver?"

"Yes, ma'am."

"Say nothing about it to anyone but me." Marut would be certain to make a considerable fuss.

"Yes, ma'am." One of Sadie's strong points was that she could be dependably closemouthed.

Turning in her chair, looking out her office window, Commander Normandy could see that one of the launches was lifting off, taking a load of cultists, some of them unhappy but all still obedient to the emperor their master, on the trip of several hours back to Gee Eye. A number of trips would be necessary to remove all who were going.

When Colonel Khodark came in, obviously ready to discuss some other business, she forestalled him by asking: "So how did Julius and his people know about our appeal for volunteers? If the communications between settlements on Gee Eye are as spotty as you say—but they must have been listening in." All communication between Hyperborea and Good Intentions had been routinely coded, as well as tight-beamed, on the assumption that berserkers or goodlife could be almost anywhere, and anything that could make it harder for them to listen in was worth a try.

Khodark nodded. "That's quite possible, ma'am. Or Julius

may have had some spy or agent in the other settlement—among the citizens who elected R and G, I mean—someone who clued him in on what was going on. All he'd really have to know is that we'd asked them for help and had been turned down. Then as soon as he found out that R and G were refusing to help us, naturally he called on his people to volunteer—just to irritate his local enemies, if for no other reason."

"But he didn't only call for volunteers among his people. He came here himself. Putting yourself in harm's way is a rather extreme step if your only goal is to irritate someone."

"All right, maybe he's serious. But is he really asking for a combat assignment, or does he plan to establish himself here at headquarters and furnish us with strategic advice?"

"If he tries that, he's on his way home, without his ship. But give the old boy credit—he sounds like he really hopes to lead his people from a position out in front of them."

People on the base who regularly paid attention to events on the surface of Good Intentions had been aware for some time of reports describing unrest, and even violence, flaring among the various factions of settlers there. When someone mentioned this problem to the emperor, he listened serenely and then went on trying to involve himself in the planning for the upcoming battle. Having left Gee Eye behind him, and determined to assume his rightful place as the supreme leader of Galactic humanity against the dreadful foe, Julius wasn't going to allow himself to be distracted by petty concerns such as what might be happening on a world in which he was no longer interested.

"I have shaken the dust of that planet from my feet."

Actually, the trouble down there on Gee Eye was nothing new; it had been endemic since the arrival of the cultists some years back, and had flared up just before the emperor's departure. Hopes that his absence would put an end to it now seemed to have been in vain.

· · ·

The cult wasn't really a new story to Harry; but still he found himself fascinated, distracted against his will.

They tended to drive Captain Marut near to a frenzy. "Why would people claim to have a fleet when they don't? Gods of spacetime, it's not as if we were enemies they were trying to bluff."

Harry shrugged, displayed a slightly crooked smile. "People are strange. You'll catch on to that eventually." Marut only turned and walked away, muttering exotic obscenities.

Every hard fact Commander Normandy could discover, as opposed to publicity statements and rumors, confirmed that the cult had never possessed any real fleet—maybe at one time a squadron of three or four ships at the most. Still, the emperor hadn't always been such a total loser as he now appeared. He and his party, or cult, had performed interstellar migrations several times over some undetermined number of years, moving from one settled planet to another, looking and looking for a place where they could settle down and live, free of what they saw as unwarranted interference from co-inhabitants and neighbors. Everywhere they'd settled, conflict with their co-inhabitants had flared up, generally sooner than later. Meanwhile, their numbers had gradually diminished. From their point of view, of course, the ideal situation would have been an entire planet of their own, one friendly and hospitable to human life. But such plums were not easy to come by.

So far, the ideal had never come close to being realized. Such worlds were rare indeed.

Twenty or thirty years ago, on a world halfway across the settled Galaxy, as some witnesses remembered, and as history in the database confirmed, almost a hundred thousand people had acknowledged Julius as their leader. And at least a thousand had been ready to hail him, with ferocious sincerity, as their god. The database had holographs of their great roaring, chanting meetings. Not really very many people, not when the Galactic population of Solarians added up to more than a trillion. Now there might be one thousand who were still faithful; only about a hundred had come with him to war, but that was probably because no more could be crammed aboard his ship.

Still, the commander did not give up all hope that Julius could prove a valuable ally. The handful of his followers who remained on Hyperborea, the people he said were essential as his flagship's crew, presented a motley appearance that did not tend to inspire confidence—but that was probably an unfair judgment, comparing them to the generally trim look of the Space Force and other mainstream units. And the emperor himself, in most of his contacts with people outside his group, proved surprisingly mild-mannered—though flashes of charisma were still to be detected.

Once the emperor settled in aboard the base, in personal quarters reserved for high-ranking dignitaries, he got out of his distinctive uniform and took to wearing a space-crew coverall, almost like everybody else. His was a civilian garment, like Harry's, sidestepping the question of rank. The admiral and his lesser followers hastily abandoned their own fine uniforms as soon as they saw what their deity had done.

Julius made matters a little easier for everyone by making it clear at the start that he had no intention of disputing Claire Normandy's authority in whatever operations might be planned. Now and in the foreseeable future, his authority would be confined to the spiritual domain. When something of the current military situation had been explained to him—as much as the commander thought good for him to know—Julius, His Imperial Highness, proclaimed himself willing to take whatever part the Space Force wanted to assign him.

If Admiral Hector was disappointed at this turn of events, he concealed it well.

Ever since the arrival of the shattered task force, the commander had been doing her best to keep higher authorities abreast of what was happening. She had fired off a succession of automated couriers, outlining her situation, to headquarters—Commander in Chief, Sector, more commonly known as CINCSEC—back on Port Diamond. The next message included all that she had been able to learn about the man who called himself the emperor.

Emperor Julius had evidently made Good Intentions the site of his final effort to establish a seat of power, to create what he and his followers hoped would be a safe haven for their now-persecuted people.

It was about five years ago that the emperor and his entourage had come to this solar system from another, at a considerable distance. Before that, his people had been on yet another world, and before that, on another.

At least on Good Intentions, the members of his sect had had plenty of room to avoid bumping into their neighbors. Not that that had prevented the outbreak of conflict. Reports from down there, readily confirmed, said that a standard year or two ago, his sect had splintered, with a schismatic faction moving away a hundred kilometers or so to establish its own settlement.

"So," the commander observed, "there are now three towns down there on Gee Eye."

"Right." Harry nodded. "The original settlement, the cultists' first camp, and now the place where the schismatic bunch has settled."

Most of the people in each of the three towns detested those in the other two, though matters had never reached the stage of actual warfare. So far, all factions had managed to share the single spaceport, under conditions of an uneasy truce. Actually, most liftoffs and landings required no such facility, and the *Galaxy* had managed quite easily without it.

During the time Harry Silver had spent on Good Intentions, he'd naturally taken note of the various conflicts among the people there. The situation held little interest for him—he found most human power struggles boring—but he could now offer Commander Claire more details than she cared to hear about the emperor and his cult. Harry's information was somewhat dated, of course—a lot might have changed in the years since his last visit.

Strangely, the emperor actually seemed pleased every time he saw or heard some bit of evidence confirming the smallness of the force that he was reinforcing and how heavy the odds were likely to be against them in the coming battle. Frequently he asked to be given more details. But neither he nor the handful of his followers who'd been allowed to remain on Hyperborea were briefed any more thoroughly than the commander thought absolutely necessary. Now the last of Julius's surplus supporters were on their way back to Gee Eye, and Normandy was confident that they could have gained very little military information to carry with them.

Unlike Harry Silver, the emperor was perfectly willing to accept on trust whatever the commander told him regarding the military situation. Captain Marut of course backed up what she said—but Julius did not need convincing.

Once the emperor asked: "Am I correct in thinking we are about eight hours in flightspace from berserker territory?"

He had begun to take an interest in the berserker situation some time ago. His interest had grown, until now he saw it not only as a menacing problem, but as a great solution to some of his other problems.

The commander's situation holostage was in her office, some distance away, and she wasn't about to bring this visitor there; no telling how many questions such a display might provoke. But she tried to be helpful. "From here to the berserkers' nearest known base is eight standard hours in flightspace, given favorable conditions. Unless that's recently changed." A flange of dark nebula creeping in between would be one factor that could drastically slow things down, and there were several others. Here was where a little more genuine weather forecasting would help.

The emperor persisted in getting a direct answer to his original question. "Which means, I take it, that they're only eight hours away from us as well?"

"In flightspace, it doesn't necessarily work that way. But yes, in this case that's approximately right. And we must assume they know we're here."

Over the last year or so, the berserkers had mounted some probing, harassing raids within the sector. Until recently, the Hyperborean system had been spared. Of course berserker recon devices might have come and gone at any time, managing to escape detection. "If they've come near, they never got close enough to this rock to activate our ground-based shields and weapons." Berserkers, like Solarians, or like any other force waging war, had to budget their available assets, concentrate their efforts in the areas judged to be of the greatest importance.

The commander went on: "So far, they haven't made any serious move against this base. Maybe they intend to do so soon. Or maybe they're content for now just to maintain an outpost on Summerland, while planning their next offensive somewhere else."

"Well, if *we* know *they're* there—?"

"Yes, they likely know this base is here." The commander wasn't going to spend any more time in explanations than she had to. She didn't want to tell these crackpot cultists any more than they needed to know to do whatever job she was going to assign them.

Yes, Commander Normandy assured Captain Marut firmly, she really did believe that Mr. Silver intended to join them as a pilot. He'd said as much, and she wasn't going to push him to go through the formalities.

"I doubt that's going to work, Commander. With a man like him."

"We'll see, Captain. It's my responsibility."

"Yes, ma'am. Until our task force moves out, and then we'll see if he's with us or not. If he is, it'll be under my command."

Another courier came in even while Commander Normandy and the captain were conversing. Sadie routinely decoded and displayed the latest news from Earth, or from Port Diamond.

The latest Intelligence reports from distant sectors were discouraging; there was nothing but bad news from the Omicron Sector, which had once contained some forty colonized systems. That territory was now, as far as could be determined, a lifeless wilderness, extending over hundreds of thousands of cubic light-years. Of the once-Earthlike planets in that sector of space, nothing was left but clouds of sterilized mud and steam. No records were available of precisely how their defenses had been overcome.

Invited at last to a formal dinner with Commander Normandy and several chosen officers—the dinner was in the commander's quarters; Harry Silver, who had not been told about the event, much less invited, was in the bar—the Emperor Julius arose to speak. No one had actually asked him to do so, but no one was surprised when he stood up and called upon such eloquence as he had at his command. Death, he said, was spreading like a river of black mud, covering up this corner of the Galaxy. "The great black pall of death, the smoke of burning human worlds and bodies, of lives and dreams, of an end that we must not, will not, allow to happen . . ." Julius could still impress many people when he spoke.

Solarian fleets operating in that particular volume of space had not fared much better. Few battles were won by the forces of life, and the survivors of the battles that were lost told terrible tales indeed. Losses totaled in hundreds of fighting ships, thousands of live crew.

TWELVE

Among Commander Normandy's skills were those of a capable and veteran pilot, and every now and then she found herself being tempted by the idea of turning command of the base over to Lieutenant Colonel Khodark and joining Murat and his people in their mission, as unlikely as their success must be. She could argue with herself that if any such desperate scheme was going to be attempted, then it was her duty, as the ranking officer on the scene, to do everything in her power to make it work. For a short time, she even considered trying out that argument on Sadie. But ultimately she simply put it out of her mind. There was one unanswerable objection: She could not possibly abdicate her responsibility as base commander.

Particularly not on this base.

Meanwhile, Harry Silver experienced another interesting encounter in the mess hall. This time it was the Emperor Julius who, carrying his own tray, stopped to inquire whether the seat across from Harry was taken. The room was more crowded than usual, and somehow the emperor seemed to have become accidentally separated from his usual entourage.

Or maybe—Harry couldn't tell—this time it was by deliberate choice that Julius wasn't sitting with his own people.

"No, it's not taken. Help yourself." Harry was aware that many eyes were turned in their direction, though he kept his own gaze fixed on the man across from him. None of the regular occupants of the base were quite sure what to make of either the emperor or Harry Silver.

"Mr. Harry Silver, I believe."

"That's right. And you must be the ruler of the Galaxy. Or am I thinking of some other galaxy?"

That didn't seem to make a dent. "Are you engaged in business, Mr. Silver?"

"Interstellar trade."

"Oh? What sort?" Julius sounded genuinely curious, in a friendly way. He took a mouthful from his tray and seemed to savor it.

"Mineral rights and related matters," Harry amplified, squinting across the table. After a pause, he added: "I understand that you're in government."

The dark eyes probed him lightly, confidently. "I do my best to serve my people."

"*Your* people, eh?"

"So I call those who have chosen freely to give me their loyalty. As I give them mine. What are your loyalties, Mr. Silver?" The question was not loud, but it carried a charge of electricity.

A sharp retort leaped up in Harry's mind, but then he didn't use it. Damn it, there was something about the man on the other side of the table that suggested that he had the best, the noblest, of reasons for everything he said, everything he did. That good old Julius was Harry Silver's best friend—or would be if he were given half a chance. More than that. That if nature and destiny were allowed to take their proper course, then soon the great devotion that they must share, an allegiance to some marvelous, idealistic cause, would bind the two of them inseparably together.

When the emperor spoke again, the momentary sharpness was gone from his voice. "Right now, it seems that all ordinary matters of commerce and business will have to wait. Until some questions of vastly greater importance have been decided."

"So it seems." Harry nodded. Then he shook his head, like a man trying to clear it of something, and started on his soup.

The man across the table said, with evident sincerity: "I look forward to our coming to grips with the enemy."

Harry grunted something. Then, after a moment's hesitation, he accepted the manly handshake offered by the emperor.

That about did it for the conversation.

Maybe that encounter was what pushed Harry over the edge. Whatever the reason, the time had come when he couldn't avoid it any longer. Harry Silver raised his hand and swore an oath, so now they could issue him a uniform. Like each of the original six Gee Eye volunteers, who'd gone through all this a little earlier, he was assigned a temporary rank. Like most of the others, he got one suitable for a junior pilot.

As soon as the oath was sworn, the commander put down the book that she had used and shook his hand. The very hand shaken by an emperor, not all that long ago. "Congratulations, Lieutenant."

"Thank you, ma'am. I guess."

Captain Murat, who just happened to be present, shot him a look of mingled satisfaction and anticipation. There'd be no more heckling from the civilian safety zone, outside the hierarchy of rank.

When the commander handed Harry the insignia to put on his new coverall, he stood tossing the little metal pins in his hand, looking at them with an expression that fell way short of enthusiasm.

A little later, Harry joined the six original volunteers in the simulator room for a joint exercise in which Captain Marut's new tactical plan was going to be tested in virtual reality.

"You don't come from Gee Eye," Sandor Tencin remarked. Most of the six had become lieutenants also. Only Havot, completely lacking in any formal training, had turned into nothing more than a spacer third class.

"Nope. I was just passing through."

"Oh. Bad luck."

"We'll see how it works out."

Karl Enomoto, the dark and serious volunteer, asked Silver: "What was your old rank, by the way?"

"I've been higher, and I've been lower." And that was all Harry cared to say on the subject.

And he got the same question once more, from Cherry Ravenau, who gazed at him with her startling blue eyes. "You didn't come up with us from Gee Eye."

And managed to answer it with patience.

"Let's get to work, people," Captain Marut urged them. "We've got a lot to learn." His gaze was on Harry as he said those last words. Harry looked back.

Already the other volunteers had logged a good many hours in the simulators. Christopher Havot, youthful and good-looking, had started training with more real, wide-eyed enthusiasm than any of the others. He looked great in his new uniform, too. They'd already given him a couple of hours of elementary pilot training, the kind of thing that all new spacers got just so they'd have some feel for what was happening aboard ship. But when it came to actually using Havot, they were going to have to find some job where his lack of crew experience wouldn't matter much.

Harry heard him assuring the captain that he was willing to try anything.

Marut seemed to expect no less from his people. "Glad to hear it, Spacer."

Meanwhile, the clock was ticking, the hours and days of the chronometer turning, the predicted estimated time of arrival of Shiva and its escort at Summerland getting ominously nearer. Commander Normandy had marked the deadline openly on the calendar chronometer for everyone aboard the station to be aware of. It seemed to her that certain security issues could now safely be set aside—even if there were a Kermandie agent aboard the base, even if there were goodlife, it would be practically impossible for any communication from Hyperborea to reach any other solar system before the deadline.

A day later, Normandy got a good preliminary report on Havot from Sergeant Gauhati, who happened to be in charge of certain aspects of the early testing and training of the volunteers on simulators.

No one had yet decided exactly what to do with Havot. "But he seems to have no nerves at all, which, in the kind of operation we're planning, is definitely an advantage."

The reports on the other new people were all at least moderately favorable. The sergeant also reported that by now, all of them had asked him a familiar question: "When are our real ships going to arrive?"

But only five minutes after Sergeant Gauhati had departed, the commander got a very different kind of report on Havot.

She knew that something must be wrong when she was told that Mayor Rosenkrantz had just arrived in low orbit, urgently requesting another short-range conference. This time, the mayor was accompanied only by a doctor, whose name Normandy did not recognize, as well as a human pilot.

"Oh-oh," the commander said to herself as soon as the bald head of Rosenkrantz appeared on her holostage. The expression on the mayor's face foreshadowed trouble.

He began without any unnecessary preliminaries. "Let me say at the start, Commander, that I have just requested, and received, the resignation of Chief Guildenstern."

The commander's relief was tempered with a sharp foreboding: *Why?* She wasn't sure if she asked the question aloud or not.

Either way, Rosenkrantz did his best to answer it. "Because of a certain matter I myself just learned about only a few hours ago. A matter that's bothering my conscience. Or it would if I didn't do anything about it. I can't let it go by, I feel I've got to tell you. The doctor here can back up what I say."

As the mayor went on speaking, Normandy had to remind herself that the image before her was only a recording; for the next minute or so, at least, it would be useless to respond to it with questions or in outrage.

Nevertheless, a moment later the commander heard herself saying, in disbelief: "Spacer Havot came from *where*?"

The full title of the elaborate hospital down on Good Intentions was something she discovered only a little later, when Sadie retrieved it from the general database. Not that the official title was alarming. But the place was in fact a high-security facility for the criminally insane—one of those facilities that interstellar councils and various other instrumentalities tended to put in out-of-the-way places like Good Intentions because the citizens and governments of real planets had too much clout to be forced to put up with them on their home ground.

Harry, when he learned of her reaction, was surprised that the commander had not known that such an institution existed on Gee Eye, that she could be so ignorant about a lot of other things concerning the neighboring community. But so it was. After all, she'd never even known about the emperor. She'd never visited Good Intentions—had felt it necessary to turn down the occasional invitation because she couldn't very well issue an invitation of her own to its citizens in return.

When the mayor had spoken his piece, he sat back and let the doctor, who happened to be the director of the hospital, do the talking.

"One of the six people who recently volunteered to join your service, this Christopher Havot . . ." The man seemed uncertain of how to continue. He had a deep voice, and thin, chiseled features that gave him an ascetic look.

Normandy flipped rapidly through records, then stared at her own copy, now showing on her holostage, of the relevant record, which was all the hard evidence she really had on Havot. "This says he's a veteran, decorated for valor?"

"He is, ma'am." The doctor ran fingers through his graying hair. "Technically, fully qualified for a decoration, because everyone who accomplishes certain things in combat is entitled to a medal. But—"

"But what?"

She listened again. And she didn't know what to say.

. . . he uses the name of Christopher Havot. I say 'uses the name' advisedly, because we know he has gone by several other names in the past. We at the hospital perhaps bear some responsibility, in not guarding our communications equipment with sufficient zeal. But the chief of public safety—the former chief—is mainly to blame, in my view. Even after Chief Guildenstern learned what Havot had done, he refused to act. The man was allowed to proceed to the spaceport, where he joined the other volunteers. Even though I warned them he was a sociopath."

"He's a what?"

"Sociopath. That's the nice word for it. What it means in

Havot's case, in everyday language, is that he kills people who happen to displease him."

"He . . . kills?"

"The way most people might swat bugs. He also tortures for amusement—though he does *that* only rarely. Technically, he's not a sadist. He was confined for life, no possibility of parole."

There was a long silence. The commander opened her mouth, intending to ask how many people Havot might have killed, but decided she didn't want to know. "Then why in God's name was he allowed to come up here?"

Now the doctor was flustered, despite his impressive looks. "Well, Commander—I found myself unable to contend with the local authorities and the Space Force too. I was given to understand that *you* insisted on having him—having *everyone* who met certain minimal requirements, and as those were stated, Christopher Havot certainly meets them as well as anyone, and much better than most."

Normandy leaned back in her chair, staring at the men as if she might be about to order their ship shot down. "Damn that Guildenstern. I knew he was up to something. He did this just to get back at me. Letting loose a homicidal maniac, not caring what harm might come to anyone."

The doctor was finishing the details of his explanation: ". . . and Mr. Havot somehow heard about your appeal for volunteers, and somehow he got access to a terminal in the hospital and made sure his name was entered."

"And his record as it was given to me? Is that accurate?"

"Far as I know. He was with Commodore Prinsep's task force three years ago, when they went into the Mavronari Nebula." That was thousands of light-years from the sector containing the Hyperborean system. "Havot was badly wounded there, fighting berserkers, and came back in a medirobot. Prinsep says: 'Speaking personally, I would not have survived without him.' "

"But the records also show that Havot has never been in the Space Force. Or in any other military organization."

"That's perfectly correct, he hasn't. It's a strange story, what little I can make of it, and not too clear."

"Doctor, we're really in a bind here, and I'm wondering if it's possible that we might find a use for him—assuming he's still inclined to be useful. Tell me more about him."

The doctor appeared shocked. "I can't advise you on military matters, Commander. I don't know what other perils your people may be facing. I can only alert you to the fact that Mr. Havot can be very dangerous."

The imaged head of Mayor Rosenkrantz continued to watch glumly.

Normandy demanded: "How dangerous, exactly? To his shipmates, to other people on this base? He's been here several days, and so far as I'm aware, no problems have come up."

The doctor sighed. "There are so many factors, it's practically impossible to say. Havot might live as a member of society, military or civilian, for days, months, even years, without harming anyone—he has done so in the past, he might again.

"He might, if he happens to feel like it, play games to entertain a baby, or gently assist a disabled person. He can be entertaining, witty. He might gleefully risk his life fighting berserkers—his record shows he's found that sort of thing enjoyable before. But don't ever cross Christopher Havot. Don't even irritate him. Or, if you must, don't ever turn your back. There are large pieces of his psyche missing. Other people mean no more to him than so many computer graphics—they can be useful, they can be sources of pleasure of one kind or another. But he considers all his fellow human beings disposable. Killing someone affects him just about as much as turning off an image on a holostage."

Wary of taking the mayor's warning, or even the doctor's, at face value, Claire Normandy set Sadie to seeking confirmation. That wasn't easy; the available database came up with nothing at all on Havot—just as it would have drawn a blank on the great majority of living Solarians scattered across the settled two percent of the Galaxy, or on most of the other people who had taken up residence on Gee Eye during the past two or three standard years.

Of the number of people on-base who were recently arrived from Good Intentions, the commander considered calling in and questioning some of them.

But first she chose to talk to Lieutenant Colonel Khodark, who had no trouble making up his mind. "Well, I don't care what kind of testimonial he has from this Commodore Prinsep—whoever *he* may be. I don't care if Havot is the second coming of Johann Karlsen, we shouldn't be that desperate for people that we could even think of using him."

"No, we shouldn't, but we are. We don't dare strip our installation here of essential people—and there really aren't any other kind aboard this base. Whether we bag Shiva or not, we can't abandon our primary mission—it's just too damned important. There are a number of positions here that must be live-crewed around the clock, even if they are desk jobs. Besides, the training of the great majority of my people, their real skill, is in gathering intelligence and decoding. They aren't really qualified for the kind of action we're contemplating. The raid will . . . it'll take a special kind of man—or woman."

"I can't argue with any of that, Commander. But it's still clear to me that Havot has to be confined."

Normandy sighed. "You're right, of course. Unless and until we find out that this is all some horrible mistake. We can't let him run around loose."

As soon as Khodark had gone out, she turned to her holostage. "Sadie? Find that sergeant for me, please—the one who's supposed to fill our military police function." The need had not arisen in the past two years, and for a moment, Commander Normandy could not recall the sergeant's name. "Have him report to my office, on the double." For the first time since she'd assumed command of the base, she was truly glad that she had aboard someone with experience along that line.

Within a couple of minutes, the sergeant, a compact, muscular man, stood before her. "Ma'am?"

"I want you to take two or three good men—they'd better be men, physically strong—and detain trainee spacer Christopher Havot. Search him very thoroughly, and put him in one of the cells. No detours for any reason, take him directly to the cell from wherever you pick him up. No discussions. Refer his questions to me; I'll be coming around to see him in a little while."

"Yes, ma'am."

"And Sergeant. Use extreme care, for your own safety—we have reliable information that he is physically very dangerous."

The sergeant's attentive expression altered slightly. But it wasn't his place to ask questions, and he wasn't easily thrown off stride. "Yes, ma'am."

When he was gone, the commander thought: Later we will have to see about Mr. Guildenstern, former chief. He's not going to get a pass on this. But it must be later.

A search of highly classified Intelligence records—much more up to date than the general historical database—turned up the fact that the berserkers had mentioned Havot in one or two of their intercepted communications. No human ever learned why, or even how, the enemy might have learned his name. He hadn't made Security's list of suspected goodlife collaborators. There was his name, but the message was in a new code, or a specialized one, or one that had so far resisted cracking.

Security would doubtless want to talk to him all over again when his name showed up on the list. Without explaining to him where the list had come from. But as matters stood, Security was far away, on other worlds, and the commander's people were going to have to wait.

Commander Normandy was talking to Sadie, because she wanted to talk to someone: "The berserkers assign code names to some of our leaders and exchange information about them, have discussions about them—in some sense—and no doubt assign them ratings for effectiveness, just as we do theirs. They evidently keep dossiers on a rather large number of human individuals, not all of whom are leaders. We have no idea why some of them are on the list."

Sadie with practice had learned to be a good listener. "Their overall lists of names include goodlife, one assumes. Their friends as well as their most important enemies."

"One supposes so. Unfortunately, in most cases it's impossible to tell what they are saying to each other *about* any individual who's mentioned, or even what category he or she falls into. But the names often come through in clear-text. By the way, Security is perfectly correct, as far as their statement goes. There's no reason to think that Havot, despite the, ah, rather obvious flaws in his character, is goodlife, or ever was. Commodore Prinsep had no discernible reason to lie about his combat record. He—Havot—seemed to view it all as an especially exhilarating game."

The only prison facilities available on-base were two cells, right next to each other on a middle-level underground, and as far as the commander was aware, this was the first time either of them had been used.

The man himself, when at last he stood before Commander Normandy when she came to stand outside the statglass door of his cell, admitted having spent a year or so in the hospital, but claimed to have been morally strengthened by his experiences. He said they had taught him something about the value of life.

His conclusion was somber and earnest, and all the more impressive in that it didn't sound rehearsed; in fact, his voice seemed at times on the verge of breaking in his apparent sincerity. "This is all a huge mistake, ma'am."

"I truly hope so. Can you explain to me how such a mistake came to be made?"

He claimed that his incarceration in the hospital on Good Intentions had been a colossal error from the beginning. There were people, highly placed officials on a distant planet, who for years had been out to get him. "Would you believe me, Commander, if I swore I am not guilty of any horrible crime? If I could give you a good, solid explanation of how an innocent man can be convicted of such things?"

Havot, the experienced institutional inmate, was standing in the attitude of parade rest, feet slightly apart, hands behind his back, in the middle of the confined space. The cell was about three meters by four. The single bunk along one wall was a gauzily transparent force-field web. Using controls provided, the cell's occupant could turn it into an exercise machine, or cause it to assume the shape of a simple chair and small table. Light in a pleasant but tranquilizing blend of colors radiated from the whole surface of the flat ceiling. The plumbing facilities, in a far corner, were exposed, and like everything else inside the cell, invulnerable to any assault that human hands might make.

"I'd much prefer to believe you, Mr. Havot, and to be able to let you out of there and put you to work. But having looked at a transcript of your record, I don't see how I possibly can."

Havot made a graceful gesture; his arms looked stronger when they moved, his hands very large and capable—probably not the effect he would have chosen to convey. All he said was: "Then I won't waste your valuable time in argument. My fate seems to be in your hands—but then, given the fact that you're desperate enough to even consider taking me on, your fate is perhaps in mine, also."

Claire Normandy was silent, but only for a moment. Then she turned away briskly. "See that he's well taken care of, Sergeant. But not let out of the cell for any reason."

"I demand my legal rights," said the voice, still calm, from the cell's speakers.

"When I decide what should be done with you. At the moment, you are under martial law." And Commander Normandy turned away again.

Was there indeed a possibility that Havot was as innocent as he claimed to be? It was hard to see how that could be, and the commander had no time to fret about it. At the moment, she had far greater worries.

As she left, his voice rose up behind her: "Innocent or guilty, I'm ready to fight berserkers, Commander. Is there a note, a comment, from Commodore Prinsep in that file? He'll tell you how well I perform."

Marut expressed his wish that at least one ship from Good Intentions would drop in at the base. "At best, we could commandeer the ship."

"I doubt they'll send a warship, they'll have them all out on patrol."

"Well, at least we might be able to send that homicidal maniac back where he belongs."

"Technically, they tell me, Havot's not a homicidal maniac."

"I've also heard that he's technically not a sadist. Tell that to his victims, they're just as badly off. I wonder how many of them there are, by the way."

"I don't know and I don't care—he's not going to add any of my people to the score. Yes, getting rid of Mr. Havot would be nice. But it's far more important to make sure that the other volunteers are going to work out well enough for us to use them."

So far, the performance of the other early volunteers in training was encouraging.

Finding himself almost immediately back in confinement after a brief taste of freedom was a far more serious blow to Havot's psyche than his attitude to the commander and the sergeant had revealed. He'd not been at all surprised, of course—the only surprise was that he'd been free as long as he had—but his reincarceration had hit him harder than he'd expected.

For a long time, in the hospital on Gee Eye, and for years before that, he had rather enjoyed it when people gave him that wary look. But in the past few months, it had started, more and more, to annoy him. Then, beginning when he'd been put aboard the ship to Hyperborea, all that had changed. It was obvious, from the attitude of the other draftees toward him, that none of them knew the first thing about his background. Nor had any member of the crew of the ship that brought him here seemed aware of his—special credentials. How glorious!

His renewed condition of freedom had been, of course, too good to last. Being locked up again had come as no surprise—yet still it had been a hard blow.

He wondered how many of his new potential comrades and shipmates had been told about his record, and exactly how much they had been told.

"Chow time."

Havot looked up, blinking mildly, at the sound of the cheerful voice. It was the sergeant, the same man who'd so capably taken him into custody, carrying a tray, accompanied by a wide-eyed spacer of low rank who, the sergeant said, was going to be Havot's caretaker from now on.

Both spacers seemed reasonably well-informed on the status and history of their prisoner. At least they knew what kind of hospital he'd been in, and why he'd been put there.

Dully, Havot studied the contents of the tray when the young man shoved it in through the slot in the wall. Well, no worse than he'd expected.

The sergeant had to hurry on about some other business, but before doing so, he gave his assistant what was obviously a final caution, so low-voiced that Havot could not make out a word.

In spite of everything, Havot could not resist a little boasting. "Did you know, Sergeant, that in the hospital, they . . . assigned me a certain roommate?"

"Oh?" Two heads turned in a wary response—naturally, neither of them could see what he was getting at. The sergeant said: "I don't quite see . . ."

"Forgive me, I'm not making myself clear." Havot gave his head a civilized little shake. Moving forward, he leaned on the statglass wall, putting his lips close to it as if in an effort to achieve a kind of intimacy. "Two of us who, in the view of the staff, presented special problems were assigned to the same room. Not by chance, I assure you. No, they really hoped that one of us at least would eliminate the other, thereby reducing the special problems by half." Havot stopped.

"And?"

The young man in the little cell raised an eyebrow. "Here I am." His voice was gentler than ever.

THIRTEEN

Today was the seventh day since the arrival of Harry Silver on the base. And it was also the day on which the new task force had to lift off if it was going to intercept Shiva at the scheduled time on Summerland.

On the morning of Harry's arrival, Commander Normandy had issued an order canceling several scheduled weekend passes. Four days ago, she had gone further. All time off was virtually eliminated, except for the minimum deemed necessary for rest and food. All of her people not actually on duty in the computer room, or working at other essential tasks, had been set to refitting pods, used couriers, and even lifeboats, as imitation berserkers, under the direction of Captain Marut and his lieutenant, or otherwise assisting at the practice maneuvers. Hour by hour, tension had grown, until now it was almost palpable.

Three days ago, the captain had urged her to order everyone on the base to set aside regular duties to help with the preparations for the sortie.

Commander Normandy had calmly and immediately assured him that that was not possible.

Marut was taken aback. "Commander, I don't know what the regular duties of most of your people are, but—"

"That's right, Captain, you don't. So you'll have to take my word for it that I must keep a minimum number of people—not less than twelve, probably fifteen—on a job that must have priority."

The captain blinked. "Priority even over the attack on Shiva?" He seemed unable to conceive of such a possibility.

Claire Normandy nodded. "Exactly."

"I don't understand. What could such a mission be?"

"Captain, I will not discuss it."

Marut couldn't understand, but he was going to have to live with it. The commander sat looking at him in steady silence. "Commander, I intend filing a written protest."

The base commander was neither surprised nor moved by hearing that; probably she had expected it. "That is your right, Captain. It doesn't change anything."

Harry had long ago ceased to pay much attention to the irregular traffic in robot couriers, coming to the base and leaving it again. He estimated the number at ten or twelve arrivals every standard day on average, and an equal number of departures. No one around him ever talked about what these busy vehicles might be carrying, but certain things were fairly obvious. Some of their cargo could of course be physical supplies—though that would be a damned inefficient way of shipping material. And if all the incoming couriers were laden with orders from headquarters, Normandy would surely be cracking up under the strain of trying to keep up with them, and she didn't give any sign of doing that.

No. The conclusion seemed inescapable that the burden of

this substantial commerce was mainly immaterial. Vast amounts of information were being sent, from a variety of sources at interstellar distances, here to Hyperborea. On this base, some kind of information-processing took place, and when that had been accomplished, the results were shipped out to distant destinations. Beyond that, Harry wasn't trying to speculate. He had plenty of other things to worry about.

The hours of the last few days had rushed by in a blur, most of them filled with planning, with frantic work to make an assortment of hardware look and act like something else, and with rehearsals. The latter were carried out mostly in the actual ships that would be used in the attack, but with control helmets connected in simulator mode. The ships stood motionless on the landing field, or hung in low orbit, while standard tactical computers worked the simulation. Only once did Harry get to take part in a real exercise in space. It was a hurried affair, lasting no more than half an hour, in which all the available armed launches, together with an odd assortment of even smaller craft, meant to be imitation berserkers, maneuvered to the far side of Hyperborea. There, in real time, scratching and banging their armor on real rocks, they practiced the landing operation that Marut hoped to be able to employ successfully at Summerland—there was no serious attempt to simulate enemy ground defenses, though everything would depend on the Solarians' ability to deceive them when the time came to do the real operation.

Harry's estimate of the chances of success plummeted, if possible, to an even lower level.

In endless debates, which seemed to Harry maddening exercises in futility, the leaders hashed over the possibilities. Harry was present during at least half of their discussions.

Whatever the layout of the berserker station on Summerland proved to be like, whatever its size, the basic unfriendliness of its design to human intruders could be taken for granted—

forget about airlocks, or supplies of air and water. Any corridors or catwalks there would be of a size and shape to facilitate the movement of the enemy's service machines, most of them smaller than armored people. Possibly there would be no artificial gravity. Even worse, and more likely, there would be a field of simulated gravity that cut in only when necessary to protect relatively fragile machines from heavy acceleration. And the level of gravity maintained when that system was turned on would probably be vastly different from Earth-surface normal. Mere space suits did not come equipped with protective fields, and their occupants might well be mangled without their armor ever being pierced.

The possibility was raised of the enemy base containing a prison cell or two, possibly occupied by captive life-forms. There was no reason to believe that the majority of berserker installations were so equipped. A great many dramatic stories, and innumerable rumors, detailed the fate of berserkers' prisoners, but only a few of them were true. In real life, cases of a death machine holding prisoners were extremely rare, and when a berserker did take them, it had clear and specific reasons for doing so.

Marut was decisive. "We've got too much to do as it is. If there are any prisoners held on Summerland, we'll just have to ignore them—until our primary mission is taken care of."

The new plan of assault, as worked out by Normandy, Marut, and their aides, in consultation with Harry Silver, called for a landing to be made by units disguised as berserker machines—but still, if possible, without even being noticed—on the planetoid called Summerland.

Every time Harry had the chance, whenever his new colleagues were willing to listen to his comments on the developing plan, he let them have the plain truth as he saw it. And he was far from optimistic about the possibilities of success.

At one point, after listening to what seemed an hour of optimistic projections, Silver threw a holostage remote control crashing across the room and swore. "How the hell are we supposed to approach and land without being detected?" There would be some kind of early warning system, probably much like the one protecting Hyperborea. And if the attackers got through that, every square centimeter of the planetoid's surface would be monitored at least by sensors.

Marut looked at him as if he had just heard confirmation that the new lieutenant's sanity was suspect. "That's the whole purpose of our program of deception, Silver."

Once a foothold had been established on Summerland, assuming that could be done, the human attackers would work their way to a good point from which to strike at the enemy base's unliving heart.

The success of the plan worked out by Marut and his assistants depended heavily on how well the individual pilots assigned to miniships could each operate a swarm of them. These devices were in large part originally berserker metal, designed and put together in the base workshop to look like berserker utility machines. There were in all as many as a dozen of the little pods. Certain individual human pilots were going to have to control as many as three, or even four.

They had earnestly considered assigning Silver to that job, but in the end had decided that his proven skill as a combat pilot was too desperately needed. He would be in the pilot's seat on the *Witch of Endor.* Becky Sharp's somewhat lesser but still formidable talent would be put to work on the pods. People controlling those miniships would have to approximate routine berserker movements up until the last possible moment—and then maneuver and fight as they never had before. Not that they would be carrying much of anything to fight with.

The more Harry thought about the plan, the less chance of success he was willing to allow it. The more ingenious new details Marut thought up, the crazier it sounded.

But Harry didn't want to withdraw from the planning sessions. If he had to go through with this, he wanted some idea of what was going on.

Marut's original plan had called for Havot, then considered a choice recruit, along with Marut himself and one or two others, the whole party shielded and armed with converted berserker hardware, to drop in their miniships from the scout or courier as it approached the berserker base from behind the far side of the rocky planetoid.

Havot being no longer available, someone else would have to take his part.

Once the landing party was on the berserker base, especially after it got inside, making its way from one point to another would almost certainly involve cutting or blasting a route through solid decks and bulkheads, not to mention fighting off its commensal machines—keeping in mind that the place must still appear as a functional berserker base, at least for half a minute or so in the interval between their own arrival in the system and that of Shiva with its presumed escort.

At that point, the intruders, or some of them, would be required to slip out of their Trojan hardware and move and fight in their own suits of space armor.

Relentlessly, the advancing numbers on the chronometer were bearing the combat crews toward the moment when they must board the inadequate ships of the new task force and lift off for Summerland. Somewhere, at some astronomical distance in space, though at no enormous gap in time, the thing called Shiva was in flight, no doubt escorted by sufficient units of mobile and aggressive power to sterilize and pulverize a planet.

Now, on the seventh day of Harry Silver's presence on the base, only a few hours remained before the scheduled liftoff for the attack on Summerland and Shiva. And Harry Silver was growing more and more thoroughly convinced, with every passing hour, that Marut's new plan of attack was completely harebrained. Trouble was, he didn't yet see a damned thing that he could do about it.

Still the only person who could stop the attack was Normandy. She could do it simply by pulling rank and refusing the newly reconstituted task force permission to lift off from her base. But she wasn't going to do that. Harry could understand her motives for allowing the plan to go forward, but he was increasingly sure that she was wrong.

The installation of the c-plus cannon aboard the *Witch* had been completed, and Harry's ship was certified as combat ready. Even the missing fairing had been replaced by a new piece, made in the machine shop. The thought crossed his mind that if he failed in combat, Marut didn't want him to have the faintest shadow of an excuse.

It might have been funny, if it wasn't tragic. To Harry, the whole plan was looking more and more suicidal. Maybe he'd felt a bit self-destructive when he signed up for it, but he sure as hell didn't now.

So far, he'd not aired his complaints in the presence of the lower-ranking Space Force people and the other volunteers. But they had eyes and ears and brains just as he did, and he could hear some of them grumbling too.

Julius had been given the brevet Space Force rank of captain—modest for an emperor, but he was going to be in command of his own ship, crewed by his own followers, and that was the only point that he had really insisted on. The captain/emperor was quite prepared, or said he was, to take the *Galaxy* into combat shorthanded if necessary. Even if he was the only live human on board. It was quite possible to do that, with even the largest carrier or battleship, but the vessel would have only a fraction of its potential effectiveness in combat.

When some of his followers objected, pleading with him to protect his glorious life at all costs, Julius haughtily accused them of wanting him to act the part of a coward.

At least one of them was then suitably penitent. Graciously, the emperor forgave him.

And he told his listeners that he had retreated far enough—his calm, thought Normandy, was that of the potential suicide. She had known one or two of that type rather well.

Some of the people who had remained loyal to Julius until now decided that they were going no farther. Then they resumed some relationship with Becky, though her reasons for defecting were a little different from the others'.

Everything besides the looming battle had now become for Julius a mere distraction.

Harry got the impression that the man really didn't want to risk sabotaging the whole effort against Shiva through his own ineptitude, or that of his faithful followers. And Harry thought that what he really did want was perhaps not all that hard to figure out. The Emperor Julius wouldn't be the first failed leader in human history whose goal in entering battle was simply to achieve for himself a sufficiently glorious and dramatic end.

Of course, if the Solarians won the coming fight, and the emperor survived, that wouldn't be too bad either. One tested way to acquire dedicated followers was to launch a crusade.

FOURTEEN

Shortly after being locked up, the prisoner had put in a formal request to be allowed to communicate with a civilian lawyer down on Good Intentions. His appeal had not been denied so much as ignored. All his objections and questions would have to wait until Commander Normandy had time to consider them, and of course no one knew when that might be.

It seemed to Christopher Havot that his best chance to make a break for freedom would come when the sergeant and his helpers showed up—as they surely would sooner or later—to take him to the landing field, or to the hangar, and load him aboard ship to be transported back to Good Intentions. How good his chance of getting loose might be would absolutely depend on how the sergeant and his helpers went about their job, and Havot was worried that the same sergeant would be in charge. Of course a real chance to get away, clean out of the Hyperborean system, would be too much to expect. That would mean somehow getting aboard an interstellar ship and riding it somewhere else—realistically, far too much to hope for. Much more likely would be a lesser opportunity, which could still be highly satisfying. An unrestricted few minutes, or even no more than a few seconds—that could be time enough to pay back some of the people who ran the system that kept him from enjoying life to the full. Christopher Havot could leave his mark again.

Yes, this was not the worst spot he'd been in, not by a long way. If nothing else, he'd be out of this cell, being transferred somewhere else, in no great length of time. The possibilities were intriguing.

Getting up from his bunk where he had been lounging, Havot stretched, doing a thorough job of it, arms, back, and legs. Tapping simple commands into a small, flat panel on the wall, utilizing the speck of freedom and authority he had been allowed to retain, he reconfigured the webby stuff of the bunk into an exercise machine and adjusted the height of its saddle to where he wanted it.

Since entering the cell, he'd spent much of his time in physical workouts. Now, as he did more often than not when exercising, he pulled off his clothes and rode the bike stark naked. When his unseen guards looked in on him, as he had no doubt they would be doing from time to time, and disapproved of what they saw—well, they could stop watching.

If, on the other hand, one or more of them became interested in his beautiful body, that could open possibilities. He knew, without thinking much about it, that his body was beautiful. He always rather expected people of both sexes to be physically attracted to him, and it seemed to him that he was often right.

Of course—and he was ready to admit the weakness to himself—he tended to forget the occasions when he was wrong.

Right now, the space given over to face-to-face visitors, just beyond the statglass wall, was deserted. Not that he'd had any visitors, except for a few official ones.

Whether or not he was being watched, at any given moment, through hidden sensors in his cell's walls or ceiling, Havot had no way of knowing. It seemed a safe assumption, in any prison, that his behavior was being recorded.

In recent years, his body had been through a lot, one way and another, but he felt serenely confident that it was still beautiful.

Havot wondered if someday—somewhere, somehow—he might have a career as a consultant in prison design.

Having spent most of his life, since the beginning of adolescence, locked up in one place or another, he'd become something of a connoisseur of cells and prisons. Many such facilities were already so well designed as to appear hopeless as far as managing, or even imagining, an escape was concerned. But the fact was that none of them had yet managed to contain him for more than about a year.

Not that Christopher Havot possessed any superhuman powers that enabled him to walk through walls. It was rather that so far the universe had seemed to be on his side. Whatever kind of hole or trap his fellow humans stuck him into, whatever walls and fields they put up to contain him, something always turned up that opened a way out. That prison hospital on Good Intentions, for example. It was about as secure a facility as human ingenuity could devise, and his chance of ever leaving it alive had been about as close to zero as the real world allowed any probability to become. Yet here he was.

His deliverance from Good Intentions was the second time in his life that berserkers had served, indirectly, as the agency by which the universe contrived to open ways to freedom for him. He supposed it would be only proper to feel grateful. But he wasn't quite sure whether he did or not.

Not that he felt any inclination to worship the death machines—or any other entity, for that matter. But it was curious. Berserkers were highly entertaining opponents, and he didn't hate them, any more than he necessarily hated people. All he asked of the universe was to be allowed to seek his own amusement from it, in his own way.

Pedaling his force-field bicycle, gradually quickening the pace, working his strong arms rhythmically against the resistance of its moving handgrips until his body gleamed with sweat, Havot thought over what little he'd learned about the military situation here, mostly gleaned from listening to others' conversations on the ship from Hyperborea. The situation must be desperate indeed for a Space Force commander to call for civilian volunteers.

Every time he had the chance, which wasn't as often as he would have liked, Havot tried to strike up a conversation with the young spacer whose name he had already forgotten, his new caretaker. There was no indication that the youth had actually been ordered not to talk to him—only to keep him locked up, of course, and to prevent his communicating with anyone else.

"I suppose the preparations for battle are coming along."

"I guess they are."

"Will you carry a message from me to the base commander?"

"Maybe. What is it?"

"Before they locked me up here, I went through a couple of training sessions. I was beginning to get a feel for what kind of operation this planned attack is going to be, how important it is . . . I'd like to tell the commander that if she happens to have some job that's really too dangerous, so bad that she doesn't even want to ask any of her own people to volunteer— Well, what I'm trying to say is, I'm volunteering for that job right now, whatever it may be."

The youth was staring at Havot, obviously undecided as to whether to take him seriously or not.

"Will you carry that message?" The truth was that Havot himself wasn't entirely sure how seriously he meant it.

The other nodded, and withdrew.

Left alone again, Havot for a time allowed himself to indulge in fantasy. Here came Commander Normandy to visit him in his cell, to ask him if he wanted to volunteer for a certain practically suicidal job. It seemed they had just discovered some kind of booby trap in the Trophy Room, and it was going to have to be disabled before it blew up the whole base. Only a human could do the job. Of course there would be some fantastic reward if he succeeded. The commander was really desperate, and she was coming to plead with him to undertake the task.

Havot could do that part of the fantasy quite realistically; over the years, he'd heard a lot of people pleading for things that seemed to them tremendously important. "Maybe if you go down on your knees," he told the commander's image in his mind, "I might just listen to you." The daydream faded . . .

While Havot pedaled his bicycle and dreamed his dreams, Harry Silver was trying to convince himself that Marut's desperately improvised plan to ambush Shiva might possibly be made to work. Harry's conclusion was that sure it could—*if* the human side was going into battle with at least three more good ships and the properly trained crews to man them. And *if* the attackers had been able to practice the assault at least once with real hardware, machines, and bodies dropping out of space onto real rocks somewhere; *and* if they had some firm idea of what the real enemy strength at Summerland was going to be . . . *and* if that strength was not simply too great.

But as matters actually stood, the harried humans of Hyperborea had not one of those things going for them.

It was going to be practically suicide. And he, Harry Silver, was actually volunteering to go along.

Over the past few days, the planners, working against the chronometer in a frenzy of anxiety, had tried to consider every possibility: What would Shiva do if it arrived at Summerland to find the berserker station under attack? It would assume leadership on the berserker side, unless the attacking force were of overwhelming strength, and if past results were any indication, it would very probably win the fight. If the Solarians could for once manage to bring crushing power on the scene—not that that would be a possibility now—Shiva could be expected to get itself the hell out of there and go on computing to fight on another day.

Marut's improvisation—you might call it brilliant, you might call it crazy—called for the humans to get themselves into the berserker base and out of sight, taking over control of the enemy installation from inside before Shiva and its no-doubt-formidable escort showed up.

There were just too damn many things that could go wrong. And they didn't even know enough to compile a list of all the ugly possibilities.

There was really nothing that could be done about that.

With liftoff for the reconstituted task force only a few hours away, now would be the time to load the miniships aboard the vessels that were going to transport them to the vicinity of Summerland.

Marut insisted he was going to be able to tow them all to the scene of action in a kind of force-bubble—but to Harry, that meant they all had to lift off from the field at the same time. There were problems, seemingly insoluble, any way he looked at it.

· · ·

Silver hadn't had a drink of anything stronger than mineral water for a day and a half, and it didn't look like his string of drinkless hours would be broken anytime soon. But that didn't prevent him from going into the lounge, when he found he had maybe a quarter of an hour of free time, and sitting down. Even if he generally had the place entirely to himself these days, he somehow felt more comfortable in a bar than staring at the walls in his little anonymous room. Or sitting in his combat chair, staring at the inner bulkheads of his ship—no, he corrected himself, of what used to be his ship. In just a few hours, he was going to have all he wanted of that scene.

When the tall, bland, pyramidal shape of the inhuman waiter rolled over to his table, he ordered something soft, only fizzy water with a little sour flavoring, just to have a glass in front of him. Then he sat there, staring into the lounge's half-real greenery, wishing that he could melt into the jungle.

All right, he wasn't really kidding anyone. Not even himself. He caught himself watching the doorway, hoping that Becky was going to show up again.

He'd got himself trapped in a bad position, and there didn't seem to be a damn thing he could do about it. He'd done it to himself of course, stuck his neck out of his own free will, signed up on the dotted line, so now things were considerably different. A civilian could get away with a lot of things that a lieutenant could not. If only they'd given him the temporary rank of general . . . fat chance.

He'd already pushed his objections to the revised plan of attack right up to the line of insubordination—had run a good distance over that line, according to Marut.

Now, unable to come up with any wiser course of action, he mentally replayed his last encounter with the captain. For the last couple of days, their meetings had tended to be very similar, and had been running along these lines:

Marut: "I am giving you a direct order, Lieutenant, to cease making these insubordinate remarks."

Silver: "Insubordination, hell! What do you think you're going to do, lock me up? Arrange a firing squad? You *need* me, Captain, if you're going to have even a ghost of a chance out there."

Marut: "If you think for one minute, Lieutenant—"

And it was generally up to Commander Normandy, who was usually present on these occasions, to get the two of them away from each other's throats and maintain at least a semblance of constructive planning in the meetings. Whether Harry was thrown into a cell or not was really going to be up to her.

That was how matters stood at the moment. Silver had to admit that the captain was right about at least one thing—if Lieutenant Harry Silver objected to the plan so forcefully that he couldn't be trusted to take part in it, the logical course for a commanding officer was to lock up Lieutenant Silver; there weren't that many cells to choose from, he'd probably be right next to the murderer, to await courtmartial. That ritual would take place as soon as possible, whether anybody came back alive from the attack on Shiva or not.

But Harry could think of another reason to curtail his arguments, one even better than staying out of jail. The time had come to put up or shut up. It was now too late to voice objections—unless he could come up with a better plan to replace the one that wasn't going to work, a feat that at the moment was quite beyond the powers of Harry Silver. Inadequate as Marut's scheme was, it represented the best chance they had to save the population of this sector, and the next one after this, and all the rest of Solarian humanity, from being ultimately consumed in Shiva's hellfire. And preparations, such as they were, had already been made, the countdown was running, and at this point it wasn't going to be turned off by anything that anyone else, except the commander, might do or say.

And Silver came around again to the unhappy fact that

Commander Normandy was going along with it. It wasn't that she was stupid, Harry told himself. It was just that she had nothing better to try, or to suggest, and for an officer of her rank to do nothing would have been criminal. Not for the first time, Harry was very glad he wasn't in her position of command, facing the decisions she now had to make.

Harry decided that he must have been a little crazy when he signed up for active duty. Becky's supposed death had hit him hard, and he'd been thinking that his life wasn't worth much. Well, he wasn't the first one to do that. Most people went through spells of depression, and it was no good claiming that as an excuse. He'd just have to live with the results. He'd raised his hand and sworn an oath, and there didn't seem to be any good way out of that.

Sitting in the bar now, sipping at his sour, watery, inconsequential drink, he was thinking that he might be strongly tempted to find some way out that was not so good—except for Becky. He'd have to get her out of it as well . . . but then he ran into the fact that subtracting two good pilots from the mix would definitely kill the planned raid's last faint possibility of success. It would definitely guarantee a berserker walkover when the stunt was tried. And Harry had to admit that a faint possibility of victory still existed. It was just a very lousy play on which to stake the survival of the human race.

Anyway, Becky had flatly refused to consider desertion when in their last talk he'd tried to hint around the subject. Maybe his hinting had been too oblique—but no, he didn't think so.

He'd been testing out the vague and possibly imaginary possibility that he could talk her away from participating in the raid while still going on with it himself. But Becky gave no sign that she was taking seriously his hints about bailing out—maybe she knew something he didn't. Like the fact that he wasn't serious about them himself.

Damn it. All in all, that woman really knew him pretty well.

And now suddenly, as Harry was sitting in the bar, she came in through the doorway he was watching, dressed in her new coverall with her own lieutenant's badge on the collar.

He thought she looked better than ever.

"Ready to go, Harry?"

"Ready as I'm going to be. How about you?"

"Same here. And the captain and his crew are ready."

"I bet. How about the emperor?"

"Oh, he'll show up. Julius and his prize crew." Becky paused. "I sure can pick 'em, can't I?"

"You picked me, kid, once upon a time. As I remember."

"Sure, Harry." Becky looked at her wrist. "Only about two hours to go to liftoff. I just had a nap. You should be resting."

"I am. This is how I rest. Sitting in a bar."

And that was the moment when all the alarms went off. Again.

People had endured their last briefing for the ordeal into which they were about to plunge, and some of them were starting their final checklists, when once more the noise and flashing lights came crashing into their awareness.

Whatever entity had triggered the alarms showed no manners at all, interrupting without any consideration. Right in the middle of someone's conversation, the first sound and visual signal of the alarm.

Harry and Becky had been trying to say good-bye, or trying to find a way to do so. They had become reconciled to the fact that according to Marut's plan, they were not going into battle aboard the same ship. But if this new alarm was the real thing, if it meant battle, it would not be the battle they had been trying to rehearse.

Harry Silver got automatically to his feet. Of one thing he was mortally sure: No one aboard the base was crazy enough to have picked this hour, this minute, to call a practice alert.

Harry's mouth was suddenly going dry. But his first thought brought with it a certain wry inward lightening of spirits: *If we're all killed here in the next hour, at least we're not going to have to carry out that damnfool attack.*

FIFTEEN

They were both headed for the door, but before Harry reached it, he was stopped in his tracks by an order from Commander Normandy, coming through on his personal communicator: "Silver, we're in a red alert. I want you to go and make sure those launches all get off." She'd discussed the difficulties in detail with him during the days of preparation, and there was no need now to spell out her doubts about the dependability of every component in the mix, from the assigned pilots through the hardware.

"Yes, ma'am."

Becky had come to a stop also, and she was looking back at him.

"Take the *Witch* for me, kid," Harry said. "Suddenly I've got another job." In the now never-to-be-accomplished attack on Summerland, she'd been assigned to fly a cluster of Marut's pet pods, but suddenly the game was drastically changed. Now no one was going to try to tow pods into action, and Becky could be vitally effective aboard a real fighting ship.

She had heard the communication, too. "We'll be a couple of minutes anyway, getting up. I'll try to wait for you."

He might be able to catch up that quickly, or he might not. There was no time for Harry to kiss her before they parted, but he took time anyway. If the berserkers were coming, they could wait ten seconds more.

Then they were both moving, running, Becky quickly several strides ahead of him. And at the last moment, he wanted to call her back, to make sure that she stayed with him no matter what happened. When their paths of duty separated, he watched her out of sight, the graceful figure moving at a flying run around a corner.

Harry moved on, at a run too, the sound of his boots joining others that were pounding through the corridors. His absence from the control cabin of the *Witch* would doubtless delay matters a little, so Becky would probably be the last to lift off. But that might not matter a whole lot. And Harry would worry less about his woman and his ship if one was aboard the other.

Of all the people on the base, only a few were wearing armor, and getting suited was the first order of business for almost everyone still on the ground.

Not all the people Harry saw were running to arm themselves, or to reach their battle stations. During the very first moments after this latest alarm had sounded, some seemed reluctant, for some reason, to take the signal at face value. Here and there, they grumbled at the annoyance. Things weren't supposed to develop this way. The damned buzzers and bells again—what was it this time? Another intrusion by a berserker scout? Maybe those crazy Home Guard people from Gee Eye, showing up where they were not supposed to be.

. . .

When Harry reached the place where the little ships were trying to get space-borne, he could see that Claire Normandy's instincts had been correct and help was needed, at least with one or two of them. One relatively inexperienced pilot was having a problem with his helmet—it turned out that he only thought he was, but his ship was just as effectively immobilized. Harry crouched beside him, describing the right procedure, step by step, in a calm voice. In half a minute, the difficulty had been solved.

Up until an hour ago, Marut had still been arguing that Harry shouldn't be allowed to lift off in his own ship. More than once the captain made the dire prediction that the *Witch* would head straight out and not come back.

Almost immediately there were indications that this berserker incursion was rather more serious than the last one. A robot voice, speaking in the helmets of everyone still inside the base or on the field, informed them that the presence of the enemy in force, in-system, was now confirmed. Six to eight unidentified objects, moving in loose formation, had emerged from flightspace about two hours ago, out on the system's fringes. The projected flight paths converged on Hyperborea.

A couple of minutes later, the number of eight bandits was confirmed.

Each Solarian reacted in his or her own way to the realization that most of their planning and effort over the past few days had been utterly wasted—whatever the outcome of this defensive battle they were being forced to fight, they wouldn't be making any attack on Summerland.

Commander Normandy's own battle station was in the computer room. An extra suit of personal armor was kept there for her convenience, and she was getting into it even while she took reports and issued orders, tuning up the big holostage that stood in the room's center, getting a picture of the immediate situation. Just as she was settling into her combat chair, some stray memory or association sent flashing through her mind the idea that she ought to consider ordering Christopher Havot released from his cell.

As far as she knew, there were no standing orders regarding prisoners in a situation like this, which doubtless came up very rarely. What was to be done in a red alert, with people who for whatever reason happened to be locked in cells, was a matter that the writers of regulations had decided to leave up to the local commander's judgment. And so Commander Normandy needed only a couple of seconds to dismiss Havot from her thoughts. Her attention was going to be totally absorbed in more important matters, and she simply couldn't afford to take the time.

Plunging into urgent business, Commander Normandy found that one of the first items on her list was seeing to it that all her spacecraft got off the ground.

Meanwhile, Sadie the adjutant was at least as busy as any of the human defenders of the base, and thinking at least a hundred times as fast in those areas of decision making where a program had been granted competence.

A certain item had been coded into the long and detailed list of the adjutant's duties: In the event of an attack, or any kind of alert, any human on the base who lacked a formally designated battle station had to be assigned one. If the subject was a patient in the hospital, then that became his or her mandated place. Sadie needed only a few microseconds to discover that the code said nothing specific about people in cells—and a quick check back showed that no one had been in either of the cells during any of the previous alerts.

Precedent was lacking. Initiative was required.

Sadie reached a quick decision. Meeting the berserker attack, any berserker attack, was all-important, and Sadie discarded from her computations all factors in the situation that she judged irrelevant to that. And bothering the human commander at a time like this was something to be done only in a grave emergency.

As long as Havot was in a cell, or subject to any kind of confinement, a major part of his mind was perpetually engaged in scheming to get free. It didn't matter that prison had come to seem his natural state of being. He'd been locked up for so long that real freedom, when he had a chance to taste it, seemed somehow unnatural, which doubtless made it all the more attractive.

Sadie spoke to him in her measured voice, unhurried and not quite human. She told Christopher Havot that as soon as she had given him his instructions, his cell door would open. His newly assigned battle station was in the computer room. She even told him how to reach it.

The artificial voice also reminded spacer third class Havot where to go to equip himself with armor. He'd been assigned a suit, a locker, and a shoulder weapon when he arrived as a volunteer recruit, and suddenly these were his once again. All humans must be able to defend themselves against berserker attack.

Havot, at the moment clothed in the standard coverall and light boots, listened, nodded, and calmly agreed to everything. He accepted almost without surprise the news that he was being turned loose. On some level of his mind, he'd actually been expecting something of the kind to happen.

The moment after the door slid open, he was out and running. He did not need to delay for even a few seconds to formulate a plan. Instead, he immediately chose, as if by instinct, the corridor he wanted and sprinted down it, running a race in which few athletes could have overtaken him. He went in the direction he had to go to collect his assigned weapon and armor—the same way he would have chosen if he were making a great effort to get into the miniship he'd begun to get acquainted with in his few days of training. It was near the place where the little ships waited to be launched.

And now the eight ships of the enemy were in range, at close range, and all the heavy ground defenses of the rock called Hyperborea opened up at once. The effect was dazzling, jarring, almost frightening in itself. And the enemy of course responded.

Watching the early minutes of the battle unfold upon her holostage, the commander was frightened, not only because berserkers were attacking, but because the ultimate terror was behaving in a way that made it still more terrible.

Whether it was necessary or not, Commander Normandy felt the need to spell it out for someone: A hundred landers and boarding machines coming down were far more unsettling than a hundred missiles, because it meant that today the berserkers were not going to be content with mere destruction. Just blowing up the base and everyone in it was not their primary goal—instead, there must be things here—machines, documents, objects of some kind—that they were going to great lengths to capture intact.

Most horribly, the death machines might have as their calculated goal the taking of certain human brains alive.

Lieutenant Colonel Khodark, who had been listening attentively from his own station at a little distance, said: "One or more of the people who handle the decoding, that's who they want. They've learned something, somehow, about our spying, and they want to figure out how much we know."

"The prisoners they took."

"Yes. You know it's almost certain that they picked up some when they ambushed the task force."

At that moment, when Claire Normandy became convinced of the enemy's objective, she was as frightened as she had ever been in her life.

But then fear went up another notch when she began to *suspect* that Shiva might be in command of this assault.

Havot, still running all-out for freedom, wondered if the artificial intelligence that had released him was now going to be monitoring his behavior. But he decided that the base must be under real attack and that under such conditions, even an A.I. system would be overloaded with other work.

Today they seemed to have a different scent in the corridors. Havot couldn't identify it, but it was something he hadn't noticed while he was in his cell.

Never mind. He knew what tomorrow's scent was going to be. What really tingled in Havot's nostrils as he ran was the smell of blood, though only in anticipation.

Of course his real objective wasn't the computer room where the A.I. voice had told him to go, or even the miniship where he'd briefly trained; not now when a vastly more desirable goal might be within his reach. It was as if a part of his mind had been preparing, from the moment of his latest arrest, for just such a contingency as this.

He'd always had a good sense of direction, and without hesitation, ignoring signs, he now chose the right branchings in the maze of corridors, eventually emerging somewhere on the flight deck, the uppermost level of the underground hangars.

He opened his assigned locker, scrambled into the armored suit in less than half a minute—he'd gained familiarity with this kind of equipment long before he ever saw Hyperborea—and grabbed up the blunt-nosed carbine that lay in its rack waiting for him, a gift from the Space Force. He needed only a moment to slam the stock against the automatic clamp on the right shoulder of his suit, select the alpha triggering mode and then clip the sighting mechanism on the side of his helmet. Now he could aim and fire almost instantaneously while keeping both hands free.

If he was being monitored, this was when they would try to stop him.

But no one tried. Everyone was naturally too busy, with enemies even more frightful than Christopher Havot.

His real objective was one of the comparatively large ships he'd earlier seen waiting out on the field. He didn't much care which one as long as it had the legs to get him out-system, away from prisons and berserkers both.

If only they weren't all up and off the ground before he could get himself aboard one. But he wasn't going to let himself think about that possibility.

In his couple of days of freedom on the base, he'd taken care to make sure of just how many ships, and what kind, were available on the field, and where they were parked. He didn't think there was much in the way of serious transport stored in the hangars.

When Lieutenant Colonel Khodark received a report that Havot was free, from someone who'd seen the cell door standing open, the colonel wanted to send out an alarm and have the prisoner rearrested. "He's a homicidal maniac!" Khodark shouted to his boss.

Normandy was listening with only half an ear. "Is that a fact? But he might be fighting on our side."

"He *might,* yes. But—"

The commander nodded toward her holostage, where Khodark's imaged head appeared only in a small compartment at the side. She said: "I've just seen a hundred guaranteed, fusion-powered, steel-bodied, homicidal maniacs hit the ground, and I *know* what they're going to do. I can't take the time to worry about one who's only flesh and blood."

No doubt, thought Commander Normandy, her adjutant had done it. Evidently, if Sadie had invested any calculation in the matter at all, she had decided that under berserker attack,

Havot was more likely to be helpful than harmful. Well, for all Claire knew, Sadie might be right.

While that exchange was going on, Harry Silver was still shouting orders at people and machines, struggling to get the pods, the miniships, which were still waiting underground, brought quickly out and properly deployed for fast liftoff. All the neatly organized countdown schedule for getting things smoothly into space had just been badly scrambled.

Havot had made an instinctive decision as to how best get control of the ship he wanted. If at all possible, he was just going to run boldly up to an open airlock and get aboard. But he didn't want to try to run across the whole field if he could help it. His gut feeling was that one running man would be too conspicuous out there, a prominent target for either side.

He had first visualized getting aboard the emperor's ship, probably because he assumed that the opposition inside would be easier to overcome. Not that Havot had any particular urge to kill the emperor. In fact, in his brief contact with the man, he had been somewhat put off by an impression that Julius was altogether too eager to get killed.

Commander Normandy would have been a good candidate for murder too, as the primary figure of authority. So would the sergeant who'd locked him up, or the spacer caretaker. But the fact that Normandy was also an attractive woman moved her up to the head of the list. As was generally the case with such people, Havot would have much preferred to seduce her first. Experience had confirmed that sometimes the most complete and satisfying success came with the most unlikely candidates. But now it seemed remote that she was ever going to see him or talk to him again.

So he ran through the echoing underground, past the waiting miniships. The servo-powered joints in the suit's legs more than compensated for the burden of the outfit's extra weight—

Havot was now running faster than before he put it on. The sensation of massive power that the suit provided engendered feelings of invincibility. He knew it was making him even more reckless than he naturally became in moments of crisis. At an intersection of corridors, he knocked an inoffensive service robot out of his way instead of going around it. There went a human who still lacked a suit, giving him plenty of room—too bad.

He loved space armor!

Now Havot began to take notice of the signs. The walls in all the corridors bore a number of them, glowing electrical symbols giving directions through the maze to every part of the base. He supposed that once the enemy had actually breached the walls, assuming they did, the signs might be turned off, or altered to provide misinformation. He shook his head in passing; if things got that bad, such tricks weren't going to help.

Here and there, a helmeted head turned to look at Havot as he ran, but no one tried to interfere. No reason why they should. Other figures were running, too. People were intent on their own jobs, on getting to where they were supposed to be.

He couldn't have remembered if he'd tried how to get to the pod that they'd assigned him to. His mind had blotted out information that he knew he wasn't going to use, and he no longer even remembered what its number was. All his effort was now focused on getting control of a real ship, some capable conveyance that would carry him away from the Hyperborean system, and its prisons and its battles, to some remote world, preferably at the other end of the Solarian domain, where no one had ever heard of Christopher Havot. And he'd noticed, during his brief spell of freedom on the base, that none of the real ships were in the hangar, but all out on the open field, where liftoff could be instantaneous.

Now he came up from underground, through an airlock and out into the open, almost staggering in his first steps as he left the zone of artificial gravity that was maintained in the hangars. Harry's ship was still out on the field, and Havot blessed the instinct that had made him take time to get himself into armor before doing anything else.

Still bounding toward his goal, under a steadily turning sky of stars and galaxies, he caught a flashing glimpse of a flying berserker. The thing was not very high, and it hurtled across the dark, star-shot sky almost like a missile, but not really fast enough for that, so that Havot knew it must be coming in to land. The size was hard to judge. All he could see of the object's shape was a span of metal legs, outstretched for landing like those of a falling cat. He thought he'd never seen one of exactly that design before, but he had not the least doubt of what it was.

It had come into his field of vision and was gone again before he could even think of getting off a shot. As always, the rush of immediate danger made him feel intensely alive.

Now fire from the attacking machines that were still spaceborne was hitting the ground not far away. He wasn't sure what the weapons were, but they were doing damage. Flares, and a rumbling sound that traveled through the rock beneath his boots.

He needn't have worried about running straight across the field. Around him, other running figures—legitimate pilots and crew members, every one of them far more experienced than Christopher Havot, but none with better instincts for this sort of thing—were trying to reach the ships almost as desperately as he was.

Luck stayed with him on his long run—through the hangar levels and up and out of them, across part of the open field. At last he reached the side of the waiting ship, and after only a moment, located the airlock. The outer door was still standing open; they must be waiting, delaying liftoff, for one more assigned crew member.

He had a vague idea that this must be Harry Silver's ship—

not that the name of the owner mattered. He knew it wasn't the emperor's—Havot's keeper had gossiped to him in his cell about Julius and his ragtag band of followers. He had no idea of how large a crew was likely to be aboard. If there were a dozen armed people inside, trying to take it over could be the last move he'd ever make, but this was the chance he'd chosen, and he'd live with it or die. The worst thing a man could ever do was to hesitate.

Havot had been afraid that he would get this far and then not have the necessary code to open the airlock on whatever ship he was approaching. But it seemed that luck was with him once again.

Without hesitation, he bounded up into the lock chamber, which was just about big enough to have held two suited bodies like his own, and slammed his armored hand against the prominent control to start it cycling. Immediately, the outer door banged shut.

Simultaneously, the inner door was opening. The device worked fast, like the locks on all military ships, relying on a tuning and tweaking of the onboard gravity field to retain most of the atmosphere in the lock chamber even when the outer door was open.

The moment the gap between the inner door and its surrounding bulkhead widened enough to let him pass, Havot stepped through, weapon ready, trying to take in the unfamiliar cabin with a single glance. Somehow, the space appeared smaller, more cramped, than he had imagined it would be, looking at the outside of the ship.

More than a year had passed since he'd killed anyone, anyone at all, and a certain need had been building up, and now suddenly he recognized the craving for what it was.

Displays assured him that the cabin he had entered was fully pressurized, but the two human figures in front of him were completely buttoned up in armor, even to their wired crew helmets. Both were intent on their jobs, their backs to the man who had just entered—no doubt they were assuming that he was someone else.

Between them stood on its short, thick pedestal an empty chair, a prominently unoccupied position. Havot quickly assumed that this would be the pilot's. A third control helmet rested there on its stalk of flexible cable, awaiting its user.

An instant later, one of the armored figures turned to confront the newcomer. The other was still facing away from Havot, evidently continuing to assume that the person who'd just entered was the one they had been waiting for.

Without a moment's hesitation, Havot shot down the first human figure that got in his way. The suited body, back turned to Havot, was lifted by the jolt, knocked spinning in midair to crash against a bulkhead amid big shards of shredded armor. What a hit—this gun was meant to kill berserkers, after all.

He'd taken great care not to miss. He didn't want to shoot a hole right through the inner hull, doing some kind of damage that would keep him on the ground—and it was almost a sure bet that his weapon as he held it now had not been turned to any particular reflective coating.

The second spacer he shot was standing up and had spun around at the sound of the first concentrated blast. This shot, at point-blank range, opened up the armor frontally and knocked the suited figure heels over head, sending it crashing into a bulkhead and falling to lie in an inert heap.

As easily as that, the ship was his. And, as far as Havot could tell, all ready to be launched. How the battle was ultimately going to come out was too remote and abstract a question for him to worry about—fighting a battle would be fun, but getting clean away in a nice ship would be infinitely more fun.

Havot hurled himself into the central chair. Somehow, that seemed to him the most likely place from which to get the ship hurtling up into space.

Now. Close the airlock—there was a manual control for that, he'd seen it worked on other ships—and get going. Later, if he got away from Hyperborea alive, there would be time enough to worry about astrogation. All these ships had good autopilots. Right now, he had to somehow, anyhow, get up into space and get going.

He thought of dragging the bodies out of the ship, but that would take too much time. Once he was well under way, he'd find a means of dumping them out into space.

Briefly, the idea crossed his mind that he ought to look into the next compartment to see if there was anyone in there. But every instinct urged him not to delay for that, not even a few seconds.

Now he was loosening the helm of his suit, lifting it off. Then he reached out to the pilot's headgear and plucked it from its stalk.

When Havot put on the activated helmet, the world around him changed abruptly. He'd more or less expected that—but not such a violent and extensive transformation as he got.

He observed the strange symbol representing the cannon, amid a bewildering array of other symbols, but paid it little attention. This display was far more complicated than the one he'd started to train on, and included a lot of things Havot didn't understand. For a moment, he came near wondering whether he ought to consider giving up.

He was certain that there ought to be an autopilot system here, somewhere, but he wasn't going to take the time right now to figure that out.

Abruptly, a host of new connections was completed, through inductance, between the synapses of his brain and the waiting, receptive hardware in the helmet. Hardware was a very misleading word for devices of almost organic subtlety. He nearly cried out as the world swirled crazily around him. Somehow, this experience was vastly, disconcertingly, different from what had happened in rehearsal. Of course, that had been only a very elementary kind of primary-school interface. Everything in this display was shudderingly faster and more complicated. Still, he thought the outline of what he had to do was plain enough. Going *this* way would have to mean going *up* . . .

His gauntleted fingers were crushing the chair arms, and his body stiffened. There seemed to be nothing to prevent him from actually launching into space. And in fact, now here he went—he was actually getting the ship off the ground.

This was it. This was going to work.

Somehow, the helmet and its associated hardware had conjured up for him the realistic image of a knife, the long blade saw-toothed and stained with the good red stuff. The picture was distracting, coming and going amid the myriad other icons the pilot was supposed to watch, and he kept wanting to get the smooth wooden handle of the weapon in his grip.

Never mind that now. Concentrate. Concentrate! The drive was already on, working, and he was space-borne. Or almost. All he had to do was put it into gear, so to speak.

Like this?

Suddenly, the ship lurched under him. Artificial gravity kept him from feeling the movement, but through the helmet he could see its violence. His mind trailing raw and gory visions that only he could see, like clouds of smoke or mists of blood, Havot managed to achieve liftoff. Not that he had a clue to where he was going. Abruptly it seemed to him that what was turning not only the knife blade red, but the whole world, was his own blood, welling out of all the orifices on his head. He screamed in horror, in terror. Only seconds after liftoff, the drive stuttered, and the ship, wildly out of control, was carrying him helplessly he knew not where.

SIXTEEN

One of the top priorities in base defense was always to get every ship capable of movement up off the field and out into space as rapidly as possible. Whether or not a vessel could fight effectively, it made a harder target, and presented the enemy with greater problems, in space than it did sitting on the ground.

Today the distant early warning array, englobing the whole solar system, had functioned almost perfectly, even if its human masters, worn by their preparations for a different kind of battle, had been just slightly laggard in reacting. By the time any berserker was near enough to strike, the machines of close-in defense were ready, the whole planetoid already shivering with the long-stored energies now being mobilized.

Several of the smallest craft intended for use in the raid on Summerland, the imitation berserkers, were already up in low orbit when the alarm sounded. Some of the defenders nursed hopes that their presence would confuse and delay the oncoming attackers, but if that had happened, the effect lasted for no more than a couple of seconds.

Captain Marut, at the first sound of the alarm, cursed in anger and ran for his ship. His immediate reaction was one of instant rage: How dare the damned machines nullify all his ingenious plans?

But even as his anger flared, he realized that no one with much military experience ought to be surprised at such a turn of events. It crossed his mind to consider how much of the whole war was nothing but sheer madness, let humans and their enemies make plans as precisely as they liked.

Marut's destroyer, with himself and all the essential members of his reconstituted crew onboard, had already lifted off. They were clear of the field even before Normandy had got herself established in her proper battle station in the computer room.

And, to the surprise of many, the emperor's ship was next off the ground, her crew evidently moving with the speed of fanatics. Commander Normandy, only a couple of minutes after reaching her battle station in the computer room, was pleasantly startled to observe the departure of the *Galaxy,* accelerating strongly upward from the field.

Actually, in terms of minutes and seconds elapsed, the emperor and his crew hadn't been all that fast. The only reason they were second off was that something must be delaying the *Witch of Endor.* Communications with the *Witch* were also out at the moment, a situation not surprising in the flare of electronic battle noise.

Now most of the remaining smaller craft were lifting off. Sadie the adjutant, in her unshakable machine voice, was calling out a litany of names and numbers.

For some reason, the *Witch* needed a couple of additional minutes to get going, and once the commander was on the verge of making a concentrated effort to call the pilot to see what was going on. But the delay, whatever its cause, turned out not to be critical, for there she went at last, apparently still unscathed, though her movement seemed a bit erratic. Evidently the enemy this time had some objective more important than smashing up Solarian spacecraft.

Relieved that at least one possible catastrophe, the loss of ships on the ground, had been avoided, Claire Normandy turned her attention to other problems.

One or two of the smaller craft were still stuck on the ground. Watching the difficulties attending a simple scramble, the commander thought the enemy might have unwittingly done her people and Marut's a favor by preempting the planned Solarian attack. Suddenly it seemed to her that Harry Silver had been right about that; there would have been no way to escape disaster.

Now and then Commander Normandy glanced at the huge computers mounted immediately before her, just beyond the conference-sized holostage on which a model of the battle was struggling to take shape. Then she turned her head to look at some of the operators who were still engaged with the computers in their decoding work. They were ignoring the battle outside to the best of their ability, and they would have to continue to do so as long as possible. Until the fighting engulfed this very room.

For the hundredth time, the commander wished that there could be some way to divert the fantastic computer power before her from its usual task, to the immediate needs of base defense. But there was none—none that could be implemented now.

Around her, the solid rock that encased the computer room was shaking, jarring with the impact of berserker missiles nearby, rumbling with the thunderous response of her own automated defenses. Nothing had yet touched or seriously disturbed her precious computers—they, along with several meters' thickness of the surrounding rock, were held nearly motionless by powerful protective fields.

Distracted by other matters, she didn't notice, until Sadie called her attention to the fact, that the *Witch* was back on the ground, if not exactly on the landing field, less than a minute after having lifted off.

Harry Silver was still struggling with the problems that a group of inexperienced pilots were bound to have in getting their launches and little shuttles up and off the ground. The major difficulty involved the unfamiliar control helmets.

It needed only one person in a panic to screw things up, and here there seemed to be at least two or three.

"Never mind that!" Harry spouted profane obscenity in exotic languages. "Get up! Get these ships off the ground!"

Harry swore at the incompetent ones, at those who were suddenly paralyzed with terror, and finally had to drag out of a miniship's cockpit one would-be pilot who was thus immobilized. He shoved the man aside so that he went staggering and bouncing in the low gravity. Years ago, experience had taught Harry that it was futile to try to punch out somebody who was wearing a helmet and full body armor, even for a puncher who was similarly equipped.

Among the group having problems was Karl Enomoto, who'd been assigned to a two-seater launch. Looking and sounding strained, though far from panicked, Enomoto announced that he'd had to abort his liftoff due to a malfunctioning drive. "I just couldn't get the bloody thing to work."

"With all the bloody tinkering that's been going on," Harry growled back, "I'm not surprised."

Then, at last, people and machines were once more flowing up into space, and Silver was suddenly free to run for his own ship. He hadn't been timing the delay, but now he realized that it had probably cost him no more than a couple of minutes; there was still a chance that he could reach the *Witch* before Becky and whoever else had got aboard gave up on him and lifted off.

Enomoto stuck with him as he ran. Well, having one more aboard wouldn't do any harm, and Harry didn't know where else to tell the man to go.

As Silver ran, he tried to call ahead to his ship on his suit radio to tell them he'd be there in a few more seconds, but getting any signal through the flaring battle noise and the berserker jamming was hopeless at the moment.

Scrambling as fast as he could move, Silver had run only a short distance when he reached a position from which he ought to have been able to observe the *Witch* directly. He saw what he had half-feared to see, that she was gone, and felt no great surprise, only a pang of mingled relief and disappointment. He'd simply been held up too long, and Becky and whoever else had scrambled aboard had taken her up.

What might be happening to Silver's woman and his ship out there in the space battle was his next concern. He had to assume they were both going to be all right. But Harry's confidence was shaken when at last he did catch sight of his ship. The *Witch* was at extreme low altitude and maneuvering in a peculiar way.

Just standing here and watching wasn't going to accomplish anything. What was he going to do now?

The hectares of landing field that stretched in front of him were now totally devoid of anything that could get off the ground. Marut's one functional destroyer was no longer to be seen, and neither was the emperor's ship. That, of course, was as it should be.

There were already missile craters on the landing surface—only the powerful damping field of the defenses had prevented the whole thing from being blown away—and Harry realized that had his ship been a minute later in lifting off, she might well have been blown to rubble.

The ominous pencil shapes of several enemy missiles just lay there unexploded in the rock, near the spot where the *Witch* had been, each another demonstration of the feats of local space-warping achieved by the defense.

It came as no surprise, but was still an ugly shock, to see berserker landers on their way down. Harry caught sight of one about to land, spreading long legs like a giraffe.

Behind and above it hurtled half a dozen others of various types, including rough likenesses of the human form.

Several times Harry was on the brink of taking a shot at the enemy. But he refrained as the chance of doing serious damage to such moving targets with only a shoulder weapon seemed wastefully small.

Running around out on the open field would make no sense, so Harry used the airlock in a nearby kiosk, and the stairs inside, to get down into hangar space. It was an unlikely chance, but possibly another ship of some kind was still available in some corner of the hangar, or behind one of the revetments on the field. He was a pilot, and in time of crisis, every instinct screamed that he wanted to be up off the ground in something.

Harry reversed the direction of his run, moving the few necessary steps to get back to the place where he'd been struggling to get the launches space-borne. Karl was sticking with him. One miniship, the one that had been giving Enomoto trouble with its drive, still had not been launched.

Harry bumped open the hatch again and wedged his armored body into the front seat. Enomoto, evidently determined not to be left behind, climbed into the rear. "Need a gunner? I'm good at that."

"Hang on, then. I'm gonna try."

Harry slammed the control helmet on his head, feeling the gentle, carefully padded physical contact—and drew a deep breath, like a man who had suddenly come fully alive. The next thing to deal with was getting launched.

Harry's regular space armor had a pilot's helmet built in, so he only needed to connect an umbilical cord. Now he could see what had held up Enomoto—there was some tangle in the thoughtware, and it took Harry only a couple of seconds to think it clear. In the next moment, they were off the ground.

The ship that Harry was now driving into space possessed only light armament. Of course it was a lot smaller than the *Witch,* no more than ten to twelve meters long, and narrow, little more than three meters wide. The launch carried two to four short-range missiles and a beam projector of modest energy. There was not much hope that any of this would work against large enemy machines, but it might be possible to do something really effective against the swarming landers.

Some cosmetic alterations had been made in the launch to try to make it pass as a berserker, if only briefly. Should the enemy be confused, even momentarily, so much the better—but Harry wasn't going to count on it.

Immediately the helmet gave him, in the form of visible icons, a complete inventory of the weapons systems aboard, as well as the available power and the current status of as many systems as he wanted to try to deal with.

Right now, he only wanted a minimum—let the automated systems manage the rest.

Harry had been relieved to discover that the thoughtware on the launch was indeed of an advanced type, much like that aboard his own ship, for use only by skilled pilots.

As he activated the controls, the world around him underwent a marvelous transformation in his perception. Stylized, vivid, very complex and colorful. Simulated audio came through, as well as video, giving him a shadowy awareness of the presence of Enomoto in the rear seat. Experience rendered as clear as crystal a display that would have overwhelmed and bewildered a neophyte.

The little world of rock that had fallen away so rapidly below him now appeared as a mass of stylized, grayish lumps. The two suns that he might normally have seen, bright white and dull brown, had been rendered invisible, being only distractions to the business at hand.

An act of will shifted the scale of the presentation in discrete jumps or, at the operator's choice, in a smooth flow of changing sizes. He perceived the berserker ships or landers, by his own preference, as slugs or insects, furnace-red outlines surrounding masses that were the empty color of the night between the stars. The few odd Solaria ships that he could see were distinct small shapes in bright pastels, a somewhat different hue for each, nothing like red among them.

Harry Silver had understood for a long time that the shapes and colors of the world, as he perceived it through his helmet, were produced as much by his own brain as by the external hardware. Thus his pilot's world was inevitably going to be marked by events in his own mind below the conscious level.

He guided the launch, controlled its speed, by another effortless act of will. The helmet and its hardware had become transparent to his purpose.

Here, logic and meaning flowed out of complexity, as from a page of printed letters.

The pilot's helmet left Harry's eyes uncovered, his head free to turn, to see and hear things in the tiny cabin around him at the same time as the helmet's augmented vision and hearing—bypassing eye and ear to connect directly with nerves and brain—brought him a clear and marvelous perception of the world outside.

And now the helmet, and the subtle devices to which it was connected, provided him with vastly augmented senses with which to look for, among other things, his own ship.

As Harry lifted off, swearing under his breath, he felt a trifle cramped, engulfed in the vague physical discomfort he usually experienced in space. But all systems were working, the artificial gravity cushioning him and his shipmate against all the gees of acceleration that he poured on. He'd *really* wanted to do whatever fighting was necessary in his own ship, and not the least of his reasons was the c-plus cannon the techs had just finished putting in it.

In a matter of a few seconds, piling on acceleration cushioned by onboard artificial gravity, he got his miniship up to an altitude of almost a hundred kilometers, enough to obtain a minimal amount of maneuvering room.

Now the launch was well up in space, and still, against all Harry's expectations, nothing was attacking it. Either the enemy's attention was focused elsewhere, or the attempt at berserker disguise was more successful than he'd dared to hope.

And now suddenly, unexpectedly, Harry caught sight of the *Witch* again, at a distance of a few score kilometers. He needed no augmented senses to see that she was in trouble, jerking and reeling drunkenly in flight. In another moment, she had vanished around the curve of the planetoid's near horizon.

"What the hell is going on?" demanded an anguished Harry Silver of the world.

A moment later, he was distracted by an urgent communication from someone on the ground.

"Armed Launch Four, who is in command aboard?"

"I am, get off my back."

"Lieutenant Silver?" It was the commander's voice. "That is not your assigned ship!"

"It is now, dammit!"

Enomoto, in the rear seat, was wisely staying silent, concentrating on his armament, which so far, he'd had no need to use.

At least one of the space-borne berserkers took a passing interest in the launch. So much for any hope of being successfully disguised.

Whereupon Harry, and his frightened and marveling shipmate, spent the next minute or two engaged in furious combat in the near vicinity of the planetoid. The onboard computer of the launch engaged in a few seconds of thrust-and-parry with its counterpart aboard the nearest death machine as Harry's lethargic human synapses, in their relatively glacial slowness, added a human-Solarian flavor to the output, tinting and toning everything, like pedals on an organ.

That clash, that small footnote to the battle, was over before either human occupant of the launch had consciously realized that it had started.

It was the kind of thing, Harry knew, that was likely to bring on nightmares later. If only he was allowed to live long enough to enjoy another nightmare—

In the shielded compartment just behind the control cabin, banks of hydrogen power lamps, all currently tuned for maximum output, flared fiercely with the flames of fusion.

The image was momentarily converted into that of lancing weaponry. First a beam, then a missile, rapidly followed by the beam again.

"Get the bastard!"

"—got him!" The gunner Enomoto, combat veteran that he was, yipped and howled with elation.

Harry wasn't at all sure of the claimed kill. But at least they had inflicted some damage, and had themselves survived.

Then, at last, on the bare-bones display that was the best this wretched excuse for a combat ship could provide, Harry again picked out the familiar code symbol of his own ship, returning from around the curve of the horizon, looping back, reappearing in the same place that it had disappeared, and still maneuvering drunkenly.

Thank all the gods the *Witch* hadn't been vaporized or wrecked! But Becky, in the pilot's seat, wouldn't be mistreating her this way. Something had gone seriously wrong.

Harry was raging now, swearing a blue streak against the fate that seemed to have sent Becky into some deep trouble and left him with a poor substitute for his own ship.

And he couldn't keep from fretting about the new c-plus cannon that the commander had taken such pains to have installed on his ship. Harry hoped to hell someone was getting some good use out of that. Maybe, he thought, someone aboard the *Witch* had tried to use the weapon and it had backfired somehow, which the c-plus was prone to do. That could explain his ship's bizarre behavior.

He couldn't figure out what might be troubling his woman and his spacecraft, but at the moment, all his energy was concentrated on simply keeping himself alive.

And his groaning, yelping shipmate, too. Both of them, along with the poor excuse for a ship that they were stuck with, were buffeted around severely; either they would make it or they wouldn't. What worried Harry, while he waited to find out, was that the enemy seemed to be putting out a swarm of landers.

Down on the ground, Commander Normandy, who ten minutes earlier had been almost in despair, was finding some grounds for hope. In general, there were certain indications, clearly visible to her in her combat control center, that the enemy was finding the ground defenses uncomfortably, perhaps unexpectedly, strong—great missile launchers and beam projectors that pounded the stuffing out of most of Shiva's tough escort machines.

A haze of dust and small parts swirled and drifted in low gravity.

Space in the near vicinity of the planetoid, out to about five hundred kilometers, was now almost totally clear of berserkers; some of them must have pulled back a little, out of close range of the ground defense—but it looked more and more like most of them had gone right down *on* the ground.

There was still one, though. When Silver looked for it, his helmet showed it clearly, up above. Right there, streaking past in a low orbit. Confusing the ground defenses, dodging everything they threw at it, changing its orbit rapidly in a tactic known as quantum jumping, after the supposedly analogous behavior of certain subatomic particles. Harry certainly wasn't going after anything that size, not with this peashooter he was driving now. He'd leave that to the emperor, if Julius wanted to die a glorious death.

But this battle was going to be won or lost right down on the surface of Hyperborea. The more Silver saw of the enemy landing machines, especially the ominous number of them—there had to be something over a hundred—the worse he felt about the Solarian chances. For once, the berserkers weren't content to strive for the pure annihilation of humanity and all its works. All those landers had to mean that the enemy was making a great effort to *capture* the base, or some important part of it, intact. And Harry had a horrible feeling that they knew exactly which part was so important to them that they were willing to make almost any sacrifice to get at it. They hadn't seen that part yet, anymore than Harry had, but like him, they had learned about the computers. From prisoners, or through sheer deduction, they knew something about the true work of this base, enough to convince them of the necessity of finding out the rest.

Silver threw the launch into the defense against the landers as best he could, though it was practically impossible to coordinate the puny efforts of the launch with those of anyone else. He aimed at the crawling, darting enemy machines, sending his agile craft screaming over the enemy units that were scrambling on the ground as he strafed them.

Other Solarian ships space-borne in the vicinity were trying to join in as well. Marut's destroyer was nowhere to be seen. Harry couldn't spot the *Galaxy* either, and was fleetingly curious as to what might have happened to the emperor. There remained the two patrol craft and a handful of even smaller units like the one that he was in. He thought he caught a glimpse of one of them in his helmet display, but he couldn't be sure.

It was at this point that Harry picked up part of a communication from Marut, intended for the base, the gist of which seemed to be that things were just about all up with the captain and his crew.

Even in the heat and confusion of battle, sending the launch darting and lunging this way and that, Silver took care not to stray too many klicks away from the planetoid, out of the zone of protection theoretically offered by the heaviest close-range ground defenses, which were mostly beam projectors. He was taking a calculated risk in doing this—it was quite possible that in the roaring fog of battle, friendly fire would kill him. But the odds were against that—and any sizable berserker entering this zone in an attempt to close in on him would have to contend with the most powerful Solarian weapons.

From time to time, he communicated tersely with his shields-and-armaments specialist, Enomoto. And he grouchily demanded that the other tone down his screams of elation when they hit the foe.

There were a few fleeting moments when communication with the base could be established solidly enough for information to be exchanged, and then only in bits and pieces.

Claire Normandy was trying to order all ships' attention to the danger of berserker landers, rallying her fleet to help defend the base.

One of the things she wanted to know was why the *Witch* wasn't performing up to expectations. Harry had to try again to explain that he wasn't in the *Witch.* And when the commander finally understood that, she naturally wanted to know why.

"Because she was off the ground before I could get to her. Can't tell you any more than that."

Silver would be double-damned if he could give any better answer yet, but he was going to find out.

The enemy did not yet seem much concerned with anything as trivial as an armed launch. The larger berserker machines, the few of them still space-borne, simply tried to kick it out of their way so they could get on with what they really wanted. Their main objective had nothing directly to do with Harry Silver, or with his craft.

The good news—there were long minutes when it seemed the only good news—was that the ground defenses were taking a heavy toll on the enemy machines in space—here came a drifting fog of small parts from another one, glowing as pieces pinged off the launch's small defensive fields—but still, it was plain that all too many of the little landers were getting through, making contact with Hyperborea's black rock, where some were digging themselves in, others making as much speed as they could toward the almost featureless walls of the base.

No sooner had Harry concluded that the berserkers were once more totally ignoring him than that situation changed drastically for the worse. Now the launch was caught up in a duel, trading shots with a superior foe that appeared to have singled out the small Solarian for destruction. In the process, Harry and Enomoto lived ten or fifteen seconds of electric intensity.

Silver's shipmate kept busy firing missiles and trying to work the beam projector. The launch's modest arsenal of missiles was soon used up, and the projector was too small to be effective, except against enemy machines already damaged, their shielding weakened.

Eventually, their latest foe, a thing that Harry would have described as a kind of berserker gunboat, was taken off their back. Harry wasn't sure if the cause was some heavy ground-based Solarian weapon or whether the berserker had simply moved on to some other objective.

Shrieking noise, and an explosion of light inside his helmet, told Silver that the miniship he was driving had been seriously hit. His shipmate was screaming, though hopefully not injured much. But Harry's helmet and his instincts alike assured him that the launch had been badly damaged.

He might have managed to stay space-borne for a long time yet, but instead decided to crash-land his crippled vehicle. To hell with this fluttering around in space in this little gnat of a ship. Nothing that anyone could do with a midget like this was going to decide the battle. His own ship, his real ship, was down, and his woman was in her, and he was going there to do whatever he could.

"Hold on, Enomoto, we're going in."

His helpless shipmate screamed something incomprehensible in reply.

"Shut up. Hold on." Harry gritted his teeth, and against the looming impact, actually closed his eyes, which of course did him no good inside the helmet. The launch went plowing in, scraping its hull right through a small squad of enemy landers deployed along one edge of the landing field. Only one leaped clear, on metal legs.

Moments later, the armed launch, causing what seemed a great disturbance for its size, went scraping and screeching and thudding to a halt, artificial gravity still holding on, saving the occupants from almost all the stress, until it had lost half its speed. Finally, the craft went off one edge of the landing field and up against a substantial rock, one of the big black buttresses like those in Sniffer's pictures.

Chunks of rock and metal flew, force fields bent and glowed. The launch's onboard artificial gravity had ceased to exist. The impact was impressive, but the two humans in their armor and their combat couches came through it in good shape.

Then everything became relatively still and quiet. One thing sure, thought Harry—no pilot was going to get this clunker off the ground again.

Harry quickly had his helmet disconnected from all the systems of the launch, but his shipmate's voice still came through on suit radio. "What do we do now?"

"Get out of this. Get out and come with me. I want to take back my own ship."

SEVENTEEN

A jet of some kind of gas was whining out into space through a rupture in the thin hull of the downed launch.

The systems on the launch were going crazy, but Harry wasn't going to worry about it any more. As soon as he'd popped his hatch open, unfastened himself from the combat chair, and got his armored body out on the ground, which was quivering and jumping with the energies of battle, he looked around again. Looking back along the scarred track of his crash-landing, he was able to observe, with satisfaction, several fragments of mangled hardware that strongly resembled certain pieces in the Trophy Room. His coming down must have made hash of at least a couple of berserkers.

Enomoto had got out of the ship every bit as fast as Harry did, and stood by waiting to see which way Harry was going to go.

Now Harry's eyes, once more restricted to the impoverished

perceptions available outside a helmet, could directly confirm the fact that the *Witch* was also down on the surface, a couple of hundred meters from where he stood and not more than half a kilometer from the base. The silvery shape, almost that of a giant football, lay in a tilted position. Looking over a small intervening hillock, he could clearly see the upper portion of her hull. The *Witch,* too, must have come down in a crash-landing, maybe on autopilot, not drastically different from the one he'd just made.

One of the frequent Hyperborean sunsets came over the scene as he was looking at it, both the big white and the brown dwarf below the horizon now, leaving the wash of light from distant galaxies and stars to serve as background for the flares of battle.

Waving Enomoto to follow him, Harry began working his way toward the *Witch.*

Whatever the cause of the abortive failure of his old ship on her most recent flight, her formidable new weapon might still be functioning, and in a battle as close as this one looked to be, a c-plus cannon could certainly make the difference. Getting her back into action, if possible, was a very high priority. Defend the base, Commander Normandy had ordered. Well, he'd do his damnedest.

A blast from an enemy lander, fortunately fired while the ground was shaking just enough to throw off the aim, narrowly missed Silver but still almost knocked him off his feet. He spun around and returned fire with his comparatively puny shoulder weapon. The berserker that had shot at him in passing, a thing almost the size of a combat tank, ignored the near miss of his counterstroke and went rolling and rumbling on toward the Solarian stronghold.

Harry and his shipmate moved on together toward the fallen *Witch.*

Several big berserker machines were down on the surface, too. Not neatly landed, but sprawled, scraped, some badly crumpled, no doubt as a result of withering ground fire. What kind of tactics were these?

Harry wondered for a moment, as everyone else on the base must also be wondering, whether Shiva was directing this assault. And if so, whether Shiva's legendary tactical skills might possibly have deserted their lifeless possessor. But maybe it was a stunning, brilliant innovation, being so prodigal with hardware, to crash-land its large machines that were the analog of troop carriers. That might be just the thing to do if its main objective this time was not killing humans, but plundering the base.

And now one of those landers, frighteningly big, reared up right in Harry's path. Karl Enomoto, the serious financial planner, fired his carbine at it, almost over Harry's shoulder. A split second later, Harry's own beam lanced out. Experienced gunmen both, they focused their weapons on the same spot, and the combined weight of radiation ate through the enemy's armor and put it out of action.

The berserker had evidently already exhausted its own beam and projectile capabilities. But before it died, the death machine did its best to kill the two men with its grippers.

Two minutes after the *Witch* came crunching down on rock, Christopher Havot came stumbling out of the airlock, feeling that his brains were scrambled. It wasn't the cushioned crash-landing in itself that had almost destroyed him; no, it was the effect of the pilot's helmet on his brain. As soon as he thought the ship was down, he'd come leaping up out of the pilot's seat, his only concern to get that helmet off his head. Fortunately, he'd remembered to put his own helmet on again before entering the airlock. Emerging through the outer door, he'd lost his balance and fallen, reeling slowly in the low gravity. He had left the airlock slightly open behind him when he came out. As far as he could tell, no one saw him emerge.

Havot, seeking shelter, looking for sanctuary, for a chance

to regain control of himself, had not stopped to try to do anything with the two bodies of the people he'd shot, still inside the main cabin.

For the moment, shocked and terrorized by what the pilot's helmet had called forth from the depths of his mind, he had abandoned hope of immediate spaceflight and only wanted to crawl under a rock somewhere.

There weren't many things that truly frightened Christopher Havot. But he had just encountered one of them. He had to admit to himself that he would face almost any fate rather than put that helmet on his head again.

He was a couple of hundred meters from the *Witch* before he was able to stop bounding, to try to pull himself together and try to think.

One decision had already been made: Someone else was going to have to pilot his getaway ship for him. Any thought of using the autopilot was only a bitter joke, when he couldn't even figure out how to turn the damned thing on.

Whatever human pilots were still alive and on the ground were probably inside the base now. Fighting was going on there—he could see the flares and hear the blasts—but Havot had never been particularly afraid of ordinary fighting.

Thoughts under control again, carbine ready, Havot started to work his way across the pockmarked ground toward the base.

Now Harry was approaching his own ship, shoulder weapon ready and Enomoto, similarly armed, close at his side. Finding the outer hatch of the airlock open, they quickly stepped up into it. As they entered the artificial gravity of the tilted vessel, the ship seemed to swing itself into a level position, while the ground beneath it became the slope of a long, steep hill.

The lock cycled quickly. When the inner door slid back to show Harry the inside of the main cabin, he stopped, the sight of the two fallen bodies, amid disorder, tending to confirm his worst fears.

Enomoto, at his right shoulder, muttered something. The internal atmosphere was still basically intact, and in a moment, Harry realized that the mess might not be as bad as it looked at first glance. A quick survey of the panel showed him that the ship ought to be operable, but there was no way to be sure of that without a trial.

Before he could take in details, before he could even see if one of the fallen forms was Becky, there was another task that must be done. Harry looked left, looked right, shoulder weapon on the verge of triggering. The berserker that had shot things up might still be here. Maybe it was in the other cabin, just beyond the interior door.

With Enomoto standing alertly by, Harry checked the panel indicators once more and made sure the airlock was secure, then stepped forward to open the door leading to the other cabin—in there, all was peaceful. Ruin had not advanced this far. A few seconds' search demonstrated that no berserker lay in ambush and that there were no other humans, alive or dead, onboard.

Now he was free to return to the main cabin, to make the discovery that he dreaded most.

There were two fallen bodies inside the cabin, but Harry paid little attention to one of them. The armor of the second one was so badly scorched and torn as to be useless for identification—but in his heart, Harry already knew that it was Becky's.

A moment later, he faced the nightmare sensation of once more discovering her fallen body. Twice now in a few days he had done this, and this time, it was for real. The position of her body suggested that she might have been seated in the pilot's chair, but now she was crumpled on the deck, close to the locker in which Sniffer spent most of his time. Now all the locker doors were standing open.

For just a moment, as Harry started to turn over the suit, he had the eerie feeling that it was going to be empty, just as empty as that other one that lay in freezing cold, wedged between dark rocks.

The servos of Silver's own suit purred and murmured almost inaudibly, multiplying his strength, so that the armored body of the other rose and turned quite easily in his grip, despite the full one gee of artificial gravity.

But this suit wasn't empty. Fate didn't give that kind of blessing twice in a row.

Something, some kind of energy or missile weapon, had hit the back with terrific force, peeling away the surface armor like the skin of a banana. Fortunately, the power supply and other solid hardware had taken the main impact, saving the human flesh inside from utter ruin. The suit's servos were dead, and life support was running only on backup batteries or fuel cells.

Even as Harry moved her, her eyes came open behind the faceplate, looking at him through a tangle of curly hair—she was still alive. Somehow, Harry accepted the fact without surprise, because the alternative would have been more than he could have coped with. Her suit's own hypos must have bitten her, because she didn't seem to be feeling too much pain, and the tourniquet pressure points were probably working, so she wasn't losing too much blood.

"Harry . . ." Her suit's airspeaker had a tinny sound. Better to stay off-radio, if possible.

"You're all right now, kid." Harry could lie in a calm and steady voice; that was one trick he could always manage when he had to. "Let me think." What was he going to try to do with her? What would be the least dangerous place that they could reach? He wasn't going to try to get the ship off the ground, not when it had just crash-landed from unknown causes, and not into the hell he'd just come out of in the launch. For whatever reason, the berserkers weren't shooting at the *Witch*, not right now. But what would they do if he tried to lift off?

But maybe it would be possible to change the odds.

Enomoto was pacing around the cabin like a man looking for a way out. Harry's gaze swept back to the control panel, where there were new gadgets and indicators he'd never had a chance to see before. If a man got desperate enough, he could fire the *Witch*'s new c-plus cannon while she was still sitting on the ground, maybe at a target within point-blank range.

There was that cruiser-weight berserker up there just a few kilometers, streaking around in low orbit, and no one else seemed able to do anything about it. So now it was up to Harry to take care of that, even if he might scramble his brains in the process, and Becky's, and the brains of everyone else on the planetoid; but he had to try, because their brains weren't going to do them much good if they were all dead.

"What're we doing?" Enomoto asked.

"Are we desperate?"

"What? I don't understand."

"Never mind. I seldom ask a question when I don't already know the answer."

Harry got into the pilot's seat, grabbed the umbilical and hooked it to his helmet, then tore it off and threw it aside with a curse. "Thoughtware's really scrambled. Don't know how the hell that happened. Have to go manual."

When Enomoto at last realized what was going on, he was suddenly worried after all. "Maybe you shouldn't . . ."

"Shut up. Should or shouldn't doesn't matter. It's a case of have to."

In the rush to get things going, there hadn't been any chance to test the weapon, which he wouldn't want to do in the near vicinity of valuable objects and people, but they'd all been going on the assumption that it, along with their other cobbled-together hardware, was going to work just fine.

Harry had seen similar weapons fired, more than once. But that had been out in deep space, with a target light-minutes distant, scores of millions of kilometers. Then the big slugs would begin skipping in and out of normal space in a freakish, half-real way, outracing light. Only relativistic time retardation allowed the mass of stressed metal to survive long enough in the real world to reach its target. In the last part of their trajectory, the slugs would be traveling like de Broglie wavicles, one-aspect matter with its mass magnified awesomely by Einsteinian velocity, one-aspect waves of not much more than mathematics. The molecules of lead churned internally with phase velocities greater than that of light.

The results of a point-blank firing this deep in natural gravity would be uncertain, to say the least. About all that anyone could count on was that they would be in some way very spectacular, and that they would probably do the user less harm than they did the target. From this close, the gunlaying system could hardly miss, let the bandit go quantum-jumping all it wanted to.

"Here goes."

And Harry fired the cannon.

The firing itself was invisible and inaudible, but even as he pressed the manual control, the world turned strange around him, the energies released passing twistily through all their bones. In the same moment, he heard Karl Enomoto cry out. Harry had been afraid that something like this, or even worse, was going to happen when he fired, but he could tell now that it wasn't as bad as it could have been. He thought he saw Becky, standing before him, or maybe it was just her virtual face. And now it was only her ghostly image imposed on his faceplate, so that he could see through her and, behind her, the black rocks where he had once discovered her virtual dead body . . . and then the effect passed; the nerve cells in Harry's brain stopped jumping, and the real, solid world was back again.

The instruments on the panel told him his shot had hit the berserker in its shrieking-fast low orbit and wiped it out. No quantum-jumping evasive tactic had been able to help against a c-plus, not at this point-blank range. The display on Harry's panel, as badly confused by the event as human eyes and ears, showed that the leaden slug had taken no time at all to get where it was going. In fact, there was one indication that the projectile had reached the target about a microsecond before Harry fired. He supposed—he wasn't entirely sure, but he supposed—that this was only an illusion.

Slumping back in the pilot's chair, Harry with a sigh of relief turned it away from the panel.

"We're not lifting off?" Enomoto demanded.

"We're not. We can't. Told you, the thoughtware's scrambled. It was, even before I fired the cannon."

"What scrambled it?"

"Can't tell." Neuroptelectronics had its disadvantages, sometimes going bad at the worst possible time. It might take ten minutes to straighten the mess out, or ten days; there was no way to tell until he tried, and it was going to have to wait.

They were stuck on the surface, for now at least, and there was no use crying about it. Maybe the base hospital wasn't the best place for a badly hurt woman, not when berserkers were threatening to overrun the base. But he couldn't come up with any better option. At least there was some chance of defending that facility. Here, the next moment might see the enemy coming in the airlock.

Now, if only he could get her there.

"Karl, stick with me. I'm going to need your help. All the help that I can get."

"Right, boss." Enomoto had the same rank as Harry, but there was no argument over who should be in command.

Harry crouched over Becky and did his best to touch her tenderly, which, under the circumstances, was not easy. "Can you move, kid? Can you walk? Maybe you could if I got you out of that suit?" Without its servos working, the thing would be a great deadweight.

Feebly, Becky was shaking her head behind her faceplate. No. Then she murmured: " . . . wasn't a berserker, Harry."

That pretty thoroughly scrambled all his trains of thought. "What?" Although he'd heard the words plainly enough.

"Not a berserker," she repeated.

Harry demanded: "What, then? Who?"

"Some guy . . . person. I don't know for sure."

It took him half a minute to remember to switch to his own airspeaker, time enough to realize that the damage to her armor would indeed be consistent with a shot from a Solarian carbine, like the one on his own shoulder.

"Who?" he demanded again.

"Might have been Havot. That crazy guy . . . came in." She winced under the impact of some interior stab of pain. "Thought he was locked up."

"All right. I'll take care of him—whoever it was. Right now, you need some help."

"It hurts, Harry."

"I'm here, kid. I'm in charge now."

The ship's medirobot was tucked snugly inside a wall, and opening a panel revealed a coffin-sized space into which he tumbled her after getting her out of what was left of her armor. He didn't try to peel off the remnants of her undergarment—the robot could do a better job of that.

Then, calling in to the base from the cabin of his own ship, Silver brought the commander up to date on what he—and Enomoto—had been doing.

"Silver, was that you? Firing the—"

"It was. Direct hit." With a c-plus, having said that much, there was no need to claim a kill.

But his main concern right now was to take care of Becky.

No point in trying to radio for help. There was no way the base could send out anyone to assist them now.

Only after he'd started moving toward the base did it occur to him to wonder if the big berserker he had just destroyed in orbit had been the last space-borne enemy. If so, that raised an interesting question—might Shiva have been aboard it?

Or had Shiva come down to the ground, finding it necessary to direct the fighting at close range?

Now that Becky was in the medirobot, the two men who were trying to save her life had to figure out a way to somehow guide the mobile device into the base.

The medirobot, the size and shape of a waist-high coffin, ran on its own beltlike tracks. It rolled along at a brisk pace when told, by voice or by gentle guidance, where to go. With Enomoto and Harry trotting beside it, they got it out of the ship and then began moving toward the base, over what had once been a smooth landing field.

Enomoto was dubious. "Won't every entrance be—"

"Covered, besieged by some squad of berserker landers, trying to force a way in? I don't know. Maybe not; a hundred landers make a hell of a formidable force, but I doubt they'll be spread out evenly around the whole perimeter. They'll be pushing hard at a few points, wherever they think the weak spots are."

They pushed on.

Actually, the entrance they used was a hole recently blasted by berserkers in the base's outer wall. Whatever units had opened the breach were gone now, either moved on deeper into the base or destroyed by the defense. At least the two men and the machine they guided managed to avoid the enemy in the labyrinth of corridors.

At last they came to an airlock that was still intact. The automated defenses holding at this point recognized Harry's suit and Enomoto's, and the coded signals of the medirobot, and since all three were together, allowed them to pass.

Once back in territory that was still held by humans, Harry guided the bed-sized vehicle straight to the base hospital—Enomoto happened to know where that was, and the shortest way to get there. Vaguely, Harry remembered seeing signs, but they'd been scrambled now.

Once Harry had done all he could for Becky, delivered her into the presence of the overworked human medics and their inhuman helpers, he took a couple of minutes out, doing nothing but sitting slumped over in a corner, before he started for the computer room. There were a lot of casualties. He couldn't help wondering how many of Commander Normandy's people were still alive and functioning—there couldn't have been more than a hundred of them to start with, at the outside.

Karl Enomoto slumped beside him, staring blankly in the direction in which the medirobot, with Becky in it, had just been wheeled away. Inside the medirobot was the box of contraband Kermandie wanted. Enomoto had been able to spot it in Silver's ship, grab it up and hide it there while the man was distracted.

Enomoto hung around the hospital for a few moments, looking for a chance to retrieve the box and hide it somewhere else until he could arrange to get it offworld and back to Kermandie.

Now Harry had somewhere else to go, and he didn't think that anyone would try any longer to keep him from going there.

EIGHTEEN

Once Harry had found his way to the deeply buried computer room, getting in was easy. He'd expected that today many of the rules would be changed. There would be no problem getting in anywhere as long as you were obviously human. In fact, the human guard at the door was glad to see any fellow Solarian still armed and active. Nor would there any longer be a possibility of keeping any of the folk who worked here isolated from combat. Combat was coming to them. It was all around them now, and might arrive in their laps at any moment.

Once the heavy door of the main computer room had closed behind Harry, things for the moment were almost quiet. The occasional blasts of battle noise seemed to come from very far away. He just stood there, looking around and feeling very tired.

The overall arrangement was reminiscent of a medical operating theater, with four near-concentric rows or tiers of stadium seating. The chamber was windowless and indirectly lighted, its surfaces predominantly gray, with a mixture of other colors in pastel and here and there, bright highlights, very small. At the moment, it was occupied by only half a dozen people, with empty combat chairs waiting to accommodate three or four times that number. Evidently what they were doing here was so important that there was no thought of calling it off, or letting it wait, even in the midst of battle. A soft murmur of activity still left the room so quiet that a modest throat-clearing sounded like an interruption.

Each duty station had a combat chair, so that Harry was reminded of the bridge of a big warship. The resemblance was strengthened by the fact that most of the people here were wearing wired helmets, much like those worn by a combat crew in space, connecting their brains ever more closely to the optelectronic hardware that took its orders from them, saving picoseconds in whatever processing the giant computers were about.

When Harry had a chance to appreciate the size and complexity of the equipment assembled here, he let out a silent whistle. It was a bigger room than he'd anticipated, large for any kind of computer installation. The machines appeared to be equipped for wrestling with truly gigantic problems.

The design of this workplace demanded a high ceiling, which was also called for by the fact that for some reason, computers of this type worked better if their modules could be stacked vertically in a standard gravitational field.

Harry assumed that normally several shifts of people crewed these positions around the clock. That would mean that perhaps half of the people under Normandy's command worked in here.

Commander Normandy looked up from what was obviously her battle station near the center of the room, saw that Harry had come in, and briefly raised one hand in greeting.

Catching his breath, he moved slowly toward the place where she was sitting in her armor. When he stood beside her chair, he said: "So this is what you people do on Hyperborea. This is the place that Shiva knows it has to get at."

Commander Normandy looked at him solemnly. "This is it."

Buried deep beneath alternating layers of steel, force fields, and native rock were massive supercomputers—virtual duplicates, at least in function, of the machines at the secret Intelligence stronghold known as Hypo, on distant, sunlit Port Diamond. Harry was no computer expert, not on any level nearly this advanced. But he knew enough to make a fair estimate of the power of devices of this size and configuration, served by as many live brains as worked in this room. He would have wagered that those human brains were also some of the highest quality. Commander Normandy had not been exaggerating when she told Harry how quickly his downlock codes would have been shredded here. Looking at the great machines, Harry could well believe they'd have disentangled his would-be fiendish mathematics like a stage conjuror snapping knots out of a rope.

He also observed, without surprise, that right in the midst of this heavy technology had been placed what were doubtless very effective destructor charges, ready to swiftly and thoroughly obliterate the computers, along with their human operators, should their capture by the enemy ever appear likely.

Taking a chair beside the commander's, Harry gave her a terse report on what he and Enomoto had been doing, and reported himself ready for reassignment.

Her first response was to send him to one of several bunks ranged at the side of the room, with orders to get an hour of rest if possible.

When Silver returned an hour later, hot-drink mug in hand and feeling greatly refreshed, she provided a briefing on the current situation. Immediately in front of her combat chair, between it and the arc of towering computer units, was mounted a large holostage. At the moment, the stage showed what was known of the progress of the battle ongoing outside and around them.

Most of Commander Normandy's people, and the bulk of the defensive weapons dug into the planetoid, had survived the first onslaught. The situation was grim from the Solarian point of view. But the fight was not yet lost. What Shiva's prisoners had never known, they could not have been forced to divulge, and that information included the status of the formidable Hyperborean early warning system and the general state of Solarian readiness.

The Hyperborean early warning system and the defenses associated with it, which were deployed widely enough to encompass the whole solar system, could give only a few minutes' warning, but that had proven to be of inestimable value. And the system still managed to inflict some damage on the enemy units pouring through.

For a short time after the landers hit the ground, it had seemed quite possible, if not probable, that the enemy would overwhelm the base before the people in it and their localized defenses could effectively respond. But that response had come in time; and after a while, a lull set in, an interval of relative quiet, that no one expected to endure for long.

It seemed to Harry that the worst possibility—and he could think of several bad ones—was that the berserkers had good reason to expect reinforcements.

"What about our side, Commander?"

"We have no such prospects, as far as I know. If any help reaches us during the next several days, it'll be purely by accident."

Shortly after the berserker assault struck home, Colonel Khodark had come up with a new idea: One of the chief assets of the base was the large fleet of robot communications couriers, designed to carry intelligence off to Earth and Port Diamond and bring back supplies and various kinds of information.

These vessels had been pressed into emergency service and launched as missiles. Most were ineffective, but the overall effect had been to help beat off the berserker attack.

By the time Harry had reached the computer room, several of the gates and locks in the base's outer walls had been forced and ruined, and much of the interior was in the possession of the enemy. But the extensive compartmentalization inside meant that a lot of rooms still enjoyed a full, breathable atmosphere. In places, the enemy seemed to have withdrawn; but that could mean only that they were regrouping for a fresh onslaught.

"What are we doing now? What do you want me to do?" Harry asked.

"Right now we seem to be holding. And I want to keep you in reserve. The books say that every field commander is supposed to have reserves, and I have none. Except my computer operators here, and they . . . had better keep on with their own jobs."

Harry said yes ma'am. He said he supposed that things here sometimes got as hectic, in their own way, as they could in the control cabin of a spaceship.

Hc said: "I'd like to try on one of your helmets someday."

"Someday." Battle-weary as the commander was, she could not resist smiling at his wistful tone. "What they show you is a lot different from what a pilot sees."

"I bet."

"And yet in some ways, not so different. I've been a pilot too, you know."

"A good one, is what I've heard."

Two or three of the people now on duty in the room looked especially busy, bodies tense, hands active in brief dancing spasms on keyboards and contact panels that must in some way complement the controls in their helmets. The remainder were simply sitting, though most of them had helmets on, staring as if lost in thought at displays that were utterly meaningless to Harry. Here and there, one of the operators looked up as if surprised to see the face of an outsider in the room.

Whatever work was going on, none of the output was visible to Harry, at least not in any form that he could begin to interpret.

Now and then, someone stood up to stretch, sometimes to exchange a few words with someone else nearby. Occasionally the commander exchanged a few easy words with one or two of the crew who were occupying the chairs and working at the consoles.

She also introduced Lieutenant Silver to a few of the operators, people who at the moment appeared to be waiting for the machines, to which they were still attached, to tell them something new.

"I was a pilot," he informed them solemnly. "My new career is security consultant. I sell a little insurance on the side. Health and accident, you know."

He got a couple of nervous smiles at that. Harry exchanged handshakes and polite murmurs with several people, none of whose names he really caught.

Someone asked him where he'd been when the c-plus cannon had fired. They'd all been able to feel it, even here.

Commander," Silver asked, "is Shiva here? On the surface of this planetoid, right at this moment?"

"To the best of my belief, yes."

"How do we know?"

"Less than an hour ago, a courier came in with some data that had to be decoded." She gestured at the machines before her. "Here."

"A courier from where? What kind of data?"

"It was an intercepted berserker communication. They are very difficult to decode. The gist of the message was that the machine we call Shiva had changed its plans and no longer intended to go to the Summerland base. Instead, it had decided to personally lead, tactically conduct, the counterattack against the badlife base on Hyperborea. I take that as confirmation that he—it—is here."

"Wait a minute, Claire—I mean, Commander . . ."

"Surprising, isn't it? But it looks like the stakes on the table are even bigger than we thought."

"Wait a minute. You said: 'They are very difficult to decode.' That sounds like you intercept them all the time."

"Putting it that way would be a gross exaggeration. But we do pick up enough to keep us busy in this room."

Harry was staring at her, an expression of bewilderment on his face that few people had ever seen there. "I don't get it. How could you bag enough berserker couriers to matter? And doesn't the enemy notice when they show up missing?"

The commander was shaking her head slowly, and her eyes were fixed on Harry's. She said: "They don't show up missing—that's the beauty and the secret of it all. Our people out in the field are able sometimes—don't ask me exactly how—to scan those couriers in passing and extract the information that they carry, without stopping them or even delaying them. Until Marut's task force was ambushed, the berserkers were unaware that any of their dispatches were being read. Of course they're chronically suspicious of organic cunning and trickery, and they change their codes from time to time, and it always takes us a while to solve the new ones. We intercept only a fraction of their messages, and we can read only portions of those we intercept. Still, that can add up to a considerable advantage."

Harry again found his lips pursing as if he were about to whistle—but he didn't make a sound.

"It must have been a bigger surprise to Shiva than it is to you. It must have learned what was going on, from the prisoners it took from Marut's task force. A very astonishing discovery, and terrible—if anything can be terrible to a berserker. Shiva evidently computed that it had to do something about it, without delay, and the thing it decided to do was to come here, after us, after our secrets."

"All your secrets are here, on Hyperborea?"

"Most of our data-stealing, code-breaking secrets. They have to be. The decoding is done here, near the frontier, rather than many days away at headquarters, because the information has to be made available rather quickly if it is to be of practical use. The task force from Port Diamond was scheduled to stop here to pick up the latest information—not on the weather, but on planned berserker movements. So, for the system to work, the machines in this room must contain analogs of the methods our spy devices use. If Shiva could capture this room intact, it would learn everything."

Harry nodded. Then he let out the ghost of a chuckle. "And I thought my downlock codes would be too tough for you."

Claire Normandy's face showed a fainter reflection of his faint amusement. "It would have taken several minutes, at least, to set up for the job, and as you can see, I'm very reluctant to divert any of my workers from their regular tasks, even for that length of time."

Harry was just starting to say something else, when suddenly he fell silent. The commander looked up startled at the first strange rumbling coming from inside the blank wall of the computer room, no more than six meters from the place where her combat chair was rooted to the floor.

People in the room stared at each other, then grabbed for their weapons.

The inner surface of the wall burst open.

Two anthropomorphic boarding machines came smashing their way into the computer room and, without pause, moved straight toward the nearest seated operator. It was plain that their orders must have been to somehow locate this Solarian nerve center, to somehow fight their way in, and to take another prisoner right from the midst of it.

Talk about audacity. Harry's weapon and several others were already blasting at the intruders. Returning fire with their built-in lasers, the machines advanced across the room and seized a cryptanalyst by her arms, trying to drag the screaming, unfortunate woman out of her combat chair.

But the human was strongly belted in, and with her body sheathed in servo-powered combat armor, even a thin-armed woman would be able to put up something of a struggle. Nor did she fight alone. Fellow workers immediately rallied around, unable to fire now for fear of hitting their comrade, but grappling the enemy with their suits' own fusion-powered arms and grippers.

A small chorus of human screams went up, on airspeakers and on radio. The berserkers howled, banshee shrieks at inhuman volume, to terrify their victims and to drown out human voices. Airspeakers became useless.

Handicapped by the necessity of taking this specimen alive, the enemy units were having a hard time.

When one of the roughly man-shaped berserkers was burned down by friendly defensive fire, a replacement came leaping through the hole in the wall to take its place. One mechanical body fell atop another, and around them lay those of human casualties in their armored suits.

The local skirmish was over in less than a minute. The death machines were finished off, and the commander called in heavy machinery to block the tunnel through which they'd somehow squeezed and dug their way. Harry saw to the placement of the blockade and stood guard for a time. The berserkers had been denied another captive, though two operators had been killed, one literally torn apart, armored suit and all, and several others wounded.

When the wounded had been carried off, it was time to tend the great machines. Not until a quarter of an hour after the last invader of the computer room had been reduced to scrap did someone notice that the back of one of the great cryptanalysis computers had actually been broken into.

One of the operators said: "They did it—Shiva did it—somehow, while we were all distracted, fighting for our lives, trying to keep Ann from being taken prisoner."

Harry asked: "How many machines were actually in here, anyway? Did anyone keep count?"

Even as he asked, he knew it was a foolish question. There were almost as many guesses as there had been observers.

"Shiva, all right." The commander nodded. "It seems that we must score one for Shiva. Assume it has obtained the information that it came here to get. So now we must make sure it never leaves." Presumably, Shiva's unique and most vital component was much smaller than the big decoding computers on the base. Evidently it didn't function continuously in the same attenuated realm of metamathematics. And with its allied machines, it had plenty of raw computing power to draw upon when necessary. Experts had been unable to form a consensus on the precise physical form of the archenemy; Harry tended to picture a solid-state slab of something dull and greasy-looking, no bigger than a briefcase.

Overall, the elaborate computer installation had suffered moderate damage, worse than many of the other rooms and systems aboard the base, though not as bad as others—but, as someone pointed out, computers were mere hardware, and could be replaced.

"Trouble is," said Colonel Khodark, "you can say the same thing about berserkers."

Spare parts, replacement units for the computers, were stored in a cave even deeper than the computer room itself, dug far down near the center of the planetoid, and so far, untouched by the enemy. People and machines were starting to make repairs even before the last berserker lander, anywhere in the base, or on the surface of the planetoid, had been hunted down and exterminated.

It was going to take hours to get the facility up and running again, days before it was back operating at full capacity. But, barring some renewed attack, nothing could prevent that now.

Commander Normandy, in odd moments between life-and-death decisions, had taken note of the fact that the emperor's *Galaxy* was back on the ground again, and wondered how much fighting the one-ship imperial navy might have done in space, and to what effect. And whether the emperor had actually been aboard his somewhat grotesque flagship when it got off the ground.

When the enemy attack swept in, the commander had briefly considered putting some of her own people onboard the *Galaxy* and ordering the emperor himself to stay on the ground, on the theory that he ought to be saved, somehow, as a rallying point for his followers.

But there had been no time for any of that. In addition, Julius had as much as warned her that being told to keep out of harm's way was one order he would not obey. If she tried to enforce it, she could be sure of a rebellion in the ranks.

She thought she was beginning at last to understand the emperor's motivation. With his empire, never really more than a dream, collapsing around him, what Julius wanted above all out of this situation was a chance to achieve a hero's death in combat. That was fine with the commander, if his heroics somehow helped win the battle.

An hour and a half after the first berserker lander hit rock when coming down on Hyperborea, not only had most of the berserker machines been wrecked, but most of the Solarian ground defenses had been shot out or turned off.

Down in the computer room, Lieutenant Colonel Khodark was saying: "If we're exhausted, so is the enemy. I mean, they're worn down. I think they no longer possess any heavy weapons with which to take advantage of . . . our weakened state."

Meanwhile, the people and the machines in the buried room worked on.

Some of the intercepts sent on to Hyperborea were extremely fragmentary, and most were of no immediate use. Still, every one of them must be mined, squeezed, wrung out in an effort to extract useful information.

"Too bad," Harry observed, "the sector commander in Omicron didn't have this kind of help available."

"He did. But evidently against Shiva it didn't do him a whole lot of good. The enemy must have been moving too quickly. By the time we got information processed and to the people who could use it, often it was too late."

The commander went on to relate how, about two standard months ago, a series of messages had been intercepted that, when decoded, proved to be of a value hard to overestimate. They indicated that the malignant machine, already christened Shiva by its Solarian antagonists, was soon going to be shifted from its outlying position to one of much greater authority—or, perhaps, it was being recalled for study and duplication.

Harry, when he heard the explanation, was impressed. "Either way, bad news for us."

"Yes indeed." Colonel Khodark nodded. "But we did in fact believe we knew, with a very high degree of probability, the very place and time where the damned thing called Shiva could be intercepted. What we couldn't foresee was that the enemy was going to change its plans. What we have here is a once-in-a-lifetime opportunity. Better than that, maybe once in a dozen lifetimes."

So Shiva decided to hit us here. But why didn't it mobilize a bigger fleet?" Harry asked.

"Evidently it decided that it couldn't afford to wait. Or—"

"Or what?"

"Or maybe, after the string of victories it's had, it's developed a certain contempt for our ability to defend ourselves."

W*hen deliberately grounding itself on the planetoid, the machine carrying Shiva had avoided actually ramming any portion of the badlife base. At that stage, it had taken great pains not to demolish the precious computer it wanted to study, the store of information it needed to extract, not to kill too quickly the life-units in whose living brains so much more information was likely to be available. Rather, it had come down on rock, in such a position that would give its landers the greatest possible advantage in assaulting that base.*

It would have come right up to the outer wall of the base, but defensive blows and obstacles had prevented so close an immediate approach.

Struggling against the force-field hammers and spear thrusts launched at it by the ground defenses, it was unable to control its path with any precision and was forced to stop at a greater distance from the walls of the fortress before it.

The landing had brought its heavy carrier scraping across the landing field, very much as Harry Silver would do with a different purpose in mind, and then crunching to a halt. Anything like precision of control was hardly to be expected, because Solarian weapons were pounding at the transport machine almost without letup, and shields were beginning to give way. And it would have to be able to count on getting away again, with its new treasure of information, or the losses sustained in the attempt would be wasted.

Humans considering this maneuver on the enemy's part found it hard to believe that Shiva, coldly aware of its own value to the berserker cause, would take such heavy chances with its own survival—unless it knew with certainty that its key features had already been duplicated in at least one other piece of hardware.

The people on the base reasoned that the bad computer had learned not only of the successful Solarian spying, but of the badlife assassination plan directed at itself. Shiva could have gained this knowledge scavenging information from the data banks of the ruined ships in the ambushed task force, and by extorting confirmation from live prisoners.

Shiva had forced its prisoners to confirm what the data captured in the Solarian astrogational banks had already strongly suggested. The intermediate destination of the task force was the supposed weather station on Hyperborea. More information on the vital subject of Solarian intelligence gathering and code-breaking must be available there. So Shiva calculated that the possible gain to the berserker cause outweighed the risk of its own destruction. It would take direct command of the units that would carry out the raid.

It seemed a safe assumption that Shiva traveled always with a strong escort. But when Commander Normandy began to compile an inventory of the types of machines that were arrayed against her, she realized, with a surge of hope, that the enemy force was nowhere near as formidable as she had feared at first. It included no machines of the heavy cruiser or dreadnought classes, nor any carriers. Evidently the enemy's main forces were occupied elsewhere, seeking the most profitable targets in terms of the quantities of life, human and otherwise, that could be extinguished. Shiva had chosen not to wait, not to delay for the time necessary to assemble an overwhelming fleet.

But in other ways, the berserker task force was alarming indeed. One question now puzzling the commander was: How had Shiva been able to equip its force, on short notice, with so many boarding and landing machines? They must have been intended for use elsewhere, until Shiva diverted them to the Hyperborea operation.

Conversely, it might have been the fortuitous availability of such a force that had decided the enemy to attack at the time and in the way it did.

The implication was that the berserker too had accepted a desperate gamble. The fact that Shiva was here, risking its own existence, could only mean that it computed that grave risk as acceptable—and the only thing that would make it acceptable was the probability of inflicting an enormous loss upon the badlife.

An hour after the first strike came roaring in, after the Solarians had survived the first onslaught, their chance came to counterattack on the ground. The space-borne counterpunch, such as it was, had been delivered by the ships that had been ready to launch anyway.

Commander Normandy would have given her right arm for a heavy tank or two to throw into the battle now, taking the enemy in the rear. But the Solarians had nothing like that available.

The same idiosyncrasies that made Shiva such a formidable antagonist also caused it to behave oddly, for a berserker.

If audacity succeeded—and it had—then next time, the enemy would tend to be even more daring.

Harry wondered how much of human history Shiva might have been able to absorb. Whether it had learned that even the greatest of military commanders, human or otherwise, tended to show some characteristic weakness.

NINETEEN

Shiva's unliving warriors had indeed succeeded in bearing their unliving master with them into the computer room. It had been possible to remain there for only a brief time, under intense Solarian fire, but those few seconds of close contact with the badlife machine had been enough. The berserkers had succeeded in at least partially achieving their prime objective—they had gained certain vital secrets.

Commander Normandy, an advanced computer expert, theorized that Shiva had chosen to put itself in the forefront of the battle because the plundering of the Solarian computers' most important secrets would be possible only if it got itself into close physical proximity with them, its circuits reacting to theirs at no more than picosecond range. And now she realized, with a sinking feeling of defeat, that during the berserkers' brief occupation of the computer room, the security of one of the machines had been breached, and vital data plundered.

Shiva had now managed to confirm, to its own optelectronic satisfaction, the answer for which it had risked its valuable existence. Across vast stretches of the Galaxy, the information cargoes of berserker couriers were being secretly copied by some new Solarian science that bordered on fantasy. By a superior technology that left no trace, no reason to suspect tampering.

The precise means by which the badlife were able to accomplish such feats of wizardry were still obscure, but the fact that they did so had now been established, beyond any possibility of logical dispute.

The deeply disastrous truth had been discovered, and any purely human psychology would have found it devastating. But berserkers were utterly immune to such blows. What was necessary now was what was always necessary to a computer: First to discover, and then to take, the next step toward the ultimate goal. In the present situation, new means of conveying information must be devised as soon as possible, and some of the badlife spy technology must be captured, studied, analyzed, duplicated, and effective countermeasures put in place.

The vital knowledge gained would be of little use unless it could be conveyed to berserker high command. Shiva moved on, with its usual nerveless elan, to the next necessary step, the arrangement of a means of escape, or at least of transmitting the data to berserker high command. Its own space-going craft were all shot up, blown to bits or hopelessly crippled, the last one blasted out of low orbit by an unexpected round from a c-plus cannon mounted on a grounded ship. Another means must be found to convey the vital data to its destination. Some Solarian equipment that was still intact must be taken over.

Alternative means of transmitting the information, dependent on radio or other light-speed signal, were hopelessly slow and inadequate over the distances involved.

Commander Normandy said: "It's going to have to steal one of our ships to get away. Looks like all of its own carrier machines were wrecked, thanks to our defenses, when they crash-landed."

Harry Silver nodded. "And we're going to have to see that it dies trying."

Only two ships remained on the field, Harry's *Witch* and the emperor's *Galaxy.* As seen from outside, neither appeared to be damaged.

Marut's destroyer had gone roaring off in the early minutes of the attack, and there was good reason to believe it had been destroyed, lost with all hands. Commander Normandy as yet had no absolute confirmation of that fact.

With the fight in nearby space at an end for the time being, a few of the smaller Solarian craft that had survived had also returned to the field. But those smaller than the patrol craft lacked interstellar drive. And the single patrol craft to come down had landed only because it needed repowering, which could not be accomplished now. Its mate had lost contact with the base, and had to be presumed lost.

"Lieutenant Silver, get out to your ship and see if you can get space-borne. If you can, stand by in low orbit to take out the *Galaxy* if the berserkers seize it. If you can't manage a liftoff, let me know."

"Yes, ma'am. But let me stop in the hospital on the way, see if I can talk with Becky—Lieutenant Sharp. She was at the controls of the *Witch* after I was. She's probably still in a medirobot, but maybe she can tell me what happened to the thoughtware."

Commander Normandy nodded her agreement. Harry saluted—some old habit surfacing, evidently—and was gone.

The commander turned back to her holostage. "What's going on with the emperor and his ship? Sadie, try to raise them, see if we can find out."

"Yes, ma'am." But Sadie's first effort to establish communication failed, drowned out by hellish noise.

· · ·

At the moment, there was little noise inside the shielded main cabin of the *Galaxy.* Only two people sat there, surrounded and greatly outnumbered by empty combat chairs, and the pair was gripped by a hushed and terrible silence.

Not that an impartial observer would have thought their situation all that desperate, not for the crew of a warship that was supposedly engaged in battle.

Admiral Hector was in the pilot's chair, with the Emperor Julius seated next to him upon a throne-like chair that had been slightly and symbolically raised above the others.

None of the rest of the crew, the people upon whom Julius had counted so intensely, had reached the ship before the emperor had ordered liftoff.

Julius had refused to delay more than half a minute for the laggards. "Lift off, I say!" he had commanded the admiral, his pilot. "The fewer we are, the greater the share of glory that must come to each."

Now, half an hour later, Julius smiled grimly, remembering the admiral's warning that it would be very dangerous going into combat with the crew short-handed. Such had been the emperor's difficulties with the single crew member who had made the trip that he was ready to believe that having his full crew might have been tantamount to suicide.

The smoothest part of the whole exercise had been the landing, handled by the autopilot. The interior of the main cabin was still as calm as his bedroom in the palace, back on Good Intentions. The Emperor Julius, conscious of looking regal on his small throne, wondered whether any of the great empires of the past had entered their final stages of collapse in such a mundane setting.

Not long ago, during most of the few days he'd spent in his Spartan assigned quarters on the Space Force base, and especially in those early minutes after the alarm had sounded, the chief and secret fear of the Emperor Julius had been that he and his fighting ship would never get off the ground at all. That his effort to find redemption in battle, like so many others he'd made in recent years, would be aborted, was doomed to die in futility and disappointment.

As recently as an hour ago, he had been proud of the fact that the training and practice in spacecraft that he had insisted on for the crew of his flagship, before ever coming to Hyperborea, had not been wasted. The immediate difficulties had been overcome, and he and his selected crew of one had lifted off successfully in their ship.

Then, with the pilot's helmet seated more firmly than any crown on the incompetent head of his chief and most loyal supporter, they'd lifted off in a blast of acceleration, and had gone roaring out at full speed, on the emperor's express orders to seek immediate contact with the enemy. This was not, of course, the battle for which they had been several days preparing, and he had received no orders from Commander Normandy on how to deal with this situation. But to the emperor, such details hardly mattered now. He had his own goal and knew, essentially, what he had to do to reach it.

At some point during those early minutes of flight, while he'd thought he was being carried into battle, the emperor's mood had soared, becoming euphoric, almost ecstatic. They were looking for a fight, as ready for one as they could be—

But somehow, in the midst of a battle, they hadn't been able to come to grips with the enemy, or even to locate it precisely. It had been in the ensuing bewilderment that his fanatical aide suggested, in all apparent seriousness, that the berserkers were afraid of the Emperor Julius. The death-machines had fled on learning that His Imperial Highness had taken the field.

Julius had not laughed on hearing this. Instead, he'd stared at Admiral Hector, who was gazing back at him, waiting to find out from him whether the theory the admiral had just put forward might possibly be true. Hector was like all the other worshipers, dependent for instructions from their god on what to say, what to think. That, of course, was what Julius wanted them to be, but sometimes, as now, he infinitely despised them all. He gave them no signal. And so none of them knew what to think.

For a horrible few minutes, the Emperor Julius had wondered whether the battle might be over before he could take part.

As the minutes passed, two, three, ten, then a quarter of an hour, with the planetoid Hyperborea falling farther and farther behind them, it had gradually become obvious that the whole berserker attack must have bypassed the *Galaxy,* left her drifting peacefully alone in deep space. They had not been defeated, but ignored by an enemy that went plunging on toward its chosen objective.

Vaguely, Julius had been picturing a thousand, or at least several hundred, berserker battlecraft swarming around the planetoid. But now it seemed that the numbers involved had to be very much less than that. And he wondered, military innocent that he was, what had prompted the enemy to attack with less than overwhelming force.

And then at last he broke his silence. "Where is the enemy?" he demanded of his loyal crew person. For a long time this man had represented himself to Julius as competent in matters of space warfare, but now the emperor could see that Hector's competence was a delusion.

The question was rhetorical, because its answer was plain for both of them to see. The wave of attacking enemy machines, intent with single-minded ferocity upon some other goal, had evidently ignored them, had gone right past the *Galaxy.* All the berserker force was now concentrated in the close vicinity of Hyperborea.

Then, lashed by the tongue of an angry emperor, the pilot turned the ship in space and headed back toward the planetoid, where the berserkers were.

It had taken them another quarter of an hour to get back

to the near vicinity of Hyperborea. And then, less than a minute more than that, to be forced out of the fight, not by direct enemy action, but by their own incompetence. Somehow, the control system, the thoughtware, had become scrambled in such a way that the autopilot had automatically taken over and brought the craft in for a landing.

Monumental futility! They seemed to be laboring under a curse. The emperor swore, in four languages, starting in a whisper and ending in a full-throated bellow.

The tirade was cut short a few minutes later, and its object saved from having to respond, by the signal of an incoming message on the main holostage.

Soon the head and shoulders of Commander Normandy appeared there, demanding, in a very military voice, to know what the hell was going on.

The emperor's expression as he faced the holostage was as proud as if he had a smashing victory to report. "Commander, our ship has experienced difficulties, but we will soon be reentering the fight."

The face of Normandy's image was blurred by battle noise, but her voice came through crisply. "I must warn you that Shiva is on the ground here. It has taken direct tactical control of the enemy forces." After a short pause, just long enough to draw breath, she also informed him of what had happened to his missing crew members. Shortly after the *Galaxy* lifted off, they had been killed en masse by a berserker that caught them milling about on the landing field. "I tell you this in case you have landed expecting more of your crew to join you. That will not be possible."

"I understand." Julius drew a deep breath of his own. He wanted to say *good riddance*—but he did not. "That was not the reason for our landing."

But Commander Normandy had broken off communication as soon as she finished speaking. Had Julius intended to offer any explanation or excuse, she would not have heard it. But that made no difference to him, because he had nothing more to say.

What he did have to do now was to deal somehow with the remnants of his incompetent crew. Turning to Admiral Hector, who still occupied the pilot's seat, Julius got to his feet and calmly ordered the fellow to take off his helmet.

With trembling hands, the admiral did so.

"Our ship is not damaged, as far as you can tell?" the emperor demanded. "It is possible for us to lift off again?"

"I believe so, Your Imperial Highness. But I must refuse the attempt. I am not qualified." This man was sobbing, his words almost indistinguishable. He wasn't going to pick up his helmet and put it on again.

"So you have demonstrated. But you drove us successfully from Gee Eye to Hyperborea," Julius mused aloud.

"I must admit, sire, that journey was accomplished largely on automatic pilot. Not all the way, only at every point where we might have encountered difficulty. But in combat, to use the autopilot is not . . . not feasible."

"I should imagine not."

Hector groaned. Obviously, he was practically dying of shame. "I should never have attempted combat flight, it is beyond my ability."

"Well," said the emperor slowly, "what you have done, you have done. There is no help for it now." He took a step closer to the combat chair where Admiral Hector sat, and standing over him, reached out a hand. "Give me the helmet."

The pilot's helmet left the admiral's face exposed, eyes behind a transparent shield, and the emperor could see him blanch. "Sire. You have not the training, not even as much as I—"

"But I have other qualifications that you lack. Give me the helmet." He was thinking that wearing the pilot's helmet ought to at least give him a good look at the ship's surroundings, a more immediate sense of what was happening than was provided on the holostage.

As soon as Julius had placed the helmet on his head, he became aware of blurry presentations, perceptions of the ship's systems and of the outside world. But for the moment, he ignored them; there was another matter that had to be concluded first. Drawing his sidearm, he lifted it, aiming it point-blank between the admiral's unprotected eyes. When the pistol came up to aim at Hector, the man closed his eyes, but he did not flinch or turn away. Such executive punishments were rare in the empire, but not unheard of.

At first the emperor thought that the gun had made no mess at all; but when he looked again, beyond the admiral's shattered and now immobile head, he saw that someone would have to do some cleaning up. Well, it would not be him. And maybe it would not be necessary, after all.

There was a crisp sound of movement, of the operation of a door, in the direction of the main airlock, and Julius turned, pistol still in hand. Someone was coming in.

"Who—?"

And then the emperor understood that he might better have asked *what.* It seemed to him that if he drew in a deep breath, he would be dead before he had the chance to let the air all out again.

In keeping with the crew's unblemished record of ineptitude—in this indictment, Julius did not exempt himself—no one had seen the enemy approaching the ship.

A silvery quartet of berserker boarding machines, moving alertly, on guard against treacherous Solarian ambush, marched into the grounded *Galaxy,* which seemed to them at this moment the most readily capturable means of transportation. Four of them, their shapes a poor approximation of the human, silvery metal showing through where some kind of outer coating, what must have been an attempt at camouflage, had been shredded. Silently, they deployed themselves in an almost regular arc, all four of them equally distant from the emperor. Silently, they thus confronted him.

Too late the sole survivor realized that the outer door of the airlock had, through yet another calamitous oversight, been left unlocked. Maybe it had automatically unlocked itself when someone called for an emergency landing.

The deep breath came and went, and was followed by another. And he was still alive.

As always, even if no one was now left alive to watch him, Julius was making every effort not to appear indecisive. But he really had no idea of what to do next.

In his quiet desperation, he was even toying with the idea of personally taking the ship up into space again. He couldn't do any worse than his supposedly expert helper had done.

The death-machines remained standing in their deployment before him, saying nothing. All was quiet in the cabin, save for the muted background noise of intermittent combat.

Deliberately, as deliberately as he had executed the admiral, the emperor raised the pistol and fired at the machine that happened to be standing nearest to him. This time, the effect on the target was negligible. Whatever came out of the barrel glanced harmlessly from berserker armor to smack into a bulkhead on the far side of the cabin.

The Emperor Julius looked at his hopelessly inadequate handgun—but any machine that calculated he was going to pitch it away was sadly mistaken. Unhurriedly, without the slightest loss of dignity, he raised it for another calculated shot at the foe.

In the time required for his arm to perform that motion, one of the machines had crossed the cabin, in a movement whose speed and fluidity took his breath away, and laid a hand of clawlike grippers on his gun. Before Julius could get off another round, the pistol's stubby barrel had been bent, the sides of the magazine, a centimeter from the imperial fingers, crushed to uselessness. Then the weapon was pulled away.

The emperor's skin had not been scratched, not a hair had been turned on his head or a thread of his clothing even rumpled. The hand with which he'd held the gun had not been damaged by the violent treatment accorded the weapon.

The man who had been ready to embrace death found that death, in its most virulent form, seemed to be trying to treat him as gently as possible.

"Remove your helmet," one of the machines squeaked at him. It seemed to Julius that the berserker was deliberately taunting him, echoing his own words spoken just before he'd shot his once-trusted second-in-command.

"I will not," his airspeakers rasped out. He thought they somewhat augmented the tones of power and dignity that he had so long and carefully cultivated in his voice.

He stood there, having got to his feet when they came in, his body tensing in anticipation of a death that did not come. He could feel his knees actually quivering, something that had never happened to him—not since the days of his little-remembered childhood. *Why would they not kill him?*

Why this further, terrible, humiliation?

Shiva, processing data as methodically as ever, paused for an unusually long time when it read a certain insignia that was new to its extensive memory. The insignia, borne by the body of the dead life-unit now lying before it, was that of an admiral—and an admiral in some Solarian fleet whose very existence had been unknown to the berserker until now.

It seemed extremely, astronomically, improbable that the badlife would have created such an insignia, endowed one of their units with an apparent rank, simply in an attempt at deception.

Remembering what Commander Normandy had told him in her latest communication, the emperor demanded of the machines that seemed to be playing the role of honor guard for him: "Where is the one called Shiva? It cannot be any one of you." Even as he spoke, Julius formed a sudden mental image of what Shiva ought to look like, regal and lethal and metallic all at the same time. No doubt his imagination was technically incorrect, but he found it inwardly satisfying all the same. None of the berserkers before him now came close to matching it.

But he had scarcely finished speaking before one of them, he wasn't quite sure which, because of course there were no lip movements, replied, "I am the one called Shiva, and I can speak to you through any of the units that stand before you."

Turning his gaze away from the machines in front of him, Julius said: "Then you are not physically present in my ship. I am Emperor of the Galaxy, and I do not deal with intermediaries. I want your physical presence. Come here, into this cabin, and stand before me. At that time, we will discuss my handing over the control device."

A moment later, when the same machine voice—he still couldn't tell which of the four machines the words were coming from, but he supposed it didn't matter—questioned Julius on the subject, he repeated in a firm voice his claim to be the ruler of the Galaxy.

A*ccording to all berserker records of Solarian behavior, the great majority of totally deranged humans were kept under confinement by the relatively rational members of the species. It seemed illogical that those with serious mental deficiencies would be allowed to pilot their own spaceships. But no completely satisfactory interpretation of badlife behavior had ever been computed.*

These machines did their best to secure the Galaxy *for their master's use. But they were unable to make a decision in the matter of this strange prisoner without consulting Shiva.*

Shiva was about to order its subordinate units to confine the life-unit for further investigation, since that could be easily and quickly done, and then to hold the ship ready for liftoff.

But the video transmitted by Shiva's servants told it that the badlife was wearing the pilot's helmet. And that put a whole new face on the matter.

The best prediction of the outcome that Claire Normandy could now get from her computers was that the battle would most likely grind down to something like a draw.

Aboard the *Galaxy,* the standoff still held, one man, unarmed now except for his thoughts, the electrochemical changes in his fragile brain, facing a row of mechanical monsters. Occasionally there was some exchange of dialogue between human and murderous machine. The thing spoke in a squeaky voice, the way berserkers generally did when they decided to speak at all—no one had ever discovered why.

Why was it wasting energy now on argument? The emperor's vanity allowed him to convince himself that even berserkers were vulnerable to his charm, his charisma.

People watching him, had there been any, would think that he was stalling for time, with nothing to lose, in hopes of some favorable event. But that wasn't really it at all. It wasn't time that Julius was waiting for, but opportunity.

And suddenly, through the helmet, he heard a voice that he was able to recognize as that of Commander Normandy.

"Emperor Julius? Are you still there? We saw the berserkers enter your ship."

"I am still here, Commander."

"Subvocalize your answers and I don't think they can hear us. What is your situation?"

Briefly, he outlined the position. "Commander, how big is

Shiva? I want to know how I might be able to recognize that device, when—if—it should stand before me."

"Do you have some reason to think that's going to happen?"

"I have my hopes. How will I know when it is in my ship?" Any ordinary human in his position, talking with the enemy, might be accused of being goodlife. But it never crossed Julius's mind to worry about such things. The Emperor of the Galaxy was above all ordinary law. Such rules could not apply to him.

The voice of the commander sounded strained. "I can't tell you what Shiva looks like, exactly what size it is. I don't mean that I refuse, but that no human being knows. There is, however, something of great importance that I must tell you. As long as you continue to wear the pilot's helmet," said Commander Normandy, speaking carefully, "they probably won't kill you. They won't even take the chance of shocking your nervous system with a disabling wound. With that helmet on, your nervous system is very closely engaged with the ship's systems, including the interstellar drive. To engage that drive while your ship is sitting where it is, right on the surface of a planetoid as big as Hyperborea, would destroy your vessel on the spot. And that, you see, must be what they are trying to avoid."

"I see," said the emperor. It came as no great surprise.

His greatness, his glory, his leadership—all that meant nothing to them. Nothing. To them, he was another badlife unit, and no more. It was the *ship* they wanted. The ship that for some reason, they felt they had to have . . .

Any combatant, human or otherwise, who had great need of a ship would be very careful not to wreck it. Just now the berserkers were being very careful about that, and it was easy to deduce that they did not want the life-unit who happened to be wearing the control helmet to die a violent death. Probably for the same reason, the intruders had very carefully taken his pistol away—they were taking no chances on his deciding suddenly to shoot up the control console.

Meanwhile, he could sense through the helmet how, outside his quiet ship, the battle flared and died away again.

Even when on the verge of its own destruction, Shiva's compulsion to learn was such that it couldn't resist trying to find out whether the whole situation that had brought it here to destruction was an elaborate trap, a hoax, a scam worked on it with fiendish cleverness by the badlife, who had been willing to sacrifice numbers of their own life-units in the process. It wanted to know if one of their computers had enabled them to figure out and work a plot of such terrible complexity.

Someone—a spacer Harry Silver could not remember having seen before—who had been shot down by a berserker lander lay dying in a corridor and had pulled his helmet off.

Harry, on his way to the hospital to interview Becky, stopped briefly to attend the dying man.

The mangled spacer gulped for air, and for a moment, Harry wondered what today's scent in the corridors might be. No one who had a helmet on could tell. It might help a little, he thought, to go out with fresh pine scent in your nostrils, or maybe oceanside salt air. Either one of those would be nice when his own time came.

Back on the *Galaxy,* Julius was thinking that this was not exactly the kind of ending he had envisioned for himself or for his cause. He had seen himself and his loyal followers as charging gloriously into battle. Over and over again he had imagined the *Galaxy* in a suicidal ramming against some kind of berserker flagship.

No doubt if any of the people on his maladroit crew had actually tried a stunt like that, they would have committed some hideous mistake and crashed into the wrong object.

And now fortune, fate, destiny—so often against him over the past few years—had now relented, had given him one last advantage. It was just that he had happened to be wearing the live control helmet when they came in—not even a berserker could move faster than human thought across the quantum interface between his brain and the optelectronic systems of the ship.

His mind went scanning through the images of controls and systems that he had been practically ignoring up till now—yes, that must be the drive, and there were the mains of power. Exactly how would one go about ordering a suicidal c-plus jump? It would be terrible, an inconceivable failure, to attempt such a stroke and then to botch it somehow. As it seemed to be his fate to botch mechanical, physical things in general.

Now he was earnestly attempting to delay the blast until he could be certain, certain enough to act, that Shiva had actually been brought aboard.

When one of the berserker units before him spoke to him again, the emperor insisted on confronting the enemy chieftain, or commanding officer, face to panel.

At last, the voice in which the enemy spoke to him agreed. It promised him that it would come aboard.

"I await your arrival," he said, and sat down once more in the pilot's chair. He seemed to have been standing too long, but even sitting, he took care to hold himself upright, as if he were on a throne. Whatever happened now, whatever the enemy might do, he must not faint.

TWENTY

For thousands of years, berserker computers had understood—to the extent that such machines were able to understand anything about humanity—that the badlife, in their swarming billions of units, often behaved and spoke illogically, in modes of thought incomprehensible to the pure computer intellect. To Shiva, or to any other berserker capable of making decisions of comparable complexity, the claim of the life-unit Julius to a certain title, and all that title implied, was irrational. But it was no less rational than many other assertions made by other units of badlife, and believed by billions of their fellows all across the life-infected portion of the Galaxy.

How many or how few life-units agreed with the claim of the one now calling itself an emperor was a question of no intrinsic importance to Shiva. Of infinitely greater moment was the fact that the self-proclaimed emperor continued to wear the pilot's control helmet of a certain ship, and that this ship was perhaps the only intact means of departure from the planetoid.

Contact with the helmet in effect placed the brain of the life-unit in intimate communion with all the systems of the ship, including the thermonuclear power sources and the interstellar drive. Activating that drive this deep in the local and systemic gravitational fields would be immediately disastrous. As long as the life-unit in question continued to wear the helmet, it could not be destroyed, or even subjected to serious shock, without gravely endangering the ship.

Shiva decided it was necessary to make some move to break the deadlock. To board the ship would be to tell the enemy its whereabouts—so it sent a decoy on first, to see what the badlife, in particular the unit claiming to be emperor, would do.

Meanwhile, Shiva waited outside, nearby, physically a small, compact unit carried in the grip of a fast-moving boarding device. If no treachery impended, a very quick boarding would be accomplished just before liftoff.

When battle noise once more broke off her contact with the *Galaxy,* Commander Normandy sat back and took thought. She no longer commanded forces or weapons capable of keeping the emperor's ship from lifting off. Had she done so, she would have used them now. But the power reserves of all her strongest weapons were now exhausted.

"What's he going to do?" Lieutenant Colonel Khodark asked.

"Your guess is as good as mine. I told him what'll happen if he takes the helmet off."

"And if he keeps it on? How long can a standoff last?"

"My guess is that they're going to make him an offer—"

"—and if he's crazy enough to take a berserker's word—"

"—not even an emperor could be that crazy. Could he?"

She really wasn't sure.

A*nother fact that still unsettled the calculations of the death-machines was their observation that one of the dead bod-*

ies aboard the emperor's ship bore a written label designating the rank of admiral. The presence of a life-unit of such status strongly suggested a whole fleet of badlife warships somewhere in the vicinity, but no such force had been detected.

Shiva had yet to make a decision on what to do with the unit calling itself emperor.

Shiva was quite ready to promise continued life to this life-unit or any other in exchange for a viable getaway vehicle. And it knew that some would always be ready to believe such a promise, even when it came from a berserker.

The emperor had no idea of when more Solarian ships might appear in the black sky of Hyperborea, nor did that any longer matter very much to him.

If only, he thought, the woman who truly loved him could be with him, she would understand. She would comprehend his motives, how he had wanted to save his failing fame, inflate his almost nonexistent reputation, by sacrificing himself to kill this worst berserker of all time . . .

But his daydream of that woman, like most of the other fantasies by which he tried to live, was fatally flawed. After many decades of life, and connections with a great many women, he still had no idea of who she was.

She was certainly not to be identified with any of his many wives. He had been for some time thoroughly separated from all of them, and it was amazing how little he felt the loss.

It wasn't the idea of the thousands and thousands of people who had denounced the Emperor of the Galaxy, deserted him and opposed him, that Julius found truly unendurable. No. Rather, it was the thought of the trillions, some dead, some living now, who had been untouched by his greatness. Before today's events, the chances had been high that they did not even know his name, and probably never would.

The four berserkers were still standing at attention in front of him, almost like a military guard of honor, and now one of them suddenly spoke. It asked him: "Arc there other emperors?"

"Does the question come from Shiva?"

"It does."

"Then let me say that I still await the personal presence of Shiva aboard my ship."

"I am on my way."

Are there other emperors? Julius didn't know whether to laugh or cry. Though usually he managed to avoid thinking about the subject, he knew perfectly well that scattered among the trillions of the Galaxy there were perhaps as many as a hundred of his rivals, other prophets, cult-leaders. Maybe none of them called himself emperor, but that was unimportant. Probably dozens of them, maybe scores, were more successful than the Emperor Julius had ever been, each claiming more followers than Julius had ever had—and the average citizen of the Galaxy had never heard of any of those scores or dozens either.

As soon as the fact and the importance of Shiva had been explained to Julius, he had understood what he must do. For a long time he had misjudged his own true importance in the universe, but now he understood at last just what his destiny must be.

For years, Julius had been isolated on the Galactic backwater of Good Intentions, with defeat staring him in the face, the bitter taste of human ridicule in his throat. But now he had left all that behind him—and his life, his career, were rushing on toward a very different sort of conclusion.

At times over the past few years, he had been strongly tempted by daydreams of someday being able to take a magnificent revenge upon the entire Solarian human population of the Galaxy, to inflict upon them a just punishment for their impenetrable deafness and blindness to his message, their invincible ignorance of his very being. Their hatred would have been a kind of tribute. What was unendurable was to be ignored.

Even now, the folk of the Galaxy in their swarming trillions were totally unaware of the glorious thing that the Emperor Julius was about to accomplish. But such a state of affairs could not persist for very long. Whether Solarian humanity was going to win the battle of Hyperborea or lose it, Commander Normandy's couriers would be going out with news of the event. The news would spread swiftly, and certainly, to all the inhabited planets of the Galaxy. And those who today fought and died for the cause of life would never be forgotten. The name of the human who succeeded in destroying Shiva would be enshrined in human consciousness forever.

And while the surface of his mind was busy with these thoughts, quite a different idea kept trying to take form beneath the surface. Suppose—only suppose—he were to form an alliance with this berserker? But it was only the ghost of a temptation, and it died completely before it could take solid shape. Ruling as the mere puppet of any other authority, human or otherwise, would be unthinkable. Julius was quite willing to play a role when his destiny required it, to take orders in battle from a lowly Space Force commander, for example—but he wanted it understood that this was a gracious concession on his part. He could not acknowledge that any other authority was really greater than his own. Besides, he knew in his heart that berserkers would betray any agreement they might make. In this, at least, they were very much like human beings.

Suddenly, quite unexpectedly, the door of the airlock moved again, and three of his honor guards walked out of his ship, as quietly as they had come. A single berserker lander stepped in, carrying a strange-looking slab of metal. Some kind of solid-state device, the emperor thought, although he was no expert. Once the newcomer was completely in, the fourth member of the original honor guard departed also.

Julius stared at the motionless form that had just entered. "Shiva?"

The speaker of the supporting figure told him: "I have come aboard."

Slowly, deeply, the emperor drew in a breath. Now that the

moment had come, he could not resist skirting once more the edges of the monumental betrayal, just to confirm in his own mind that the possibility existed. Feeling reasonably confident that no humans could hear him at the moment, he cleared his throat and said: "A question for Shiva."

"Ask."

"What will you give me in return for an alliance? For control of this ship?"

Shiva needed no time at all to think the proposition over. "Whatever you ask, if it is in my power to give."

Julius felt deep satisfaction. At long last, a truly great Galactic power, and the berserkers were certainly that, was taking him seriously—even if the offer was only to install him as their puppet ruler. And even if he did not believe their offer for a moment. His importance, his own Galactic stature at this moment, was proven by the fact that Shiva was taking him seriously enough to make a very serious effort to deceive him.

Suddenly he hoped devoutly that Commander Normandy and her people had somehow overheard the proposition made him by the enemy. Then history would be sure to grant him the full glory and credit for having turned it down.

Slowly he drew in breath, then let it out in a long, long sigh. His place in Galactic history was now secure.

"Welcome aboard," he said. "I am very glad that you are here." And turned his attention to the mental intricacies of activating his spaceship's c-plus drive.

What was that?"

Even down in the computer room, the ground shook violently with the detonation.

"That was the *Galaxy.*" Normandy had been watching through a remote viewer as that last machine had gone in through the airlock and the others had played out their act of departing. Moments later, the ship had seemed to dissolve into pure light.

"What about Shiva?" Colonel Khodark was almost hanging over her shoulder. *"Was that really Shiva that just went on board?"*

"I wouldn't bet on it."

Karl Enomoto had had to leave the hospital at about the same time Harry Silver did. Since there was no longer any ship for Enomoto to pilot, he was ordered to join in the ground defense. And since people were watching, he'd had no choice but to obey the order.

But he'd been steadily on the lookout for a chance to get back to the hospital, to get the box of contraband out of the medirobot in which he'd hidden it while he and Silver were out in Silver's ship. That box would be worth a fortune to the authorities on Kermandie, and Enomoto did not intend to let that fortune slip through his hands.

The attempt to take control of one of the remaining Solarian ships had failed, but Shiva could not know disappointment, any more than it could know fear. Only one lander unit had been lost in the explosion, while Shiva itself had remained outside the ship, waiting until the true intentions of the badlife unit at the controls could be confirmed. Many badlife, when facing destruction, promised cooperation, but few indeed could be relied upon. The blast had not damaged Shiva's computational ability, or altered the purpose of its programming. Shiva felt nothing. The impact had been violent enough to cut off all sensory input, severing communication with the outside world, including all of its supporting machines.

Shiva could no longer receive information, or issue orders. It knew nothing of the current status of the battle, or even whether it was still on the surface of Hyperborea. Blind, deaf, and dumb, it could only wait, with nerveless patience, for one of its auxiliary machines to find it and reconnect it to the world.

· · ·

Karl Enomoto arrived at the hospital carrying his helmet under his arm and wearing on his face what he hoped was just the proper expression of concern.

In leaving his assigned post, he was taking a chance on being accused of desertion. But it was only a chance—and right now he didn't see any alternative.

Trying his best to achieve a winning smile, he calmly asked the robot desk clerk for information. "I'm looking for Lieutenant Becky Sharp. I'm one of the people who brought her in."

The human nurse who soon appeared recognized Enomoto as one of the heroic volunteers and was willing to go at least a little out of her way to try to help him.

"Good news for you, Lieutenant! Lieutenant Sharp isn't in the medirobot any longer! The unit was needed for someone worse off, and she wasn't as badly injured as you must have thought at first."

"That's great. Where can I find her, then?"

"I'm not sure where she is just now—"

"That's all right. As long as she's okay, I'll track her down." Enomoto paused to draw breath. "About that medirobot." He had memorized the serial number, just in case, and now was able to rattle it off. "Actually, there was an item of mine in that unit—a box with some stuff in it—it has some personal value to me—"

The nurse directed him.

Passing through the indicated door, he saw before him a long room filled almost to capacity with rows of medirobots, devices like elaborate coffins with clear panels on the top so the body inside was visible. In most units, the glass was opaque up to the neck of the occupant, but this sheetlike modesty covering could be turned down by the movement of a human attendant's hand over the outer surface.

The adjoining ward, or room, was ordinarily reserved for people who were well enough to occupy ordinary beds but still were considered better off here than in regular quarters.

Enomoto started down the line of medirobot units, looking at the inconspicuously engraved numbers. He needed only a few seconds to locate the medirobot in which he'd concealed the box of contraband. Quickly bending to open the storage compartment in its base, he reached inside.

He brought out what he had been looking for—

One of the berserker landers, seeking another way to approach the computer room, detoured through the small base hospital. Recognizing the space for what it was, it began slashing through the power cables of medirobots to right and left as it progressed. The damned thing, already damaged before it got this far, was conserving its dwindling energies, saving its remaining capacity for violence for use against a harder target. It went rolling down the central aisle, between rows of units, like some deranged attendant.

Becky, less seriously injured than had first appeared, had shown strong signs of recovery and was now more or less up and about, but still in the hospital. When the tumult in the adjoining ward told her what was happening, she grabbed up a weapon and took an active role in the defense of the hospital. Or tried to do so.

There were some twenty or thirty patients, survivors of Marut's ambush as well as fresher casualties of the fighting on the ground. When the marauder appeared in the doorway, those who were able to run, or even to crawl, ran screaming, or dove under their beds in a futile search for shelter.

The killer machine need delay only a moment to hurl a bed aside and crush the cowering form beneath.

Heroic human medics tried to stop the invader, shoving furniture in front of it and uselessly smashing and spraying containers of chemicals on its back.

One lunging attendant carved a hole in the back of the invader, using a neutron scalpel. But a fraction of a second later, that valiant human was smashed aside, scattered and spattered, by the swing of a metal arm.

Enomoto was on the scene and fully armed, and he opened up with his carbine at once, conducting what looked like a fierce and almost suicidal defense of the helpless wounded.

Of course he stood his ground and fought, because that was the best means of preserving his own life. Nor did he want any berserker to destroy the smuggled box, not after he'd come this far in his scheme to get away with it.

Then the berserker was suddenly right on top of him, and something smashed with crushing force at Enomoto's armored legs, which broke like dry sticks inside their armor, collapsing under him. He could feel himself falling, going under momentarily with the pain and shock of his wounds.

His last thought before losing consciousness was of the box.

Harry Silver heard the sudden uproar from some distance down a corridor and came on at a dead run. By the time he reached the scene, the invading berserker was down, its legs shot out from under it, its armor breached, and then a finishing jolt administered through the hole. Patients were being wheeled and carried away from the steaming, glowing wreckage. He could see Becky at a little distance, out of her medirobot and looking to be in amazingly good shape.

The next thing that Harry noticed, lying inexplicably right on the floor of the hospital ward, was a small box of distinctive shape. He had last seen that box several days ago in the cabin of his own ship. Now it was simply lying there, and he picked it up.

"That belongs to Lieutenant Enomoto," said a nurse. She held out a hand. "I saw him holding it a moment ago. I'll see that he gets it."

"Like hell it belongs to him." Harry tucked the object tightly under his arm. "Who told you that?"

"Why, the lieutenant came here asking about his personal property. And then I saw him with the box in hand."

"Ah. Interesting. Very interesting. I see now why he was so gung ho to come with me to my ship. He must have found this lying around and just stuck it inside the medirobot while I was looking after Becky. And it rode into the base that way."

Harry and some others stood guard in the hospital for a while for fear there might be another invader coming through. Commander Normandy was soon present on the scene by means of a holostage. After more important matters had been dealt with, the controversy over the box was brought to her attention.

Turning to Harry, her image demanded: "If it's yours, why would Lieutenant Enomoto claim it?"

"Only one good reason I can think of. Because he's an agent of the Kermandie government."

"That's a strong accusation. When the fighting's over, I will have to have some explanation of this, Mr. Silver."

Some time ago, she had begun to wonder privately whether one of the six brave volunteers might not be the Kermandie agent that Intelligence had warned her to expect. There were, after all, very few ways for an outsider to obtain entry to this base. But she hadn't wanted to disrupt the battle preparations by an investigation.

"I can give you one right now, Commander. You told me your secrets, I'll tell you mine. Actually, that box, or what's in it, has a lot to do with my being here on Hyperborea." Harry shook his head slowly. "It's a long story."

Commander Normandy said: "Perhaps I'd better take custody of the property in question until this can be investigated."

Silver said: "I don't think that would be a good idea, Commander. It's mine, and it goes with me when I walk out of here."

"Before I can agree to that, Lieutenant, I'll have to see what its contents are. If they are contraband of some sort—" Claire was shaking her head.

"Only by Kermandie rules—I wouldn't call them laws. Want to see?" And before anyone could respond to the question, Harry was working at the latch that held the container shut. He said: "I expect that the dictator's people would pay pretty well for what's in here."

Commander Normandy was scowling. "The authorities on Kermandie are offering a reward for contraband? And you mean to take it to them?"

Silver exploded in three foul words. Then he added: "Just take a look, Commander. That'll explain things better than I can." Moving in front of an empty table, he flipped up the lid and dumped the box's contents out.

Normandy for once looked stunned. Instead of the drugs she had been expecting, she found herself gazing at what appeared to be a modest collection of personal belongings, including some torn and bloodstained clothing. Harry held up a long shirt of some fine, silky fabric, running the material through his fingers, displaying the ugly stains for the woman on the holostage to see.

Silver was saying in a tight voice: "They belonged to a man whose holograph I've seen hanging on the wall of your office. Most decent folk think a lot of that man. The Kermandie government had him murdered some years ago."

"Hai San?"

"Who else?"

There were beads and other small objects, some less easy to classify, strung into a kind of necklace. No spacefarer's garments here. Nothing of real intrinsic value. A long shirt, with rents in the fine fabric, showing where and how the fatal wounds were made. A pair of pants, made from the same thin stuff. A few small coins. A leather belt, some sandals—

"As I told you, this was stolen from my ship, and I claim it as my property. By the way, I resign my commission."

No one paid any attention to his resignation. Well, if they didn't take him seriously, they wouldn't be able to say later that he hadn't warned them.

Hai San's relics, if they could be authenticated—and Harry knew these could be—ought to have enormous psychological value to certain factions of the population in Kermandie. The current rulers would go to great lengths to prevent their being found, or to discredit them.

"But you're not taking this to Kermandie," Normandy observed a little later, when they had a chance to talk in private.

Silver shrugged. "I know some other people who'll pay me pretty well."

"Probably not as well as Kermandie would."

He squinted. "Am I going to have trouble with you, too? By the way, have we heard anything recently from Mr. Havot?"

Havot, after getting out of Harry's ship, had felt it necessary to return to the base. In doing so, he was taking a chance on being locked up again, but this was the only way to get someone to pilot his escape.

Way down on the list of possibiiities was trying to force someone, at gunpoint, to pilot an escape ship for him. Havot had left behind his shoulder weapon in his panicked flight, but had been able to pick up a replacement dropped by some fallen spacer.

Being reluctant to use threats or force meant he'd have to find another man, or woman, who also had a good reason for wanting to get away. But Havot wasn't too worried. He thought that could be practically anyone, when a berserker attack was on.

TWENTY-ONE

When Harry and Becky met again, they rushed into each other's arms.

The emergency at the hospital having been dealt with, they had a chancc to talk, and Becky told him what little she could about the thoughtware on the *Witch.*

A little later, as soon as he was free to think about extraneous matters, Harry gave Becky his box of contraband. "See what you can do with this, will you? Repack it in some other container."

"I can do that—is Enomoto coming looking for it again?"

"Not for a while. He's going to be in the hospital for a couple of days at least, and Normandy's going to charge him with spying, soon as she has time." Harry paused. "He's a piece of scum, but he's not the really scary one. Is he?"

"You mean the one who shot me."

"Tell me about him."

"There's not much I can tell. Everything seemed ready for

liftoff, all systems go, and we—Honan-Fu was the man with me—we were just waiting another minute, hoping you'd show up. The airlock was unlocked. And then *he* came in."

"Havot."

Becky nodded.

"Sure it was him? Could you recognize his armor?"

"He was just wearing standard stuff. The only thing I could really recognize was his face. He has this little smile that seems to say, 'Look how cute I am.' " Becky shuddered. "I know it was him, Harry. But if they put me on the witness stand, a good lawyer could make it sound real doubtful."

"Yeah, tell me about lawyers. Where is Mr. Havot now—or is it Lieutenant Havot?"

Becky frowned. "No idea. And he's only a spacer third, isn't he?"

"Thought he might have got a battlefield promotion."

When Harry asked around some more, it appeared that several hours ago, Spacer Havot had been seen on the base, armed, apparently unhurt, and ready and eager for combat. He'd been ordered to occupy a certain advanced observation post, and after sounding the alarm, to do his best to defend it if the enemy appeared. Mostly it meant sitting motionless in one of the machines that was supposed to be used in the assault on Summerland.

"Exactly what do you want him for, Silver? Shall we try to call him?"

"No. It can wait."

Harry supposed that by now there was an excellent chance that Havot was dead. It was a good bet that many of those on the "missing" list were no longer breathing.

"Well, we can hope," he said, to no one in particular.

By now, the enemy attack had been drastically slowed down, though not stopped. Here and there, the enemy, as always, moved and killed as opportunity arose. The possibility of a crushing defeat still existed for each side. Each had been much weakened.

The commander had rescinded her earlier orders to Harry. Rather than get the grounded *Witch* up into space, she wanted to keep it on the ground for now, encircled and defended by most of her remaining forces. If Shiva had survived and wanted to get offworld, it would have to fight its way somehow through them. Even if Shiva had not escaped the blast, the captured Solarian secrets might very well have been passed on to some anonymous berserker second-in-command.

To the small group of aides that served as her council of war, she said: "We've got to understand that in some very basic ways, Shiva is, was, has to be, like every other berserker. For one thing, it places no intrinsic importance upon its own survival. To our enemy, no object in the universe, itself included, has any value except as it may contribute to the success of the grand plan, the destruction of all life.

"If berserkers were at all susceptible to mental, emotional shock—and we know they're not—the news that the badlife meant to ambush their most successful field commander, and knew just how to go about it, would have hit them a nasty blow indeed.

"I can picture in my mind—or at least I think I can—how they must have chewed that one over among themselves, in some kind of exchange of information in their strategic council: '*The badlife might have deduced the existence of Shiva from our suddenly increased rate of victory in battle. But how could they have known—our interrogation of prisoners shows they did know—at what point in time and space Shiva could be found?*'

"And the berserkers not only knew there was going to be an attack directly against Shiva, an assassination attempt if you want to call it that, but they knew the badlife base from which it was going to be launched. So they supposed that a quick strike at Hyperborea might well succeed in gathering that important information.

"But it looks like Shiva decided to take that decision on itself. It simply didn't have enough time available to discuss it with the berserker high command—wherever that may be currently located.

"And what Shiva decided was to strike quickly at this base. Not only strike to destroy, but to invade the place in force. It knew that the knowledge it had to have was here, and it could still calculate that we were unaware that it had found out. Audacity had won for it before, time and again. And it very nearly won this time. But it hasn't won, and now we may have the damned thing trapped."

Not everyone was sure it hadn't.

Meanwhile, intermittent gunfire, crashes of destruction, testified that several remaining berserkers, presumably not possessing any stolen secrets, and likely out of communication with their leadership who did, were not devoting their considerable computing power to the problems of escaping. They, the berserker infantry, liked it right here on Hyperborea, as they would have liked it anyplace where there were life-forms to be discovered and killed.

Havot, sitting in his assigned observation post, had taken several shots at distant flashes of movement that he thought were probably small berserker units. On the strength of this activity, he was ready to claim a couple of probable kills, and he was finding the game of berserker-fighting every bit as enjoyable as he remembered it. This was fun! For long moments, he could even begin to lose himself in the game.

But for moments only. No game could long divert him from his real and terribly urgent need to get out of here, away from the people who were soon going to want to pop him back into a cell. When he figured enough time had passed, he moved out of his post and spent about an hour just hiding out in a piece of wreckage, waiting until the fun was over. Of course, if the machines won, there'd be a little more fun yet, for the last human who was left alive. But then they would be quick and efficient in what they did. He had no military secrets.

The clear thought came: Maybe they'll kill me soon, one side or the other will. Then he wouldn't have to worry anymore about trying to escape.

Havot thought he might have something in common now with whatever berserker stragglers might still survive. He and they both wanted a good ship and a clean getaway.

Listening in on his suit radio, though careful to maintain radio silence himself, he was somewhat put out when he heard that Karl Enomoto was now wounded, confined to the base hospital, and would soon be charged with spying for Kermandie. If Havot could have guessed that Enomoto was a spy, he'd have tried somehow to work out a deal.

Not that he would have had any intention of going to Kermandie. He'd heard too much about that world—they'd have no reason to treat him well once they had everything they wanted from him.

He could imagine how the game might have gone with Enomoto. Likely, the agent would have had a plan for disposing of him once they were aboard some ship and on their way. Well, that would have been all right. With the ship cruising steadily on reliable autopilot, Havot would have been quite ready for such games. He could play them better than anyone he'd ever met.

But now Enomoto was gone, and the berserkers—even if he'd been willing to risk, and able to make, a bargain with one of them—would probably be all gone, too. It seemed that the only available ship was the one belonging to Harry Silver.

Havot knew that as soon as everyone felt about ninety

percent safe and secure, reasonably sure that all the berserkers had been disposed of, the next thing that would occur to them was that Havot, the dreadful murderer, ought to be locked up again.

Well, if worse came to worst, he'd have to come up with some scenario to explain what he'd been doing during the battle, and he wasn't going to admit that he'd been anywhere near Harry's ship, let alone trying to drive it. Because he knew that there were two dead humans in there. There were of course dead humans scattered all over Hyperborea now, and everyone knew the berserkers were to blame. But still . . .

He heard first, and then saw, a suited human approaching. So, it looked like the people were winning, as he'd thought. When the man got a little closer, Havot saw that it was Harry Silver.

Surveying the field and what he could see of the underground hangar space, Havot observed that the most notable feature of both was a profound lack of available ships. Well, the only thing to do was wait and see. He didn't think his chances were too bad, and if he couldn't get off on the *Witch,* something else would turn up.

The truth was, he was glad that the berserkers were here. Their presence actually made him feel good. He was no damned goodlife, but the fact was that berserkers were lucky for him—always had been. Once, several years ago, they'd inadvertently got him out of what should have been foolproof life imprisonment. And now again today. Maybe the third time would be the charm. Somewhere, somehow, a berserker was going to get him out of trouble yet again.

Harry Silver, cautiously leading a small squad on a search-and-destroy mission, said quietly on his suit radio: "You people wait here. Stay alert, just in case something's been following us. I'll take a look in there."

A procedure had quickly been worked out by the people

with the most combat experience. Machines, tame robots, Sniffer's cousins, rather simpleminded for the most part, did the preliminary searching of the station. Then people. Then the machines again, this time going over everything in excruciating detail.

Now Harry, advancing with extreme care, and for the moment alone, took note of the fact that the lounge and the adjacent areas were relatively undamaged. Part of the high, arched ceiling had fallen in, creating random rubble on the floor, but enough of the gadgets and programs were still working to maintain something of an atmosphere—though it wasn't quite the one the designers had intended. When Silver stepped warily over the threshold, the housekeeping systems, all thoroughly deranged, took no notice. But they were already doing their best to reestablish a bright and cheerful environment. Something in the background was making an occasional little hissing, steaming noise. A mottled sort of light—it might almost have been real sunlight—came down, penetrating a network of branches. The brook, idiotically cheerful, went babbling along over its natural and artificial rocks.

Some member of the human scouting party Harry had left outside the lounge called in after him: "Silver? You all right?"

"Yeah, yeah. Just taking my time."

Now and then, once or twice a minute, the artificial gravity in the social room became confused about exactly how it was supposed to perform and underwent a great, slow pulsation, briefly turning the brook into slow amoeba-like bulbs of water that went drifting through the air. Each time, the glitch lasted for only a second, and then—splash!—gravity was suddenly back to normal. Weight came back, the floor pushed up again on the soles of Harry's boots, and on the legs of all the furniture that was still standing. Most of the floor was wet, most of the water draining back into the little winding channel.

Harry, eyeing the devastation around him, thought it amazing that any of the systems were still working at all.

As he took his second step inside the room, one of the bland-mannered pyramidal waiters came rolling forward, bumping over a new unevenness in the floor. But the machine, unable to recognize any figure in space armor as a potential customer, offered Silver no greeting. Advancing a couple of steps farther into the big room, he could see that the fighting had already passed through here at least once. The waiter's inanimate colleague, lying partially behind the bar, had been shot into ruins, possibly by sheer accident or else mistaken for an enemy by one side or the other. Bottles and mirrors and glassware lay about everywhere in shiny, rounded, safe-edged splinters. Liquid from smashed bottles puddled on the floor, little streams of diverse colors trickling toward the brook, then rising up in small colored blobs when the gravity stuttered again. When that happened, the waiter steadied itself by grabbing at a corner of the bar.

Cautiously, his carbine ready, still set on alphatrigger, Harry continued moving forward, looking around. At last he'd had a look at the whole room, and it was a place that made him uneasy, what with the virtual decor still functioning, trying to make battle damage look like pleasant woodland.

There was only one other casualty in the lounge. It wasn't human either, though its shape more closely approximated that ideal than did the waiter's.

A roughly man-shaped berserker boarding machine, one leg blown clear away and its torso riddled by fierce gunfire, had come into view lying behind some bioengineered ferns. Evidently it hadn't fired at Harry because all it could do now was to lie there, like a failed dam athwart the brook, partially blocking the current. The water hissed whenever a ripple carried it deep inside the ruined metal torso, and when that happened, holes in the fallen body jetted a little steam, like living breath on a cold day.

A moment later, Silver saw with a faint prickling of his scalp that one steel arm of the thing still moved—the machine wasn't totally out of action yet, though too badly blasted to drag itself within reach of another human being, or even to get at any of the robots that served humanity. Impotently unable even to blow itself up, the berserker lay there with the water gurgling musically around and through it.

Still, the death machine was keeping busy, using its one functional limb as best it could, methodically crushing all the plants that grew within reach of its steel fingers. Harry realized for the first time that the stream contained small fish—exotic, multicolored products of some bioengineering lab; the berserker was just squeezing one into paste.

From somewhere overhead, a virtual songbird twittered now and then. No doubt saying, *Cheer up, things could be worse.* Each time the gravity stuttered, the body of the moribund berserker lifted from the deck as if making an effort to get up. Each time, it fell back a moment later with a crashing, splashing thud. It wasn't only the arm, Harry observed now, that was still alive. On the right side of the thing's head, one lens the size of a fingernail was swiveling in its little turret, watching, alert for anything that might help it to get on with its job.

Eventually, the lens found Harry and stayed turned toward him, even when he moved again. Meanwhile, the good arm suddenly ceased its patient, industrious murdering of leaves and fish. Probably the berserker's optelectronic brain was still clicking away, at least enough of it to calculate that the intruding badlife might not have spotted its activity. It had to be hoping that he might step close enough for it to grab an ankle.

Harry drew a bead on the functional metal arm, then let his weapon rest. He didn't want to make any big noise in here until he'd looked around a little in the next room—and maybe the Trophy Room experts could extract some useful information from this unit.

Now suddenly, from outside, Harry's mates were calling to him urgently, but very quietly, on suit radio. Their whole party was being summoned to help surround a fully functional berserker someone had run into in a distant quarter of the base.

The thing on the floor in the lounge didn't appear to be any immediate danger to anyone. Assuming a human victory, the mop-up squad could get it later. Harry went out of the lounge, retreating through the door by which he'd entered, and went loping down the corridor after his mates.

He should get a medal," Harry Silver said.

Someone else, who didn't know what had happened to Becky, looked at him, struck by something in his tone.

"I'll give him his due, all right," Harry muttered, not loud enough for anyone else to hear.

By the time the battle had passed its climactic stage, the humans' defensive perimeter had been steadily constricted, forced in by the untiring pressure of the enemy. Now the situation display on Commander Normandy's big holostage, down in the middle of the battered computer room, showed that the battle-worn human survivors, their numbers reduced to about half the original strength of the garrison, were still defending only about half a dozen rooms, including the hospital, the big central computer chamber at their center.

At the high-water mark of the berserker attack, some of their boarding machines had overrun the commander's office, where before their arrival, all of the functional controls and information sources had gone totally dead—Sadie had seen to that. They had fought their way not only into the computer room, but through the hospital and social room, disposing of all the life that they encountered—whenever that life, aided by its loyal slave machines, did not first dispose of them. Wherever the invaders found that a corridor had been effectively blocked, they burned or blasted their way through doors and walls. In every quarter, almost at every step, they met exceptional resistance. The base had been constructed to serve as a fortress, in addition to its other functions.

At almost every stage of the berserker advance, the machines sustained heavy casualties. Nevertheless, Shiva, exerting thorough, effortless control, calculating its losses as carefully as possible, had at first refrained from using extreme violence against the base. The objective, a goal worth many risks and heavy losses, was the capture intact of at least one of the big cryptanalysis computers, and/or one of that machine's human operators alive.

There was no single, pivotal moment in the battle when success or failure was decided. Rather, the attackers' chances slowly diminished, while the defenders' gradually improved. By the time the berserker leadership was ready to use extreme violence, it was no longer an available option. All their heavy weapons had been destroyed.

All throughout the base, alarms kept at their useless, mindless task of making sure that everyone had been alerted.

When he went out of the computer room to look around again, this time with a slightly different purpose in mind, Harry was walking by himself. He had walked a hundred meters through winding corridors, all battle-scarred but quiet now, when someone spoke his name. Harry spun around, his weapon at the ready, and saw that it was only another suited human standing there, carbine ready but not aimed. Marginally, Harry relaxed.

"Hello," said an almost-cheerful voice. "It *is* Lieutenant Silver, isn't it? Spacer Third Class Havot, reporting for duty. Everything's been quiet around here."

TWENTY-TWO

There was definitely a bad side to fighting a decisive battle on the home front. Shooting it out there, the primary question to be decided was inescapably that of your own survival. But being on the defense also conferred a few advantages. Every spacer in Normandy's command was a frontline soldier now. Even those whose normal duties saw them completely deskbound had weapons in hand, and their training had been such that they knew how to use them.

Every spacer on the base was also aware that he had nothing to lose by fighting on to the last breath. The people on the planetoid had their backs to the wall. There was no way any of them were going anywhere.

Yeah, I'm Harry Silver. Been kind of looking for you."

"Oh?" Havot relaxed minimally; he didn't think they would ever send just one man out to arrest him. He very sincerely hoped that the truth about his two most recent killings never came out. Because if it did, that would make it absolutely imperative for him to get away.

Havot was no stranger to Solarian laws in their numerous variations, and he needed no lawyer to explain to him that the conditions under which he'd done his latest murders were very different from those surrounding any similar events in the past. For one thing, these made him not only a common murderer, but goodlife, which on many worlds was considered a worse offense. For another, and more important, his legal guilt was compounded by the fact that he was now a sworn-in member of the Space Force, subject to military law.

If he should be brought to trial on Hyperborea—and he still thought the odds were against that—a military court would hear his case. With only doubtful and disputed evidence to go on, conviction might not be likely, but it would be a disaster if it came. The penalty imposed for desertion, treason, and the instrumentality only knew what else, would *not* be merely one more term of life imprisonment layered on top of those—he'd really lost count of how many—he was already supposed to be serving. Instead, the punishment would be death, and between the moment when he heard his sentence pronounced and the moment when he stood before the firing squad, the delay would be no more than a few hours, perhaps no more than a few minutes.

More likely, in Havot's estimation, was that the shooting of two people on Silver's ship had been attributed to berserker action, and the authorities simply intended to send him back to the prison hospital on Gee Eye. He had every intention of avoiding that fate, if at all possible. If Harry Silver's ship was the only interstellar vessel remaining intact, then he was going to have to deal somehow with Harry Silver.

Buy you a drink?" suggested Harry. "I think we've got a little time."

"Sure."

"Some of the frangible bottles in the bar were still intact when I came through there. Amazing luck. Come along and we'll discuss space travel."

"I'm your man." They were walking now, and Havot stepped over the detached arm of someone's armored suit; he gave no thought to the question of whether there might be a real arm inside. Human bodies and enemy machines lay scattered about in fragments, indoors and outdoors, along with pieces of every type of component of the base, including maintenance machines and blasted robot couriers. Only the built-in high redundancy of systems now kept the installation functioning at all.

No one had yet managed an exact count of how many berserker landers had reached the surface of the planetoid, though the commander had one member of her staff doing little but trying to fix that number; nor could the total so far destroyed be fixed with any precision. Therefore, no one knew just how many might still remain unaccounted for.

But in the Solarian fastness of the computer room, hopes were rising that their archenemy Shiva had been caught in the emperor's suicidal blast. At least the deadliest berserker was missing, and humans could hope that it was out of touch with its legion of killers.

How many hours the entire battle lasted, from the first sighting of the enemy to the last shot, Commander Normandy could not have said. When later she read the numbers in the final, official summary, they seemed meaningless.

Hour after hour, her brave troops, outnumbered at first but with heavy automated support, blinktrigger and alphatrigger weapons at their shoulders, had fought the intruders, up and down the corridors, in and out of private rooms and meeting rooms. A lot of the real estate was now in very bad shape, though some portions of the base were amazingly untouched.

Human reflexes were of course too slow to come in first in such a contest, but their efficiency was augmented by mechanical and optelectronic aids—and inside these walls, humans possessed the considerable advantage of knowing the territory.

"Lieutenant Silver will want to take a look at this." The commander was looking at a holograph recording that she meant to show Harry when he got back.

Marut himself had transmitted the message from his dying destroyer, a couple of million klicks away, drifting now in a slow orbit of the great white sun. Marut reported that he didn't think any of the enemy engaging him had got away, but his ship wasn't going to make it either. Whatever the captain's last message, he was already dead before it reached the base.

In the recording, Marut finally admitted that Harry had been right about their planned strike against Summerland—it would have been a disaster.

"Maybe a disaster as bad as this one." The dying spacer on the holostage managed a faint smile.

Normandy shook her head. "Disaster for you, Captain, but we're still here. Any berserker fight that anyone lives through is a victory."

It was impossible for anyone to be sure whether time in this case was on the side of life, or working to death's advantage. Which side could reasonably expect the first arrival of reinforcements?

There was no way to be sure if Shiva was counting on more bad machines to show up or not, but human aid had been summoned and was bound to arrive during the next few days.

Robot couriers were still coming in, on the usual fairly regular schedule, from other bases and from the far-flung network of Solarian spy devices.

Every now and then, small groups of heavily armed Solarians sortied out of the computer room at the commander's orders, making their way in single file through some concealed passage whose designed purpose had to do with utilities and maintenance. Other small groups came back to grab a little food and rest. Their continuing objective was to make sure that enemy access to the grounded *Witch* was effectively blocked. When that had been accomplished, it would be necessary to hunt down whatever units of the enemy survived.

The enemy's radio traffic had been gradually dying down, slowing from a ragged torrent to sporadic bursts of mathematical code. Now none of the commander's monitors had detected any berserker signals for ten full minutes.

At one point, the Solarians, probing to locate the enemy, tried the familiar tactic of sending a robot ahead of them, hoping to trigger any booby traps the enemy might have put in place. Trouble was, the regular service and maintenance robots were too naive, not capable of deliberate stealth. And the enemy was too clever to reveal its position until it could get more life within range of its destructive force.

Moving as silently as humans could manage in armor—and still, inevitably, making more noise than man-shaped berserkers—the armored bodies of the squad emerged, single file, around a corner in one of the regular corridors, on a journey that had already taken them through manholes and ductwork, through gaps blasted in what had once been solid walls and floors. Everywhere they went, they encountered ruin in its various stages, as well as a great many patiently flashing alarms.

The hunters had become the hunted, and vice versa. Now and then, they flushed out a berserker.

Once, an ordinary maintenance machine, innocent but not too bright, skittered by and a nervous Solarian wasted a shot, blasting it into fragments.

A Templar veteran advised him: "If you have time enough to watch it move, and if it's moving away from you—not likely it's a berserker."

Elevators would become traps for any inhuman presence

trying to use them. Certain massive, almost impenetrable doors had revealed themselves when the shooting started and had gone into action, solidly closing off corridors at strategic places so that the base could be sealed into several domains, each independently defensible, though still connected by hidden communication lines. The base commander knew how to generate a set of keys by which the doors could be opened again.

Harry, in his bad moments, was sometimes perturbed by the idea that Summerland, in its new mode of existence as a nest of death, probably had its own kind of Trophy Room. And his earlier vision of that place had changed—now he saw human bodies, especially brains, well preserved for study. Beautifully preserved, but thoroughly dead, along with the bacteria that would otherwise have destroyed them with decay.

The enemies invading the human base had done their best to shoot the lights out when and where that was feasible—when the machines calculated that they could see better than the defenders in the dark—wreck the power supply and all the systems of life support. But the designers of the base had made the key components of those systems extremely hard to get at, and had provided redundant systems.

In many of the rooms and corridors, the furniture and equipment, the walls and floor and ceiling, were all badly shot up. Air kept leaking out from a dozen comparatively minor breaches, but so far, the generators and emergency supplies were making up the losses. Alarms, unheeded now for many hours, were still sounding everywhere, and maintenance robots ran or rolled about in dithering uselessness. Or worked, with insanely methodical patience, accomplishing one modest repair at a time, while all around them, the world of the beings they served was still being torn apart.

TWENTY-THREE

Several times in the course of the battle, the berserker attack on Hyperborea had come very close to succeeding, gaining an advantage that would not only doom all life on the planetoid, but would send some inner secrets of Solarian intelligence to exactly the place where they could be expected to do the most harm.

But gradually, at first imperceptibly, the balance had tipped, and now it seemed that not only could the secrets be saved, but there was a good chance that the archenemy Shiva might have been destroyed, or possibly blasted into orbit by the violence of *Galaxy*'s explosion in the low Hyperborean gravity. Of course, no one could be sure that the berserkers had not already made another copy of that evil miracle—but at least there were some grounds for hope.

Everyone who had gone space-borne on Captain Marut's destroyer was now counted as missing and presumed lost. It was remotely possible that some crew members from that vessel, or from one of the lost launches or patrol craft, might have survived and could be picked up alive if a search were to be made. But that possibility was already vanishingly small, and diminishing with every passing hour.

Commander Normandy, who had survived without a scratch even the irruption through the wall of her computer room, was putting together a list of casualties, in which "missing" was still the largest category.

As far as the commander could tell at the moment, none of the people who had come to Hyperborea with the emperor had survived.

The question was whether the emperor's grand gesture at the end had succeeded in its purpose. If not, the glory he had spent his life in seeking might very well still escape him at the end.

"What price glory, Lieutenant Ravenau?"

"I've heard the question asked before."

Harry predicted that some members of the cult down on Gee Eye would soon be saying that Julius wasn't dead, that he'd only been carried or called away and would return someday in glory to lead his people to a final triumph.

And someone, more than one, would be putting in a claim to be Julius's anointed successor.

"Meanwhile, it would appear that he found what he was looking for."

Lieutenant Colonel Khodark, one of the last Solarians to fall, ambushed when he decided to lead a foray out of the computer room, had spent the last couple of hours, and was going to spend a few more days, unconscious in a medirobot. The berserker that had struck the colonel down was disposed of soon thereafter.

Eventually someone noticed that both confinement cells

were empty—the accused spy Karl Enomoto was still in the hospital—and thought to raise an official question as to what had happened to the earlier prisoner.

When the commander asked around, as Harry had asked earlier, someone remembered sending Havot to occupy a forward post. "We've lost contact with him? Put him down as missing, for now."

Sadie, when questioned on the subject of Spacer Havot, promptly acknowledged that she had released him as soon as a red alert had been declared.

"Oh, yes," said Commander Normandy, now with a vague memory of Khodark telling her something about that, way back at the start of the festivities. Normandy still wasn't going to devote her full attention to that problem, if it was a problem. Not when there were likely to be live berserkers still loose in her base. But she did comment. "Probably wasn't a good decision, Sadie. Shows stupidity, somewhere."

"Yes, ma'am," said the A. I. adjutant. Sadie spoke in her normal voice. There was of course no question of any emotional reaction on her part. Sadie understood as well as the commander did that "stupidity" was a quality that could be attributed only to human beings.

Basically, the secrets of Hypo and Negat did not appear to have been compromised; if any berserker machine had learned them, that machine was destroyed before it could get away.

Still, people wondered whether what kind of a berserker it was that had apparently been blown up with the emperor's ship. They could only hope that it had been Shiva.

A long time would have to pass before humans could be sure about that.

The Gee Eye Home Guard, unable to shake their indecisiveness, mobilized, but then just kept milling around in their own small sector of space, closely guarding their own planet—staying too close to it to be effective in case of a real attack.

During the hours of battle on Hyperborea, the ships from Good Intentions spent their time occasionally firing at shadows, setting off alarms at the sight of passing asteroids, trying now and then to call the base on Hyperborea with questions. Their calls were not returned—not until several hours after the shooting on the planetoid was over.

The next courier that Normandy sent off to Port Diamond went plunging through flightspace with figurative banners waving, carrying a report of victory. She looked forward to being able to begin a thorough search among the scattered berserker wreckage for some kind of optelectronic brain that might be identifiable as Shiva.

"I think we got it," one hopeful officer commented. "I think the emperor really bagged it."

"How in hell can we be sure?" her colleague asked.

A considerable time would pass before anyone began to feel really confident. It seemed that whatever quantum arrangements had made the brain of Shiva unique among berserkers were probably gone beyond the possibility of recovery.

As he walked toward the social room with Harry Silver, Havot was saying: "Soon—maybe less than an hour from now—things on Hyperborea will once again turn very civilized. Which means I'll be locked up again. Also, I'll be demobilized, returned to civilian status. I do believe I like being a civilian."

"But not being locked up."

"Very perceptive of you, Lieutenant. I suppose you have an aversion to that as well? Didn't I hear your name mentioned somewhere in connection with some vague talk about a smuggling charge?"

"Not a lieutenant anymore. I resigned my commission,

which means I'll have to go back to making a living. In my business, a man like you could be quite useful sometimes, so I think that you and I have things to talk about."

"Sure, thanks. Your ship all right?" Havot asked lightly.

"Yeah. All ready to go, as a matter of fact. There was a little ruckus on board earlier, but that's all been straightened out."

"Glad to hear it. That it got straightened out, I mean. Anybody hurt?"

"Two people shot. One pulled through."

"Friends of yours?"

"I wouldn't say that." Harry looked up at him briefly, vaguely. "She saw the man who shot her."

"A man? She thinks it was a man?"

Harry nodded.

"Silver, you've probably heard about my background. I don't know what this woman thinks she saw, but they're not going to stick me with something like that. All the shooting I did today was at berserkers, and I fought well. Damned hard, and damned well, if I do say so myself. I think there might be pretty good legal grounds for a review of my whole case."

"Yeah, I could go along with that. You want me to put in a word for you, I'll say I think maybe your whole case should be reviewed."

They had reached the social room by now, and Havot paused in the doorway, alertly inspecting the interior before he entered. There was, not surprisingly, no one else in sight. "It'll have to be in a civilian court. I expect to be out of the military within an hour. And, no offense, but I'm not sure your putting in a word for me would help. Somehow I have the feeling that you're on the run yourself. Or just about to be. Don't get me wrong, I'd rather be going with you."

And Havot thought to himself, too bad that the woman was still alive, but there didn't seem to be any safe way of finishing her off now. One risk that was certainly not worth taking. And the situation was complicated by the fact that he couldn't be entirely sure that she could identify him as the one who'd shot her.

That would make it all the more imperative to get away. Things got a little more urgent when you were facing a firing squad, not just a cell.

"All right, Silver, let's talk business. You say you might be able to use a man with my experience. My own fundamental need is for a pilot. I've only tried once in my life to fly a real ship—and it didn't work for me. Maybe because my thoughts were . . . busy with other things." And Havot smiled his nice smile.

"If you're flying a ship in combat, a clear mind is necessary, though not sufficient."

On entering the social room, Harry went directly to the bright ruin that had once been a proud display behind the bar. It took a little searching to find the intact bottle that he wanted. Somehow, bottling the stuff in casually breakable material had come to be seen as a warrant for its authenticity.

Havot brushed some debris off a table and sat down, opening a container of snacks—wild nuts, fresh and self-drying fruits—from the bioengineering labs.

Harry soon joined him, bringing a couple of glasses and a bottle of Inca Pisco brandy, imported all the way from Earth.

Havot, evidently craving something else, got up and went to look for it behind the bar. He carried his carbine with him, holding the weapon in a relaxed and expert way, but left his helmet on the table where Harry sat opening his bottle of brandy.

Now that the shooting was over, or almost over, Harry could recognize the stages that people tended to go through after a fight. It was starting to feel safe to set his helmet and his weapons down out of reach, at least briefly. He allowed himself to put down his carbine, at just a little distance. And no one could drink with a helmet on.

In another hour, the cleanup machines would be starting

an enormous job. Before the day was over, people would probably be expected to pay for things they took.

Fumbling with gauntleted fingers inside the belt pouch of his armored suit, Havot brought out some money and laid it on the bar. "Wouldn't feel right if I didn't pay." Then he came back to the table with his own bottle, some label Harry didn't recognize.

Harry wondered just where and how the other had obtained the money. But he wasn't going to ask. Instead, he inquired: "Did the commander tell you about my downlock codes? They gave her engineers some trouble at the start."

"No, she didn't mention anything like that." Havot poured stuff into his glass. "The codes must be pretty tough if they gave her people a hard time."

"Oh, they're totally disabled now."

"I see. Then your ship really is ready to go."

"Right."

Both men's helmets now were off, sitting on the table where they could be grabbed quickly should the need arise.

"Here's to safe flight," Havot proposed, raising his glass.

"I'll drink to that." Harry said. Then, as if merely continuing some unspoken chain of thought, he added: "But shooting down two people, just like that. Why do you do that kind of thing? It's not nice."

The handsome face looked pained, though not terribly surprised. "Any man or woman who suggested I did that in your ship is crazy. It was probably a berserker, and if it was a human, it couldn't possibly have been me."

"I look at it this way. If it was a human, it was someone who badly wanted a ship to get away in."

Havot smiled. "I still want a ship—or a ride, rather. I'll make it worth your while to give me transportation."

Harry didn't sound interested in discussing any deal. "Y'see—right after the shooting, someone tried to lift off in the *Witch,* and just made a hash of it. And you said just now that you had tried, once in your life, with a real pilot's helmet on. Now that didn't happen before you came to Hyperborea, did it? So it was today that you didn't do very well as a pilot. Not with your head full of all the garbage that seems to grow in thcrc."

Havot just sat where he was for a few seconds, shaking his head silently. It was impossible for Harry to tell whether he was denying the accusation, trying to shake the garbage loose, or simply marveling at the strangeness of things in general. At last Havot said: "Don't get me wrong, Silver, I'm no damned goodlife. But I'm glad the berserkers came."

"I bet they love you, too."

Havot tasted the stuff in his glass and smacked his lips appreciatively. "Why do you say a thing like that?" He had it down so well, the tone of sounding nobly injured.

Harry said: "Berserkers don't insist on doing the killing themselves—as long as it gets done. Unlike crazy people, they get no personal kick out of it. All that matters to them is the final body count. So the more humans slaughter each other, the better berserkers like it—saves wear and tear on them."

Havot didn't really seem to be listening. Staring into the distance, he took another sip of his drink and said: "But the truth is that berserkers are lucky for me. Always have been."

"That's all right. Sometimes I think crazy people are lucky for me."

"I'm glad to hear," said Havot, "that the autopilot on the *Witch* is now working just fine. Because that means I don't need a live pilot any longer. I do know that much about ships." Now he looked around, smiling. "Harry, it's really dangerous not to carry your weapon with you. No one's called off the alert yet. There could still be a berserker here—somewhere." And he knocked Harry's helmet off the table.

Confronted by that quietly happy gaze, Harry, unarmed and helmetless, unable to protect his head or to radio for help, his own weapon hopelessly out of reach, jumped up and dodged and sprinted around a curving corner into the other wing of the social room. When he got there, he pressed his body back against the wall in what seemed a pathetic attempt to hide.

But the look on his face wasn't pathetic, or even very scared. He said: "It won't work, you know."

"Oh?" Havot had jumped up too, carbine in hand, and moved with long, purposeful strides, knee-deep in ferns, to cut the other off from the door leading to the corridor. Now Havot had reached the precisely correct spot to allow him to aim a neat shot into the corner, from a nice, convenient distance.

"No it won't," said Harry. "While you were rooting around in the bottles back there, you left your helmet at the table, and I reached inside and got a good grip on a couple of things." He raised and wiggled ten servo-powered fingers. "Bent those things, just a little. Enough to screw up the whole system slightly—even the manual triggering on the hand-held unit. Your carbine won't work now. If you ever get back to your helmet, just feel with your hand inside it. Maybe you could tell what I did. It hardly shows."

"Is that so? Then why are you trying to hide in the corner?" As Havot spoke, he raised his weapon, eyeing the helpless-looking figure before him. "Nice try, Harry," he added sarcastically. "Oh, very cool thinking."

Then Havot tried his blink-trigger, and nothing happened. He groped for the manual trigger and tried that, with no more success.

The gravity stuttered. Harry was ready for that, having seen it happen before in this room, but Havot wasn't. It only made him sway slightly on his feet, and did not shake his aim.

Still, Harry just stood there calmly, as if they were getting ready to play some game. "Reason I'm back in this corner," he said, "is that I wanted you to come after me, and to stand just about where you—"

At that moment, with the speed of a sprung trap, what felt like the grip of death itself locked onto Havot's left ankle. If not for the hardness and toughness of his armor, the bones of his leg and foot would have been crushed. Only one mode of death struck in this way, and immediately Havot's mind and body were mobilized for a maximum effort to survive. But he was tossed by a giant's strength, berserker's strength, his armored body flung spinning in the air before he could brace himself and exert the full power of his suit's servos. His eyes kept on blinking madly, even if he couldn't aim, but still his weapon refused to fire.

Spinning flight ended in a sprawling crash, leaving Havot flat on his back on the uneven floor. In that instant, the fallen berserker, thrashing its one useful limb, dragging its crippled body along the deck, struck out once more with its one good gripper . . .

Harry, advancing warily out of the corner of the room, could see that the berserker didn't have the best possible hold—but after a couple of seconds, it was apparent that the killing machine was going to manage quite satisfactorily with the one it had.

The water in the brook flowed red.

There was Havot's carbine—not in working order just now, and Harry let it lie. Edging sideways, he picked up his own functional weapon from where he'd earlier placed it, a little out of easy reach. Cautiously, he circled around until he could feel a chair behind his knees, and then he sat down with a slight shudder.

The gravity stuttered again, and a great blood-tinged water bubble became briefly airborne before splashing back. The general shift of position caused by the stutter gave Harry a better look. The steel claw had Havot by the lower jaw, metal fingers rammed into his mouth, thumb forced in under his chin. A number of his white and shapely teeth were being scattered around, and no one was going to admire his beauty anymore.

By now, Havot had got a two-handed, servo-powered grip

on the steel arm that was killing him—but too late, too late. The berserker's fingers had already found a major blood vessel and were doubtless going for the spinal cord. Now the whole metal fist was forcing its way right down the throat. The dying man made noises for a little while, and kicked his legs, but soon was quiet.

"You shot her down, you son of a bitch," Harry told him. He spoke almost conversationally—only a little short of breath. "Becky, and I don't know how many others. Just like nothing, you tried to kill her, and then you let her lie there."

The deck beneath the lounge gave another little upward lurch, once more gently tossing the two bodies so it looked like the dead man and his last antagonist were both trying to come to life. Then gravity held everything smoothly again. Tall ferns hid Havot and his killer and the curve of the small stream in which they lay.

Drawing a deep breath, Harry Silver leaned back in his chair and ordered himself a drink, calling for Inca Pisco. Then he woke up and remembered that none of the waiters were ambulatory, and he got to his feet and searched for a bottle other than the one he'd offered to share with Havot.

Just a minute later, two minutes ahead of the appointed time for her arrival, Becky came in and found him sitting there, glass in hand. Harry could hear the mop-up squad, murmuring on their radios at no great distance behind her.

He raised his head. "You're looking good, kid. Still got the stuff?"

"Sure I've got it." Becky patted a kind of saddlebag slung round her armor-suited shoulder. "Along with various of my own personal possessions. I discharged myself from the hospital, Harry. And I resigned my commission at the same time. I don't know if they heard me or not. They didn't seem to be paying attention."

"That's how it was with me." Harry started to throw down

his carbine, then decided he'd better hang on to it till they were safely aboard ship. Becky was carrying hers, too. "I guess they're too busy to pay attention. Let's go somewhere else." He wanted to get his woman out of the social room before she happened to discover what lay behind the ferns; she'd had enough unpleasantness to last for a long time. "How about the two of us taking a little ride?"

An hour later, the official mop-up squad, on making its careful way through the social room, discovered, with not much surprise, one more berserker to be finished off, and one more human victim. Parts of the former would be preserved, naturally, for the Trophy Room. It was with some relief that the squad leader reported that the escaped prisoner had now been located. Havot's weapon lay near his body, and evidently he'd shot the berserker at close range, but had carelessly taken off his helmet too soon, and the thing got him before it died.

People on the station would still be going armed and armored for several more days at least, in case one more deadly machine might still be lurking somewhere.

Commander Normandy, by this time somewhat groggy from lack of sleep, was distracted and stimulated by the news that a large, strong human fleet had just come roaring into the Hyperborean system. Evidently one of the ships in Marut's original task force had managed to get a courier off at the time of the ambush, with a message of disaster. But no one had known, until now, whether that courier managed to get through.

By the way, Commander?" It was an admiral who asked the question, a couple of hours later. Claire had to keep reminding herself that this one was real.

"Yes, sir?"

"What happened to this Lieutenant Silver?"

"I don't know, sir. I really haven't been making an effort

to keep track." Under the circumstances, that was quite understandable.

What had happened was that Harry Silver was in flight again, having sneaked a liftoff in his ship before anyone else thought it was ready. Ten minutes spent with his familiar pilot's helmet on had proven long enough to straighten out the thoughtware.

Now, at a light-year's distance from Hyperborea, he and his companion could console themselves with the thought that it was only the Space Force after them now, and not berserkers. Harry knew they'd be after him for something, and had decided not to wait around to hear the specific charges. Probably not Havot—that would be charged to berserker action. But there was sure to be some legal tangle with regard to the Kermandie agent, Enomoto. And some Kermandie thugs might be after him as well.

Well, Kermandie thugs would have good cause to be upset. He was determined to see to it that the relics of Hai San found their way into the hands of the rebels, who would know how to put them to good practical use—as psychological weapons, in rituals, and on display. And Harry had been telling the truth when he said he hoped to collect a good price for Hai San's relics—though not as much as the other side would have paid him, to make sure they were destroyed.

When he raised the subject with Becky, she quickly came up with a corollary to the scheme of selling the relics to the rebels. "Harry, how would it be if we first contrived some fakes? Good enough so that the dictator's people would fork over a good price for 'em?"

Harry stared at her with something approaching reverence. "Gee, we'll have to think about that. Hey, kid, I'm glad you're back."

"Me too, Harry."

And now he supposed he was a good bet to be charged

with stealing the Space Force's c-plus cannon, which was still riding in his ship. Well, he didn't really want the damned thing, but getting rid of it in any kind of responsible fashion was going to be a job.

"We'll have to be careful where we try to sell a thing like that," Becky mused wistfully.

"We will indeed."

After running for another couple of hours in hyperspace, Harry mentioned that he was considering doubling back, just enough to observe the *Witch*'s trail for signs of a pursuit.

Becky suggested that there would be no point in doing that. There was no need, because they had no doubt of what was happening.

Harry Silver nodded slowly. "You're right, kid."

The pursuit was on. Harry had known for a long time now that it was always on. That all you ought to ask of life was the chance to do some real good things before it finally caught up.